THE ELUSIVE BILLIONAIRE

HAPPINESS EVER AFTER
BOOK 2

AVERY MAXWELL

That's What She Said Publishing, Inc.

THE *Elusive* BILLIONAIRE

ISBN: 979-8-88643-889-5 (ebook)

ISBN: 979-8-88643-888-8 (paperback)

averymaxwellbooks.com

102925

PLAYLIST

When I sit down to curate a playlist for a book, I spend weeks pulling songs that I think will fit the vibe of the story.

Greyson and Savvy's happened a bit differently. I started with just four songs that I played on repeat while I was planning. Then, at the end of some chapters, a song would pop into my head.

Unfortunately, I seem to remember every lyric to every song, but never the title, so I ended up singing very badly into my phone to find each one.

Luckily for you, I'll only give you the actual musicians' versions.

Each song matched a specific emotion for me. I hope you love it as much as I do.

Their story is one of complicated, messy, truly raw love. It's fire and ice with all the spice, and I think that is reflected in their playlist.

Throughout the banter and the bickering, Greyson and Savvy learned to not only love each other, but to love themselves, and that makes this one of my favorite love stories I've ever written.

I hope you enjoy the soundtrack to their story. You can download it here:

https://geni.us/TEBPlaylist

I spent my twenties starving myself, my thirties hating myself, and the first part of my forties exhausted and wondering why.

This story is for anyone who has ever wanted to love themselves but didn't know how to start.

The answer isn't easy, but it is simple: You just have to choose it.

Choose to love yourselves, luvs.

Then choose yourself every day for the rest of your life because if you give yourself a little luv...you'll realize you deserve a whole lot more.

AUTHOR NOTE

Dear Reader,

Much of my twenties was spent starving myself, hating myself, and hiding it all from everyone who loved me.

In fact, I hid it so well, I even tricked myself into believing the lie—I didn't have a problem. What problem? At six foot one and a size zero, all I saw were my flaws. It's devastating to write that sentence now, but it was my truth for many, many years.

It wasn't until I was faced with a wakeup call that I admitted it to myself. But even then, it was another fifteen years before I ever spoke the words aloud and told my therapist.

To this day, I've struggled to speak about what I've put my body through in pursuit of the elusive idea of perfection.

And it's because of my silence—my *shame*—and others like me, that Savvy's journey with disordered eating and abuse looks the way it does.

Not everyone talks about it. Not everyone seeks help. Not everyone is a textbook case.

We all have our journeys, our hardships, our stories...

and this is a version of those experiences as seen through Savvy's fictionalized life.

It is not a one-size-fits-all disease. There's no one right or wrong way to depict it, therefore I didn't try to be perfect. I simply told the story as I knew it.

A very special thank you to Nadia, my sensitivity reader, who offered a different perspective from my own. Because of her, I was able to navigate Savvy's story with love and care.

If you or anyone you know is struggling with disordered eating or abuse, please reach out for help:

https://www.nationaleatingdisorders.org
https://www.thehotline.org

And if you need a friend, please join us in my reader group:
https://geni.us/AverysLUVclub

CHAPTER ONE

SAVVY

Eight Months Ago

Awareness shoots up my arms—electricity racing across each tiny hair as though it's a pinball bumping against every follicle. Even the damn air is thicker, more potent, alive.

Greyson Reyes is in the room.

I know it without turning around.

I feel it—a phantom itch I can't, shouldn't, scratch.

He's a possession that invades every molecule and pore on my skin until pain and passion are braided together into a corset made just for me.

We fight to fuck, or we fuck to fight. I don't even know which came first anymore, and my emotions for him run the gamut of hating to love him and loving to hate him.

Madi eyes me suspiciously and I quickly drop the thumb I was chewing the hell out of. My entire cuticle is probably bleeding, but I tuck it below my leg and hope that no one else notices.

My best friend's future brother-in-law is so magnetic that every head in the Chug turns his way when he enters.

It's as infuriating as it is mesmerizing, but the last thing he needs is one more person propping up his ego, so I intentionally don't seek him out.

The Chug is Madi's coworking space. Her grandfather owned the building, an old train station, for years, but she recently repurposed it, and it quickly became a gathering place for the residents of Happiness, Georgia.

"Geez, could you imagine having that kind of confidence?" Clover whispers.

Elle snickers. "If I looked like that, I'd be walking with much more swagger."

"You're married, Elle." Damn. That came out harsher than I intended. Her smirk tells me she knows exactly what she was doing.

Dropping my head, I focus on the task before me—scheduling out the next three episodes of my podcast, *Can We Talk About That?*

I read the same sentence three times before Bethany's voice digs at my spine with the finesse of a rusty knife.

"Oh, Grey. I didn't know you'd be in here today." Her voice drips with so much sex, I think I need another shower.

"Have a good day," he says dismissively.

That makes me feel marginally better.

God, this is so bad. The last time I got this excited by another human being, I almost lost my life.

And isn't that a depressing thought? But it's one that hasn't been far from my mind lately because I know Riley, my ex, will be out of prison soon.

My stomach cramps as old habits try to take shape in my subconscious.

It's the reminder I need to keep the boundaries in place where Grey and I are concerned.

Fuck buddies, not friends.

Cinnamon fills my nostrils, telling me he's entered my space, and since my podcast is doing a shit job of giving me a distraction, I grab my phone and open the app that is my current obsession. There's no way ChasingColors42 hasn't responded yet.

I'm not trying to lead this guy on. We've been talking through a surrogacy app for about two months, but I have no intention of becoming a surrogate if I can help it. Yet somehow, he's become the friend I need.

Signing up with Ray of Hope last year had been a panic response after receiving the call from my attorney that Riley would likely get out of jail at his next hearing.

I have no idea what kind of fight Riley or his family will bring to my doorstep, but with only $4000 in the bank, I needed a way of getting a substantial amount of money should the time to fight come. Again.

Where Grey makes my pulse race, ChasingColors42 just makes me feel...determined. He seems lost to me, lonely. I want to know what makes him tick, what makes him so sure that becoming a single dad is what will fulfill him, but it's not my place.

I have told him that I'm not the surrogate for him, but he's nothing if not persistent.

A small smile plays on my lips when I see his name on my screen.

The sound of wood scraping on the floor has me looking up from my screen. Grey's joined our table with a moody scowl on his face, but he says nothing.

"Braxton will be here soon," Madi says, mentioning

Greyson's brother and her boyfriend in a soothing tone he doesn't deserve.

I like the secret thing we have going, but he's a total asshole. Grey smiles pleasantly at Madi though, so maybe he truly does save his surly assholery for me.

Regardless, I'm not in the mood for his shit today. I'm about to open my messages when he leans in to my space.

"Miss me?" His gravelly tone has me sitting up taller as my entire body comes alive in a way it's never done for anyone else.

"Not even a little." The lie tastes bitter, but I ignore it. We have a physical connection, nothing more.

"So you're not pissed that I snuck out of your bed this morning?"

I scoff, and my friends lean forward, attempting to eavesdrop on our whispered confessions.

"I appreciated it. It was an act of kindness I didn't think you had in you." I press my lips closer to his ear. "Any time you want to sneak out in the middle of the night so I don't have to see your smug face in the morning is just fine by me."

My breath hits the sensitive flesh of his ear, and he shivers. It's an involuntary reaction I take great pleasure in.

"I'm only smug because I made you come three times last night." He leans even closer, his lips ghosting the shell of my ear. "And you begged for it."

"I don't beg." *Liar, liar, pants on fire.*

"Oh, but you do. And it's my second-favorite sound on earth."

Do not ask. Do not ask.

"What's your favorite?" *Damn it, Savannah.*

His hand falls to my thigh under the table, out of sight of our friends. "I'm more of a show than a tell kind of guy. So, when I knock on your back door tonight, trust that I'll show you the second I strip you down."

"Awfully presumptuous of you. I never said you could come over tonight." I hear Madi and Clover giggling in the background, but I'm addicted to the way Grey's heat fills in my cold, dead cracks. "We're not exclusive." My gut lurches, but it's the truth.

Greyson freezes. It's a momentary blip in his shield that he quickly reinforces with steel.

"Beautiful little liar. You know I can't stay away from you any more than you want me to. Our...fighting during the day only makes our nighttime activities that much hotter." His voice drops with each passing word. "And if you were seeing anyone else, I'd know about it, since I'm in your bed every fucking night."

"You are the most irritating man on the planet, you know that?"

He chuckles. It's low and deep in his chest. My eyes close as I fight the way my body reacts to him.

"And you're the rudest, most annoying woman I've ever met. It's all that...hate that makes us so explosive, and you know it."

I do. Jesus, do I know it. Except I'm not entirely sure it's hatred I feel when he's in my presence—not that I'll ever admit that to anyone.

He runs his nose along my jawline. It's the most physical contact we've ever displayed publicly, and I know I'll get an inquisition from the girls the second he's gone, but I couldn't pull away even if he was literally on fire.

"It is...it is hate, right?" It's the first time I've ever heard Greyson be anything but one hundred percent confident, and the red flags start waving in both hands.

Of course it's hate, what else could it be? We fight any time we're fully clothed. It has to be—

"Sorry I'm late," Braxton says. "Pops was...er...causing trouble over at Huckabee's Hardware. I had to sort that out on my way over."

Madi groans and drops her forehead to the table. Her grandfather, Pops, is worse than a drunken frat boy out causing trouble. And that's on a good day.

My phone vibrates in my hand, so I pull away from Grey, thankful for the reprieve a little space affords me, and unlock it.

> ChasingColors42: Are you around?

> Firefly12: For you? Always. Did you pick a new surrogate yet?

> ChasingColors42: How could I when you're the one that I want?

> Firefly12: (eye roll emoji)

> ChasingColors42: I won't even drop off my semen or choose a donor egg until you've agreed to be mine.

My chest buzzes with warmth. I know he doesn't mean *his* his, but dang, it's been a long time since I ever associated belonging to anyone with anything other than dread.

> Firefly12: Told you, while I love babies, this is a last resort for me. I won't be accepting anyone unless life takes away my choices, and if you knew me, you'd know I'll fight like hell to make sure that doesn't happen.

ChasingColors42: You make me want to fix shit, and I don't even know what's wrong.

Firefly12: Because you have a God complex?

ChasingColors42: Something like that.

Damn. This got heavy fast.

Firefly12: What are you up to today? Got any good stories for me?

Sometimes he'll regale me with stories of his grandfather that could rival Madi's stories about Pops. It always makes me laugh.

ChasingColors42: Have I told you about my nephew?

I nearly drop my phone. So far, he's kept his personal life private, except for his reasoning for wanting a child—his family has moved on without him, and he has a giant gaping hole in his heart where they used to reside.

My words, not his. I'm not sure ChasingColors is self-aware enough to make that connection.

Firefly12: No! I'd love to hear about him.

I settle into my seat and pull up my knees so my heels rest on the edge of my chair and my shins press into the table in front of me.

It has the added benefit of blocking out Grey.

He grumbles something I don't hear, and I'm thankful that something has finally dragged his attention away from me.

I watch the bubbles move across my screen as Chasing-Colors types. It feels like an eternity before his message appears.

> ChasingColors42: He's a genius. He's been taking college-level courses since middle school, but now he wants to attend college. And play football.

My feet fall to the floor with a loud thunk, and my face nearly smashes into the table.

"You okay over there, Savvy?" Grey's voice swims in my ears as I stare at my screen.

"Yeah, sorry," I croak. "I just booked a guest I was excited about. Um, excuse me for a moment."

I don't wait for a response. My fingers clench my phone so tightly they turn white as I skirt around table after table and hide in the room Madi has designated as quiet space. From here, I can see Grey sitting at our table, and I swallow hard.

> Firefly12: He's playing football? That's great. What position?

If he says kicker, I will throw up.

Grey and Braxton's nephew moved here with Grey four months ago. And he recently started college. And he's playing football for the first time ever...as their kicker.

> ChasingColors42: You know football? I played when I was younger. I'm just getting back into it now that he's playing.

> ChasingColors42: He's the local university's new kicker.

I press my nose to the glass door and watch as Grey types on his phone.

Holy shit. Holy shit. Holy shit.

> ChasingColors42: I'm really happy for him.

> ChasingColors42: I gave up a lot for my family.

> ChasingColors42: I never want him to have to make the same sacrifices, you know?

I can't respond.

Grey is ChasingColors? What the hell are the chances of that? One in a million? A billion? There can't be another man in the US who wants a baby but not a wife and has a nephew with the exact same background, right? That's too coincidental to happen twice.

> ChasingColors42: He's growing up and I'm…

What? He's what?

I lift my head from my phone and find Grey staring at me. No. No, no. Does he know it's me? The intensity of his glare sears me. I'm a filet left on the pan too long, and sweat gathers on my spine.

He shakes his head with a frown that fits him like sadness, then he drops his gaze.

A moment later, my phone buzzes, and I sink down to the floor, unable to stare at Grey a moment longer.

I feel dirty and guilty as hell.

ChasingColors42: I'll never admit this to anyone else, but since you're so adamant that we'll never meet, I'll say it to you.

Please don't. Please, please, please don't.

ChasingColors42: I've spent so long fearing I'd end up like my father that I've forgotten how to make real connections with people anymore. Even when I want to.

Oh, Grey. That's not true.

ChasingColors42: I'm lonely. Isn't that the saddest fucking thing you've ever heard? Thirty years old, and I'm lonely but too untrusting to let anyone in.

Greyson Reyes just decimated my soul with that one admission.

He wants love but doesn't know how to accept it.

We're more alike than he'll ever know.

I can't let him into my screwed-up life. Hell, I've had Madi, Clover, and Elle for ten years, and I've never once asked them for anything. Instead, I've made myself invaluable to them. I'm the friend they go to when all hell breaks loose. I'm their guardian angel, their sounding board, their rock.

It's the only safe way for me to experience love now.

ChasingColors42: Did I scare you away with my neediness?

This is a sad version of Grey that he doesn't share and I never would have imagined. He needs someone. No, he needs me.

This will undoubtedly come back to bite me in the ass, but how can I leave him in pain and all alone?

Lifting to my knees, I chance another peek at him. His brows are furrowed, and his mouth is set in a grim line, but now I've seen beneath the mask to the sadness he hides beneath.

I can't leave him all alone, I just can't. I'll have to be the friend Grey needs but will never ask for. If he never finds out it's me who's supporting him as Firefly12 and also pushing him to open up as Savvy, we'll be just fine.

This is a secret I'll take to my grave, because if Grey learns to let someone in, he'll be the hero every woman deserves but most never get. I know that in my soul, and he deserves to love and be loved that way—even if it'll kill me to see him happy and in love with someone else.

Because the other thing I know for sure is that Grey can never be mine.

> Firefly12: Never.

> Firefly12: And I understand that kind of loneliness more than you'll ever know.

> Firefly12: I'm jumping into a meeting, but I'll check in with you tonight, okay?

> Firefly12: Thank you for opening up to me. I'm honored. Truly.

A moment later, my phone buzzes, but I pocket it, suck in a deep breath, and then chase after Grey so I can find a way to push him out of his online chats and into his real-life relationships.

Who knows, perhaps if I can help the storm cloud that is

Greyson Reyes, then maybe, just maybe, there's hope for me too.

CHAPTER TWO

GREYSON

Six Months Ago

GUILT.

It sits heavy and solid in my gut.

It always has.

It always will.

That's what happens when your sister dies a senseless death you couldn't—didn't—prevent.

Or when you witness your father do despicable things, expecting you to follow in his footsteps, but you're too young or too weak to speak up—that shit changes you.

Too bad for him, I've done everything since to be the exact opposite of him.

Until now.

Because of *her*, I've turned into someone I said I would never be. I hate myself for it, but I hate her too.

And now she's here. I sense her before I see her—I always do. We're connected in a way that shouldn't be possible. She's my missing piece, and I feel the ghost pains of her every time she comes near.

My thumb hovers over the send button, the sick feeling of betrayal washing over me for the second time in less than a minute. It doesn't help my mood that we're standing in a park in the middle of January and I'm freezing my ass off to celebrate something as fickle as love.

Fucking weddings.

"Pops," Savvy hisses. "I swear to God, if we can't get the soot off your suit, Madi will lose her mind."

My fingers clench around the phone until the whooshing sound starts, then I relax my grip. Shit. Message sent.

Guilt grows spikes and claws its way up my throat, but I pocket my phone and rush to Savvy's side—I always do.

I'll unpack my screwups later. Right now, I need to focus on whatever's happening on the lawn. If Pops hurt Savvy, I'll string the guy up by his old pointy elbows. I've never met someone who can cause so must destruction under the misguided muse of concern.

The park is decorated for Braxton's wedding, with white lights that twinkle like stars while we stand here waiting on his bride, but Pops is leaving a trail of smoke in his wake, and my nerves get the better of me.

Lifting Savvy's arms, I inspect her skin and see no burns, cuts, or other injuries, but she has soot on her face, neck, and the left side of her body.

What the fuck did this old fool do now?

"What the hell are you doing? Let me go." She wrenches her arm free and glares at me.

This is why I'm wearing guilt like a second skin. I should not be lusting after Savvy Monroe—when we barely tolerate each other—while aching for the connection I have with a faceless woman I'll never meet but can't stop texting with either.

But night after night, I fall into bed with Savvy as though a rabid force of nature is pushing us together, only to wake up searching for a message from my Firefly.

Self-control has always been paramount for me, but where Savvy is concerned, I appear to have none.

And it's so very wrong.

We want completely different things.

We're not even compatible, for fuck's sake.

Fighting is not foreplay...except in our case, it's not only foreplay, but also the accelerant to our most deviant desires.

"It's not me. Pops set his suit jacket on fire over at the Chug." Savvy waves her hands in front of my face, and I tune everyone else out. Even Braxton, my half brother, best friend, and tonight's groom.

I forget everything as Savvy ramps up. Her arms wave wildly as she speaks. I like when she gets worked up like this, her cheeks tinging pink. It reminds me of the color of her skin when she comes.

And just like that, my cock jerks in my pants as though she's reciting a magical incantation to lure him to her side.

It makes no sense at all. I don't even like her...do I?

Savvy's loud and demanding. She pushes my buttons just to irritate me. She forces me to communicate and engage. She's nothing like my Firefly.

I'm so goddamn confused, and I hate myself for it.

Savvy or Firefly? Firefly or Savvy?

My nephew, Sage, thinks I should see a therapist. If he knew half the shit flying around my head, he'd surely force the issue.

I study Savvy's reaction as I lift my thumb to wipe away the soot from her cheekbone. Her expressive green eyes grow large, but it's the sharp intake of breath that I love.

My gaze darts lower as the column of her delicate neck

works to swallow. I'm itching to wrap my hands around it, and when she shivers, I groan low and deep in my throat because I know she's thinking the same thing. Braxton's audible gasp brings our situation back into focus, and I drop my hands. He's never seen me react this way because no one has ever fractured my control the way Savvy does.

Once again, she's forced me to lose all restraint around her.

"Tell us what you want us to do." It's shocking how calm my voice sounds because the internal battle I'm experiencing is overriding all common sense.

I'm an asshole for loving how I fluster her yet doing it anyway.

She blinks.

"Fine. Ah, hold this stuff so I can wash the soot off Pops before he ruins Madi's dress." She shoves all kinds of shit into my hands. A hairbrush, her phone, some sticky tape that says it's for boobs—where the hell did she get this, and what exactly is it doing?

Leaning back, I scan her long, lean form. Her emerald dress hugs the slight curve of her hip, and the long brown hair I love is pulled high on her head in a sleek ponytail that has my blood heating—I can't wait to wrap my fist around it later. Her tits are the perfect size, and now I'm imagining removing tape from her naked skin.

At least until Pops gives her a hard time. He's a seventy-year-old menace.

Braxton says something that I answer on autopilot. I keep my focus on Savvy as she ushers the old nuisance toward a tree.

"If my phone rings, you have to answer it," Savvy calls over her shoulder. "Moose said he'll call when he's around the corner with Madi. The code is 5212 if you need it."

Who the hell rides to their wedding on a horse and carriage in January? That's a hard fucking no for me. Especially when I can practically see my breath every time I open my mouth.

"You really are an arsehole," Cian mutters in his thick Irish brogue.

"Why am I the asshole again?" I couldn't tear my attention away from Savvy if I tried.

"Because you're still secretly trying to get a baby via surrogacy instead of putting yourself out there and finding a loving, stable relationship with some nice girl," Sage says, joining us. "Someone like Savvy, maybe."

Jesus Christ. Not this again. Why did I ever blurt my innermost wish to a crowd full of dickheads? I should have just shown up one day with my baby in tow instead of filling them in on my intentions to have a child of my own—my way.

And Savvy is not a nice girl. She's the spawn of the devil...and sexy as sin.

My so-called friends laugh with Sage, but I'm saved from more hazing when Savvy's phone pings. Shuffling all the shit in my hands, I turn her phone over.

She has a new email notification, but also...

No.

Just...no.

This can't be happening. It...can't.

Using the palm of my hand, I press hard into my eyeballs because I'm seeing things—hallucinating from the cold, maybe. That's possible, right? But when I remove my hand and blink rapidly, Savvy's screen doesn't change. There's an older notification too.

New message from ChasingColors42

My fingers are stiff as I type in her passcode. It takes me

three tries to get it right, but when I do, the ground sways beneath my feet.

Without remorse, I find and open the app for Ray of Hope, the surrogacy center I've been working with.

The guilt I've been carrying morphs into something much darker, angrier. It's violent in a way I've never experienced as messages between me as ChasingColors42 and Savvy as Firefly12 fill the screen.

She knew.

All this time. All these messages—she knew she was talking to me—she had to have known.

I scroll back to the beginning, where I told her I had just moved to a small town after my grandfather passed away. To where I told her about Sage, and when I told her I'd just found out that my best friend was also my brother.

Where I told her the real reason I wanted a baby of my own.

I haven't cried since the night my sister died, but emotion pricks at the corners of my eyes now.

I've spent months worrying that I was growing feelings for both Savvy and a faceless woman I was determined to make my surrogate, only to find out that they're one and the same.

I've been tearing myself up for turning into what I feared most—a cheater, a liar.

Savvy's eyes meet mine, and hatred stronger than the devil himself consumes me.

Betrayal is the one thing I can never get over.

Now she's become the one person I can't forgive. Or forget because with one lie of omission, she made me believe I was turning into the one person I hate most in life —my father.

But she's done more than betray me. She might have actually succeeded in what my father never could.

Savvy now has the power to destroy me with my vulnerabilities, my secrets, my truth.

I don't remember moving, but Savvy's worried stare stays locked on mine as I march through the park. When I'm close enough to touch, I shove all her shit into her hands, then grab her chin between my thumb and forefinger.

Keep it together, Grey. Keep it together.

She tries to pull away when I spit on my pocket square, then roughly wipe away the remaining soot from her face, and I should let her go. I should walk away, but the hurt that's currently feasting on my heart won't allow me to.

"Stop it, Grey. That's disgusting."

"Wouldn't be the first time we've swapped spit." I narrow my eyes and lock my jaw. "Firefly12."

And this, right here, is why I'm still touching her. I needed to feel her reaction. See the truth in her face, breathe it in when she gasps in the knowledge that she's been caught. Witness the moment she realizes she's sealed our fate as enemies.

"What? How?" Her gaze darts back and forth between my eyes at lightning speed, and I simply point to her phone.

"What the hell is firefly? And do we really have to do this now?" Braxton pleads.

"No. We don't have to do this. Ever." I don't even attempt to control the ice in my tone.

Savvy and I are done.

I sense Braxton walking away from me, but Savvy stands before me with tears in her eyes.

Too bad for her because tears mean nothing to me. After listening to my sister cry behind her locked bedroom door for months, I'm immune to them now.

"Grey, wait. Let me explain," she pleads.

"No." The word is yanked from the deepest recesses of my chest. "You've betrayed me in a way I didn't even know I was vulnerable. There's no coming back from that. You thought we were enemies before?"

Someone clears their throat, so I lean in as close as I can without touching her and lower my voice until it's no more than a threat on a breeze. "Stay the fuck away from me, you fucking liar, or I will destroy you. Enemies is too tame a word for what we are now, and believe me, you don't want to see what I do to those who betray me. This was your one and only free hit. Stay away from me."

Her chin trembles—something I've never seen before. Savvy is one of the strongest, most pig-headed women I've ever met. And I'm a depraved asshole because it gives me the slightest hint of satisfaction as I push past her to take up my duties as best man.

Before I step next to Braxton, I shoot off a text to my assistant, Quinn.

> Me: Come up with a believable emergency that will get me the fuck out of Happiness, Georgia and back to California by sunrise.

> Quinn: Done.

> Quinn: What did Braxton do now?

What the hell is she talking about, what has he done now? Braxton is the only one who's been by my side since the day I lost it all.

> Quinn: Is he leaving you to clean up a mess again?

Again? I'm too angry to deal with this bullshit.

> Me: I want to be on the plane in six hours.

> Quinn: I'll send you details shortly.

Pocketing my phone, I inhale a breath so deep my lungs burn, then release it slowly and plaster on the fake smile I learned as a child.

"Everything okay?" Braxton whispers.

"Never been better," I lie. "Let's get you married."

My best friend and brother smiles so broadly that I'm surprised sunshine and fucking rainbows don't shoot from his mouth.

He looks like an idiot, but even as my insides rot with lies and betrayal that fester like cancer, I'm relieved that he's happy.

Some of us are just not that lucky.

CHAPTER THREE

SAVVY

THE SECOND THE CEREMONY IS OVER, I RUN STRAIGHT FOR THE bathroom.

I'm going to be sick.

As soon as my knees hit the tile floor of the Chug, a familiar sense of control washes over me.

I haven't thrown up in years, but the combination of learning earlier today that Riley is now free and the image of Grey's face as he spat the word "firefly" from his beautiful lips has me dry-heaving until my stomach cramps, my throat aches and my nostrils burn.

My carefully crafted life is starting to fall apart, and once the pieces crash this time, there won't be any glue strong enough to put me back together again.

I messed up.

I know I did.

But it was for a good cause—at first. Then it spiraled into something I couldn't get out of. So I did the best I could.

I supported Grey as Firefly via text and pushed him in person as Savvy until I got a clear picture of the whole broken man that he wouldn't share with any individual person.

He needed a friend.

Greyson will never admit that, but he did, and I was there for him.

"Sav?" Clover's voice trembles.

Shit. I didn't bother turning on the lights. She's probably imagining all the ways a mass murderer could lie in wait in this dark room.

"I'm here. Sorry. Something wasn't—" I choke on a sob that startles even me.

The overhead lights flicker to life, and Clover enters the room with me. She debates sitting on the floor next to me for half a second, then reaches into her bag and pulls out a single graham cracker package and some hand sanitizer, then hands them to me.

She's never pushed for details or asked questions about the silent battle I've had with food since I was a teenager, but she's always been in silent wait, watching, helping, offering quiet support. While I've been happy and healthy for six years now, I understand why she'd make the jump to this being a relapse.

"I'm fine, Clover. I promise. I just had way too much coffee and not enough food. It all caught up with me."

She tucks her thick wool coat tighter around herself. "Are you sure that's all it is? Things have been...intense with Grey lately, and you've been really jumpy, almost like you expect someone to reach out and grab you at any moment." If she only knew how likely that scenario actually was. She fans her face. "And whatever happened before Madi's ceremony, well, that was explosive."

Regardless of what Grey thinks, I have never and will never spill his secrets, so instead, I lie to my best friend again. "Oh, that? Pfft. He's all wound up over being in Happiness. It's nothing. We fight like brother and sister because we're both button pushers who can't help ourselves. I promise, it's not that deep."

The lines between Clover's brows deepen as she stares at me.

"So his returning to California tonight doesn't have something to do with you and him?"

I forget how to breathe.

He's...leaving?

Rubbing my tongue along the roof of my mouth, I attempt to add enough moisture back so I can form words. It only makes my dry mouth worse.

"N—no," I say. "I'm sure he just has an emergency to take care of."

She quirks a brow, and I stand to avoid meeting her eyes, hand her back the sanitizer and crackers, then move to the sink because I wouldn't believe me either.

Splashing cold water on my face does nothing to cool my overheated skin.

He's leaving.

I know it's because of me, but I can't be the reason he runs away from his family. Braxton and Sage need him, and if I have to eat crow and be the person he hates more than anyone else to make that happen, then so be it.

Ignoring how painfully my heart is beating, I swallow all the usual comments I want to make about him running away and dig deep for an apology that will hopefully make him stay.

When I finish washing my hands, Clover holds out a tiny bottle of mouthwash.

"Just how much shit do you have in that big bag of yours, Clover?"

She laughs. It's a dainty, jingling kind of sound that suits her. "Every bag I own doubles as a go bag. You know, just in case a murderer chases me out of here, I'll be ready for anything."

Clover writes thriller novels for a living, and sometimes I worry she doesn't always see the line between fiction and reality.

"Come on. Let's get back before we miss Madi and Braxton's big entrance."

I quickly rinse my mouth with the mouthwash, toss the tiny bottle in the trash, then plaster on a fake smile that fools everyone. Well, almost everyone. But something tells me Grey no longer cares what's behind my mask.

"Let's do this," I say, then guide my curious friend back to the wedding.

I feel his presence the second we step into the park where the reception is being held under big, beautiful tents. He's somewhere to my left. If I had to guess, he also clocked me the moment I walked in, and he'll do everything in his power to avoid me.

But I can be relentless.

And tonight, I need to be because I owe him an explanation and the biggest apology I can muster.

"Oh, there's Elle and little Keela. Let's go say hi." Clover releases my arm and drifts away.

"I'll meet you over there in a second," I say to the back of her head. Ever since our friend Elle had Keela, everyone in this town has gone baby crazy.

Especially Grey, who announced the very first time he saw her that he was "getting himself one of those."

It's not my fault that he chose Ray of Hope.

It's not my fault that he got stuck on my profile.

It's not my fault that I never had any intention of being a surrogate if I could help it.

But it is my fault for continuing to text with him after I realized ChasingColors was him.

So that's what I'll apologize for.

Squaring my shoulders, I prepare to face him, except when I turn to where I'd felt him, he's gone. And a quick scan of the crowd doesn't show him. There's no way he's left already. Braxton would kill him.

"Can I have this dance?"

I tilt my head up to find Grey's nephew, Sage, smiling down at me. The kid is eighteen, but he has the soul of an eighty-year-old.

"I'd love to, but I need to talk to your uncle Grey first. I actually have to...apologize." My face scrunches as I say it, no matter how hard I try to keep my expression neutral.

Sage's face falls, and my chest bursts with pain. "I don't think that's a good idea tonight, Sav. I don't know what happened between the two of you, but he needs some space. I—I don't think I've ever seen him like this."

"You've betrayed me in a way I didn't even know I was vulnerable. There's no coming back from that."

Grey's words taunt my mind like a fucked-up fairy tale where everyone dies in the end.

I'd seen the pain in his eyes as he told me to stay away from him.

I hurt him, and I despise myself for it.

"Let's dance," Sage says again, this time drawing me onto the dance floor.

"I have to apologize to him, Sage."

"I have a feeling there will be a lot of apologies made in the coming months, but tonight, you have to let him go."

"But..." I look away. Sage looks so much like his uncle in

this moment, I swear my soul is tearing in two. "He's going to leave. I have to speak to him before he does."

"He won't stay away forever. Uncle Grey is a lot of things —tortured, protective, stubborn—but he's not an idiot. He knows he needs us as much as we need him. Whatever's going on between the two of you will be resolved, but first he'll need to tame some of his own demons."

"I just..." I finally peer back up at this amazing young man. "I can be prickly too, but I messed up this time. I owe him an apology, Sage."

"And you will. But tonight is about Braxton and Madi. Uncle Grey can be a grumpy bastard sometimes, but he's a good man. He'll come around, but Madi may never forgive us if we don't have the times of our lives tonight."

He leads me in a circle to see my best friend. Madi is happier than I've ever seen her, and I know Sage is right.

Grey and I may have a rocky road ahead of us, but we aren't getting rid of one another anytime soon.

Eventually, he'll have to forgive me, and eventually, I'll have to admit that it was never just about sex with him.

Thankfully, neither of those things has to happen tonight.

Soon, but not tonight.

Tonight is all about happiness and love.

Elle pushes baby Keela into my arms.

And apparently, babies. Lots and lots of babies.

CHAPTER FOUR

GREYSON

Present Day

Rain falls in a wall of water so thick that I can't see more than a few feet in front of me.

Standing on my front porch with a cup of coffee, watching it come down is fascinating. The power of it. The raging energy. Yet I'm calmer than I've been in months. Leaning my shoulder against my new porch pillar, admiring the riotous view, I'm almost relaxed, something I thought would never be possible now that I'm back in Happiness.

But it's a vast improvement over the last few months, where everyone around me thought I'd snap like a twig at the slightest provocation.

Even the mountain of dirt Cian left on the side of the drive that's quickly turning my private road into a mosh pit and will likely create a few thousand dollars in damage doesn't deter me from studying meteorological savagery with mild enjoyment.

Witnessing Mother Nature ravage the area as Hurricane Isolde warnings blast through my cell phone is an apt representation of what's been happening inside my mind since returning to Happiness, Georgia a few days ago.

I don't belong here.

But I'll live here for Sage and Braxton.

I fight back a shiver because thinking about my lifelong best friend as my half brother is still messing with my head. He seems to have adjusted to this particular betrayal much better than I have.

We've been best friends for twenty-five years. His grandfather, Ace, adopted Sage and I after my father went to jail for the death of my sister.

The worst part is, people knew we were related, but no one bothered to tell us until last year.

Since Ace passed away, our lives have been upended. First, he threw us curveballs with his will. One sent Braxton here, to Happiness, to essentially find and fix the heart and soul of the town, which ended up being Madi Ryan, his new wife.

My mission was slightly...different. And twofold. First, he wanted me to run Omni-Reyes Media on my own. While that's daunting, fine. I'll never back down from a challenge. It was his second request that's still haunting me.

The mistakes of youth and misplaced trust weigh heaviest on innocent souls. When Sin turns to sadness, don't allow her to break. Be stronger than those before you. Choose love, and light, and laughter. Choose Happiness, Greyson. Choose to let go in order to move on.

I'm certain he wanted me to choose this godforsaken little town too, with all its intrusive residents, fucked-up festivals, and absolutely no privacy, but his words were written in secret codes I can't decipher.

Sin? Who the hell is that? And why will she be sad?

None of it makes any sense.

But I chose Happiness for him. I'm here. I tried.

And I failed.

Or more accurately, Savvy fucking Monroe failed me.

Fool me once, shame on me, but you won't get a second chance because you're instantly dead to me.

And that's where I stand with my new sister-in-law's best friend. She's dead to me.

It's my own fault. I never should have gotten close to her. I never should have confided in a stranger I met online, and I sure as hell never should have announced to half the town that I was getting a baby of my own.

Not because I'm embarrassed by that, but because they've put up roadblocks at every turn. They want me to be happy, but they don't want me to be happy on my terms.

Braxton and Sage have moved on with their lives, and I'm happy for them. Truly.

After my sister died, Braxton and I took on the burden and the privilege of raising Sage. Ace was there for moral support, but every decision we made from the time we were twelve on was done with Sage in mind.

Braxton's married now. Sage is attending the local college here and is treated like a superstar on the football team.

They moved on without me, but the one thing I've done right in my life is Sage. I want that again. I want to be responsible for someone. I want to give a child everything I never had growing up.

I want a little girl, though another boy would be fine too. The only logical way to make this happen is through surrogacy.

The last thing I expected was to form a connection with a woman via the surrogacy app, only to find out that the woman I spilled my secrets to was none other than Savvy Monroe.

That's the real reason I fled home to California as soon as I could. Savvy made me question who I am at my core. I felt as though I were cheating on her when I would talk to Firefly and vice versa.

It makes no logical sense, and I'm always logical. Savvy and I weren't dating, we were never exclusive, and she made sure I knew that every chance she got. We weren't even friends with benefits. We were...benefits.

Liar.

Fuck me and my conscience.

I didn't want to feel anything for Savvy.

Slightly more truthful.

But she always, always showed up when I was at my weakest point. And now I know why. She got me to open up to her as Firefly, then used that information to—to what exactly?

I still don't know. She didn't take advantage of me with the information. She just...showed up.

It's so damn confusing. All I know for sure is that when I saw that message on her phone, betrayal like nothing I'd ever felt before cut me to my very soul.

After six months, I'm no closer to finding answers, but I also couldn't stay away from Braxton and Sage any longer. I'd already cut out on Sage's football team, where I'd agreed to help coach, like a class A asshole. Sure, I flew back to work with the quarterbacks once a week, but I never stayed more than a day.

I never gave anyone a straight answer either, and I know they're fed up with my bullshit, especially now that Braxton is going to be a dad.

The worst part is, I've never in my life backed down from a challenge or a fight.

But Savvy broke something I don't know how to fix, and it's slowly killing whatever kindness I have left.

Something moves in the distance, a flash of yellow through the sheets of rain. What the hell is out there?

There's no way though. Someone would have to walk up my mile-long driveway in this weather, and it's—

For fuck's sake.

I set my mug of coffee on the porch railing, then stand straight with my arms crossed over my chest.

If that's who I think it is, I might actually kill her.

Why is she on my property when she knows I've blocked her number and have actively avoided being in the same space as her since Braxton's wedding?

In the middle of a severe weather advisory.

Another flash of yellow, and I squint my eyes, attempting to follow her. The shock of color comes and goes, but if it's because she keeps falling or because of the rain patterns, I can't be sure.

Then the wind blows from the opposite direction, clearing a path to her in time to see her go down face-first into the muck. My muscles clench as I wait for her to lift herself up. She's the only woman stubborn enough to believe she can outrun a goddamn hurricane.

Savvy pulls herself up, only to fall again a few steps later, and a gnawing guilt outweighs my anger when she's close enough to see she's missing a boot. It was probably swallowed by my mud sea, so I stomp down into the rain with every intention of sending her away.

I'd just finished a workout when I came outside, so steam rises from my bare chest and arms when I hit the chilly rain, even though it's humid as hell out here.

No one on this planet can piss me off as much as this woman does simply by existing.

I sink into the mud up to my shins, the mountain of dirt looking more like an anthill now.

Savvy stands, and I'm not sure what happens, but her eyes flash brightly, the entirety of her face caked in mud except the whites of her eyes. She steps forward and right out of her pants that get swallowed into the earth. It trips her up, and she wobbles through an ungraceful spin before falling backward onto her ass, and it's then that I see the first signs of defeat in her shoulders as her entire chest cavity appears to sink into itself.

Lost to her own mind, and honestly, probably exhausted from her hike up my driveway, she hasn't noticed me yet as she lies back and...and cries. It's raining so hard I could have missed it if it weren't for the quiver to her chin and the complete and utter despair on her face.

A porcupine releases all its quills in my throat. In the time that I've known this woman, she's been strong, stubborn, independent—painfully so. She doesn't break down, and she doesn't give up.

Seeing it happen now, just yards from my house, causes my heart to pound violently against my chest.

Get up, Savannah. Get. The. Fuck. Up.

She doesn't move.

I should have known that she wouldn't let me cut her out of my life forever. I suppose I should be thankful for the six-month reprieve I've had because apparently, our standoff is over.

For now.

Shaking my head, I trudge through the mud that gets precariously deeper the closer I get to her. With her eyes closed, she can't see me coming. Her tears and the rain wash her face clean of mud, but nothing can erase the sadness, the complete sense of defeat in her expression.

It's something she would never willingly show, and I almost feel guilty for intruding on this moment, except I won't because she's the one trespassing.

Right. She's the one who doesn't belong here. It helps me hang on to my anger with a little more force as I bend, then lift her over my shoulder.

I almost toss her too far and have to readjust my grip. She's lighter than I remember, and I hate that.

My hands land on her bare, muddy thighs, and I hate that I remember how good her skin feels beneath mine.

That's another thing she stole when she betrayed me— the best fucking sex of my life.

She wasn't looking for anything serious, and I'll never be a forever kind of guy, so it was perfect. The way we hate each other ninety-nine percent of the time only made the sex that much hotter.

"Gr—Greyson. W—what are you doing?"

I slide her off my shoulder and into a wedding hold, then nearly drop her when I realize her lips are blue.

"How long have you been out here? Are you trying to get yourself killed?" I take quick but careful steps toward my house.

"C—Car...s-stuck. E-e-eleven." The chattering of her teeth is a knife to the gut with each stuttered syllable.

I pause as her words register, then I pick up my pace and come close to jogging the rest of the way to my front porch. "You've been trying to get up my driveway for two hours, Savannah? Two fucking hours with a hurricane warning in effect?"

Granted, it's not hypothermia-type weather, but she

grew up in Vegas, and she's cold when its seventy. Wet and muddy? No wonder her entire body shivers now.

"T—two hours?" she asks as I walk us around the porch to the outdoor shower, but I'm too angry to respond.

Savvy is a smart woman—her podcast listeners call her brilliant—yet she does the stupidest goddamn shit sometimes. It's as though she never learned to properly care for herself.

"This is going to suck," I say through clenched teeth. The outdoor shower doesn't currently have any hot water. It's on Cian's list to fix, but my priority was finishing the small apartment and putting in an elevator in the workshop of the detached garage for Moose first.

It's the least I could do for the old guy who sold me his dream home that he had no intention of ever selling.

I walk us into the shower, turn on the spray, and do my best to get most of the mud off us as she gasps and shivers in my arms.

Instead of bothering with towels once she's mostly clean, I march us straight into my house, up the stairs, and into my room and the attached bathroom.

She doesn't protest or even make a sound except for her chattering teeth. Her condition is much more precarious than I first thought because Savvy Monroe will fight me to her death just for the fun of it if given the chance—it's probably why I liked her so much.

But she ruined that, and I can't do second chances.

Setting her on the bench in the large walk-in shower, I blast the hot water while hosing off my legs and torso, then adjust it so it doesn't burn her. With my luck, the hot water would send her into shock or something.

I'm pulling down the showerhead, and her eyes widen when she realizes my plan.

And my entire being feels lighter as I turn the spray on her and hose her down from head to toe until she's warmed enough to stand on her own and fight me for the showerhead.

"Stop," she gasps as warm water splashes her face.

"Sorry, you've got a little mud..." I spray her in the face again. "Right there."

Savvy stalks forward, the usual fire returning to her blazing green eyes, and rips the shower nozzle from my hands.

I simply smirk and walk away, not giving a shit that I'm soaking my floor.

"Hurry up. You've got a long walk home," I call over my shoulder, then slam the bathroom door.

In my closet, I strip naked, tossing my wet shorts into the laundry basket and slipping on some lounge pants. A suit would feel like necessary armor right now, but I know putting one on will only lead to questions, and I just want her out of my home as quickly as possible.

And, because I'm not a complete asshole, I also grab Savvy one of my T-shirts and another pair of loungers.

I'll never get them back, but it's fine. The sooner she gets out of here, the sooner I can go back to reminding myself why I hate her in the first place.

She's not going anywhere in this storm, you dingledick.

Opening the bathroom door without knocking, I ignore how she sits on the floor of the shower under the hot water —even though my stomach turns at the sight—and drop the clean clothes on the vanity for her.

"Don't use all the hot water. I've got shit to do today."

"Grey..."

Whatever she's about to say won't undo the fact that for months, she talked to me as Firefly12, that she broke my trust, or that she might have even broken my cold, dead heart.

This time, when I exit the bathroom, I slam the door so hard the walls around it shake, then I retreat to my office, where I can hopefully get lost in work while she figures out how the hell to get home.

My world no longer includes Firefly12 or Savannah Monroe, and I need to keep myself busy so I don't forget that.

CHAPTER FIVE

SAVVY

This is not how this was supposed to go.

I'd wanted to confront him at his office, but when I got there, his bitchy public relations lady told me he was working from home.

So my contingency plan was to drive up here, tell him to unblock me because we do have to coexist now that our best friends are married, and get home before the storm got too bad.

Freaking Mother Nature hates me.

With a sigh, I lift myself off the floor, strip out of my shirt and panties, then use Grey's body wash to scrub my skin free of the mud that's caked itself beneath my fingernails, up the crack of my ass, and even in my flipping ears.

It's like a mudslide rolled down the side of a mountain and deposited it all in front of his house.

Defeated doesn't begin to cover what I was feeling when he hefted me from my muddy grave. It had been raining so hard I couldn't see his house, so I had no idea how far I'd gone or how far I had left. The trees lining his ridiculously long driveway gave nothing away either.

I had only planned to rest in the rain and mud for a few moments, but then emotions crawled up from hell and dragged me under in a way I never allow.

Grey and I have never been friends, but I'm grieving the loss of him like a death.

Which doesn't make any sense. How can it hurt so much to be cut off by the one person who feels more like an enemy than my actual enemies?

The thunder overhead is so loud it shakes the walls of the house, and then the lights flicker, so I hurry through washing. It doesn't matter if I'm still dirty. It'll only get worse when Grey tosses me out of here anyway.

I'm under no illusion that he'll offer me safe harbor during the storm.

"Get out of the shower," he growls from the doorway. I don't bother covering myself up. It wasn't that long ago that he had his mouth on every inch of my body, so it's not anything he hasn't seen, and truthfully, the task of getting home is daunting.

My life has spiraled out of control, and I fear that this storm is only the prequel of what's to come for me. I'm already exhausted by life at thirty years old. That doesn't bode well for my future.

"A tree behind the house was struck by lightning." He's staring at me in the mirror, and somehow, the redirection makes his heated glare sting even more. "I have no idea if it's true about not showering in a lightning storm, but I'd rather you didn't die in my home. You haunt my life enough as it is."

He spins and strides back out the open door.

But I do shut off the water because he's right.

Typically, I would toss him the middle finger for bossing

me around, but he's also right in his feelings. I did this to whatever fledgling situationship we once had.

It's my own fault he hates me, so it's up to me to help us move past this before my life completely and irrevocably implodes.

A large white towel flies into the room, and I frown.

"I was doing laundry," he barks. "Try not to soak my floors."

Okay, he's moved from asshole to dickhead. At least it's movement, but it's anyone's guess if it's progress or not.

He has the softest towels I've ever used, and I bring it to my face with a sigh.

It smells like him, and my stomach clenches with nerves.

I'm not this girl, and the fact that he can make me want to be is even more reason to justify what I've done—it was the right thing for the both of us.

He'll never see it that way, but I know it's true.

The towel soaks up the excess water from my hair, then I run it all over my skin before dropping it in his hamper and slipping into the clothes he left me. Of course even his lounge wear is designer—this outfit he so casually tossed my way probably cost more than my car payment.

Thank you, childhood insecurities—some remnants of being the poor girl never fade, like how I still notice every piece of clothing I could never afford.

For someone who hates me, he sure goes out of his way to care for me, even now.

When I exit his bathroom, he's a tight wall of muscle standing in the hallway.

"What do you want?" His left hand balls into a fist while he weaves his lucky coin through the fingers of his right hand.

"First." My hand falls to my hip, while the pointer on my

free hand wags in his direction. He makes me so damn angry. "The weather app said I had four hours before this—"

Lightning lights up the sky, casting shadows through the windows and doors. But it's the thunder that rivals a rickety old wooden roller coaster that causes me to gasp.

Freaking hell.

Before I can open my mouth, a deafening crash has me clutching the walls.

Greyson appears to fly down the stairs, his feet touching down on every third step, propelling him faster, until he lands at the bottom with a thud.

I follow at a more reasonable pace, but I know we're in trouble when I see him running from window to window, cursing loudly and muttering what sounds like threats under his breath.

I'm still two steps from the bottom when he rushes me, takes me by the hand, and drags me deeper into his home.

He swings open a closet door under a staircase. "In," he grunts.

"What?"

He doesn't wait another moment, choosing instead to two-hand shove me inside, and then I'm surrounded in darkness when the door slams shut.

Sensory deprivation is my Achilles heel. My breathing turns ragged as I feel along the walls for a light switch.

Come on, Grey. Don't do this to me. Not this.

Stars flash in the darkness of my mind, and I'm forced to crouch low, drop my head between my legs, and attempt to breathe.

He isn't holding me captive in a confined space. He's not Riley. Find the door, Savannah. Find the—

The door opens, then closes just as quickly. The flash of

light is enough to see Grey for a moment before we're plunged into darkness again.

"We have to get under the stairs."

A small lantern flickers to life.

"For fuck's sake, Sav. What the hell?"

Greyson's large fingers wrap around my biceps, lifting me to stand, and shaking me a little when my eyes take too long to focus.

The anger creasing his forehead softens the longer he stares at me.

"What caused it?"

He's the only person to witness a flashback since Ace.

"Th..." My voice wobbles, and I suck in air through my teeth. I'm not weak. "The dark. Sensory deprivation."

"Another secret you're unwilling to share?"

I nod, just once, and the hard lines of betrayal reappear on his handsome face. He releases me, and my traitorous body follows as though it misses his comfort.

"I don't owe you anything, Grey."

A sheet of ice falls over him, an impenetrable wall, and he takes a step away from me, hinges at the waist, and opens a door that only reaches his shoulders.

"No, you just stole all my secrets while hoarding your own. In."

"I'm not going in there." Tight spaces. Sweat. Fear. The sounds of crunching metal, suffocation and pain.

"The hurricane took out half my backyard. We really don't have time for this shit, Sav. Get in the fucking shelter. It's the only safe space right now."

A loud crack outside makes me jump, and I move on autopilot, through the mini door that opens to a tiny room under the stairs.

Small fabric chairs embroidered with the names Finn

and Rory line one wall. On the floor opposite are crates marked *food*, *water*, and *flashlights*.

Greyson steps in behind me so his front is pressed against my back, and I scoot forward, then fall into a navy-blue chair made completely of fabric and foam.

The click of the door echoes in the small space, and I fight to control my fear.

Grey moves about the room, pulling blankets from one bin and bottles of water from another. I don't say a word as I track his efficient movements.

Before long, he drops into the green chair next to me, his large frame taking up his space and mine.

"When Moose built this house, he made sure this was up to code for natural disasters."

Moose is a seventy-year-old giant. He's friends with Madi's grandfather and a staple here in Happiness. He must have chosen these small chairs for his grandchildren.

"I still can't believe he sold you this place." Idle chatter is my go-to when stressed.

Moose built this place for his wife, but she passed away before it was finished. He never even moved in. He just visited the property whenever his kids were in town.

"It came at a cost," Grey says with none of the anger he directs at me. "He's puttering around in the workshop every morning at seven."

"I heard he brings you breakfast."

His large shoulder lifts and rises against mine. "I hate breakfast."

The noise of the storm is suddenly so loud, I can't focus. The house groans as though it's being trampled by a giant, and the airhorn noise rages on.

"Are we going to be okay in here?"

"Yes."

"What did you see outside?"

Hatred burns brightly in his eyes when they fall on me. "A fucking hurricane."

No. I've lived in Happiness since college. We've never had an actual hurricane, especially not in July.

A loud bang shakes the interior walls, and a whimper escapes me. Another crash and howling winds unlike anything I've ever heard before set off the panic I've worked ten years to manage.

All my carefully crafted facades, the walls I've created, the thick skin I sewed for myself, they all crack and peel away, leaving me raw and exposed.

"Listen, I'm sorry, okay?" I babble. "I'm so, so sorry. I never meant to hurt you."

Glass shatters somewhere, and I shriek.

Oh my God, we're going to die.

"I know you think I lied about everything, but I didn't."

"A lie by omission is still a lie." His voice is razor-sharp. "You didn't tell me who you were on the surrogacy app. That's a lie." A loud crack makes us both jump. "Jesus," he continues, as though I didn't just shriek my throat raw. "When I was pouring my heart out to you about Ace's death, you had every opportunity to be honest with me, to tell me about your relationship with him. For fuck's sake, Savvy. I was sharing my pain, and you just sat there, hiding behind your screen, pretending not to even know him. As far as I'm concerned, that's another lie. How many others have piled up while I was feeding into your bullshit?"

Words tumble from my lips as though I have no control of my mouth. "I didn't lie about Ace. He helped me out in Vegas eight years ago, but he said it was my story to tell, and I didn't have to tell anyone if I didn't want to. And I never took advantage of his kindness, if that's what you're thinking."

I hadn't meant to bring this up, but now that he knows I'm Firefly, he's also put two and two together to realize that in the heavily edited story I told him, it was Ace who came to my rescue. He probably thinks I used Ace. At the very least, he's pissed that I never mentioned just how much he meant to me.

Grey leaps to his feet while the rattling around us shakes so violently that it matches my internal storm. Knowing we're about to die, my mouth takes on a mind of its own.

I couldn't shut up now if I wanted to. "I made a really bad decision when I was sixteen, and it led to two years of bad decisions. One of them almost cost me my life, but it cost others so much more." My lungs attempt to deflate, making proper breathing painful. "I tried to make up for my mistakes and got stuck in a shitty situation with the wrong people. But when Ace found out, he protected me. That's all you need to know."

"Why are you telling me this?" He growls.

"Because even though Ace saved me once, I know how these people operate, and it's only a matter of time before I'll have to return to Vegas because they'll never accept that my debt is paid. So two years ago, I signed up with Ray of Hope. I needed an insurance policy, not that you would understand that. But I'm not cut out to be a mother, Grey. Becoming a surrogate was a means to an end, a way to save myself. It was never about you."

Wind like I've never heard nearly drowns out my words. The floor shakes as though we're in the midst of an earthquake, but I keep speaking. "I was with Ray of Hope long before you even moved to town. I didn't join to mess with you."

More glass. More screeching winds. More violence rages on around us.

"Yes, I should have told you when I realized you were ChasingColors42. I should have done a lot of things differently, but you opened up to me there. You acted human and didn't shut me out. I was trying to be your friend, Greyson."

"My friend?" he bellows over the destruction outside.

"Yes, your friend." I'm shouting too, but I just want to be heard over the storm. My voice is already raw from the effort. "You can acknowledge it or not, but you were struggling with your new family dynamics, and you needed someone in your corner. I knew you wouldn't let it be me in person, so I was there for you the only way I knew how. It's what Ace would've wanted. It's what—"

He sways on his feet, and then I realize it's the house moving as if we're on a ship out at sea.

Cracking wood splits the violent sounds of destructive wind, and it's as though my mind goes on hiatus. A high-pitched sob works its way up into my throat and escapes before I can wrestle it back.

Grey's eyes widen before he drops back into the chair next to me. Pulling me into his side, he cocoons my body with his.

"It's okay, you're safe." I don't know if he whispers or if it's just so loud that I can barely hear him, but being wrapped in his arms calms something deep inside of me.

"We don't have to be friends, Grey, but we should be civil, have some sort of politeness, or we'll lose Madi and Braxton. It's not fair to make them choose between us. And I—I can't lose Madi. I can't."

"Hush."

Any other day, I would roundhouse a kick right to his neck for that. But when he says it with a soothing hand brushing back my hair, and his cinnamon-and-citrus scent enveloping me in his strength when I have none of my own left, I let it go.

If I allowed it, I think I'd probably let a hell of a lot go for him.

I sway, but not of my own volition. Grey rocks me as you would a small child, his warm body pressed to mine, determined to keep me safe.

If only keeping me safe were always this easy.

"You'll be a good dad, Grey. Sage is amazing, and any child will be lucky to have you."

He grunts in response, but his muscles stay relaxed.

"How long do you think this storm will drag on?"

A huff of air swirls the hair at the top of my head when he sighs. "Even when the storm passes, I don't think we'll be getting out, or anyone will be getting in, for at least a few days."

The muscles in my neck and shoulders flex. "A few days?"

"The logging road in back is already unpassable. If the sounds ripping apart the earth in the front are any indication, both our evacuation routes will be destroyed. And we have no idea how the rest of the town will fare."

"I hope Madi keeps Pops locked up somewhere."

His chuckle vibrates into me. "I'm sure Brax has him tied to the storm shelter. When he renovated the inn, he made sure to update their stairwell shelter too."

My shoulders tense, and he isn't able to rock me as effectively.

"They'll be safe, Sav. I promise. Their shelter is five times the size of ours to accommodate all the guests at the inn. So, I know that they, and Sage with a few of his teammates, are and will be safe."

"Oh, God. Clover." Jumping to my feet, I spin in place. How the hell could I have forgotten Clover? Where's my phone? "She's terrified of her own shadow. I promised I'd be back before the storm hit. I have to—"

"You have to what?" When the hell did Grey stand up? "You're not going anywhere. Clover will be fine." He doesn't sound as reassuring as he did when talking about Braxton and Madi though. "She's an adult. She'll be fine."

"No. You don't understand. She—she has reasons to be afraid. This might— What the hell was I thinking? Clover needs me."

"And you'll go to her as soon as it's safe."

"No, I—"

"Do not argue with me, Savannah. Not now. If you leave, you die. That's the reality, and if you think I'm going to stare at your best friends' faces for the rest of my life, knowing they blame me for not keeping you safe, you're out of your fucking tits."

"But Cl—"

Soft, firm, demanding lips crash into mine, and my eyes widen to uncomfortable dimensions.

This man, the one who is actively hating me on purpose, is kissing me.

And I do the stupidest thing I could possibly do—I kiss him back.

CHAPTER SIX

GREYSON

Fuck, she tastes good.

I hate that she tastes good.

I hate that she fits against me as if God molded her at my side.

I hate that her soft moan urges me to continue.

I hate that my tongue commands hers in the only way she'll allow me to dominate her.

I hate that I like dominating her.

I hate that I have no self-control around this woman.

I hate that my body does whatever the hell it wants the second her belly presses against my erection.

I hate her.

I hate that she lied.

I hate that I allowed myself to be hurt by her.

I hate that she mewls, and scratches, and writhes against me as though I'm the only one who can bring her pleasure.

I hate that I don't hate her nearly as much as I should.

"Fuck." I hiss as sharp nails trail a line down my bare chest, then clench my teeth when my cock bobs angrily in my lounge pants.

Savannah Monroe is my damnation, my ruin, my eternal light.

Her tense muscles turn pliable in my hands, and it sends a rush of power through me.

I absolutely cannot fuck my sworn enemy. Again. I cannot fuck her again.

"Grey." Sav doesn't whine, she doesn't beg, but my name certainly sounds like some sort of prayer from her lips.

"Why do I have to want you so fucking badly?" The anger in my tone is directed at myself, but she flinches as though my words struck her.

Guilt is a sensation I've been actively attempting to ban from my existence, but she manages to wrangle the devil out of me every time. In every situation besides ones involving her, when I see a problem, I fix it, then I move on. I don't allow emotions to tangle up my life. I don't allow distractions.

My entire adult life has been about raising Sage to be the complete opposite of my father, and I've done some pretty questionable things to ensure he grew up in a safe, loving environment.

But then Sav struts in here, caked in mud, and sets fire to all my carefully laid plans.

"Say yes," she mewls, rubbing her body against mine.

This is the Savvy Monroe I know. This is the voice I listen to every night through AirPods so no one finds out I'm slightly obsessed with her podcast. This is the voice that guides couples through sexual doubt, self-exploration, and mutual masturbation—that was last night's podcast, and I nutted in my hand like a goddamn teenager.

One more time. This is the last time I'll be weak around her.

"I thought I was clear on this. You don't control these encounters, Sav. I do."

She gasps as I spin her, pressing her back to my front. She kicks over the battery-operated lantern, causing shadows to dance across the tight space, but I created the map of her pleasure. I could make her come without a speck of light.

And she is going to come. If nothing else, it'll make her fucking apologies stop.

"Get on your hands and knees with your face in the blue chair."

Her sharp intake of breath feeds the dragon that apparently only surfaces for her. Add that to the list of things I hate.

"Now, Sav."

The storm raging outside has yet to move along, but it has nothing on the one dismantling me from the inside out.

I will not fall for a liar. I will not fall for a liar.

A groan of pure satisfaction rattles my ribcage when she drops to her knees and presses her face into the cushioned seat of the foam chair. She has the most perfect ass.

I hate that I love her ass.

"Lower your pants and remove the shirt." I also hate that she looks so damn hot in my clothes.

"Bossy freaking asshole," she mutters just low enough I strain to catch the ending.

But she follows my directions beautifully, and pre-come soaks the soft material of my pants.

She's wet.

Closing my eyes, I drag in oxygen through my nose to calm my wild thoughts.

When I open them, they track the ladder of her ribcage —reigniting a protective flame I shouldn't carry for her. She's lost weight she didn't have to lose. What the hell has she been doing for the last six months?

Savvy arches her spine, and the air hangs thick with mutual desire. Shoving my pants down, I get to my knees behind her. My fingers trace the indents of her spine, silently cursing each and every one.

Delicate.

Fragile.

I don't like seeing her this way.

Why has she lost so much weight? I can't even begin to estimate how much, but I memorized her figure and could sketch it in my sleep. It's changed since I've been gone. Why?

"Have you been with anyone else since Christmas?" Christmas—the last time we had sex, and it feels like a lifetime ago.

"No." She gasps when my fingers separate her pussy for my viewing pleasure. Sexual desire wars with my incurable disease to fix what I perceive as broken, and seeing every knob of her spine tells me something has broken her.

Or someone.

"You're still on birth control?" My voice croaks, so I clear it.

"Always." She pushes back into my fingers, and I decide right then that I'll deal with her issues later.

"This is the last time we do this, Sav."

Her long brown hair splays out over her back when she cranes her neck to look me in the eye. "That's my line," she says, wearing a smirk that brings other men to their knees.

Fuck. It is her line. It's what she's said every time I was drawn to her under the cover of darkness.

"It is." My left eye twitches. "Luckily for both of us, I have more self-control than you. So, when I say it's the last time, believe that it will be."

"The almighty Greyson Reyes has spoken."

Anger, desire, and a small amount of respect tingles in my fingers right before I slap her ass. I've never understood why her talking back to me makes pride flood my veins, but now I'll never have to explore that uncomfortable sensation again.

My hand connects with her reddened flesh again when she doesn't immediately respond.

"Jesus, okay. Last time. Obviously, last—"

I cut off her words by surging forward, impaling her on every inch of my cock.

"*Grey*." Her needy groan pushes me to move faster.

I don't tell her that I haven't been with anyone else either. I'm just petty enough to keep that information to myself. Telling her would only raise more questions anyway. Like why I still haven't picked a surrogate, or why I haven't fucked anyone but my own hand in months.

"Harder." Her pleading turns me on like nothing else ever has. The near-feral reaction I have should be criminal.

Savvy is the first woman I've ever been with who has a full and complete understanding of her sexual needs and desires.

And the confidence to act on them.

"My—my throat." She grunts each word in between the slapping of my hips against her ass. Harder and harder I thrust, until her screams and moans block out the literal hurricane threatening to rip my house apart nail by fucking nail.

"You don't make the decisions here, Sav." Yet I give her exactly what she wants.

The second my fingers wrap around her throat and squeeze, she comes. Hard. Hard enough that her pussy grips my cock and I see stars.

Pure bliss snakes up my spine while her pussy flutters and spasms around me, but I bite my tongue to keep from coming.

Her fingers claw at my hand around her throat, not pressing it away, but forcing me to squeeze tighter.

Why does she have to be so damn perfect?

I fall forward, my front pressing into her back, so my lips land near her ear, and I slip my free hand around her thigh to pinch her clit.

"That was just a warm-up, Sav. Now fuck me like you've missed me."

She knows what I want, but she's just stubborn enough to fight me for it.

This is a war she can't win though. Once my trust is gone, it's gone forever, so this thing between us will be all about my wants and needs now.

Being selfish is the only way to rebuild my walls.

With my arms wrapped around her belly, I lift her, spin, then sit in the chair that's wet from her drool with my dick still ensconced in her heat.

She sits on my cock, a little dazed, with her back plastered to my sweaty chest, and I slap her thigh just hard enough to make the cracking sound on her skin vibrate through the air.

"Move, Sav. Your turn to do the work."

My hands fall to the sides of these idiotic stuffed chairs I never got around to replacing and I jerk my hips upright, just once, to spur her into motion.

Her pussy is swollen around me. She might even be sore, but she loves it. And when she starts to ride me, her sighs and gasps of pleasure prove it to be true.

"What is it you want today, Grey?" She rolls her hips in a slow seduction meant to torment me.

My chest rumbles. "Sweet and slow is for good girls who know how to tell the truth, and that's not you. Fuck me, Sav."

"I didn't lie to hurt you." I want to believe there's honesty in that tone of hers, but she's proven to me that she can't be trusted, so I ignore her, thankful when she slams her tight pussy down onto my lap.

"I'd have to care for the lie to hurt me, Sav. Play with my balls."

She cries out when I spread her ass cheeks. The sight of my cock ramming into her each time she bounces down makes me even harder—so hard I actually hurt.

Everything with Savannah Monroe hurts.

The soft pads of her fingertips play with my balls before slipping lower.

"Don't," I grind out. But it's too late, her finger dips back, rimming my ass, and I come with violent spurts that suck the air straight from my lungs.

Goddamn, she's infuriating.

I thrust up because even though I just came with enough force to put me in a momentary coma, I'm still hard inside her.

Savvy attempts to take control, but I hold onto her hips to keep her still and hovering above my cock as I rut into her like a man possessed.

A purging. That's what this is.

Her hands fall to my thighs, nails digging half crescent moons into my skin. It only makes me thrust harder, faster, deeper. I'm aware enough to know that I'm trying to imprint myself on her, so she'll never forget, but also, if this is truly the last time I'll have this woman, she'll feel every ounce of her betrayal the same way I did.

She's already taken the rest of me.

"Grey. Oh, God."

I tug her down so she's sitting in my lap, and I tuck her thighs over mine, keeping her open to me as I continue to thrust up.

My fingers roam her slick skin. Finding her clit, I flick at it ruthlessly until I hit the threshold she loves so much. The one bordering on pain and pleasure that has her head falling back to rest on my shoulder. She turns her face into my neck, and irrational anger festers in my chest.

That's a place for a lover, not whatever this thing is between us now. With my free hand, I roughly turn her head away from my neck, then I rub small, tight circles on her bundle of nerves, and she explodes around me, taking me with her into a momentary daze of bliss.

One where she didn't betray me.

One where if she'd only made a different choice, things might have been so very, very different.

I sink into the chair with her on top of me. We're both catching our breath as the reality of our situation sinks in.

I fucked her. Again. After telling myself it would never happen again. While our lives are in imminent danger, but my mind replays only one thing on repeat—why did she have to betray me?

"That was probably a mistake," she whispers, and my entire body turns to steel. Well, everything except my cock that deflates instantly and slips out of her, pulling our joined come with it.

With a clenched jaw, I lift her from my lap and drop her into the chair next to mine.

"Yup."

I don't want to see her face while my chest is fighting off a heart attack, so I stand and dig through a container in search of baby wipes. When I find them, I toss one package to her and then clean myself up with another.

Mistake. Yeah, and where Sav is concerned, they just keep piling up.

———

I WENT FROM HATING SAVVY TO HATING MYSELF.

She's sprawled out on the floor next to me using the seat of her chair as a pillow.

Thankfully, she didn't say another word after she informed me that we were a mistake—again—she just passed out the moment her head hit the cushion.

Sleep is an elusive bitch though, and I'm forced to stare into the dark as the storm circles us hour after hour.

What will be left of my house, my property, after this?

It could be the perfect excuse to head back to California, but I won't do that to Sage. Not when he's found his place on the football team here. And even if I'm loath to admit it, helping coach the quarterbacks has given me back a piece of my life I'd refused to acknowledge I'd missed.

"I am sorry." Her soft confession picks at my conscience like a child plucking at a newly formed scab.

"Are you hungry?" I ask, ignoring her statement. There's no going back, so I will no longer weigh myself down with her nonsense.

"No, thanks."

"Stop doing that," I hiss.

"Doing what?" She sits up, my T-shirt so large it hangs off one shoulder.

"Being...demure. This isn't you. You're loud and brash. Just stop fucking lying."

My eyes widen as her face turns a shade of red that makes me almost fearful that she's not breathing.

"I'm not lying, Grey. I don't apologize either, yet here I am. I'm trying because I know I screwed up. I know I broke your trust and that I'll never fully get it back. But I'm here, throwing myself at your mercy because the only people I consider family live in this town and I will not be the reason they can't have all their friends and family in the same place."

I stand, reaching for my lucky coin, only to remember I left it in the nightstand upstairs.

"Apology accepted. There, now will you cut the shit?"

The heat from her body alerts me first. When the air shifts and I catch the scent of her and sex, I know she's directly behind me.

Looking at her now would be the equivalent of staring straight at Medusa herself, so I keep my gaze on the bare wall in front of me.

"There's a reason I don't tell anyone about my past, and if you can't accept that, then fine. But when it comes to being a surrogate, it had nothing to do with you. You can believe that or not, I really don't give a shit at this point, but we will not be the reason my best friend doesn't get her happily ever after. Do you understand?"

"Perfectly."

She sighs, and it feels fragile as it hits my back. *It's not my responsibility to fix her.* If I say it enough, perhaps I'll finally believe it.

Everything suddenly falls silent. The wind that's been pelting my home for the last two hours disappears like a whisper. No glass breaking, no sounds of wood or metal hitting the walls.

Eerie, deadly silence.

"Do you think the storm's over?" There's fear in her tone, and if I were a nicer guy, I'd face her and offer comfort.

But she had the nice version of me before, and look what she did to him.

"No, I think the worst is yet to come."

Her fear is alive, and it takes every ounce of control I have to ignore her and grab a protein bar before sitting back down to wait this shit out.

CHAPTER SEVEN

SAVVY

GREY WAS RIGHT.

As the hours went on, the storm became angrier, ruthless, and relentless. The longer the silence stretched between us, the more my fears took control, until I was once again sitting with my head between my legs, breathing into a paper bag that he handed me.

As much as he hates me, he also can't suppress the good guy he attempts to shield under his pissed-off assholery facade.

"We can't stay in here forever." Ugh, that came out bitchy. This man pushes my buttons even when he isn't trying.

We've been sitting in silence for close to an hour now, and I'm getting antsy.

He grunts but opens the door, pokes his head out, then exits our shelter. I scramble up to grab a flashlight and follow him.

Crickets chirp loudly, as if they're in the house, and a few more steps reveal why. All the windows on one side of the house are shattered, glass shards littering every flat surface. Where the heck did these little critters ride out the storm?

"Don't move."

I open my mouth to argue, but he points to my bare feet, and I freeze.

He walks down the hall with careful steps, opens a closet door, and pulls out a pair of sneakers and tosses them to me.

"I think they belonged to Moose's daughter, but they should work for now."

Lowering them to the floor, I slip my feet into them, then trail Grey through the house.

The power's out, but the moon is eerily bright and low in the sky, casting shadows everywhere I turn.

I gasp when he opens his front door. "Oh my God."

Greyson is silent as he takes in the damage. It's a war zone. Trees are broken at odd angles and lie like dead wood, bobbing in at least five feet of water. His SUV is on its side, bent around what looks like a telephone pole, but the most concerning thing is that his house is now an island surrounded by water, mud, and debris in every direction.

Defeat smacks into my chest as I stare at Grey. His shoulders slump, and his eyes shine brighter than normal in the moon's reflection.

"Are you okay?" I ask quietly.

He doesn't look at me, but I carefully cross the porch to scan the area where Moose's workshop used to be. Now it's just a sea of rubble.

"We've never had a storm like this, at least not in the time I've lived here," I say.

"Moose will be devastated." His tone is quiet, subdued. Before I can offer any words, he turns and stalks back inside.

With a parting glance at the swampy yard, I follow him. I only make it two steps inside before he turns to me.

"If the upstairs fared like the downstairs did, the primary bedroom should be clear of glass and debris. You might as well get some sleep. We're not getting out of here any time soon."

"What about you?" I may have shown up here not quite myself, but I'm not a damsel in distress most of the time. I can help...if he'll let me.

"What about me?" he barks.

I'm proud of myself for not flinching. "I mean, what are you going to do? I can help."

He studies me as if I'm dog shit he can't remove from the bottom of his shoe.

"Go to bed, Sav. I'm going to find the satellite phone in the storm shelter and try to reach Braxton. Then I'll make sure the rest of the house is safe."

"I can do one of those things or at least start the process."

"I'd really prefer you to just go the fuck to bed."

"Right, go to bed so you don't have to face me. Well, Grey, I hate to break it to you, but if me showing up here in the middle of a hurricane didn't clue you in to the fact that I'm not going anywhere, I don't know what will.

"We have shit to work out, yes, but a natural disaster just touched down in the only place I've ever been truly happy, so if you think I'm just going to go to sleep while you worry about my family and my town, you can seriously just fuck off."

I stomp past him and head for his kitchen, where I know he has a bunch of notepads stored.

"Whatever," he calls to my back. "Just don't die on my property."

I snort, and it turns into a full belly laugh. We've always had a precarious relationship, but I'll be damned if I allow him to turn us into lifelong enemies now. He may think of me as his devil, but he'll never be mine.

He storms off, and I get to work. Until the sun comes up, it's probably safest to stay inside, so I start in the mudroom by his garage in the back, taking notes of damage and any strange scents. Luckily, I don't smell gas or anything toxic, but something in his fridge has most definitely gone bad— I'll leave that investigation to him.

The windows on the north side of the house are all blown in, but other than a little wind damage, it doesn't seem too bad. Using a broom, I sweep up broken glass the best I can, then drop towels from his laundry room on the places rain has entered without the glass to stop it.

All things considered, especially after getting a short glimpse of the outside, the inside of his home really isn't that bad.

"She's here," I hear him say.

Scooping up some wet towels, I stand just as he enters the great room.

His intense stare freezes me in place, then his focus shifts to the wet towels in my arms.

The muscles in his bare chest pull taut as he strides into the room. He takes the towels from my arms, then hands me a phone that appears to be straight from the early '90s—far too big to be new.

My brow is furrowed as he stalks away from me toward the laundry room.

"Hello?" I say, hitting the speakerphone button.

"Savvy? Oh, thank God. We didn't know where you were." Madison's voice quivers, and I imagine her chin trembling as she attempts to hold it together. "It's bad, Sav. Happiness has never seen a storm like this."

"I know. What about Clover?" Guilt weighs me down, and I sink to my knees.

Clover isn't strong like Madi and me. She carries demons stronger than anything I could ever imagine.

"She's fine. Chief was doing his patrol. He saw your car on the side of the road near Grey's place but couldn't get up the driveway, so he went to your house to check on you. He found Clover and then stayed with her because the storm hit so fast. It sounds like there's some damage to your side of the duplex, but she and Chief are okay. Brax said it's not safe to do inventory yet, but as soon as the sun comes up, we'll start gathering the troops and checking on everyone."

"It's going to be a few days before anyone can get to us," Grey says from the doorway. He avoids eye contact, but I hold the phone out, and he repeats himself. "From what I can tell, the hurricane ran in a circle around my property. No one is getting in, and we're not getting out until the water recedes and we get some chainsaws up here."

Without looking at me, he leans down, places his hands under my armpits, and hauls me to my feet as if I'm a rag doll.

"At least you're together." Madi has always been a glass-half-full kind of friend.

"Has anyone heard from Moose?" Grey asks as though he didn't just manhandle me to my feet.

"Yes, I was able to get to Cian and Elle's house. Moose is there with them," Braxton says.

"And they're okay?" I ask.

"Everyone seems to be good. We'll know more in the morning. Grey, you said something about water?"

"Yeah." He sighs and steps closer to the phone I'm still holding. We're shoulder to shoulder now, but the icy vibes ricochet off him. "The levy at the dam must have broken.

The house is raised just enough that it didn't flood. I've got maybe twenty feet of grass before it hits water, and judging by where it hits the tree line, it's probably six to ten feet high."

"Holy shit." Braxton sounds as though he's pacing. "You have supplies, right? Moose said he left the house in good shape for you."

Grey looks down at me, and I swallow hard. Why must I stare at this man all the time?

"Yes," he says, never breaking eye contact. "He was taking care of the place while I was in California. We're fine for at least a week."

"A week?" Madi and I squeak in unison.

"I didn't say we *would* be here for a week, I said we *could* be here for a week and be fine." Grey's eyes cloud over as he glares at me.

"Let's touch base in the morning then, yeah?" Braxton sounds as tired as I feel. "Just…"

"What, Brax?" At least I'm not the only one Greyson barks at.

"Don't kill each other before we can get to you."

A muscle in Grey's jaw jumps, and I decide to push him —just a little.

"Oh, Brax," I singsong. "Don't worry about us. We're reconnecting just fine. We'll be BFFs before long."

Grey's growl echoes in the large room.

"Right." Braxton laughs. "Like I said, don't kill each other. And get some sleep. I have a feeling the next few days are going to be hell."

"Agreed. Hell is exactly where I've landed." Grey takes the phone from my hand. "Tell Sage I love him, and I'll be in touch soon."

He disconnects the call before Braxton can reply.

"Reconnecting?" He squares off to face me, his shoulders tense around his ears. "To be very clear, Savannah. We're stuck together because even Mother Nature is a crazy bitch sometimes. I don't forgive you. I won't forgive you. We will never be friends."

God, why is he such a little baby?

"Screw you, Grey. If I'd known you were such a little bitch, I never would have slept with you in the first place." He pulls back, eyes wide and twitchy. It feels like a small victory for me.

"I'm the little bitch?" His tone is a low, dangerous warning I don't heed. The heat from his anger soaks into my borrowed clothing that hangs off me like a wet towel.

"That's what I said." Lifting my chin, I cling tight to my defiance. "Did you ever once stop to consider that not everything is about you? While you were tucked away in your ivory tower of guilt and greed, some of us were forced to make decisions no one should ever have to make. But that's the thing, Grey. Not all of us are given a choice. Some of us only have the option of survival. Does that sound like much of a choice to you...you overbearing, condescending, arrogant prick?"

A vein in his forehead bulges, and his nostrils flare. "You want to talk about choices, Savannah? You spout off about ivory towers of greed and guilt, but you have no idea the sacrifices I've made. You can call me whatever names you want, but the fracturing of you and me? That all stems from the one time I let down my guard, the one time I let someone in, and you shat all over my vulnerability, then had the gall to react as though I'm the one in the wrong. So yeah, fuck me for trusting you. But fuck you for hurting me."

Silence. Thick, debilitating silence hangs heavy and

resolute in the room as his words play on repeat in my mind. *But fuck you for hurting me.*

It's the truth. The most honest thing he's told me in months, and I see it written in the lines of his face as clear as an opera singer standing center stage after the love of her life falls on his sword.

"I know you don't believe me," I say as he storms off, his shoulder brushing mine on his way by. I raise my voice. "But I am sorry. Nothing I've done ever had an ounce of malice in it." The sound of bare feet slamming against the steps has me raising my voice even more. "Not everything was about you, Grey. I was trying to be your friend while saving myself. I never meant to hurt you."

A door slams.

"Fuck." His curse carries an edge of violence I've never seen from him. Another door slams, and another, and then one more. "Looks like we're sharing a bed, Savannah. I'm not sleeping on the floor, and as much as I hate you, I don't want to upset Madi. But so help me God, I don't want to hear another lame-ass excuse from you. In fact, I don't want to hear anything for the rest of the night. If you can't do that, then find your own damn place to sleep."

"I—"

Another door slams.

I have no idea what time it is, but it feels late, so with a lump in my throat, I follow the pissed-off man-child up the stairs.

It only takes a few moments to confirm what he said. His three guestrooms are covered in glass and rain. I bet they never thought placing the beds under giant windows would end like this.

If Greyson and I must learn to coexist, what better way to do it than sleeping with the enemy?

Sticking out my chest and lifting my head, I march toward his bedroom, determined to make the most of this mess.

I enter his room, climb onto the side of the bed I know he doesn't sleep on, then settle into the mattress with the sheet pulled up to my chin. It smells like him—a mixture of clean laundry and cinnamon.

He must be in the bathroom, though he doesn't make a sound.

But fuck you for hurting me.

A familiar pang pinches and claws at my rib cage—it's a painful sensation I taught myself to forget a long time ago—but it comes at me with a vengeance now.

I was five years old when I stopped trying to make people like me, six when I stopped begging for love and affection. I found my worth, and I clung to it because it was all I had.

I've lost it once before, and I can't allow myself to do it now.

Somehow, this man who stares at me as though all he can see is the worst type of monster has turned me back into that love-starved little girl who just wanted someone to care.

Funny how the heart always wants what it can't have.

The bathroom door creaks open, and I roll to my side. Over the years, I've trained myself not to cry, but I haven't slept very well since Madi's wedding, when the news of Riley's release and then the obliteration of Grey and me sapped me of any remaining reservoir of control I ever had. I knew I was spiraling after the wedding, but now, the events of this storm have the frayed edges of my soul unraveling faster than I can cauterize them.

I'm not sure how many hits one person can take, but I think I've found my limit.

The bed dips silently with his weight, and then it bounces as though he's punching the mattress.

What can I say, I'm a nosy bitch too, so I roll to my back and nearly laugh as he places pillows down the center of the bed, then punches them into submission.

"I don't think they're going anywhere."

"No talking."

"Asshole."

He sneers, then places a final pillow barrier near our knees.

"I'm not a cuddler, if that's what you're worried about." Perfect eye roll tone, if I do say so myself.

"I no longer trust your words, Monroe. You showed me who you really are, and I listened. It's all actions from here on out."

I don't bother responding. Nothing I say will make him grow up and listen to me anyway. I'll need to come up with a different plan because we can't go on this way, and for the sake of our friends, we will learn to coexist.

"Try being nice to him." Clover's words grate on my conscience.

I'm always nice. Except when he pushes every freaking button I didn't know I had.

With great effort and a very deep breath, I say, "Thank you for retrieving me from the mud, and for...distracting me when my anxiety got the better of me."

The blankets are tugged off my shoulder, and I sit up in time to see him holding them tightly as he rolls over. Freaking blanket hog.

"You've lived in southeast Georgia long enough to know better than to head so far out of town with a hurricane on the way."

Yes, asshole. I know this. But the freaking weather app said it was still hours away.

"Regardless." Oops, that was full of snark and sass. I try again. "Thank you. Getting up your driveway was..." *Be honest with him.* "I was scared—and it takes a lot to scare me. I didn't even know how long I was out there, but I couldn't see through the rain, and I got disoriented. It's— I..." my throat tightens around my words.

"You're welcome." It's the softest he's spoken to me since Christmas, and it does something pitiful to my spirit. I drop my fist to my chest, feeling for a stab wound, but come up empty. "You're just lucky I happened to be on the porch after my workout, or I never would have known you were there. Don't take risks like that, Monroe. It would kill Madi, and she's been through enough."

There's that jackass tone of his. At least it irks my anger, overpowering the stab to the heart of a moment ago.

"Good night, Greyson."

My head sinks into the down pillow that cradles it like a loving pair of hands.

I know he won't respond, so I allow myself to drift off.

Right before sleep takes me, I swear he whispers, "Good-night, Monroe."

Monroe I can handle. At least he isn't calling me a liar anymore. Perhaps there's hope for our coexistence after all.

CHAPTER EIGHT

GREYSON

A LONG, LOW, SATISFIED MOAN PULLS ME FROM THE LAST lingering grips of sleep. The sun filters in through my bedroom windows, attacking my sleepy gaze, so I allow my lids to fall closed again.

A few more moments of sleep won't kill me.

This time the moan is softer, and I realize my hand is...

I open my eyes and take in my surroundings. My lips, *my* fucking lips, are on sun-kissed skin that doesn't belong to me. It takes less than a second for the events of yesterday to crash into me, and I wrench my head back.

I was kissing Savvy's neck in my sleep. Her hand presses against the back of mine, and I give an involuntary squeeze to her tit. My fingers are wrapped around her like she's a goddamn lollipop, so I attempt to wrench my arm away, except she's lying on it, so I can only let it fall to the bed beneath her.

"What the fuck, Monroe? I thought you said you weren't a cuddler?"

She jerks awake. Her silky brown hair's a wild mess on top of her head as she stares over her shoulder at me. Sleep lingers in her eyes as she licks her lips. It takes another three seconds before her brain catches up to her surroundings.

"I— I'm not a cuddler."

"Then how do you explain this?" I shake my head between the two of us a bit aggressively. I should tone it down, but I can't seem to control anything around this woman.

"This, as in you pressing your cock into my ass, with one hand on my breast and another cupping my pussy? Is that what you mean?"

Horrified, I remove my other hand, then glare at the back of her head.

"Or this, as in you're on my side of the bed?"

I jerk away and sit up, and sure enough, three-quarters of the bed is empty, and we're crowded on her side.

"You don't have a side in my bed," I grumble.

"True. But it doesn't negate the fact that you're on the side I was sleeping on. Are you, Greyson Reyes, a cuddler?"

Am I? I don't think I am, but admittedly, women never sleep over because I didn't want to set a bad example for Sage.

"No."

Her smile broadens to show me all her very white teeth. I wish she didn't have such a sexy smile—especially first thing in the morning.

"Are you sure?" She bumps my thigh with her leg, and my body jolts to attention, ready and wanting whatever she'll give me.

Morning wood isn't usually this complicated. Just chalk it up to yet another thing she's ruining for me.

"I'm sure, Monroe."

"What's with the last name?" She tilts her head to study me as I slide back to my side of the bed.

Monroe is safer. It puts distance between us...much-needed distance.

I get out of bed, actively avoiding looking at her. I have to piss, so I head to the bathroom, but that's difficult to do with a hard-on, so I think of every unsexy thing I can.

Madison's grandfather, Pops, is a great boner-killer. He's always on my ass about something. Moose is too, but at least he's mostly silent in his disapproving glares. Then there's old man Cracken who is a real ballbuster, but truthfully, I don't think he's half as cranky as he pretends to be. Pops' other friend, Chief, who is the retired police chief that refuses to give up his badge, is probably giving the actual chief of police a run for his money this morning.

Imagining the chaos the old geezers are creating makes me chuckle to myself, but it's also what endears them to this town. They love and they love hard, even if they're wildly inappropriate with their perceived duties sometimes.

My cock deflates enough that I'm able to piss without pain, and because the water is out, I search the cabinets for hand sanitizer, then leave it on the counter for Savvy.

She probably needs a toothbrush too. She's lucky Braxton made me go to a warehouse that sells everything in bulk. Rooting around in a drawer, I pull out a new toothbrush, still in the box, and set it on the counter.

The last thing I need is Savvy believing I'm being nice to her. So, without a word, I exit the bathroom, then the bedroom. We'll need bottles of water to brush our teeth, so the kitchen is my first stop.

I'm not doing it for her—she just happens to benefit from my own need to remove my funky morning breath.

In the kitchen, I grab a few bottles from the pantry, then pause. Women are always washing their face and shit, at least on TV. *Why do I even care about this?* Even as I think it,

I'm already backtracking to the laundry room to grab her a fresh washcloth and towel before returning to my room.

Savvy stands in my bathroom with the door wide open, and she's topless.

I like to believe that I'm an evolved man, but her tits have the power to turn me into a Neanderthal.

"What are you doing?" I grunt as annoyance takes over.

She jumps, crosses her arms while staring at me, then she shrugs. "I thought you were done in here."

Focus on her eyes, Reyes. Focus. On. Her. Eyes. Exceptional peripheral vision can be a hazard at times.

I drop the bottles of water on the counter harder than necessary. "You need water to brush your teeth. Here." I hold out a bottle in her general direction.

I know she's going to do it before she even drops her arm. There's a spark in her eyes that flashes when she's ready to fight—or fuck. Right now, it could go either way, except that I decided we weren't having that type of relationship anymore.

She drops her arms, and the stupid organ in my chest jackhammers against my ribs, silently telling me which direction every molecule in my body would like this to go. Thankfully, my mind is a stubborn ass, and I stay rooted to my spot, angry that she's topless, thankful that she's topless, and annoyed that her being topless is the only thing I can focus on.

It's impossible not to stare, so I turn away and grind my teeth until my jaw aches. The faster we're done in here, the better.

"Grey?"

I face the mirror, grab my toothbrush, and she holds hers out next to mine. Because I'm already fighting my instincts to lick her nipples, I place toothpaste onto her toothbrush as well.

Do not react, Greyson. That's exactly what she wants. Savannah is a woman who knows she's sexy as hell, and she'll use it to her advantage in the smartest possible ways.

Some women shy away from their sexuality, but not her. It's what drew me to her in the first place. She knows what she wants, and she doesn't hesitate to take it.

It's also what annoys the hell out of me.

"Oh." The surprise in her tone forces me to look at her in the mirror. That's mistake number one because, try as I might, her breasts are a masterpiece, begging for attention. "This is why you always taste and smell like cinnamon."

She's talking with her mouth full of toothpaste foam. It covers the corners of her lips and reminds me what she looks like when it's my come she's holding in there.

This, us, we're so messed up. We aren't compatible, but I can't stop envisioning sex with her either.

"It's kind of weird," she says, then spits into the sink.

My cock decides it really likes seeing her spit. Maybe even more than swallowing because when she spits, the muscles in her neck are on display, and her lips purse in the sexiest way.

"What's weird?" Damnit. I forgot I don't like her.

"I've never actually known anyone who uses cinnamon toothpaste."

My mother used it, but I'm done sharing personal shit with this sexy little Benedict Arnold.

"Your limited world knowledge is none of my business." I jam my toothbrush against my gums so hard they're probably going to bleed.

"You know what I think?" The woman fucking purrs as

she rests her ass on my counter, close enough that my arm would brush her tits if I leaned over.

"I don't care what you think, Monroe."

She pushes her breasts higher when she crosses her arms under them.

"Where's your shirt?" I bark.

She points to the shower, where the remains of her clothes lay in a puddle.

"Where's my shirt?" My resolve is crumbling. If she stays in my space, I'm not sure what I'll do.

"I forgot the water wasn't working, and when I turned it on to brush my teeth, it spluttered and spit out brown shit all over me. I had just wiped up the counter with it and tossed it into your hamper when you so rudely barged back in here. I figured since the last time we had sex you left bite marks all over my boobs, it didn't matter if you saw them again now."

"It doesn't matter. And that was at Christmas, not yesterday."

"Right." She smiles, and I get the impression she's forming a devious plan right in front of me.

"I don't really give a shit if you prance around here naked, Monroe. Our physical relationship is a thing of the past."

"Right," she purrs again. "Because you said we're done."

"Yes."

Her shoulder tips up, and from my exceptional peripheral vision, I see her reach for the ties of my pants she's wearing.

I lift the bottle of water to my lips, rinse, then lean to the side to spit right when she allows the pants to drop. Then I chug the rest of the water and exit the room.

I need fresh air. Savvy makes it too hard to breathe, so I

find myself on my front porch. In the morning light, everything comes into stark, depressing focus.

My land is destroyed. After promising Moose to take care of it, one hurricane touches down and decimates the land he was building his forever on. The water has receded, but not nearly as much as I would've liked, so I can't tell what we're dealing with beyond the house.

"What is that?" Savvy's voice carries humor I don't feel, and I'm instantly on alert.

How can she find anything about this funny?

"Is—is that Moose?" She joins me on the porch and leans forward on the railing. I grip the hem of her T-shirt and haul her back to me.

"Don't lean on that. We don't know if it's structurally sound."

She shrugs me off, her face still pointed to the lake that used to be a yard. Her scent wafts into my space when she waves with both hands, and I need to get away from her, so I step to the side. Then I see what she's waving at.

"What the hell?" My feet hit the stairs before I finish speaking because, sure enough, Moose is in a canoe, and he has a passenger.

"Savvy." Her friend Clover waves excitedly, causing the canoe to rock and Moose to chuckle.

Moose is in good shape, but for fuck's sake, he's got to be close to seventy-five. What the hell is he doing, canoeing in floodwater with a passenger known for dramatics?

"Oh my God, Clover. What are you guys doing here?" Savvy bounces happily next to me, and I ignore the warmth that settles in my chest.

One of the most stubborn people I've ever met also has a vulnerability made of glass when it comes to loving and being loved.

Most people never see it, but I have from the moment I met her. She wants to be loved more than anything in the world. The kind of love that has no boundaries. The kind that makes you feel safe.

Only someone with the same affliction would be able to recognize it.

Moose gets the canoe as close to shore as he can, but he's still a good twenty feet away from us.

"She had to see you for herself, or she'd keep making herself sick," Moose says with a disapproving glower at Clover.

"Clove." Sassy stands with her hands on her hips.

"Don't you 'Clove' me. You knew better than to head out into this storm."

I stand back and watch these two friends scold each other for doing different yet similarly stupid things.

"How ya doing, Greyson?" Moose's voice is aged with wisdom. He's not a big talker. Like me, he believes actions speak better than words, so when you do hear his voice, you're compelled to listen.

My gaze instantly darts to his old workshop—or where it used to be. When he sold me the property, it was with the condition that he could continue to putter around in there. He makes furniture. Sometimes he just whittles wood and whistles, but it makes him feel close to his deceased wife, and it's not something I ever wanted to take from him.

It's why I was putting in an elevator and renovating the second floor into an apartment. He has arthritis in his hips, and he won't be able to live on his own forever. I wanted him to be where he's happiest.

"I should have had Cian reinforce your workshop, Moose. I'm—I'm sorry."

"You're doing it again." He tuts. "Everything in the

universe is not your responsibility to control, handle, or fix. Ya can't control a hurricane any more than you can control the chemistry blazing between you two knuckleheads."

Savvy smirks up at me, and I think my face flushes. What the fuck?

"Trust me, Moose. It's not chemistry, it's a nuclear bomb." At some point, Savvy has turned me into a ventriloquist—my words are clear as day as they hiss through my clenched jaw.

He shrugs, his face hidden behind his giant beard, but I get the impression he's smiling.

"We brought you some supplies." He lifts a large Styrofoam cooler and places it in the water. He's attached a rope to it, which Clover hangs on to while he gently pushes it toward us. Then he puts a smaller one in, attaches it to the same rope, and nudges it toward us.

"What's this?" Savvy asks. She's way too excited about these packages.

"Some fresh fruit, a couple of sandwiches, and alcohol." Clover laughs. "Braxton's still worried about you killing each other. He figured if you were tipsy, you'd have a better chance of survival."

"How did you even get through the downed trees?" I ask, hip-checking Savvy out of the way and wading into the murky water to reach the delivery.

"Not my first rodeo, son. I've been through worse." Something tells me my friend Moose has a life story that would make Hollywood froth at the mouth.

"How long until the water drains?"

"No tellin'. My guess is a couple of days, but the mud and sediment it'll leave behind will be the real issue."

"Great." My eyes narrow in on his canoe. "Wait. Take Savannah with you."

Clover bites her bottom lip and stares at the murky water as if she's searching for a mermaid. Knowing her, she probably is.

"No room," Moose says, even though he just emptied two coolers from it. "No offense, Sav, but we're close to weight capacity with the two of us in here."

My bedmate shrugs as if she expected that answer.

"Well, can you drop Clover off and then come back for her?"

"Jesus, Grey. Your desperation to get rid of me is charming." Her eyes sparkle with mirth, and I'm right back to my mental hate list.

I hate that even when she's aggravating, she's beautiful.

Hauling one of the coolers to dry land, I lower my voice so only she can hear. "Charming has never been an aspiration of mine. But getting rid of you? It's in my prayers every thirty seconds."

Her lashes flutter, and she swallows hard.

And now I feel like an asshole. This is why I put space between us. I can't trust her anymore, and apparently, I can't trust myself to be a goddamn adult in her presence either.

"Can you do that, Moose?" she asks, but her glare never wavers from mine.

"Either of you ever been in a canoe before?" my old friend asks.

A delicate line appears between Savvy's eyebrows as we stare at each other. I shake my head. When would I have ever been in a canoe? It's not like my father was putting me in outdoor clubs or taking me fishing when I was a kid.

"No," Savvy answers for us both.

"Well, it's a weight issue. Can't have just one person in a two-person canoe or we'd go around in circles."

Something in his tone is off. Is he trying not to laugh? If I had cell service, I'd be googling the shit out of that answer, but we're literally stranded on an island right now.

"Is that true?" I ask, trudging back into the water, hoping I don't get some weird staph infection as I pull the second cooler to shore.

"'Course it is. Well, I gotta get Clover back. I'll come check on ya again tomorrow, long as the water's still high enough."

"And if it's not?" Savvy asks.

"Then we'll start working on getting some mudrunners up through here."

"Madi threw in some condoms too...just in case." Clover laughs while Moose turns them loose in the water.

"Unnecessary, Clover." My words sound a little like when Sage had whooping cough as a baby.

"Don't growl at her." Savvy swats my chest, her skin hitting mine with the intensity of static magnified by a trillion. "They just want us to get along, Grey. Like it or not, our families are now forever connected."

Before I can stop her, she lifts the larger of the two coolers and stomps back toward the house.

Stubborn. Sexy. Seductive. Sassy. Snarky.

Savannah Monroe has turned me into a walking thesaurus—a thesaurus that follows her like a baby duckling.

I'm so screwed.

CHAPTER NINE

SAVVY

WE SIT ON OPPOSITE SIDES OF THE BED IN SILENCE. THE ONLY light comes from the battery-operated lantern that sits between us on the pillow wall that Grey insists on recreating.

Tonight, he's reinforced it with extra blankets. I'm not sure if he's pissed that over the last three nights, he's found out he's a cuddler or if he's pissed because it's me that he's cuddling with. It's probably both.

"I have to proof this," I say, holding up a recording Madi stuck into the cooler for my latest podcast. If we weren't trying to conserve battery life, I would've taken my work downstairs. The last thing I need is his commentary on the one thing I've ever been successful at.

He shrugs as his hands fly across the keyboard of his laptop, but he says nothing. As soon as he realized Braxton sent him a battery backup and an external drive, he went to work on spreadsheets and emails his assistant had down-loaded for him.

My shoulders droop, and I mentally berate myself. We don't have to be friends—we just have to be civil.

If you told him why you applied to be a surrogate, he might understand.

Or he'd judge me just as everyone back in Vegas did.

I've spent too many years outrunning my past. The very last thing I'm going to do is give someone like Greyson Reyes the power to ruin that.

My stomach growls, and I quickly recall what I've consumed today. An apple, half a sandwich, and some protein drink Grey insisted I have.

You're good, Savannah. You're not hungry, you're nervous.

My bedmate turns my way and glares at my stomach. Awesome.

"Ah." I fidget with the edge of my laptop. "Do you have headphones? I don't want to bother you."

His fingers curl and uncurl as though staring at me physically pains him. "You don't want to...bother me."

Jesus, the ego on this guy. "Not everything has to be an argument, Grey. Either you have headphones or you don't."

My mind and body are at an impasse the second his narrowed gaze lands on the computer in my lap. He's wearing an expression I can't decipher, and my stomach cramps tighter, but as quickly as it covered his face, it's gone, and he goes back to his work.

"I don't have headphones here. I live alone so have no need for them. Do what you need to do, I've gotten really good at blocking you out."

Damn. Words from haters should never be able to penetrate your armor, but Grey's are laced with painful poison that cuts me to the quick every time.

That probably means I liked him much more than I allowed myself to believe, but that line of thought is useless, so I press play instead.

Lowering the volume as much as I can, I lean back against the headboard and rest the computer on my chest.

"Welcome to Can We Talk About That? *I'm your host, Savvy Monroe."* God, I sound so stupid. I study Grey out of the corner of my eye to see if he's listening, but his brow is furrowed, and he appears to be deep in thought as he scans his screen.

"Tonight's episode is about trust."

Greyson snorts, and the bones in my spine click into place as perfectly as the teeth of a zipper.

"Relationships, even one-night stands, require a certain amount of trust. Most women can't climax without some level of it, and so tonight, we're going to deep dive into all your questions about building, maintaining, and enforcing trust from the first kiss to the final thrust. So sit back, grab your drink of choice, and let's dig in."

"Classic." Grey's muttering slaps my already bruised ego.

Pausing my recording, I glare at him. "Something you'd like to say?"

"No."

My lips press together to the point of pain. Why did I ever like this asshole?

Because he wasn't always an asshole. Scratch that. He wasn't always an asshole all the time.

My finger is hovering over the button to start the recording when Grey slams his laptop down onto the bed between us.

"The few podcasts I've listened to, you've been smart and honest." He's angry but complimenting me. I can't wait to see where this goes. "People respond to your advice because it comes from the heart, and you've truly got this shit figured out. But now you're going to sit here and lecture people about trust? Trust, Monroe? What the fuck do you know about trust?"

I shake my head. "Until you can learn to step outside yourself and see our situation from all sides, you'll never understand, so it's not worth my time trying to explain it to you."

Look at me, staying calm and collected while my insides burst into flames. Go, me!

"Step outside myself?"

A bolt of electricity rolls through my bloodstream. This is where we thrive. Somewhere between banter and bickering, we come alive with the kind of truth we can't say out loud, so we bury it in sarcasm and sparks.

This is us, and I feel stronger in this moment than I have in months.

"Your habit of regurgitating my words is beneath you, Grey. If we're going to fight, at least attempt to be creative."

His eyes are huge in his skull. "How do you expect me to step outside myself and look at our whole situation when you won't give me the goddamn details? Of course I'm pissed off, Monroe. I have one side to go on—my side—the side that you screwed over as if I'm an emotionless monster."

His breathing is heavy and erratic as he keeps going. "How can I make informed choices when the only information I have is that you lied to me for months, even knowing my history and hang-ups, huh? You tell me it's your story, and it's apparently a sob story, but you won't share a goddamn thing with me."

He's agitated and fighting with the sheets tangled around his legs. "So no, I don't believe you should be lecturing anyone on something as precious as trust when you pretended to be my potential surrogate—the only one I wanted to match with, by the way—then mined personal details I've never shared with anyone else to use against me when you came at me as Savvy. Yet you keep your secrets locked up and expect me to just get over it?"

My heart grabs hold of my ribs and shakes them as though they're the steel bars of a prison I built myself. It hurts. His words hurt because he's not wrong, but he's not entirely right either, and the anger builds in my limbs, searching for an outlet.

"Mine isn't a sob story, Grey, it's a cautionary tale." My voice wavers, so I clear my throat and call on my feminine rage. "One that brings out the witch hunts and the pearl clutchers. And I don't lecture. I listen, I reflect, and I give the most knowledgeable answer I can based on years of experience, years of training, and years of working my ass off in school. So yes, you may never be able to trust me again, but I do know about trust and relationships, so you can fuck right off to the hell you've locked yourself in."

Agitation isn't the right word for the swirl of emotions inside me, but I feel it, the shakiness in my chest, the inability to take a full breath, the panic simmering just below my surface.

"Something tells me our pasts, while different, probably left very similar scars, Greyson, so before you throw stones, just remember we both come from glass houses, and once the cracks begin to show, it's only a matter of time before complete and total destruction follows."

Without waiting for him to answer, I press play...or I start to, and realize I accidentally hit record at some point. "Shit." Checking the time stamp, I make a note for my sound engineer to have our little war of words removed from the podcast. Then I turn up the volume and completely tune him out.

"This question comes from Jaida M. from Boston. Hi, Jaida, what have you got for us tonight?"

"Oh my God. Hi. I'm such a big fan. Okay, so I've been reading a lot of romance novels lately that make me question where my limits begin and end. I know that reading romance is an escape from reality, but for months, I've been wanting...more in the bedroom. I never thought of our sex life as vanilla or boring, but now I'm having trouble climaxing because my brain won't let go of all the things I want to try. My husband makes fun of me for reading smut already, so how do I approach this with him?"

Grey shifts next to me, and the air grows thicker. Did he just slide closer to me? Against my better judgment, I chance a peek to find he's staring at my screen. That's... interesting. Technically, he owns the platform that airs my podcast—well, Omni-Reyes does—but it never occurred to me before now that he might actually listen to it.

Something about that makes my skin flush hot.

"Well, Jaida. First, reading romance is not smut or something to be ashamed of. Sex is a healthy, normal part of life, and while I agree with you that many romances push the limits of fantasy— don't get me started on a guy who can have three orgasms in a row or go all night—the stories you're reading are about love first. They're about relationships and human connection, so don't you dare let anyone shame you for your reading preferences, not even your husband.

"Second, what kinds of things are we talking about? A little light spanking, or are we going straight to whips and ball gags? Give me a reference point."

Grey lifts his knees and rests his arms on them. He

seems uncomfortable, and it makes me want to laugh because this podcast went deliciously off the rails.

"I want him to pull my hair a little. Tell me what to do in the bedroom. I want him to... I don't know." Jaida's face is obscured for her privacy, but the way she touches her forehead tells me she's embarrassed to ask for what she wants.

"You want to be dominated in the bedroom, is that it?"

Her heavy sigh carries through her microphone. "Yes, I think so."

"Are you embarrassed by that?" I ask on the screen. Grey's unruly dark blond hair catches my attention as he leans across his wall of pillows to look more closely at my screen.

"I work in a very demanding, male-dominated field. Asking for something like this does make me worry about my career and what the hell's going on in my mind after fighting for twenty years to get to the top."

"I get that," podcast me says. *"But this is where you need separation in your life. Work you is not bedroom you. You're allowed to have different personalities. Put it this way—would you speak to a child the same way you speak to your employees?"*

"No, of course not." Jaida sounds appropriately freaked out. *"I've had to create a very tough exterior to claw my way to the top. Men in my field don't always appreciate taking directions from a woman, especially when I'm so much younger in comparison, so I have to be in control of everything I do and say at work. There's no room for softness in my career."*

"It sounds as though you have to be in control seventy-five percent of the time. That's a lot of pressure for anyone, regardless of gender. And I will say, there's freedom in the perception of giving up that control. Allowing someone else to make those choices for you is the ultimate act of trust."

I steal a quick glance at Grey. Does he have any idea how much trust I've placed in him? Does he care?

His carefully curated mask is impenetrable, but his eyes dance across my screen. What is he thinking?

"By handing someone else the decision-making power, it allows you a break you don't otherwise get. And I think you'll be surprised by how much better this can make your life, so I suggest this: approach your husband with honesty and vulnerability. Explain the pressure you're under at work. Explain how giving up control to someone you trust explicitly will be beneficial to you and to him. I would go in slowly, with very clear expectations. Talk about what you want, ask for it, and then compromise until you both feel comfortable."

"What if he shuts down the conversation before I can get into details of what I need?" Jaida asks, her voice much quieter than before.

"Then give him time to cool off, but do bring up the conversation again another time. Make sure you're clear that this is something you need, not just want. And if he still resists, then you have some choices to make." I look away from the screen and get locked into a trance when I find Grey staring at me as if he's trying to solve world hunger. *"You deserve, we all deserve to have someone support us in life, in work, and in the bedroom. It's about intimacy as much as trust. Too often, women hide away from their wants and needs because of how their partner may view them. And if that's you, I encourage you to dig deep for your self-worth. Hold on to it with both hands, and ask yourself the hard question: what do I need to be happy—truly happy and at peace?"*

"You trust me." Grey's voice is warm and so dang inviting.

I shrug, refusing to commit to his assumption, focusing instead on pausing the podcast and making a note for my engineer.

"When we have sex, you're letting go," Grey says. His tone is low, husky, but also a little wary.

I nibble on my thumbnail, and his focus shifts to the action. Damn it. I bite my nails when I'm nervous, and he twists his lucky coin through his fingers when he's thinking. We both have tells and have spent enough time together to know them.

Closing out of the podcast, I wiggle out from under the covers. I'll proof the rest of it tomorrow, when Grey isn't glued to my side.

"Tell me one honest thing, Monroe." The hesitancy in his tone has me pausing my hasty escape. My bare feet press into the cool hardwood floor, searching for grounding that won't come, and I wait for him to continue.

"What?" I ask without turning to face him when the silence becomes unbearable.

"Have you ever let go with anyone else the way you do with me? Have you ever given up control like you do with me?"

The air I'm breathing suddenly burns like fire. My chest rises and falls in rapid succession. It hurts. My entire chest cavity feels as though it's collapsing under the weight of my insecurities.

I swallow three times before I remove the sawdust from my mouth, then, without turning around, I say, "That's two things, but the answer to both of them is...no."

The laptop in my hands may as well weigh one hundred pounds, considering the way my arms tremble. I'm quick to set it on the nightstand, and even quicker to round the bed and lock myself away in the bathroom.

My ass hits the cold lid of the toilet, and I drop my face into my hands as my panic attack winds through my nervous system.

I only gave him a small truth—it's not the end of the world. Our relationship is already in the gutter, so one brief moment of opening myself up isn't going to change anything. He's not the kind of guy to weaponize my words—not normally anyway. If he were, I wouldn't have already told him more than I've ever told anyone else.

It's just not who he is.

So why does it feel like I just handed him the ignition to the bomb that is my heart?

CHAPTER TEN

GREYSON

Time passes slowly while I wait for her to exit the bathroom, but it's fine because she set off a war inside my head.

This obnoxiously stubborn woman handed over her body to me, trusting me to take care of her on numerous occasions—something she says she's never done before.

And against all odds, her own actions warning me otherwise, I believe her. It shifts something in my chest—bricks reorganizing themselves to create a little shelf with her name on it, and I don't know what to make of that.

Sex like ours doesn't happen often. Well, it's never happened with anyone else in my experience, but I had assumed that was because she's so aware of her sexuality. It never occurred to me that our infatuation with each other might be caused by something...deeper.

My head hurts, a migraine looming just behind my eyes.

I can't ignore the way I connected to her, and if I'm honest with myself, it's not just the physical connection. Our bickering and banter fed into it too.

Jesus, I love the way we challenge each other. Does that make me a sick fuck?

But then there was the sweet, gentle side she gave me as Firefly. Does anyone ever get to meet that version of her?

I wanted them both desperately. Did my obsession with not becoming my father cloud my head so much that I couldn't see all sides of this complicated woman?

Is it because I was exhuming demons buried deep while laying them at Firefly's feet or because Savvy was there to meet me head-on when I felt so raw after those conversations, I didn't think I could give anyone more?

Does it make any difference at all that they're the same person? Both of them were there for me in different ways, even if I didn't know it until I'd already been cut open by the betrayal.

At the center of all my anger is...her. Both versions of her. I was angry with myself for being like my father, emotionally stringing along one woman while having a physical connection with another.

I more than hated myself for that, but I also couldn't give either of them up.

Then I found out they were both Savvy and allowed my pain to override every other emotion and logical train of thought.

And then I ran.

The bathroom door creaks open slowly, as if she's hoping I'm asleep. It's too dark to tell how long she was in there, but my guess would be over an hour.

She pads quietly across the room, then pauses at the foot of the bed. There's a seismic shift in my chest as she stares at me as intently as I'm studying her. She inclines her head, as though she's peering through the darkness, searching for answers to questions she won't ask.

I refuse to acknowledge the disappointment that rolls through me when she continues to her side of the bed before I can call her to me.

Once she's settled, my shoulders melt away from my ears.

My stomach twists when she releases a shuddering breath that goes on for so long, I'm afraid she'll pass out.

"It was different with you, Grey."

I can't breathe. She's whispering so quietly, I don't believe she even wants me to hear her. One breath from me would block out her voice, so I stay silent.

"When you've had control stripped from you in every way, it's nearly impossible to give it up once you finally have it again. But with you?" She sighs, and it feels like it weighs more than she does. "I don't know. I felt free for the first time since I was sixteen."

Sixteen again. It's the second time she's mentioned that age. What happened to her at sixteen?

The muscles that had relaxed as she made her way to me from the bathroom coil and tighten again, waiting for the right moment to strike.

Fucking sixteen? The way she talks about control digs at a distant memory, picking at it, until a vision of my sister portioning her food stabs me in the eyeballs.

It's not unlike the way Savvy has been playing with her food since she's been here.

"I was never going to be the type of woman you could settle down with. My past is...tainted. But I'll remember our time together for the rest of my life. You...gave me hope when I had none. You're a good man, Greyson Reyes, and I'll always regret hurting you, but I'll never apologize for being the friend you needed or how I went about being that person for you."

The bed trembles, just the slightest movement that makes me think she might be crying, and I silently curse. I may think I want to hate her, but feeling her cry is worse than death—it's torture.

Frustrated with myself, with her, with our situation, but mostly because I can't make a decision where Savvy Monroe is concerned, I angrily toss my pillow wall to the floor, slide to her side, wrap an arm around her middle, and forcefully drag her body into mine as she gasps and hastily wipes at her face.

She was crying. Silently fucking crying. How often does she fight her demons alone, in the dark, with no one there to hold her?

"W—what are you doing? I thought you were asleep."

I huff through my nose. "Of course you thought I was asleep. That's why you finally told the truth. Go to sleep, Monroe."

"But…"

"Go. To. Sleep."

"You're cuddling me."

"Cuddling is for couples. I'm holding you together so you don't fall apart before I can return you to your friends. There's a big difference."

"What does that make you then? If we're not a couple and you're not my friend, why would you hold me together?"

Why does she have to talk everything to death?

"Just because I hate you doesn't mean I want you to be in pain."

"Y—you hate me." It's not a question. It's words filled with sadness that make my pulse skip three painful beats.

Irritation prickles every pore in my body. "Honestly, Monroe, I don't know what I feel for you. We're not friends, but I won't let you fall. I don't care about you, but I don't want you to get hurt. You're not mine, but I want to rip out the eyeballs of every guy at the pub who even looks at you funny. You drive me crazy, but I think I'd ruin anyone who tries to break you. I don't want you to have bad days unless I've caused them. I don't like you, but I want you where I can see you. You asked, Monroe. There you have it, and I don't know what to do with any of it. So please, for the love of God, just go to sleep."

"That was...honest."

I grunt.

"Thank you, Grey."

I hold her pressed so tightly to my front that not even air could slip between us until her breathing evens out and she finally goes lax with sleep. Only then do I ease my grip and allow myself to drift off too.

"HERE," I SHOVE A PLATE ONTO THE COFFEE TABLE BESIDE Savvy. "Eat it."

"How—" She stares at the plate of pasta.

"I boiled water on an old charcoal grill I found in the attic. It took for-fucking-ever to boil, so eat." The sofa creaks with my weight as I slip in beside her.

She's sitting on the floor with her legs crossed like a five-year-old's and has papers scattered all around her. An array of sticky notes assaults my eyes—it's like a rainbow threw up all over her work.

I should have chosen another seat. One as far away from her as I could get, but she's been avoiding me all day, and my indigestion is acting up because, for some fucked-up reason, she's the antidote to my discomfort.

I swear I might actually breathe fire if she pushes me tonight.

Shoveling the pasta into my mouth is another form of heaven. After eating protein bars and whatever unperishable shit Moose had stocked for so many days, a hot meal settles the beast inside me.

"Eat," I say again through a mouthful of food. I'm hungrier than I thought because manners don't even cross my mind as I speak with food squirreled away in my cheek.

My muscles tense as she pushes the pasta around on her plate.

Violet did that too, but I was too young and too unaware to know what it meant.

"Stop staring at me," she grumbles.

"No. Eat."

This sexy, insufferable woman growls like a gladiator but brings a single piece of ziti to her mouth and bites it. She only eats one-third of the tube, and my frustrations grow.

A memory blurs my vision—Braxton and I in the library of my childhood home, researching ways to trick a teenage girl into eating.

I can't blink fast enough to bring the present into focus. The memory transposes itself onto the view before me, Savvy blending into a version of my sister I no longer recognize.

In my dreams, Violet is healthy and happy. But the reality of her was so...different—sunken eyes and cheekbones that could cut glass. I don't even remember when Brax and I caught on that her relationship with food wasn't healthy, but once we did, all we wanted to do was fix it.

Nothing we did made a difference. Not until she became pregnant with Sage. If my father hadn't been so crazy, I think having Sage would have saved her from some of her demons.

"Grey?" Savvy kneels in front of me, and if the expression on her face is any indication, she's called my name more than once.

Is it stress causing her to play with her food, or did I miss all the signs again?

My brain works to recall everything I know about eating disorders before neatly categorizing and storing the data to be called upon in an instant.

Don't call attention to the meal. Don't comment on how much she's eating. Don't judge.

Distract.

Distract.

Distract.

"Want to play a game?" It's out of my mouth before a full thought has formed.

She sits back on her heels, blinking as though she doesn't understand my question.

"A game?"

I nod in response.

"What kind of game?" Her head tilts as she chews on the inside of her lip.

Leaning forward brings me into her personal space, but I press a little more so I can drop my plate on the table behind her, basking in the hitch in her breath when my forearm skims hers.

"I don't know. Let's see what Moose left behind." Reluctantly, I pull away from her and stand.

The sound of her fork against the plate causes me to glance over my shoulder, and my suspicions rise even more as she pushes food all the way to the edges of it.

The cabinet under the TV squeaks as I force it open and begin removing board games.

The first game I pull out is Monopoly, and I instantly toss it into the empty fireplace.

"Not a fan?" Savvy snickers.

"No."

The next is the game of Life. Fucking hell. Who chose these things? The box shifts in my hands, but it makes no sound, so I carefully lift the cover to find it empty.

Not Life then.

Guess Who and Checkers are also empty.

Pictionary has the board, but no cards.

Uno is filled with flashcards for division.

"What the hell?"

Savvy laughs, and I realize she's standing behind me, looking over my shoulder. "I bet Moose's grandchildren are responsible for this."

"Animals."

"Oh, come on. Like you always put the pieces away correctly when you were a kid?"

I must flinch, because Savvy's gaze softens.

"There were consequences in my father's house, so I never even took the games out to begin with. Once I moved in with Brax and Ace, I felt such relief, and...gratitude, that I vowed to always take care of my belongings."

Silence cloaks the room with uncomfortable tension. Fuck. Once again, I've lost control of my mouth around her.

Fabric shifts behind me, and I imagine her moving even closer to me, so I drop my head inside the cabinet, desperately searching for another game.

An uncharacteristic snort escapes me as I lift the last remaining box.

"Twister." Savvy laughs, and it's a magical incantation

that diffuses the tension of a moment ago. "That is not in your wheelhouse."

My shoulders stiffen, and the unhealthy competitive streak I inherited from my father rears its ugly head as I lift the lid and quickly scan the contents. Of course this would be the one game with all its pieces.

"Who says?" I ask without facing her. I need to get a handle on my reactions and keep a cool head. After all, this is meant to be a distraction so she'll eat the food that's quickly getting cold.

"Oh, come on, Grey. You're seriously telling me you've ever played Twister before? That would require you to remove your tie and, gasp, get on the floor."

The fabric of my T-shirt feels tight around my biceps. When I glance down at the sleeve, I find I'm flexing, but not to show off. No, my muscles react this way because Savvy has the ability to get under my skin, causing my body to react as though it's being attacked.

We played tons of games all the time with Sage growing up. He's been my main priority for more than half my life, but there's not a chance in hell I'll tell her that.

"I'm not wearing a tie now." My voice is ten octaves too low, but when her nipples pebble beneath her T-shirt at the sound, I bookmark the tone in my mind for future use.

"I'm surprised. You're always wearing a tie." Her gaze drops to my lips, and energy buzzes through my bloodstream.

One step, that's all it takes for me to be in her sphere. "There's a lot you can do with a tie, Monroe. Perhaps I just like having options."

"You get a lot of girls willing to be tied up for your kinky fantasies?" Her mouth snaps shut with an audible clashing of teeth.

She doesn't want to hear about other women any more than I want to hear about her with other men.

Before this can go off the rails, I give her a sliver of truth. "No, Monroe. That would open me up to a potential scandal. But just because I haven't done it doesn't mean I haven't thought about it..." I allow myself to slowly scan the length of her figure, my cock responding with each inch discovered. "Perhaps I've just been waiting for the right person to trust with my...needs."

Her gulp is loud in the quiet room. I might even be able to hear her heart beating. Or maybe that's mine.

"You said this..." She attempts to wave her hand between us, but there's not enough room. Her fingertips brush against my chest, and even my ass muscles clench at the contact. "Us. You said our physical relationship was over."

Savvy's lips spread into a knowing grin that has the hair on my forearms standing on end.

"You also waxed poetically about how much self-control you have." Her confidence grows with each word that tumbles from her pillowy lips. "And what did you say? Oh, right, it's over because you said it was over."

The corner of the game box stabs into my palm as I clench my fingers around it, reminding me of my objective in the first place—distract her enough that she'll eat something more than part of a piece of pasta.

"I didn't say we were going to fuck, Monroe." *Who am I kidding?* "I said we were going to play a game."

She narrows her eyes and presses her body into mine. Minx. The contact short-circuits the pathways to my brain.

"What are the stakes?" Sultry seduction. That's what she sounds like.

Hmm...there are so many ways this could go, and in my

head, all of them end up with her having a full belly while naked and riding my cock.

Damn it. I should have kept my big mouth shut. Me and my goddamn self-control. Is throat-punching your past self a thing? If not, I'd like to start the movement now.

"If I win, you beg me to fuck you." Well, shit. There goes my self-control and maybe a little of my pride.

Her hand falls to my shoulder as she holds herself up while laughing so hard tears slide down her cheek.

She's a pain in my ass.

"And—" She gasps for air. "And if I win?"

"What do you want?" I sound like an aggravated teenager, but it appears to sober her, and she drops her hand away from my shoulder. Cold slithers onto my skin in its place.

"If I win, you admit that you made a mistake."

I rear back. Surely, she's joking. "A mistake about what?"

Something sparkles in her eyes—something I can't read but sure as hell want to.

"About ending our physical relationship. You may have restraint, but not enough to deny the chemistry of us forever."

She's right, but I won't admit that.

"Rules," I snap. "I'm starving, and our food is getting cold. So here's what we're going to do." Her eyes widen as I drop the box to the floor and begin spreading out the plastic sheet full of colored circles. "Before each move, you must feed the other person a bite of pasta. If you can't get the food into their mouth, you lose."

"Your plan is faulty." Goddamn. Her tone ignites fire in my balls.

"How so?" Grabbing her plate, I dump all its contents

onto mine, then set the plate and one fork on the edge of the mat.

"You'll have to feed me in order to advance in the game. You didn't say anything about me having to make it easy for you. What if I just keep pulling my head out of your reach?"

Unable to control myself, I leap to my feet and wrap my hand around her waist, pulling her against me. Hard. Hard enough to knock a shocked gasp from her lungs. My free hand knots in her hair at the base of her neck.

"I think you're underestimating just how far my reach extends when I want something badly enough."

"And I think you're underestimating just how stubborn I can be when I'm right."

Lowering my face until my cheek rests against hers, I breathe in the sweet scent of her skin with a deep inhale that has her shuddering in my arms.

Peace. It happens here in these stolen moments with her. The realization nearly knocks me on my ass, but I'm on a mission and need to focus.

"Game on, Monroe," I whisper darkly. "Remember this when you're begging me to fuck you later—I never lose. Especially when it comes to something..." With a hand splayed to her lower back, I press her into my hard length. "I can't stop thinking about."

"What..." Warm, moist air brushes my neck with her heavy breaths. "What is it you think you want here, Grey?"

You.

That one word screams in my head as though it's the only truth worth telling, but I don't say it—I can't.

"I want to win, Savvy. I always want to win."

Her shoulders sag, and her eyes flash with disappointment, but there's nothing I can do about that right now.

I don't know how to trust her anymore, and without trust, we have nothing—even if my body and soul are already begging for hers.

CHAPTER ELEVEN

SAVVY

I DON'T THINK EITHER OF US TRULY THOUGHT ABOUT THE repercussions of this game. I know I didn't.

My muscles ache as I hold a twisted version of a lunge. My left foot is on a red circle on the middle of the mat, while my right foot is on a green circle at the bottom. My left arm is pressed against Grey's cock so my hand can be on a blue circle, and I've got my right arm over the top of him for a yellow circle.

And the asshole is sprawled out underneath me like he's doing a crab walk without breaking a freaking sweat.

"Aren't we supposed to have another person here to spin the wheel?" My hair drops into my face and sticks there because I'm sweating more than when I go to hot yoga. I swear Grey is a human sauna.

"We've only been playing for thirty minutes, Monroe. Are you giving up already?"

Never.

Ignoring him, I tighten my thigh muscles to hold me steady as I spin the wheel. Right arm green. Damn it, this is going to hurt.

Grey grins up at me. Not a single muscle on him is shaking.

The pasta has long since gone cold, but he insists it's the rules, so I stab as much of it as I can get and bring it to his mouth. He wraps his lips around the fork with a grin.

He probably got lip injections. If he didn't, God definitely plays favorites because women everywhere would kill for his lips.

"Right arm green, Monroe."

Shit. My gaze snaps to his, and I want to scream. He caught me staring at his lips. Again.

I toss the fork to the plate, but it releases none of the tension that's coiled around us, then I spread out over the top of him even more. Now I'm in a strange version of a plank, our bodies are pressed together from shoulder to knee with my left arm crushed between me and his cock.

My left foot slips, pressing my weight more firmly into his. His cock throbs against my arm and he groans. We're so close, his breath warms my cheek.

"Ready to give up?" He doesn't whisper, but his words are low and husky. If I didn't know better, I might think he was hanging on by a thread. But when I scan his face, all I see is stupidly aggressive determination.

"Grey, if you think I'm about to beg you to fuck me, now or in this lifetime, you're dumber than I thought."

He grins, the smile blazing across his face like an out-of-control brush fire prepared to jump streets if that's what it takes to feed its thirst for destruction.

Somehow, he manages to lift his hips, pressing more tightly into mine, sealing us together. A slight thrust tells me he knows exactly what he's doing. With his lips hovering near my cheek, he leans toward the wheel and spins. Right foot blue.

The fork clinks against the plate that's finally nearly empty, and then he's dropping his neck to give him room to offer me the pasta.

If I'd known being fed by Greyson Reyes would create an erotic scene that will forever play in my fantasies, I probably wouldn't have agreed to this game of his.

We're so close that his stare sears into my soul as he studies my face. Each time he feeds me, the muscles in his jaw tick as he draws circles around my face with his eyes.

I swallow, and he follows the movement.

"Do you have any idea how sexy you are?" he growls.

Swallowing again removes the remnants of pasta but also takes all the moisture in my mouth with it.

"Right foot blue." I remind him.

He moves on autopilot, never once breaking eye contact with me. The new position gives him even more leverage, and he uses it to his advantage, pressing himself more tightly into my body.

"Pasta's gone." His words are rough against my ear, and my breaths expel in short, harsh pants. "Maybe it's time to up the stakes."

Dear God, I don't think I can handle more stakes with this man.

"What are your terms?" Oh, Lord. Was that my voice? What is he doing to me?

"Getting naked."

I scoff, but he grinds his hips against my center, and the sound dies in my throat.

"Y—you're serious?"

"Desperately." His whispered word against my ear sends a rush of lust straight to my core.

"How does that even work? You're not thinking with the right head."

His lips move against my cheek, and I know without looking that he's smiling again. I need to start choosing circles that get my face away from his.

"You spin the wheel. Whatever body part you land on is the article of clothing you have to remove from the other person. So, if you get left leg, then you have to get my left leg out of my shorts."

I quickly scan our positions. There is no way we make it through enough rounds stripping each other to wind up completely naked without someone falling. I'll give it two rounds, tops.

"One article of clothing at a time. You can't remove shorts and underwear at the same time. You have to go layer by layer," I counter.

"You say that as though it'll be a deterrent."

"Just making sure we're on the same page."

"Your turn, Monroe." He thrusts his hips, and I swear the only part of him I've never hated just keeps growing.

The arm of the wheel goes around and around after I flick it, finally landing on left arm red.

Thank God. I don't think I could handle another moment of feeling his thickness and not being able to do anything about it. Reaching over the top of him, I smirk.

"Try not to fall over," I say.

He shifts his weight to his right arm, then lifts his left as though he hasn't been using every muscle he possesses for the last half an hour.

It takes me a moment, but I finally wrestle his arm out of his shirt sleeve, then place my arm on a red circle above his head.

He has the face of a hunter as he stares at me, so I'm thankful when he drops his gaze and spins the wheel. Left foot green.

He looks down at the mat, then to where my legs are spread on red and green circles. "Now we get to see just how flexible you really are, Monroe."

I gasp when his hand slips below his boxers that I'm using as sleep shorts. His palm skims my ass, my hip, down to my outer thigh. The thin cotton stretches as far as it will go, but he continues to drag his palm down to my shin, then lifts it, causing me to lose my balance.

He catches me with his hips and chest, holding me steady until I regain my posture. "Slip your knee out of the shorts."

"Who said I'm supposed to help you?"

His pale blue eyes darken, and his entire body seems to vibrate.

"Have it your way."

I'm about to ask him what he means when there's a sharp pinch to the skin on my hip when he tugs the boxers I'm wearing past their breaking point. In the same breath, the silence in the room is shredded by the distinct sound of fabric ripping.

Craning my neck, I find his thumb sticking through a hole in his underwear. Motherfucker. "Don't you—"

He jerks his thumb down, and I watch in horror as he rips the material straight through the leg hole, leaving the fabric to flop open on either side, revealing my black lace G-string.

"Are you kidding me?" I pin him with a look, but all he does is shrug. "If you rip my panties, I will knee you in the balls. They're the only ones I have."

"It's not my fault you're not a team player. Spin the wheel, Monroe."

"I'm serious. If you rip anything else, this game is over."

"Negotiations ended when you spun the wheel. Rules

are rules. If you quit, you lose." He lifts his head so his mouth is pressed to the corner of my lips. "In fact, I hope you quit because I can't wait to hear you beg."

Tearing my face away from his is harder than I want to admit, and it takes me longer than it should to locate the wheel. Right foot yellow.

Without making eye contact, I reach into his shorts and instantly pause. "You're not wearing any underwear."

"Never said I was." He presses his hips up, so his cock pulses against my belly. "You can quit at any time."

"I'm not ever going to quit," I grumble under my breath. But of course he hears it. His booming laughter grates on my nerves as I tug and pull on his shorts.

He gracefully lifts his foot, then bends his knee to accommodate me removing his clothing. Freaking pervert.

As soon as they're off, we replace our respective limbs onto the colored circles.

This game is lasting way longer than I'd hoped.

Left arm blue.

Left foot yellow.

Right foot yellow.

Left arm green.

Left foot red.

Right arm blue.

With each turn, more skin emerges until a thin sheen of sweat covers both of our naked bodies. Every time Grey moves his hand, he finds a way to graze my nipples, my clit, my ass.

I'm primed for whatever he'll give me, but neither of us is willing to lose.

Left foot green has me straddling his face.

"Sixty-nine is my new favorite number." His breath skates across my clit, and I can't hold back a moan.

"Give up, Monroe. You know you want me to tug this needy little clit into my mouth and suck until you see stars."

Yes. Yes, I do want that. But I'm also more stubborn than a professional athlete on a winning streak.

"Asshole." My eyes widen when his cock bounces in front of my face. Hmm, turnabout's fair play.

Pressing up onto my toes, I lean forward so every exhale lands on his dick.

"Careful, Monroe. You don't want to play this game with me." He shocks the hell out of me when his tongue darts out to taste me in one quick lick from my opening to my clit.

We both moan with an overload of sensations.

"It's your turn to spin, Grey." As soon as the words leave my mouth, I fill it with the tip of him. His salty, earthy flavor hits my tongue, and my lips clamp shut around him.

"Fucking hell, Sav." His words are as tortured as I feel. "This is how you want to play? We always seem to be bending the rules. That's fine, though. I'm prepared to win."

The sound of the spinner urges me to move faster on his cock before he's forced to move into a new position. His groan is all the encouragement I need.

I've never cared for giving head before, but with Greyson, it's different. Watching this control freak lose control is an aphrodisiac I'm quickly becoming addicted to.

"Right. Hand. Yellow," he grunts, and then makes good on his promise.

He sucks my clit into his mouth, holding it hostage with his teeth, and I cry out. He's relentless in his domination, and it's only sheer will that keeps me upright.

"Spin the wheel." His demand vibrates against my sensitive flesh. My eyes roll to the back of my head when he flicks my clit with a stiffened tongue. "Now, Sav. Spin."

I'm losing control of myself faster than my brain can

keep up. His tongue dives deep into my core, and I cry out as the first spasms of an orgasm huddle together, waiting for his next move.

"Do you give up?" He growls.

I remove his cock from my mouth just long enough to utter, "N—no."

"Then spin the fucking wheel."

I reach blindly with my left hand until I find the small piece of cardboard and spin it. My gaze is fuzzy and unfocused. Then Grey curls his tongue inside me, and a full-body tremor rolls through me.

But when he licks down, down, down toward my ass, every muscle threatens to give out.

"Right. Right foot blue." I don't move. I can't. Sensations override common sense, and all I can do is hold still and accept my fate as an orgasm calls on every nerve ending I possess to wake up and get ready for detonation.

"You didn't move."

"I—I..."

His tongue rims my ass, and I jolt forward before pushing back against his face.

"If you come, you lose, Monroe."

Oh shit. Shitty, shit, shit.

"And then you're going to beg." He says it with reverence, as though it's a wish coming true.

"I don't...I don't beg." I do, however, pant. I can barely get words out.

"You haven't moved to your new position, and you're about to come."

"Does that mean if you come first, you lose?"

He grunts into my wet flesh. "I never lose."

Game. On.

I take Grey's cock into the back of my throat, then push a little more, forcing him past my gag reflex.

"Fuck me," he roars.

That's the plan, Greyson. That's the plan.

As if he heard my unspoken thoughts, he dives in harder, more relentless than before, causing me to double down on his cock. I suck harder, move faster, greedy in my pursuit of his orgasm.

It's a race to orgasmic bliss, and I don't know how we'll ever decide a winner and a loser here.

My knees fall to the floor and Grey's grunt of approval sets off new sparks deep in my belly.

I'm not sure what happens next, but his hand is suddenly locked around my back, holding my core to his rapacious mouth. Two thick fingers plunge inside me, and I scream around his cock. He works me with fingers and lips, using my dripping wetness to his advantage.

I can't catch my breath, and it's like he senses it as he rams into my mouth over and over again from below.

"Come for me, Sav."

"No." It's a garbled sound that's mixed with so much saliva it comes out in a sloppy cacophony of noise.

"Fuck, you're stubborn."

He sucks my clit into his mouth again and keeps sucking. He doesn't give up, and he doesn't back down as pull after pull assaults my aching little nub.

Then his fingers, wet with my arousal, slip to my back hole, and tears form in my eyes.

I'm going to lose this battle.

But I won't go down without a fight.

I slide down his cock until he fills my throat, then I reach around to cup his balls with one hand, while my free hand explores his body, searching for that spot I know will set him off.

"Come," he demands.

His cock swells, and I press my finger to that sensitive spot he hates so much because it makes him lose control.

"Now, Sav. Come on my face. Let me taste you."

He slips his finger into my ass, and I'm done.

We come in a violent torrent of groans, screams, and shaking muscles. Hot cum slides down my throat, but I'm too lost to my own orgasm to swallow properly.

Grey doesn't relent either. He sucks, nibbles, and fucks until I know he's going to drag a second, more devastating orgasm out of me.

At some point, I forgot how to breathe, and all I can do is soak up the sensations.

His cock, still hard, slips from my mouth, yet he continues plunging his fingers into me while pressing on my back and flicking my clit with his tongue.

"Grey," I scream loudly enough for the roof to cave in around us. "Please."

"Closer."

I have no idea what he's talking about.

"But not good enough. I want you to beg me, Sav. Beg for my cock."

If I do, I lose.

But is it really losing if I get a mind-numbing orgasm out of it?

I've lost the ability to think clearly. Somewhere, just out of grasp, I know there's a reason I shouldn't cave to his demands, but for the life of me, I can't recall what it is.

All I know is I need what only he seems capable of giving me.

"Please, Grey. Please fuck me. Hard." He flips me like a

pancake. "Fast." His hips line up with mine perfectly. "Rough." It's the last word I utter before he enters me in one beautifully ferocious thrust.

He cups my head in his hands and stares down into my eyes as though I hold all the secrets of the world while his cock pistons in and out of me at an animalistic pace that sets my core on fire.

"Fuck, baby. You and your magical pussy."

My eyes roll to the back of my head as my muscles seize around him. This orgasm might be the end of me.

"Why." Thrust. "Do you." Thrust, thrust. "Have to be." Oh hell. He's going to break me. "So damn stubborn?"

He pinches my clit, and I writh below him.

"Why couldn't you just be honest with me?"

Thrust, thrust, thrust.

"Why do you have to be mine?"

He consumes my body, my soul, my heart. His thumb and forefinger tweak my nipple, and he bites down on the sensitive flesh of my neck.

His words blend with my own wanton pleas, and his moans roar through my veins as though he's the very thing pumping my blood throughout my limbs.

He owns every inch of me.

And it's with that thought that I black out as the best orgasm of my life pulls me under and into the blissful darkness of ecstasy.

CHAPTER TWELVE

GREYSON

"Omni-Reyes took, ah—a small hit since the closure of Montgomery Media." Quinn, my long-time assistant, is obviously flustered. But we've known this was the likely outcome for months.

It's nothing new, and it's pissing me off that she's bringing it up. Again. Braxton's adoptive father was a piece of shit and deserved every blow we hit him with.

"But the move, and the ah...scandal is now—"

I've already asked her to repeat herself three times since my attention keeps drifting to the floor, where only last night, Savvy and I played the most intense game of Twister known to man, so this time I just tune her out and let her babble.

If you give people enough silence, they'll speak to fill the uncomfortable void anyway.

The Twister box catches my eye. It's tucked under the coffee table, and fuck me, I might need to burn that game now too.

I'm still not sure how things spiraled so quickly last

night. My intention had just been to distract her enough that she'd eat a full meal.

What we got was that and an orgasm I'll probably never be able to beat. And I've had more than a few spectacular ones with Savvy...always freaking Savvy.

Sex with her breaks every rule I've ever set for myself.

Condom. What condom?

No kissing. I can't get enough of her lips.

No cuddling. I wrap myself around her like a goddamn koala bear every single night.

"Greyson?" Concern bleeds into Quinn's tone.

Get your shit together, Grey. You're better than this.

"It's been long enough since Madi and Braxton took on Montgomery Media and exposed all their secrets," I say, unable to lift my gaze from the floor. "No one cares about what they're up to except when Brax does an over-the-top good deed, which we're working on controlling. But I'm also not going to tell him to stop giving back. It's something he needs to do."

"No, Grey. Not—" Quinn's voice drifts away, and irritation works up the back of my neck. If we were on a video call, I'd be able to see what she's doing. Why the hell is she multitasking right now? Jesus, I'm not only an asshole but a hypocrite to boot.

"Ah, right."

I'm not sure I've ever heard Quinn this flustered, and I sure as hell don't like it. I pay her to keep her shit together.

"We'll make up the loss by next quarter. Mostly. I sent some paperwork that needs your signature, and some other...time-sensitive information to Braxton. I'm guessing he hasn't gotten it to you yet?"

Jesus. Is Quinn only competent when I'm next door micromanaging her?

"No, Quinn, he hasn't. Things are a mess around here. Anything urgent should be directed to him." Thankfully, Moose has made a few return trips in his canoe, so at least Savvy and I are able to keep on top of the most important aspects of our respective businesses.

"But you're the CEO now, Greyson, not him."

"And he's my brother, equal partner, and perfectly capable of handling anything in my absence." I rarely get this annoyed with Quinn. She wouldn't have lasted this long if I did, so what's changed? Ever since Braxton moved to Happiness, she's had a stick up her ass about him that doesn't make any sense to me.

Quinn Holloway has been a fantastic assistant, although I almost didn't hire her. She met all my criteria—except she was only ten years older than me. I'd wanted someone in their grandmother era, but I was stuck and gave her a trial run. Fortunately for her, she turned out to be too good to let go.

Another way my father fucked me up. No assistant was safe from his harassment, and I always feared I'd end up like him, so the safest thing to do was hire someone I had zero attraction to.

Quinn is probably beautiful in her own way, but luckily, her personality put her strictly in the no-go category for me very early on, and we've had a peaceful working relationship ever since.

"Grey, can you throw me my underwear from the laundry room? It should be hanging on the drying rack," Savvy yells as though she forgot I was in a meeting.

"Who is...so it's true. You're not alone." Quinn says. There's something teasing in her tone that draws my attention from the forms I'm signing. This shit is so much more efficient when I can do it electronically.

I lift my head just in time to witness Savvy freeze at the bottom of the stairs, wearing only a towel. Water cascades down her skin from her hair. I would have paid good money to see her washing with the gallon jugs I carried up earlier.

Her collarbones protrude with sharp angles that have me staring more intently. It's been six days since her confession in my bed. Less than twenty-four hours since I broke my own rule and made us both lose ourselves to multiple orgasms, yet my mind is no clearer where Savannah Monroe is concerned, and nothing about that sits right with me.

At least she's back to her flirtatious, confrontational attitude, and secretly I'm relieved. The fragile version of her was...difficult to witness.

But there are still times when I catch her lost in thought that I fear this outspoken version of herself is a mask she wears to hide her vulnerability. We're together twenty-four hours a day right now, and I haven't figured out when she removes the mask. When is she allowing herself to just...be?

What worries me the most, though, is her eating habits. It reminds me of my sister and the way she'd grapple for control of anything because my father took away so much of her autonomy. Starving herself had been the first way she regained control, and I was too young to help.

I'm not saying Savvy's the same, but there are a lot of little signs that have me paying closer attention.

"Well, this is interesting." Quinn snickers, but it makes Savvy frown, so I mute the call. The power came on this morning, but my Wi-Fi and cell service are still down, so the satellite phone is our only means of communication with the outside world.

"Sorry," Savvy whispers. "I just need to get my underwear."

"Savvy." My voice is raw as she creeps closer. I love how

she moves like a dancer but hate how fragile her bones appear.

Will it always be this way with her? This love and hate, push and pull that drives me crazy?

A gasp comes through the speaker, and Savvy's scowl deepens just before she scurries out of sight.

Fuck. I guess mute doesn't work on this dinosaur of a phone, but what the hell was Savvy's reaction about?

I wait to continue my conversation with my assistant until Savvy is safely back upstairs.

"Braxton mentioned you were…not alone. The *sex therapist*, though. Huh. Never would've seen that one coming."

I don't like the way she mentions Savvy's career, but I can't quite place why.

"Her best friend is now my sister-in-law." The watered-down version of our relationship feels safer. "The hurricane destroyed everything on this property, and we're stuck here until someone can clear a path to us."

"Is that why you're not in the office?" Quinn asks. It instantly raises my hackles.

"Why else wouldn't I be in?"

There's a long pause. Long enough that I confirm the battery on the satellite phone didn't die.

"Quinn?"

"You don't have access to…anything out there?"

"No." I grind my teeth. "We're completely shut off from the outside world save for the satellite phone, so if you have something to tell me, just say it."

"This really should have come from Braxton days ago." She's obviously annoyed, but I don't give a shit.

Her recent distaste for Braxton has been a mystery to me, and perhaps I need to start paying attention. Regardless, she should know me well enough to know that she's walking on thin ice where my family is concerned.

"We're in the middle of a natural disaster. Braxton is being pulled in a million different directions, and I'll remind you that he's also my brother and the rightful heir to Omni-Reyes, so tread very carefully here. What is it *you* think he should have told me?"

"I didn't mean anything by that, Greyson. But..."

Irritation picks at the beginnings of a migraine, but she knows I'm right. Ace was Braxton's grandfather on his mother's side, while we share DNA from the morally decrepit Darren Wells. I'm almost glad we didn't find out we were related until we were in our thirties though—it saved Braxton from ever getting too close to the monster I once called dad.

"There are some things..." she continues.

"Just spit it out, Quinn."

"You and your houseguest are currently embroiled in a national scandal, which is reflecting poorly on Omni-Reyes, Sunshine Studios, and...you." It rushes from her mouth like a tidal wave.

My blood pressure spikes, and tension in my skull blinds me. "What the hell are you talking about?"

"Her past is—"

"None of your fucking business." The protective feelings that have always existed for Sage and Brax roar to the surface now, but they're for Savvy. It's new and completely unwelcome.

"I'm your executive assistant, Greyson." She adopts a haughty tone. "It's my job to keep you abreast of things. This *thing* happens to have taken on a life of its own while you've been playing house, and Braxton not informing you of it has made it worse. I suggest you distance yourself from the *sex therapist* the second you get off that godforsaken property."

"Grey?" Savvy's voice sends my pulse skyrocketing.

"Call Braxton," I bark into the phone, then disconnect the call before facing Savvy.

Her brow is raised, and her arms are crossed. She's pissed. "Your assistant has a possessive streak."

I can actually feel the shock registering on my face because that's not true at all. "Why would you say that?"

She carefully shrugs one delicate shoulder that's bare—my T-shirt once again dangling precariously from one side.

"Women's intuition. Why does she want you to distance yourself from me?"

The need to fix something overpowers me. The problem is, I don't yet know what needs fixing, though I have a sinking suspicion it has everything to do with my little troublemaker.

"I'm honestly not sure. She said there's a..." I blow out a breath that puffs up both of my cheeks, then drag my fingers through my hair. I desperately need a real shower.

Savvy stands rigidly, dropping her arms to her sides like lead weights. "There's a what?"

"Quinn said there's a scandal."

The woman before me goes eerily still as all color drains from her face.

"What kind of scandal?" Her chest rises at an alarming pace. It's the only thing on her that moves. She doesn't even blink, for fuck's sake.

Why am I the one to give her this news? Of all people, it has to be me? She just got back to her ball-busting ways—the way I like her.

Damn. I do like her this way, but I don't know her demons well enough yet to know what will weaken her.

"What scandal, Greyson?"

I stare blankly at a point on the wall just above her head. With a heavy sigh, I finally look at her. "She didn't say. Just that it was something to do with your past."

Visible tremors start in her fingers and race up both arms, and nothing I can do will tear my gaze away from her outward signs of distress. My palms itch with the need to set things right.

"My past." Her words are wrapped in arsenic, and she nods with one aggressive tip of her head.

I study her, waiting for any direction on how to proceed, but all she does is walk woodenly toward the front door in silence.

Do I follow? Do I call Braxton and ask him what the hell is going on?

I'm out of my element with her. Generally, when a problem presents itself, I act on it, then move on. But there's a looming sense of dread that I can't see through. Calling Braxton seems like a safer bet right now, but when I lift the phone, Savvy's heavy footsteps on the porch call to me, and I follow her instead.

She's staring out at the swamplands my property has become. She hasn't noticed me on the threshold yet, so I take my time studying her.

My fingers itch to tug her thumb from her mouth. Biting that nail is a bad habit, but it's also her tell that not everything is calm in that mind of hers.

"How do you even have any nails left?" I ask after a long beat.

As expected, she jolts in place, her eyes blinking rapidly as though she'd zoned out.

Her thumb curls under her fingers as she forms a fist around it, and she shrugs.

"It seemed weird that no one came out here the last couple of days." She scans the property from left to right and back again.

I'd been thinking the same thing, but I don't admit it. The last thing I need is to fuel her fears.

But she's not wrong. We've been stranded here for six days now, and someone got as close to us as they could every day right up until two days ago.

"I spoke to Braxton and Cian yesterday. I hate talking to Cian on the phone. I can't understand a word the Irish ass says."

Her lips curl up with the tiniest glimmer of a grin. "You get used to him. He's a really great guy. You should feel lucky he considers you a friend because he hates most people."

I don't think he hates them—he just has a very low tolerance for stupid. The guy would do anything for just about anyone as long as you're not a dick.

"Yeah, well, I've never needed many friends." I keep my focus on the upturned trees on the other side of the new pond.

The heat of her stare sets fire to the side of my neck. My pulse beats erratically, and I know it's because everything in me is screaming to look at her. But I can't think clearly when I do, and it's become a daily internal battle I lose every time.

"You'd have more if you let people in." Before I can formulate a response, she continues. "What else did she say? What's going on out there?"

"She was a little cagey about it, to be honest. But now that I think about it, so were Braxton and Cian."

"Do you think they're keeping us out here on purpose?"
She's cute when she's flustered.
Can Stockholm syndrome happen when you're stranded

with someone during a natural disaster? *She's cute when she's flustered?* What the actual hell is happening to me?

I like her, I hate her, I want to fuck her into submission until she says she's mine.

Wait. What? I'm losing my goddamn mind.

"They are, aren't they?"

I forgot what she asked me.

"Why would they keep us out here?"

Oh, right. I tug on my T-shirt, missing my suits more with each passing conversation. "I don't know," I say. "Brax just kept saying this was the best place for us right now and that they're working on cleaning up the mess. The way he said it was...odd."

Feisty Savvy rears to the forefront, and she taps one of her feet, hands on her hips, a slight scowl pulling at her brows. How do you not stare at her when she prowls like a goddess of war?

"Clover said something similar. But she made it sound like it was a problem with the road they had to clear before they could get up here."

I nod. That's what Cian implied too. Unfortunately for them, Braxton is a shit liar.

She begins to pace. Six days cooped up with her hasn't been as terrible as I thought it would be. After our bedroom confessional, something in me shifted. I still don't trust her, but perhaps I'm evolving and at least attempting to understand her more.

"Savvy, you've actively avoided talking about your past, but Quinn explicitly mentioned it. What the hell could you have done that could evoke a—what she called a nationwide scandal."

Her teeth dig into her bottom lip, and then I realize it's because she's trying to keep her chin from quivering.

"Jesus, Monroe. I'll fix it, just tell me what it is." As soon as the words are out of my mouth, it hits me just how true they are. My mind may want to hate her, but my heart wants to fix her entire world and then wrap her in bubble wrap coated in titanium so nothing can get to her again.

"Tell me your honest opinion, Patch."

I rear back. Is she drunk? "Patch?" I grind out. "What's that about?"

Her smile is sad. "You're a fixer, always trying to patch the holes in the ship before anyone realizes it's sinking. But some people are destined to go down with the boat, and you have to let them."

That's never going to happen.

She shrugs. "Plus now that I know it annoys you, I think I'll stick with it. It's better than the other names I call you in my head."

Heat curls around in my stomach, and my throat tightens. "What names, Monroe?"

"Drill Bit, for one. Because you're always forcing your nose where you don't belong."

"Or because my cock drills into you like no one else ever has." And now my cock is hard. "What else?"

"There was Patch Daddy, but I thought you'd like that too much. Then Commander, but it felt like too much of a compliment. Mechanic was in the running for a while too."

My lips curl. She has me so damn curious all the time. "Why Mechanic? Because I like to dirty you up?"

"Jesus, no. Because you think you can fix the whole damn world."

I suddenly feel lighter than I did moments ago. She did that. She breathes fresh air into my stale, stagnant life.

"You've put a lot of thought into a nickname for me." It's

as though she's injected me with the swagger of Iron Man, and I stand a little taller.

She grumbles and looks away. "I had to. If I kept calling you *Crotch Rocket* in my head, it would've eventually slipped out, and Madi wouldn't have thought it was as funny as I do."

A bark of laughter rips from me, shaking my shoulders and causing a stitch in my side, but she frowns—the seriousness of earlier circling back and hitting me square in the shoulders.

"Do you think our friends have left us out here to try and clean up whatever mess is out there?" she asks. "Or do you think we're still here because of the hurricane?"

The collar of my T-shirt presses against my throat tighter than the tie I once allowed Sage to tie on me when he was seven. I miss my suits, but it seems out of place to wear them here while she's stuck in my oversized T-shirts and lounge pants.

My suits are my armor, protection. And my gut says she's going to need all the protection she can get.

"I don't know," I say.

She shifts back to the swamp-like pond before determination wraps her entire form in Kevlar. "Are you up for a hike?"

She can't be serious.

"You don't have to come, but I can't just sit here anymore either. Not if..." Her beautiful green eyes connect with mine, and the pain I find hidden in their depths steals the air straight from my lungs. "It doesn't matter. If Madi is trying to protect me, I just— I can't, okay? If she and Brax are doing something to shield me..." Her throat works hard to swallow. "Madi has been through enough with the media. She doesn't deserve to go through my shit too."

"What shit, Monroe?" I'm officially losing my temper with her, and my voice rattles Mother Nature's soothing sounds. "What the hell kind of skeletons could you possibly have?"

When she looks up at me with so many painful secrets swimming in her beautiful green eyes, terrifying sensations swirl in my gut.

Ever since my father locked my sister, Violet, in her bedroom for the duration of her pregnancy when she was just seventeen years old, I haven't handled having choices taken from me well.

After Violet went into early labor and passed away from the lack of medical care, the will to protect has become my entire personality. And staring at Savvy now, every molecule in my body says that she needs my protection.

I failed with my sister—I won't allow that to happen again.

"The kind I'll do everything in my power to keep from the people I love." She glances back out over the swamp, and sadness I've only ever experienced firsthand envelops her in a cloud of grief. "Even if that means I have to leave them to protect them."

Panic. That's the uncontrollable heat feeding on my veins like cancer. "Fuck that, Sav. You're not that dumb, are you? Have you met any goddamn person in this town? Not one of them is going to let you just walk out of here to deal with anything on your own."

Especially not me.

As if she can hear my unspoken words, she drifts closer. Close enough for me to see the dash of gold in her left iris. She pats my chest, twice, then walks into the house.

"Stay here, Patch." Her smirk is an injection of adrenaline straight to my soul. "I've never counted on a white knight, and I don't need one now. I'll call you from the inn if I find out it wasn't the storm holding us hostage."

I growl like a bear in her direction, and it vibrates through each vertebra of my spine.

"Fuck you, Monroe." I lower my voice—a warning that makes most people back up a step. But not her, no, never her. She moves closer. "If you think I'm letting you walk out into the unknown alone then you don't know me at all."

She pauses, and we meet at the stairs, her chin dipping toward her chest. "Does anyone know you? Really know you?"

Flames lick at my ribs, the fire in my veins flooding my system. She's trying to pick a fight, and I can't allow it. Not now. "You almost did, Monroe. Almost. Now pack a bag and grab the first aid kit from my bathroom. We have no idea what we'll encounter—if we can even find a way around the remaining water. Even the driveway that we can see on the other side of the pond is corroded, and who knows what will happen once we meet the main road."

"You really don't have to come with me." She sighs, and it feeds my own frustration. "I'm perfectly capable of figuring out how to get through mud on my own."

"Oh, because you did it so proficiently the last time?" So much for not falling for her antics.

Her hip snaps to the left. "It was a hurricane. Rain came down thick as walls. It's sunny out today, and I'll be fine."

"Fine or dead, and it's not a risk I'm willing to take, so get your ass moving. We're doing this together."

She takes one step before stopping again. "Have you decided yet?"

"Decided what?" Irritation has me reaching for my lucky coin. Could you imagine if I was actually in a relationship with this woman? I'd either wear out my lucky coin or break my fingers. She's seriously the most frustrating human on the planet.

"How you feel about me? Love or hate? Friend or foe? Do you want to keep punishing me for being your friend or spank me...for fun? You're very divided in your words, Patch, but your actions? Those are crystal clear."

I recoil at the word love, grow hard at the vision of spanking, and no, I'm not one step closer to having any damn idea how I feel about this insufferable woman.

"Wear pants," I grunt, then hurry to the kitchen to pack some supplies. "We leave in ten minutes."

"Yes, sir, Mr. Reyes, sir." She's so damn fresh—but *sir* from her pouty lips is something I could get on board with —permanently.

I may not know what I want to do with her, but right now, yeah, I know exactly what I want to do to her, and it involves her silent and on her knees.

This woman is going to break me. I feel it in my bones.

CHAPTER THIRTEEN

SAVVY

I KNEW IT WAS A MISTAKE AFTER THE FIRST TWENTY MINUTES. Two hours later, covered in mud, grass, and debris, I'm ready to throw in the towel.

"It's not that much further," Grey says from where he's standing. "I swear you're part baby giraffe. How have you possibly made it through life walking on your own?" he asks before reaching down to offer me a hand.

"A, I'm not wearing my own shoes, and B, we're slipping and sliding around in brown snot. This shit is nasty, so do you truly believe I'm not trying to remain standing?"

He shakes his head, hauls me to my feet, then drags me forward.

"Just hang on to me, and we'll be to the main road any minute."

I take two steps before I lose my borrowed shoe in a squelching, slurping mudhole. I attempt to release his hand, but he stubbornly holds tighter, and we both tumble to the muck. Again.

"Jesus, Monroe. You're built like an athlete but with none of the coordination."

He's not wrong, and the absurdity of the situation makes me laugh.

Grey pauses, his pale blue irises glued to my lips, and the laughter dies away with the heaviness of his stare. He's done this before when I laugh, and each time, my stomach tightens with worry and something so much stronger than desire that I can't put it into words. What is it about my laugh that has him studying me this way?

"Are we going to end up with a parasite from all this mud and gunk?" I ask. I'd likely say anything at this point to steer us away from the intensity of his appraisal.

He shrugs but manages to gracefully launch himself back to his feet while I slip and slide on my hands and knees.

Please, please, please do not throw up. Who knows what the hell we're actually walking through, but the rotten scent that wafts through the air occasionally isn't helping me. My gag reflex is more than triggered.

"Probably." He grabs me under my armpits before lifting me again.

"Think we'll end up quarantined together?"

Grey has upped his side-eye game since we've been stranded together. And when he uses it now, I can't hide my smirk.

"Monroe, I don't know what to do with you." Exasperation has never sounded so sexy.

"It's not the first time I've heard that one," I say. His fingers twitch. It's the same motion he uses when he's rolling his lucky coin through them. I'm nearly certain he's not even aware he's doing it.

We manage to walk for almost fifteen minutes without me falling. It's a new record.

"What the hell are you two doing out here?"

I recognize the Irish brogue, and my head snaps in a full circle, trying to locate Cian. I find him about twenty yards to the left of us, and just as I'm about to run, Grey grabs me by the shoulders to hold me in place.

"Don't even think about running. The last thing I need is you breaking a leg out here." Grey's words are a hypnotic warning, his breath is warm against my ear, causing a shiver to overtake my limbs.

"Question is, if you're here, why have we been cut off from all communications?" Grey directs the question to Cian, but his gaze and hands remain on me.

"Christ on a turd loaf." Cian's cursing always makes me chuckle.

"I thought you weren't supposed to curse anymore?" I tease, knowing full well that his wife, Elle, has put a moratorium on swearing since they brought Keela home from the hospital.

"Mind your own damn business," he mutters. "I knew this cockamamie idea was rubbish."

The smile slips from my face.

"Cian," I warn. "What are you talking about?"

"Fecking bubbletwits. Come on. I'll take you to town, but I'm warning ya, it's as loony as I've ever seen it."

He motions for us to follow him to the ATV that's parked beneath a line of trees. Grey keeps his hand on my upper arm until we're seated.

"What's going on, Cian?" If my hands weren't covered in muck, I would be biting the hell out of my thumbnail right now.

His sad frown falls to mine. "Just remember, their plan was to protect you both, and their hearts are in the right place, even if they've lost their damn minds."

He starts the ATV and hits the gas. With no windows or

walls, I'm assaulted by fast-moving air as he maneuvers the thing through the mud, effectively cutting off any meaningful communication.

By the time we reach town, it feels as though we've entered another world. While Grey and I were stranded, the rest of Happiness appears to have doubled in size.

Emergency vehicles line main street, with pop-up tents littering the sidewalks, but structurally, the town itself is unharmed.

"Most of the damage is superficial, but Stillwater was almost completely destroyed," Cian shouts above the ATV's noise. Stillwater is the next town over and even smaller than Happiness. "The hurricane lost steam after surrounding the woods by Pride Peak and your place, but FEMA's here, and we've been taking a census of locals while searching for Stillwater residents. West of Bitter Creek was hit the hardest, while everything from Envy's Edge on is untouched, so most of this is for Stillwater." He shifts gears and presses on the gas, but not before something catches my eye.

"Did that sign say Rent-a-Womb?" Grey rumbles, his voice like thunder, cutting through the air like a knife.

I tilt my head toward him, but whatever else he says is lost to the wind tunnel we're in. His face, on the other hand, tells a thousand stories, and none of them are good.

Turning back to the town as we pass by, I catch sight of another sign that reads: We Vote Real Love.

No. No, no, no. This can't be good.

On the corner of Main Street and Joy Junction are picket-style signs. *Savvy Monroe for Town Sweetheart. Rent-a-Womb or Mistress-of-Doom. Vote for Love.*

By the time Cian pulls into the parking lot of the Hideaway, Madi's inn, my head is spinning with all the ways my day is about to implode.

"Why are so many people here?" Grey asks, jumping down from the ATV and standing at my side.

"Emergency shelter has been set up at the Chug." Right. Madi's coworking space is the perfect venue for that. "And this is a private business, so it keeps out..." Cian pulls on his neck and won't make eye contact.

"Keeps out who, Cian?" Grey demands.

"The media. You fecking fools are magnets for that shite, I swear. Just get inside, would ya, before someone sees ya."

Grey ushers me up the front steps, his movements mechanical as he takes in our surroundings. Even after almost a week, I'm still not used to seeing him in casual clothing.

The second he opens the door, I inhale the scent of sugar and spice—the result of years' worth of daily cookie baking that even a full renovation couldn't erase—and hear an argument. A rather loud argument that suddenly falls silent when we step over the threshold, looking as though we've been wrestling in the mud.

Madi has lived here in her grandparents' inn since she was ten. Over the years, it's become a home base of sorts for metaphorical orphans like Clover and me too. Muscle memory made up of comforting senses invades my mind, willing it to calm and find peace.

My pulse syncs to the ticking of the grandfather clock in the corner like a personal metronome. The relief of feeling safe within these four walls eases my shoulders away from my ears. The fresh flowers that get replaced each Sunday sit on the entryway table, welcoming everyone with their bright, cheery colors.

The familiar sense of happiness and belonging has never felt this fragile though—a foundation crumbling to the ground with me standing in the center of it.

"Told ya we couldn't keep them locked up there for long," Cian says, turning sideways and scooting past me.

I scan the crowd, recognizing most people, but for the first time since moving to Happiness for college, not everyone greets me with warmth.

A long-repressed anxiety bubbles to life in my gut. Why are they looking at me like that?

"Meeting adjourned," Moose calls in his booming voice. "We'll pick this back up tomorrow. Everyone out and remember, we take care of our own. Always."

Grey fists the back of the mud-covered T-shirt I'm wearing and hauls me back to him while all the usual suspects of Happiness, Georgia filter by. Most wear a small smile, but a few, like freaking Bethany Price, are filled with scorn.

It's the scorn that makes it hard to swallow.

"You're filthy," Madi says, hugging me anyway.

Clover, who's scared of everything from clouds to germs, opts for a high five, then immediately pulls hand sanitizer out of her bag.

"Start at the beginning," Greyson demands. He hasn't released the back of my shirt, and oddly, I'm okay with that.

Braxton hands us each a couple of towels, then sits at the large dining room table.

"Do you want to get cleaned up first?" he asks.

"No." Grey takes one of the towels and wipes off my back. I'm clearly the disaster of our little excursion today.

"Okay." Braxton waits until we've wiped ourselves down and fresh towels are wrapped around our chests. "There's no easy way to say this."

Greyson and I sink into chairs across from him as Madi hands us each a cup of Blissy's coconut-coffee-bean something.

"Just say it." Grey must practice speaking through his teeth—he's shockingly good at it.

"Right before the hurricane hit, a story broke." Madi's eyes cut to mine with something like pity, and I accidentally fist my paper cup of coffee so hard that the top flies off, and scalding liquid flows over my hand. I don't feel any of it.

"Shit," Grey mutters, quickly mopping up the mess while I stare at my best friend.

"What story?" The words feel deceptively calm as I utter them.

"Well," Madi says. "An 'insider' told liplocked.com that Grey was stranded with a mystery woman from the storm, and some sleazy reporter snuck into the diner. Betty didn't know who she was talking to, and they weren't asking a lot of probing questions, so she felt safe, you know? Since Savvy was named as the sweetheart this year for the town fair, she got excited." Madi speaks so quickly that her words all blend together.

I'd groan if my throat wasn't in the process of closing up on me. The last thing I need is to be the town sweetheart. Attending the fair as a resident and all its booths, stands, and rides is chaos enough, but becoming the focus of the entire event is more than I can handle.

"Once they got Savvy's name, they did some digging," Brax says, not meeting my eyes.

"I'm sure it's just someone looking for a payday, you know, since your podcast is doing so well," Clover says on a shaky breath.

"I'm not following," I admit.

"Short version." Braxton sucks in a gulp of air. "When Grey went 'missing' during the storm"—he uses air quotes, but I'm still struggling to follow along—"Betty let it slip that Grey was getting himself a baby. That, coupled with the two of you shacked up together during the hurricane, got mouths talking. But then, somehow, your latest podcast had a personal conversation between the two of you, and everything blew up. Almost immediately, there was a security breach at the surrogacy center and...both of your profiles were leaked."

"And then photos started circulating online," Clover says. Her voice quivers, and I know whatever she'll say next will be bad. "You look so young in them, Sav. Too young."

No. No, no, no.

"Now we have media here, covering the destruction of Hurricane Isolde, and the savages who pretend to be reporters but are really just searching for clickbait." Braxton's tone carries a bitter edge. It wasn't that long ago that the same tabloids harassed Madi because of his family.

Moose steps close and quietly slips an iPad in front of me, open to a webpage for celebrity gossip with an image of me dancing topless. The headline reads "From Center Stage and Crashing Cars to Rent-a-Womb: How Savannah Monroe Snagged the Elusive Billionaire."

As my worlds collide, my vision blurs, and my lungs burn as though I'm inhaling battery acid. Madi, my best friend for over ten years, swims in front of my face as I get lightheaded.

Secrets I've tried to keep buried and far away from my new life are now in vivid color for the world to see and judge.

"The scornful glares make sense now," I whisper to no one in particular.

Grey swipes up on the iPad, and the screen goes blank.

"Someone had better start explaining what the fuck is going on," he roars.

If it were anyone else, I'd fight the hostility in his tone, but I'm numb. My limbs tingle; even my lips feel cold.

There's only one man who would've had access to those photos.

And I happen to know he was released from prison not that long ago.

I stand, and the world tilts, or maybe I do, because everything quickly goes peacefully, thankfully, black.

———

A LOW RUMBLE OF WORDS STIRS ME FROM A RESTLESS SLEEP. The second I open my eyes, I find my legs ensnared in twisted sheets.

Wait.

The light blue walls and the matching coastal bedding tell me I'm at the Hideaway, but why?

My stomach revolts as images of the day come back to me.

"Do you often pass out from stress?" Grey's low voice has me clutching my chest.

"Why are you sitting in the corner like a creep?" The bed is covered in mud. Shit. So am I.

It takes thirty frustrating seconds to unwind myself from the sheets, but when I attempt to stand, Grey places a hand on my shoulder and holds me down.

The guy moves like a freaking ninja.

"What are you doing?" I hiss. "I'm ruining all Madi's new linens."

"She's married to a billionaire. She'll be fine." He's so droll, I could scream. "We need to talk."

My throat instantly closes.

"It seems we're the new talk of the town. And not just

small-town talk, but worldwide, and now we have a predicament."

"How long have I been asleep?"

"Less than ten minutes, but when I tried to tuck you into bed, you kicked as though I were trying to tie you down."

Well, the tangled sheets make sense now.

Ugh, focus. I wish my brain didn't feel like mush, because I need to be on my A-game with this guy. As much as I love annoying him, I can't trust him with my past. If I do, I run the risk of losing the only family that has ever loved me. I have to spin this.

"You were probably dehydrated because you don't drink enough water, and I know you haven't been eating enough. Then our...situation, and well, here you are. Clover is so freaked out, she let Chief drive her to Walmart to get you some hydration packets. Now answer me, do you faint often?"

Not in years.

"It's nothing. Don't worry about it."

He raises one perfectly sculpted golden brow. I bet he gets them waxed. There's no way that arch is natural.

"Tell me about the pictures."

My pulse increases, and dizziness makes me nauseous.

"Lie down, Monroe." He hovers over me, but my eyes must be out of focus because I see two of him. "What the fuck is going on?"

"Nothing." I attempt to shrug him off.

"It's not nothing. You looked this way when I first found you in the storm too. What the hell is happening?"

"It's called vasovagal syncope."

He repeats the words under his breath. "And?" His hands smooth down my arms until his fingers press against my wrist.

Is he— "Are you taking my pulse?"

He nods without speaking.

"I said I'm fine." Tugging on my arm does nothing to release it from his hold. The guy has inhumanly strong fingers. "It's something that happens sometimes in extreme stress. It's not even that dangerous. It's like my nervous system overexaggerates, and I pass out to protect it."

"Monroe, I've gone nose to nose with you over admittedly stupid shit, but we've battled, and you've never passed out. What's going on?"

"Exactly what I just told you."

"You're fighting with me now, but your pulse is evening out, not escalating. So what happened earlier to make you pass out to protect yourself?"

"We're not friends, *Patch*. I'm not someone you can fix." The acid in my words doesn't even faze him. "I don't owe you a goddamn thing."

He releases my arm, and my heart starts hammering in my chest again. It's not fair that he's the one who holds the salve to my anxieties.

"No, you're right." He takes a step back. "You're not my friend." His towering form retreats, but as he reaches the door, he casts a devastatingly alarming grin my way. "Now you're my problem."

The bedroom door slams before I've fully processed what he said. It's so preposterous that I laugh, slightly hysterically. The man has a severe savior complex.

"Savvy and Grey are getting married?" Pops shouts and hoots downstairs with so much glee in his tone that I bolt upright in bed and scramble to the door. I've never taken the stairs so quickly in my life, and when I skid to a stop in the family room, all eyes are on me.

Pops sits proud as a peacock in his recliner. "Hands

down, this will be the most explosive wedding of the century."

"There's no wedding. Who says there's a wedding?" My voice cracks with disbelief, and Madi starts rapidly plucking her hair elastic on her wrist until Brax wraps his hand around it to stop her. Somehow, I know this was her idea, but no matter how well-meaning she is, a marriage to Sir-Fix-a-Lot will never happen. "Grey, tell them."

He says nothing, and when I find his glare across the room, my eyes widen. I'm shaking my head as though I can see the trainwreck before it actually happens.

"It's not the worst idea in the world," Braxton says.

"Not the worst idea? Did you hit your head or something?" The mud that's dried to my skin cracks with every movement. I feel like a snake shedding its skin, except what's beneath the scales is raw and too exposed.

"Ya know it's right, Mr. Fix-It," Pops taunts, and I'm normally his biggest cheerleader, but this time, I'm in the crossfire too. "I can see your head spinning over there, trying to solve everyone's problems. Come on, Fix-It. We've all seen the way ya pine after our girl. It's no secret y'all been fooling around for months. We're old, not blind."

"Mind your business, old man," Grey growls. They've formed a very strange affection with each other since Braxton first moved here. They drive each other up the wall for sport but have an understanding that works for them.

"I'm not marrying him."

The side conversations carry on as though I'm not even here.

"I bet ya couldn't handle it anyway," Pops says, garnering a soul-crushing glare from Grey. "Marriage or Savvy Sweetheart."

"Sweetheart. Huh." Grey scoffs, but I know Pops is antagonizing him into action. "If I were to ever marry, it would last forever because I don't fail."

Pops stands from his recliner and rocks back on his heels. Madi's grandfather has never met a boundary he couldn't scale, not even Grey's seemingly impenetrable walls. "Prove it."

God, these two revert into derelict teenagers whenever they're in the same room. Pops doesn't surprise me a bit, but Grey? Never in a million years did I think I'd see the day that someone goaded him into childish behavior.

I honestly didn't think Grey had it in him. From everything I've heard, he's never behaved like a child, not even when he was one.

"What the hell is happening?" I say with my arms raised. Someone has to be the adult here and defuse these two, it might as well be me. "We're not placing bets or daring anyone into marriage. Especially not when it's me you're talking about."

"You've been lurking around here, fixing everyone and everything 'xcept yourself since you arrived." Pops steps closer to Grey. "Ace said it was 'cause you were hiding."

Oh, shit. Pops causes enough trouble on his own—Madi has the receipts to prove it—but Pops and Ace together was like kicking a hornet's nest and expecting not to get stung.

Grey flexes, strength rippling through him as though he's one corded muscle. "Don't push me, old man."

Freaking Pops holds out one bony finger and does just that—he pushes Grey in the shoulder with enough strength to move his arm if only an inch, but it's the action that pushes Grey into motion.

He stalks me slowly in full predator mode. Even Madi takes a step away from him. His arm wraps around my waist, he bends his knees, then his warm breath hits my ear.

"We're in a shitty predicament here, *sweetheart*." His words are barely audible, but I feel them everywhere. "Do you want to explain your past or focus on the smoke screen a fake wedding would provide? The choice is yours, but it's my world that's put you on display, so I'll be the one to protect you." I shudder involuntarily against him. "The choice is yours, past or future?"

"What kind of choice is that?" My words aren't whispered, and it has all our family staring at me like I have twelve heads.

"Yours, Monroe. The choice is always yours. Past or future sounds a hell of a lot better than secrets or lies, don't you think?"

If only I truly had a choice.

"Past or future," he repeats, this time loudly enough for the room to hear.

"I don't like being backed into a corner, Grey." The steel of my conviction is finally forcing the wobble out of my tone.

"I'm not the one who backed you in, *sweetheart*. But now I'll be the one to pull you out. It's up to you how we go about that."

"What happened to you hating me?"

A slow, methodical smile tugs at the corner of his lips.

Then, his mouth is at my ear—it's a seduction all its own. "What happened to Patch Daddy?"

"Not going to happen."

"Oh, but it will. And I don't hate the way we make up." Did he just...moan into my ear? "But I do hate that you're in a scandal because of me, and I will correct that. With or without you."

Pressing both hands to his chest, I attempt to shove him away, but he's like a flipping mountain, and the frustration of his strength seeps into my tone. "It's not because of you, you egotistical narcissistic twat-goblin."

"Twat-goblin. That's a favorite of mine." Cian chuckles.

Grey releases me so suddenly, my limbs fall to my sides as though he dipped them in cement.

"We're getting fucking married," Grey announces as though he's the dang mayor, then slams the door on his way out, while I stand in a complete stupor with everyone looking to me for answers I don't have and can't begin to know where to find them.

CHAPTER FOURTEEN

GREYSON

"Say that again?" Quinn says.

She's sitting across from my desk, tapping a stylus against her laptop, but her pinched voice is grating on my nerves, so I stare out my office window.

"Savannah and I are getting married. Put out a press release." My flat tone is at odds with every emotion I possess—they're firing on all cylinders inside my mind.

The moment Savvy fainted, I knew, in my gut that she was hiding more than a past—she's hiding a demon she can't fight on her own.

Could it be stress that caused her reaction? Maybe. But it's more likely that she hasn't been taking care of herself properly.

Thanks to my father, I never got to find out if my sister would have overcome what haunted her, but I'll be damned if I sit by and allow our friends and family to lose Savvy to a disease I know she can beat, even if that means I stay by her side twenty-four seven to ensure that she does.

Then there's the issue of the pictures. Those goddamn pictures the world should never have seen. She's definitely underage in some of them, and I will bury whoever thought it was a good idea to publish them.

"That's what I thought you said." Quinn's voice registers, but I'm only partially listening. "But exactly how is this supposed to solve anything?"

I'm still working that out. Pops backed me into a corner, and my competitive side overrode all common sense. Why the hell do I rise to every challenge Pops sends my way? It's as though that old man reverts me into a squabbling prepubescent with every conversation.

There's just something about Savvy—the weaknesses she fights hard to never show—that has me in a constant state of reaction instead of pro-action.

"Greyson, I told you that Omni-Reyes was taking a hit. This scandal isn't helping. Since you took over, your... history has made people question the integrity of Omni-Reyes, and Braxton leaving you on your own to handle every obstacle is, quite frankly, selfish."

By history, she means my DNA. Darren Wells, my father, is a monster, has always been a monster, and will always be a monster, but her verbal attack on Braxton is a line I won't allow her to cross.

Regardless of how far I go, I'll never outrun Darren's shadows, but Braxton has always been the one to turn on the light and fight them at my side.

"You will not disrespect Braxton again. Is that clear?" It's a demand, not a question, so I don't give her time to respond. "You and your godforsaken crisis PR manager are the ones who suggested flaunting our happy family in the first place, Quinn. Isn't this exactly what you wanted a few months ago? A solution for public perception? What better way to show I'm a committed family man than with a wife? It did wonders for Braxton's reputation."

"Understood," she bites out. "But Braxton isn't the head of Omni-Reyes anymore—you are. This company was built on the foundation of traditional family morals, so showcasing *that* family you've fought so hard to protect makes the most logical sense, considering your...past. But when Kristen suggested this, she didn't mean you should marry a stripper."

"She's not a stripper." Aggression swirls in hazy grays around my vision as I speak.

"Not anymore, but after this article came out, I did some digging. She was, in fact, a topless dancer. Omni-Reyes built its reputation on loyalty and family. We're the number one source for information because people trust us. We are the Heartmark of news. Tying yourself to her goes against everything this company was built on."

Truthfully, I don't give a shit if Savvy was a stripper, an exotic dancer, or a fucking circus clown. My gut tells me there's more to this story, and I won't walk away from her now.

"It's done, Quinn, and I suggest you watch the words you use when speaking of my fiancée and my brother. Tell Kristen to make the announcement. I'll handle the rest."

My office door nearly comes off the hinges as it crashes against the wall. Even Savvy seems surprised by the force of it as she enters my office like the goddamn hurricane that forced us together.

My fists tighten on the towel that's draped around my neck. I hadn't expected Quinn to be waiting for me in my office when I came out of my private shower, so I hadn't finished getting dressed yet.

The skin around Savvy's eyes pinches as she stares from my naked torso to Quinn.

Interesting.

Jealousy looks good on her.

"You arrogant piece of shit." Savvy came for war. "How dare you decree anything regarding my life? This isn't a fairy tale, and you don't get to pretend to be the white knight. You don't even like me half the time."

"Oh, I think he likes you just fine," Sage says, entering behind her with Braxton and Madi on his heels.

My nephew is a modern-day Einstein, and he has the highest emotional IQ of anyone I've ever met. It would make him dangerous if he possessed even a single malicious intent.

"We are not doing this," Savvy hisses. "This is the worst idea I've ever heard in my life. We'll kill each other."

"From a strictly professional standpoint, if you're discussing the pending marriage, I have to agree, Greyson." Quinn steps forward but smartly retreats when Savvy's fiery glare lands on her. "This won't help the situation."

"This has nothing to do with their engagement, Quinn." Why is Brax lying to my assistant? Savvy opens her mouth to fight him, but he's focused on Quinn. "Can you give us a moment?" Braxton poses it as a question, but the order is clear. "This is a family matter first and foremost." Quinn's entire form stiffens. "We'll worry about the professional side of this once my family is on the same page."

A year ago, I would have argued that Savvy isn't family, but since Braxton found Madi, his definition of family has expanded from Sage and me to an entire community that gives me a headache.

"Of course." Quinn's words are clipped, and while I appreciate her ability to reason without emotion, Braxton's family is an emotional tsunami. "Family stands by family, or at least they should," she mutters. "Who was there for Grey when you left him all alone? Me, that's who."

I furrow my brow as Quinn gathers her things. What the hell is she talking about? I'm about to ask when Savvy's movements catch my attention. She's a caged tiger pacing the room right now. If we were alone, the sex might actually bring down the building.

The second the door closes behind Quinn, Savvy—raw and unfiltered—explodes.

"You don't make decisions for me, Drill Bit." She shakes her head. "I mean it, Greyson."

"I prefer Patch Daddy."

Madi and Braxton sit on the sofa across the room chuckling, while Sage slips into a chair positioned in front of my desk. The kid's put on a lot of muscle since he's been working out with the football team, but sometimes when I look at him, all I can see is the five-year-old who used to crawl into my bed in the middle of the night because he was scared.

"Monroe." I pinch the bridge of my nose and turn back to the window. "It's not a real engagement." Damn it. This woman is giving me indigestion again. I press a fist to my chest, but it only causes my pulse to quicken even more.

"Obviously. But it's not a fake one either. I'm not doing this with you. Not now, not ever."

My gut clenches as though someone kicked me, and I reach for my lucky coin. Rubbing my thumb along the raised words, I allow the familiar motion to soothe my rough edges.

Why is her dismissal of me so damn irritating?

"What are you trying to fix, Grey?" Braxton knows me too well.

"Everything."

"Everything." Savvy snorts.

My muscles release, knowing we're about to get into it.

Fighting with this woman is better than meditation—I can't deny how my muscles and my mind relax with each shot fired, regardless of how fucked-up that is.

A smile tugs at my lips, and I allow it to grow as I turn to face her. Standing with a hand on her hip, her shoulders squared, and a toe tapping against my floor, she's a goddess.

An infuriating, lying, sexy, stubborn goddess.

"Yes, Monroe. Everything."

"Ah, care to elaborate?" Madi asks.

"Sunshine Studios' stock tanked three days ago and isn't projected to recover in the current climate. Omni-Reyes slipped to second place on Forbes for the first time in over twenty years. Someone is personally attacking your character, Monroe, and with the way the story took off when my name was attached to it, it means I'm the accelerant here. I'm the common denominator in all of this, so I will fix it however I see fit."

"I—"

"*Can We Talk About That?*" —I say, interrupting her—"is still number one on the podcast charts, but *The Matchmaker Manual, Flirting with Fear*, and all the other podcasts Sunshine Studios has acquired have fallen in ratings and lost sponsors. Do you know what that means?"

"Sunshine Studios is still new, Grey. Even under the Omni-Reyes umbrella, we're bound to have some boomeranging." Braxton doesn't sound confident, and Savvy catches it too.

With measured steps, I stalk Savvy. It appears that's the only way I'm capable of approaching this woman. "It means that people are tuning in to listen to you because of the media shitstorm, but that frenzy is also hurting everyone else, and when it dies down, so will your ratings."

"I don't care about ratings," Savvy snarls. "Not mine, anyway."

Of course she doesn't. She's consumed by trying to protect everyone around her, but I don't know why. Though she doesn't care that *Can We Talk About That?* might fail, she's worried about Madi's podcast, *The Matchmaker Manual*, and Clover's *Flirting with Fear*.

"I know you don't." I soften my tone, even though it takes great personal toughness to do so. "The problem is, you're now associated with me, and the Wells name is biting us both in the ass, but I promised Ace that I'd never allow our family to fail. Unlike you, I don't lie."

"Time out," Madi says, standing. She's snapping the elastic on her wrist—her anxiety is in control now. "Do you know something we don't, Grey?"

"Only that we're in need of a reputational rehab."

Savvy's snarl makes me chuckle.

"And what better way to do that than with a fairy tale?" I say. "After all, it worked for you and Braxton, right?"

"No." Savvy digs in her heels—literally and figuratively. She's widened her stance like a fighter, and sadness hits me hard in the chest. She strikes me as someone who has fought for everything she has, and I know firsthand how utterly draining that can be.

Everything I thought I knew to be black-and-white about this woman turns out to be various shades of gray.

"Braxton and I weren't trying to kill each other though." Madi's gaze darts between Savvy and me, but her smile radiates across the room.

"This has nothing to do with any of you." Savvy slips her thumbnail into her mouth, and I swat it away. Not only is it disgusting, but she makes herself bleed every time. She gasps, and adrenaline spikes in my bloodstream. I shouldn't enjoy taunting her this much.

"This is..." She steps back, putting space between us. "I should have anticipated this, but I don't need you saving the day. I promised myself after Ace helped me that I wouldn't put myself in that position again. That I would save myself —always."

"From what?" Madi asks, hurt coating her words. As close as these women are, it's becoming painfully apparent that Savvy has kept a whole life hidden from those who love her most.

I should hate Savvy for hurting Madi this way. But like all the other times I should find myself hating this woman, the only verb I can grab ahold of is *protect*.

I have an unfounded need to protect her. It's the only explanation for why all her faults irritate the hell out of me yet keep me coming back for more. And I blame it on Ace. He had a soft spot for her too. I must have adopted it on his behalf when he passed.

"I—I can't tell you, Madi. My life before I met you was all kinds of messed up."

Acid bubbles in my gut. Savannah Monroe has devils on her heels, and she's unwilling to let anyone in. Too bad for her that's a boundary I'm more than happy to demolish.

"What do you mean? You can tell me anything." Madi crosses the room and throws herself at Savvy. "You've seen me at my worst, Sav. Geez, you're the sole reason I made it through my early twenties. Nothing you can do or say will ever change how I feel about you. Is this about the photos? You looked hot in them, by the way. Young and too thin, but hot."

That's my thought exactly. Savvy didn't just look young in those photos that were posted. She looked...fragile. I just

don't know how young or fragile she really was—or potentially is.

Yet.

"Please, Savvy." Madi is on the verge of tears as she begs
her best friend to open up, but I can tell by Savvy's stubborn
stance that she'd rather run through fire than put her friend
in the crosshairs of whatever plagues her.

When Savvy doesn't speak, I take preventative measures
of my own. "She thinks she's going to run away from Happiness to save you all from her troubled past."

I've seen Savvy truly angry, but when she spins on me
this time, it's anger and betrayal that cause tears to well in
her beautiful green eyes—and they aren't tears of sadness.
They spit accusations she won't say: *How dare you? It's not
your story to tell. Stay the fuck out of my business.*

Too bad for Savvy, I've already made her my business.

"No." Madi gasps. "You... Why, Savvy? Why won't you let
me help you like you've always helped me?"

Savannah trembles—the war she's fighting is coming to
a head—and her pain sits heavy and unmoving in the back
of my throat.

She casts frantic looks around the room. It's as though I
can see the fight-or-flight response brewing in her mind,
and the only reasonable answer she can come up with is
flight. She wants to run. She wants to do everything she can
to keep her pain from Madi.

I stand helplessly as Savvy's eyes glaze over and her face
flushes. The pulse point in her neck beats faster than a
hummingbird's wings. She sways on her feet, and the
tremble in her limbs rolls as violently as ocean waves in the
middle of a storm.

My chest roars out to fix this. Save her. Fix her. Love her.
But I'm frozen by the fear I see in her eyes. It's the kind of

fear you expect when someone is scared for their safety, their life, and it gives me one tiny glimpse into what she carries with her. The sadness of it all is devastating.

And then, it's as though she crumples under the weight of her own expectations as she slides to her knees...and cries.

My soul shatters at the sight, piercing skin and slicing through bone. I don't ever remember a pain so visceral.

This beautiful, stubbornly broken woman destroys my resolve with each tear that slides down her face. I don't understand it or even appreciate the reactions she pulls from me, but I can't deny that they're there, at least to myself.

The day I met her, I thought she was talking badly about my brother behind his back, and I've judged her on that perception ever since.

It never occurred to me that she was just like me—looking out for those she loves with little to no regard for her own well-being.

"God, Sav. What is it?" Madi falls to the floor beside her, cradling her in a motherly hug that makes her cry even harder.

"It's—it's not what it seems," Savvy stutters.

I meet everyone's gaze over Savvy's head, each person more confused than the last, and then cross the room on autopilot because when shit hits the fan, I'm the one who springs into action.

I reach her in three strides, bend to remove her from Madi's arms, lift Savvy, and carry her to the sofa, where I sit with her in my lap.

Sage stares at me as though I've lost my mind, and perhaps I have because I'm no longer consumed by thoughts of what I've lost or how I'll move on by creating a family of my own. The only thought in my head is getting Savvy back to being my equal, my sparring partner, my own personal headache.

For the first time in over a year, getting a child is not my top priority—it's my beautifully broken pain in the ass Monroe.

Madi stares at her friend with so much heartache that I look away. Braxton smirks at me as though he's figured out a secret, but I'm unwilling to entertain him. Instead, I focus on the woman in my arms who's fighting a battle with herself.

Compromise has never come easy to me, but if I don't offer her something, we may never find a resolution that involves her and me in Happiness long-term.

"Let me in," I demand in a voice low, soft, and steady, but with enough control that it breaks through her internal battles. "Please. We're in this together now, regardless of how you feel about that. The only way for both of us and our families to come out of it unscathed is for you to tell me what haunts you so we can blow that shit up together."

My words seem to snap her back to this reality, and she scrambles from my lap, but I only allow her to slide onto the cushion next to me.

Braxton stands to give her space. He, Madi, and Sage all pull up chairs to face us.

"Please, Sav. Talk to me." Fear and love battle for dominance in Madi's tone.

I've never even considered compromising for a woman before, and it shocks the hell out of me as I do it now for Savvy by angling my legs toward her and offering a bit of my past. "My father is a piece of shit, Monroe. He took the jewelry emporium that had been in our family for generations and turned it into a bloodbath. He was unethical in his sourcing of diamonds. He cut corners by going into business with known criminals. He killed my sister with his neglect because he was more concerned about appearances and crooked loyalty than he was about his own daughter.

"I'll never wash the blood from his hands off our family name, and that will always follow me. So don't tell me that my history has nothing to do with the media frenzy stirred up by my choice to remain elusive over the years."

Her shoulders tremble. If I could imbue her with my confidence, I'd attach an IV myself.

"I've been on display but just far enough out of reach that the public has nothing on me, and now, the first sign of scandal in eighteen years, they blow it up as though we're royalty. So please tell me how anything you could have possibly done in your past can even compare to my history. Because from where I'm standing, I'm the one the media is after."

She shakes her head with a quivering jaw.

Desperation and fear bleed from her eyes, and I feel it deep in my gut. Savvy opens her mouth, but no words come. Whoever has the power to break my woman this way will meet my wrath. I swear it.

It feels like an eternity before she speaks. "My childhood best friend is paralyzed from the waist down...and it's all my fault."

The pain that she exudes hits me square in the chest with sniper-like precision, and the list of ways I hate my honesty-challenged angel is instantly wiped away.

Childhood trauma has a way of allowing you to see the most damaged souls, especially when their pain mirrors your own.

CHAPTER FIFTEEN

SAVVY

"My childhood best friend is paralyzed from the waist down...and it's all my fault." Electric shocks straight to the heart would be less painful than what I experience the moment I admit it.

Run.

It might be the first time I've ever uttered those words, and now I'm terrified to make eye contact with anyone.

Hide.

I barely survived the hurtful comments and vicious glares from people in Vegas when I was a teenager, and I never cared much about most of them. Receiving the same treatment from people I love will be my undoing.

Protect yourself.

I have to get out of here.

Outwardly, I'm steady and calm as I attempt to stand, but Grey knocks all the air from my lungs when he tugs me back to the sofa next to him. His large fingers remain wrapped around my wrist as if he knows I'm seeking an escape. The soft fabric of his designer pants slides across my fingertips, making the threads of my shirt feel like sandpaper in comparison.

Don't react. Don't show weakness. Run.

"You're not running away. These people love you, Monroe. You will give them the opportunity to be to you who you have always been to them." His words are harsh, but his soothing tone makes my stomach flip and flop.

"Savvy." Madi says my name hesitantly, and when I glance up, I'm forced to witness the pain my secrets have already caused. "What do you mean, it's all your fault?"

Am I seriously considering telling them everything? I can't do that, right? The control Riley's family has reaches too far. It makes them dangerous—I know that now. If they're behind this, then everyone I love could be in harm's way.

We will ruin you someday, little girl. You don't get to do this to our children and get away with it. We'll take everything and everyone you love until every last drop of hope is eradicated from your life.

A chill works through my body at the memory of the vicious glares Riley and Paige's moms had leveled at me as they hurled never-ending threats. They'd cornered me in a bathroom stall at the courthouse before Riley's trial had begun.

Don't react. Don't show weakness. Run.

Shaking my head, I bite the skin around my thumbnail until the taste of copper fills my mouth. Grey curses, then grabs a box of tissues from the table to his right and wraps one around my bleeding appendage. But he doesn't let it go. He holds pressure to it while gently caressing the inside of my wrist with his thumb and simultaneously managing to look pissed off.

What the hell is happening right now?

"Sav, you know you can trust me," Madi whispers.

The log in my throat rolls over, lodging itself painfully and making it impossible to swallow.

"It's not that I don't trust you." *It's that no one has ever believed me...not when it mattered, and now, I fear for your safety if I say anything at all.*

Grey stops his ministrations, his hold on my wrist becoming tighter, as though my words triggered him to react. "You're scared of someone."

I can't control the way I flinch.

Don't react. Don't show weakness. Run.

I'm well beyond slipping into old self-destructive habits, but all the coping mechanisms I've learned over the years are unraveling with the weight of my past.

"Savvy," Braxton says in a strangled tone, "we have the means to keep everyone safe, but we can't protect anyone if we don't know what we're up against. Madi and Clover will be safer if we can plan appropriately."

Shit. Is he right? Of course he's right, but it doesn't make it any easier. They're richer than sin. *They'll* be fine.

It's just me that'll get buried. Right? Helena DeVane and Corrine Ashford have money, a grudge, and a mean streak that strikes harder than a bolt of lightning, but Braxton and Grey have the means to shield themselves and the people they care about.

"What are you so scared of?" Greyson whispers. He's tense, prepared for a fight. "If it's all coming to light anyway—and trust me, if there's a public record anywhere, the media will find it—allow us to help you before we find out on some website."

I think I'm going to be sick. My stomach clenches, and it takes everything in me not to wretch. With all the strength I have left, I yank my hand out of Grey's grasp.

The last thing I deserve is comfort.

Especially from someone who says he hates me half the time.

"Savvy." Sage is only eighteen, but he might be wiser than all of us combined, and it shows in his calm, even tone. "I know Grey can be...well, Grey, but there isn't a more protective man on the planet. If he says he can handle your trauma, you should let him."

"It's not trauma if you created it yourself," I mutter.

"Did I create my trauma by not getting my sister out of her prison cell of a bedroom before it was too late?" The power behind Grey's question chills the room to arctic temperatures.

"No, of course not. But it's not the same. That wasn't your choice, you tried. I...I didn't try at all, not really."

Madi stands, then practically falls onto the sofa beside me. I'm sandwiched between her and Grey, their comforting heat surrounding me in a protective shield I almost believe in.

"I think Grey's right, Savvy." Madi continues to snap the elastic band around her wrist as she speaks. "It's only a matter of time before it all gets released to the press. While Grey has always had media attention, he's never had a scandal, and with him tied to you, they won't stop digging until they find out every sordid detail. If I've learned anything over the last ten years, it's that it's better to control your narrative. Don't allow someone else to rewrite your story. Please, let us help."

Jesus. I know she's right, but I'm not ready to lose these people either. Then again, I might have to walk away to protect them, so maybe telling them what I've done will help diminish their pain when I do.

After all, how could they love me once they know my truth—what I've done?

It's why I never told them, right? They could never love me the way I love them if they knew.

I was only ever meant to be a supporting character in their story, never the main attraction because if they got too close, they'd find my foundation built on a pile of lies.

And now, here we are.

Corrine and Helena sold every story they could after the accident happened, but I was a no-name kid who came from nothing. It wasn't sensational enough to keep the traction going once Riley was found guilty.

But now that I've been linked to Grey? *Oh my God.* This is what they've been waiting for. This is what they meant when they said they'd wait however long it took to take away everything I've ever loved.

This time, I have everything to lose.

Grey was right. He's the accelerant they were waiting for.

My insides swirl as though they're inside a blender, so I stare down at my lap. After years of friendship, I can't look my best friend in the eye. If a goodbye is in our future, I need her to hear my side of the story first.

"When I was sixteen—"

"Fuck," Grey curses beside me, but I attempt to shrug him off.

"I met this guy. He was...older than me, but he made me feel special, and my parents never gave a shit as long as it didn't interfere with their *free love* and *if it feels good, do it* lifestyle."

Grey stiffens beside me, and I focus on how he fists then flexes both hands.

"My parents are...different. I didn't grow up with rules. They idolized the '60s and raised me and my brother as free spirits, but to the extreme. I was a little girl who craved attention, and begged for love, and when I didn't get it..."

Shame wells in my chest. I can't look at anyone, so I close my eyes for a count of three. When I open them, I feel more robotic, less connected to the scene before me. "I rebelled," I whisper. "I was going to parties at twelve. Shoplifting by fourteen. Staying out all night by fifteen. They didn't know where I was half the time, and truthfully, it never crossed their mind that they should."

Madi presses her hand to mine and squeezes gently, but now that I've started this, I have to get it out, so attempting a smile that feels more like a grimace, I tuck my hands under my legs and continue.

"I was labeled the 'bad kid' the 'troublemaker' even though Paige—she was my best friend—dragged us into half the shit we got into. Her last name got her a rideshare home, while all mine did was get me thrown into the back of police cars. But we fed off each other. She loved that I had freedom, I loved that she had parents who cared."

Internally, I fight the sensation of fire ants crawling along my exposed skin, but when it becomes unbearable, I release my hands from under my legs and begin to pick at the skin around my thumb.

"My parents never came to get me when I'd get in trouble for shoplifting food or tampons. It was always my brother. When police would raid parties, it was Austin who would promise to keep a closer eye on me, but he was busy building a better life for himself, and he left home the moment he could."

I chance a peek around the room to gauge everyone's reactions. I wish I hadn't. Madi's skin has gone pale, Braxton's eyes are pinched at the corners, and Grey's jaw ticks like the second hand of a clock. Inhaling, I stare at my hands while I collect my thoughts.

"Austin was always a rule follower, the extreme opposite of my parents, and I was acting out, doing anything I could to get the attention of anyone who would care. My brother is probably the only reason I'm still alive, but even he could only take so much shit from me."

Madi shifts next to me. She's wearing her sadness like a heavy cloak that's weighing her down.

"When everything was spiraling beyond what I could handle, he didn't believe me." I can't help the detachment in my tone. It's been a long time since I've gone to this place in my mind, the one that protects me without judgment— the hidden garden I would seek solace in when I needed to still believe that someone, somewhere would care about me.

"I asked for help with Riley DeVane, and Austin shut the door in my face." A sob catches in the back of my throat, and I wrestle it back down to my stomach. "I can't even blame him. The only thing he asked of me was to stay out of trouble, and I just couldn't do it."

"What did you ask him to help you with?" Grey asks through gritted teeth.

"That's not— Is Riley one of *those* DeVanes?" Braxton asks, and my neck crackles as I whip around to stare at him.

Those DeVanes? What's that supposed to mean?

"Yes," Grey answers cryptically. I open my mouth, but he continues before I can form words. "Continue your story, and then I'll explain."

The urge to gulp is strong, but my mouth is suddenly as dry as the Vegas desert.

"Um, well. So, I'd been with Riley for two years. He got us into clubs—"

"I bet he did." Braxton spits the words as though they personally insulted him.

I frown in his direction, but he makes a rolling motion with his hand for me to continue.

"We got into clubs, but he also found ways for me to work in them when I needed money, even though I was obviously underage. But my parents would take off for weeks at a time, and I'd be left on my own with cans of soup if I was lucky or nothing at all if I wasn't. Looking back on it, I know the entire thing was wrong, but I was a dumb teenager, and Riley was this twenty-two-year-old with money and power who gave me the affection I'd never had. He gave me experiences I longed for but could never afford."

"For fuck's sake," Grey mutters before taking my hand in his again. His thumb hovers over the pulse on my wrist, and I swear his lips twitch when my pulse begins to slow.

"When I was seventeen," I say, staring at the floor again, "Paige's parents found out I was dancing in one of Riley's clubs to pay my living expenses and to save up for college, and they rightfully forbade her from going anywhere near me. They always assumed anytime we got in trouble, it was my doing.

"Riley's mom and Paige's mom are best friends, and they had plans for their children that didn't involve a kid who had to steal tampons or cereal, so they told them both to stay away from me or there would be consequences. They didn't know that Riley was obsessed with me or that Paige wanted freedom from her obsessively strict parents. But..." My chin quivers as memories of a lost friendship assault my mind.

"But Riley wouldn't give me up. Paige and I had made a pact to never leave the other person behind. We were going to college together. We were going to experience life to its fullest and make sure that we both got everything we ever wanted. We just had to get through high school first. So, when Riley would pick me up, she would sneak out and come too. We looked out for each other always. Paige…Paige wasn't like her family."

Madi hands me some tissues and gestures toward my face. Jesus, Monroe. Get control of yourself.

Don't react. Don't show weakness. Run.

I've come this far, now I have to finish getting this story out. It's been weighing on my heart for so long, it's as though I can almost feel it lifting, and even though I don't deserve the reprieve, I need it like the air I breathe.

I'll take the repercussions of my actions as I always do. This time, it'll just be a whole lot harder to rebrand myself because the loss of the family I built will leave me as a shell of who I could have been, of that I'm certain.

The air is thick, and all the eyes on me make my skin crawl, so I focus on my fingers instead.

"Riley was pissed off the night everything fell apart. He found out I was planning to go away to college. He picked me up and saw a stack of acceptance letters in my room, and he just…lost it.

"Paige wasn't feeling well and didn't even want to go out that night, but I sort of guilted her into coming. When she saw Riley though, she was worried about getting in the car with him, but I was terrified of what would happen if I didn't. He—he could get so mad. I convinced her it would be fine, and we went with him to a party in one of the suites at the DeVane Casino, but it wasn't like any party I'd ever been to."

The sickness in my stomach swirls and swishes hotter than lava, and I clutch it to ease the pain.

"The vibe was…off," I say quietly as I recall the horror of that night. "The girls walking around seemed scared." The contents of the breakfast Grey made me eat want to stage a revolt, but I force them down. "Paige knew something was wrong too and told me we had to get out of there. It sent Riley into another rage. I—I think he wanted me there to see whatever was happening to scare me into submission, and we didn't know what to do. When I finally convinced him that Paige's parents were looking for us, he insisted on driving us to her house. I didn't know he'd already taken something."

Memories I've attempted to avoid fly across my vision in a sick highlight reel.

"Paige didn't want to get in that car." A painful hiccup rips through my chest. "R—Riley threw me in the passenger seat so hard my head hit the dashboard, and I saw stars. I only remember him telling Paige she had one second to decide if she was getting in or not. Everything was so blurry, but I remember Paige standing on the sidewalk with tears in her eyes.

"We didn't leave each other for anything, but I couldn't get my words to work. I wanted to tell her to run, but she— she got in the car. He drove too fast."

The sounds of crunching metal and shattering glass reverberate through my memory as though it's happening again in real time, and my body constricts, attempting the fetal position as though I have no control of my limbs.

"The next thing I know, I'm suspended in the air, the car crushed in on all sides. I couldn't see or breathe. All I could smell was gas and blood."

Madi sniffles beside me, but I can't look at her.

"Then I woke up in the hospital. Paige's parents told me

they hoped I died in there for what I did to their daughter, and they would press charges if I ever attempted to see her again."

"Jesus, Savvy. I'm so sorry." Madi wraps both arms around me. *Don't get too close, Madi. I cause mayhem wherever I go.* She squeezes tighter. Why would she hug me after what I just told her? After all the shit I did? The stealing, the lying, partying, the police, and the chaos I've created.

"That's not the end of it though, is it?" Grey is scarily composed. "There's an age span in those photos of you dancing at DeVane's. What happened between the accident and some of those photos?"

Peeling Madi's arms off me, I straighten my spine. This is one part of my story I will never be ashamed about.

"My brother's now a police officer in Vegas. He was the first one on the scene after the accident. I told him and his partner...everything. But he—he was also best friends with Riley's older brother. Austin didn't believe me, and the DeVanes and Ashfords spun stories so well that even I started to question my reality."

"Oh, Sav." Sage has been quiet, but when his expression falls into a face full of compassion, I wish he weren't here. He's too young to be tainted by my past, but now that I've started, I just have to get it all out and then plan my escape.

For their safety, I have to run.

"Austin demanded that I recant my statement, though I don't know if that was because he knew what those families would do to me or because he truly didn't believe me. I refused. I testified against Riley. His mother and Paige's threatened to take everything away from me, no matter how long it took."

"How did you end up *back* in Vegas, Savvy?" Grey's voice

sounds as though he's about to snap like a bungee cord pulled past its limits. "What did Ace have to do with this?"

Madi and Braxton watch me, their concern piercing my exposed wounds with a million tiny needles.

"Paige's mom called me and said that Paige wanted to see me, and they were going to allow it just once so she could have closure, but when I got there, they gave me an ultimatum."

"What did they do, Sav?" Madi is rubbing my back in slow, soothing motions. Almost as though she expects me to break out in a panic attack at any moment.

"They said I owed retribution for ruining both of their children's lives. I could either work off my debt in the Dove Cage—it's their main attraction, and the girls who dance in the cages easily make thousands of dollars in one night. I could do that to repay what they thought I owed them—or they would systematically take away my degree, my license in psychology, and my podcast. So I took the deal."

Madi's gasp has me looking up from my hands. "That's when you flew to Vegas with Ace."

I nod but break eye contact with everyone. "I came to the Hideaway to tell you I was going home for a couple of weeks, and Ace was there. He said he had a meeting and was headed in that direction anyway, so he offered to fly me there. That was supposed to be the end of his help."

A slow, sad smile creeps onto my face. "But nothing ever went to plan with Ace. He was always ten steps ahead of me. I had arranged to work in the cage again for what I thought was two weeks, and I'd only told Ace I was helping a friend out at a club.

"What I didn't know was that Helena and Corrine were making their next play to ruin and humiliate me—that had always been their favorite method of punishment."

"Why would they go to all that trouble?" Madi asks, squeezing my hand in hers.

"Riley had just been denied early parole, and his family was pissed. My podcast had started to pick up some momentum then, so they thought they could swing the court of public opinion against me. According to them, I should be paying for Riley's crimes. They're...vile human beings."

I suck in a breath, thankful when Sage hands me a bottle of water. I chug greedily.

"They thought they could break my spirit, but they didn't know my spirit didn't exist anymore. They got me back into the Dove Cage but stopped seating their wealthy clients in my section. I was dancing for a percentage of what I had made as a teenager, and at that rate, I would never reach the impossible quote they'd given me, so after a few days, I started taking double, and sometimes triple shifts, pushing through exhaustion, sneaking naps in the locker room between shifts, and that's when Ace found me."

"Jesus Christ." Grey stands, fists clenching.

"Vegas has a lot of clubs. How did Ace know where to find you?" Sage asks.

"When I asked him, he said my face was plastered all over Vegas seemingly overnight. The DeVanes were promoting "Sin's Retribution" all over the strip with images of me and the car accident."

Grey paces the floor next to me, his skin a little paler than before, but his eyes are a fiery laser cutting through what's left of my heart.

"What about your brother?" Madi asks.

God, the way Austin must hate me. That was my first real loss in life—the protection of my big brother.

I'm burning up. My skin itches as though I've been rolling around in poison ivy for days, and my stomach cramps like it's the worst period I've ever had. The guilt of my actions is slowly killing me from the inside out.

"He was livid that I didn't try to help Riley, and he blamed me for Paige's condition. I tried to talk to him multiple times. I tried to tell him my side of the story. But by the time the accident happened, he was either tired of trying to save me from myself or he thought I had cried wolf one too many times, I'm not sure."

"The crash, then the cage," Grey says, low and deep in his throat. "That's why you panic in tight spaces. Darkness too. Your sensory deprivation attacks—it reminds you of them."

I wish he didn't know me so well, but I nod in response.

"And they called you Sin."

"It—it was the stage name Riley gave me when I was sixteen."

"How did Ace get you out of there?" Braxton asks, his tone strained.

I shrug. "I'm honestly not sure. He just showed up one day, opened the cage door, handed me some clothes, and took me out of there, telling me I never had to worry about the DeVanes or the Ashfords again."

The rustling of fabric has me once again looking up from my hands. Grey stands before me, sliding on a crisp white button-down over his broad shoulders. The fact that he's been shirtless this entire time is not lost on me, but the way he methodically loops each button makes me nervous.

"The bathroom is over there," he says, pointing at a closed door across from his desk. "Get yourself cleaned up, and then we'll make a joint statement."

I look down at myself, confused, because I already showered at Madi's.

"A joint...what?"

"Ace may have saved you, Monroe, but it also put a target on your back because of the blood that runs through my veins and my new last name. The Wells family alone had more zeros in the bank than the DeVanes and the Ashfords combined. Factor in my adoption into the Reyes family, making me a Reyes family heir too, and it's more than enough to get greedy hands grabbing. Those families have a reputation for being—"

"Unethical at best," Braxton supplies. "Criminals for sure, and covetous enough to think they deserve whatever they can blackmail out of any situation."

Greyson leans down, planting his hands on either side of my lap, and instinctively, I lean away from him.

"So herein lies the problem, Monroe, because, as I said before, that makes you my problem to fix. In fact, even Ace told me in his final letter not to let Sin break, so I'll hold you together with my bare hands and get you through this if I have to drag you kicking and screaming to the altar. Because even though they want to mess up our world, not even the DeVanes would dare fuck with my wife."

"Your—your wife? Are you having a breakdown of some kind? I'm not marrying you. I'm not carrying your baby. And I most certainly am not a damsel in distress in need of your intervention."

Except, perhaps I am.

God help me, Grey smiles. It's a smile that takes over his entire face and changes the atmosphere in the room instantly.

Somehow, he sucks all my fears and worries into his vortex and swirls them together to make me feel something else entirely—something far too similar to *safe* for my liking because I know safety is an illusion meant for other people.

"Wanna bet?" Those two words whisper over my bare skin like a lover's caress but sharpened by the tongue of an anti-hero. They're devastating in their destruction because I know without a doubt, Grey isn't going to back down from what he perceives as his fight.

The only way out of this is to make him regret his decision to strong-arm me into a fake marriage.

This maniac of a man just managed to turn my fear into determination, and as much as I want to hate him for not giving me a choice in the matter, all I can feel is grateful—freaking asshole.

My smile now matches his because if there's one thing Grey and I know how to do, it's push each other's buttons. I may be his enemy—who he also happens to love fucking—but I'm about to become his worst nightmare.

My battles are meant for me and me alone. I learned a long time ago that relying on anyone is like digging your own grave—and I'm not about to get my hands dirty again.

I give this fake fiancée thing one month, tops, before he's running as fast as he can in the opposite direction.

And then I'll figure out how to handle the shitstorm Riley is undoubtedly ready to rage on my life.

"Game on, hubby." I stand on shaky legs, but he doesn't retreat, our chests pressing together because neither of us is willing to back down.

He's much better at masking his emotions, and he knows it. His resulting grin is downright feral.

This man has pushed and shoved me right into the corner he was constructing. Now the only thing I'm focused on is winning this battle with him, not the bombshell of a confession I just made to one of my dearest friends.

And Greyson Reyes smirks as though that was his intention all along. That asshole just got a point, and I didn't even know we were keeping score yet.

Game on, indeed. Greyson Reyes is going to regret the day he forced a metaphorical ring on my finger. I'll make sure of it.

CHAPTER SIXTEEN

GREYSON

Sin. Of course she's Sin. Who else would it have been? Ace was always playing puppet master with our futures when he was alive, why wouldn't he do it from the grave as well?

I remove the coin he gave me eight years ago. I didn't understand what it meant back then, but maybe I'm starting to now.

"Grey, you okay?" Braxton asks. I'm standing in one of our conference rooms because the second Savvy went into my private bathroom, I needed space. Space to think, to breathe, to make a fucking plan.

"Did you know?" I ask.

Braxton read my letter from Ace's will, just as I read his.

He slowly lowers himself into a chair opposite me. "No, but I had my suspicions, as I'm sure you did."

Yeah, I had them. But no one in their right mind would ever think Savvy and I could be... Jesus, I'm trying to protect her, yet she challenges me as though I'm the enemy.

"This is so fucked-up, Brax."

"I don't believe the DeVanes made any connection to us

until Ace showed up to get her," he says. "And the Ashfords are known to be patient vipers. I'm sure they've been lying in wait for a moment to strike, so the instant a romantic connection between the two of you was leaked, they struck."

Braxton frowns, tugging at the back of his neck with an aggressive grip. "They've probably been secretly watching her since the moment Ace rescued her, if not even before then. Moving Omni-Reyes to Georgia probably piqued their interest even more, but the gossip sites were definitely the catalyst for this attack. There's no denying they were behind the photos being released, and I doubt they would even try. They want everyone to know they're coming for her."

My skin crawls, and I want to peel it off layer by layer until I'm no longer coated in the sins of assholes.

"You're right," I say. "But they have no idea who her family is now."

"Greyson." Quinn steps into the conference room and shuts the door. She visibly stiffens when she spots Brax in the chair.

"What?" I've lost the ability to control my emotions, and my lethal tone is the only warning I give.

Braxton watches us both closely, too closely. Does he see something in Quinn that I've missed?

Quinn smooths down her skirt. "I have the press release you asked for, but Kristen is suggesting I implore one more time that you truly think about this, and she is the only crisis PR specialist here. You have a company depending on you, and this is the kind of scandal that won't go away anytime soon. After the mess with..." She waves an indifferent hand in Braxton's direction.

"After the mess with my father, and our grandfather's company, you mean?" Braxton's cool demeanor is a shock. The guy goes around doing daily good deeds for strangers, for fuck's sake. Unlike me, he doesn't have an assholish bone in his body.

"Well, yes. We're still trying to recover from all the... changes, and to be frank, Grey has been forced to handle a lot on his own. I believe another scandal will push us to a point of no return. Ace built this company on honor and integrity. Marrying a goddamn stripper is just reinforcing the narrative that all the gossip columns and competitors are perpetuating about you."

The way I suddenly want to fire this woman has me clenching my jaw so tightly I might crack a molar. If I open my mouth, a lawsuit will undoubtedly follow.

It's my own fault, perhaps. Over the years, I've given Quinn more responsibilities and freedoms than most. When I ran back to California, she's one of the only reasons I didn't fail. She stepped in when I was at my lowest with no one to turn to. She's essentially become my executive assistant at the office and the COO of my messy family life.

That's why I'm surprised when Braxton stands slowly and with purpose, making him seem even bigger than his six feet four inches.

"Let me explain something to you, Quinn, about *our* grandfather's company." Braxton's voice is rough, as though he's containing a terrarium full of venom beneath his words. This is not the Braxton she's ever met before. Hell, I've only seen him come out a handful of times.

Braxton's methodical as he rounds the table to stand at my side, a visual representation that we're on the same team.

"It doesn't matter that Grey isn't related to Ace by blood. Family is family, and our great-grandfather, our grandfather, and now we have built this company to be what it is for one reason and one reason only. Do you know what that is?"

Quinn visibly swallows even as her posture screams her displeasure.

"No?" Braxton's tone is mocking, and again, I wonder what I'm missing between these two. "This company was built on and thrived because of the love we have for the women in our lives. Great-grandad started Omni-Reyes so his wife could publish whatever she wanted in a time when women weren't supposed to have a voice. Ace transformed the company so his wife could direct film and television projects before society thought women should be in control. And us?"

"We're evolving again to build Sunshine Studios into the platform best suited to help our wives succeed," I finish for him. And nothing has ever felt more right. Savvy Monroe may not want to be my wife yet, but sometimes destiny is more powerful than our own stubborn minds.

"That may be true, but your grandparents were acting on love. Love makes you go to unimaginable lengths. What happens when this—this farce implodes, and the world feels betrayed by your lies?"

"Fortunately for you, that irrational fear is above your pay grade." The jab hits exactly as Braxton intended. "As you've said a number of times, this is a family business, and you are not family. Your job is to assist Grey in whatever he deems appropriate. Are you able to do that, or should we reassign you?"

"I'm excellent at my job, Braxton, and I've more than proved that every time you shirked your responsibilities."

"Hmm," he hums. "We might need to agree to disagree here. But perhaps it's time that some lines were rebuilt. Mr. Reyes seems appropriate here from now on." He turns to me with a raised brow. "For both of us."

It feels as though he's daring me to contradict him, but

I'll never go against my brother, and I will find out what the hell's going on sooner rather than later.

"While the engagement may be sudden," I say, needing to defuse the situation, "I assure you, there's nothing fake about my impending marriage. Savvy and I have been in a relationship almost as long as Brax and Madi have."

It feels like the most honest statement I've shared in a long time, and if there weren't already such a shitstorm waiting for us, I might have dug deeper into the hidden meaning behind it. But for now, all she needs to know is that I mean it with my whole fucking chest.

It's not Quinn's business that the relationship I speak of has mostly consisted of sex and verbal sparring. If I can make her believe it, then we'll have no problem convincing the world too.

Quinn raises a skeptical brow, but Braxton chuckles. "I told Madi it wasn't a coincidence at Christmas when Savvy went into the kitchen put together and came out with her pants on inside out."

His words seem to irritate her more, and she pales.

"That's all for now, Quinn." My tone is dismissive and unyielding. "Please leave the press release on the table, and I'll call if I require anything else today."

She opens her mouth to speak, then appears to think better of it because she tosses the folder onto the table and walks out without a word.

I follow her to the door and quietly shut it.

"Care to tell me what the hell that was about?" I ask. My voice isn't raised—Braxton and I will always be a team, but he has some explaining to do.

"Madi has always gotten a weird vibe from Quinn. Then when you went back to California, she started lashing out at me with little barbs, like she did today about not being there for you. Almost as though she took it as a personal affront that I didn't chase after you. But after all of today's revelations, I realized something."

"What?"

"Well, for starters, the photos of Savvy didn't circulate until after someone announced that you were stranded during a hurricane with a mystery woman. The moment Savvy was exposed—all her secrets leaked—almost as if someone had an entire press kit ready to go." He tugs on his earlobe, and it's so close to what Sage does when he's thinking that it makes my chest ache with memories that will never again be a reality.

It's another reminder that we're all drifting apart and I'm not always going to be part of their day-to-day. Then a flash of Savvy's face enters my mind, and the void I've been attempting to fill suddenly feels less like a black hole and more like a pinprick.

Jesus. I rub at my heart with my knuckles. It's racing as though I just ran a marathon. Just thinking about Savvy gives me heartburn.

"True," I say. "But wasn't it Betty at the diner who outed Savvy?"

"But how many people knew you canceled your meetings with Quinn at the last minute? The rest of the executive team had already been sent home, and as far as they knew, you were heading to the inn to be with your family, so who else knew you were at home and not at the inn with the rest of us? The story that you'd 'gone missing' was out there before anything was released about Savvy. And what better way to spread that particular gossip than by stopping in the diner and letting it slip?"

He's right. I had planned to ride out the storm at the inn

with him and Sage, but it hit so suddenly, I'd decided to stay home right before Savvy turned up.

Braxton stares at me as though I'm missing something important. "The stories, the podcast, the photos, they were all rapid-released after someone let slip that you were stranded with a mystery woman. The information that was leaked wasn't hearsay. It wasn't random town gossip. They had details, receipts. They had access to Savvy's unreleased podcast."

My mind swirls with scenarios—each one more dysfunctional than the last. "There's no way anyone could have predicted my land would turn into a literal island, and Savvy didn't tell anyone that she was coming to my house. It's why she was so freaked out about Clover."

"That's what I mean. Someone had access to the details, and Madi has a pretty good read on people. My gut is telling me that someone has been building a case against Savvy— and possibly you—for a long time. If it's not Quinn, it's someone else that's close enough to us to know the intimate details. Someone willing to sell you out. Someone willing to work with families like the DeVanes and the Ashfords."

I nod as suspects form before my eyes. Quinn knew Savvy was with me, and her voice is ice-cold anytime she mentions Savvy's name.

"What could Quinn possibly gain by doing that?"

Braxton's chuckle tells me he thinks I'm being obtuse. "Money, your attention, you," he lists as though they're the most obvious things in the world. "Take your pick. Why does anyone do anything?"

I snort out a wry breath. "I think it's well-documented that I'm far from a prize to be won. But it doesn't make any sense, regardless. These attacks feel personal to Savvy, but I can't tell if the hits are meant for the both of us or if I'm just the accelerant used to hurt her."

"Greyson, I love you, but you're an idiot. People, women especially, adore you. I don't know what the endgame was, but let's talk in absolutes. In your email to our employees, you specifically mentioned riding out the storm with family. Only a handful of people knew you were home alone, and Quinn was one of those people."

Braxton stands and paces as he talks. "Yes, the attacks feel personal on Savvy because other than the perception of you marrying what the media is calling a stripper, nothing has been personal to you."

I scoff. Everything about Savvy is personal to me.

He says, "The DeVanes want to make her pay, and they've proven they'll take their time to make sure they cause her the most amount of pain possible because they've known for years that there was some connection to Ace."

"Right," I say. "If they've been patiently waiting, they could've been searching for a way to hurt her since he took her from Vegas. They've probably been putting out feelers, biding their time for the right moment, and that right moment exposed itself when news of our...relationship was made public."

It's all very plausible, but is it realistic?

"It sounds to me like they found a mole willing and able to help take her down, and you're just a casualty they were willing to lose."

"A mole? Seriously?" A migraine tugs at my eyelids. How many punches will I take today?

"As I said, I don't know what the end goal is, but I do believe the stories being presented to the press were preplanned, so we need to be open to the possibility that we might have a traitor within our company."

"Let me guess." Savvy barges into the room as though she owns the damn building. She's a walking contradiction —fragile in body yet fierce in mind. "Quinn is your prime suspect?"

She's touched up her makeup, and she stands before me as the worthy adversary I know her to be. Pride makes my fingers twitch, and my brain nearly combusts at the realization.

My, how quickly I've converted to the dark side.

"There are no suspects," I say. Quinn has been my assistant since I was in college when Braxton and I first took over Omni-Reyes. I refuse to believe there's not some loyalty there. If this is all true, I've failed every promise I ever made to Ace.

"There are no suspects yet," Braxton says. "But we're not taking it off the table. Until we have a better handle on what's going on, all conversations should be kept to our family."

"Clover—" Savvy starts, but Braxton doesn't allow her to finish that train of thought.

"Clover is and always will be family, as are Pops, Moose, and Chief," he says.

"But we should probably keep some details away from Pops," Madi says with a grin. I've been so focused on Savvy that I didn't even see Madi hiding behind her. "We can't trust him to keep any kind of secret."

"Agreed," I say. The man's middle name is *menace*.

"So...what now?" Madi asks. She's practically bouncing on her toes. Giddy is the word I'd use to describe her, and it makes me uncomfortable as hell.

"First, I think the fake part of this relationship should stay between us," Braxton says, eying me curiously. "It is fake, right?"

Savvy nods while scowling at me. "Obviously."

Why does her anger make me feel like a little kid on Christmas morning for the first time in my life? I never had a traditional Christmas morning as a kid, and by age thirteen, all holidays were focused on Sage.

"It can't get out to anyone else then," Braxton says.

"I won't keep it from Clover or Elle." Savvy crosses her arms, the same way she did during the bathroom incident a few days ago. Her cheeks flush when she catches me staring at her tits, and she's quick to drop her arms to her sides. Is she remembering too?

"Of course." Braxton smiles at Savvy, and she visibly relaxes.

It makes me want to punch my beloved brother in the throat. I don't like that he gets her softness while I'm stuck with the thorns.

It's your own fault. Fucking conscience.

"Moose and Pops will have their suspicions though." Madi's scowl now matches Savvy's. "Especially since Pops pushed all Grey's triggers to get us to this point."

"That could be a problem." Braxton chews on his lip while he thinks. "We have to convince everyone that this is real. The chemistry between you two should do the trick, but that means you need to really pack on the PDA."

"No," Savvy all but growls.

I shrug. "Fine by me."

She narrows her eyes and purses her lips. "We just spent nearly an entire week with you telling me how much you hate me. Hate. With a capital H. Why are you suddenly so keen to be my husband?"

Why, indeed? I don't have an answer for her, but I do know that witnessing her struggles changed the chemistry of us—of me—and now I'll burn the world to the ground to keep her by my side where I know she'll be safe and cared for.

It's that fire that matches hers that has me lurching forward, and before I know it, we're standing toe-to-toe as I lower my voice to just above a whisper. "Maybe I like the idea of watching you...submit."

She snorts, and spittle hits the side of my face, which makes her laugh out loud. But when she reaches out and wipes it away, I lean into her touch as though I'm helpless to do anything else.

"The day I submit is the day I die." Can she hear the lie in her words? Because I can.

"So...morbid, dear wifey." I lean in, fully aware that we have an audience, just not giving a shit. She fills a void that's resided in my soul for months, possibly even years, and under the guise of helping her, I allow myself to explore it. "But you do submit, Monroe," I rasp into her ear. "Even if it's in private, you're still submitting. In fact, that might be how I like you best."

"Y—you're an asshole." She shoves me away with two shaky hands on my chest.

Point for me.

"I'm really going to love this game of ours, Monroe. I think you will too."

"Not likely."

A knock on the door interrupts us, and we all turn to see Quinn and Sage enter the room. She's visibly annoyed, but I don't comment on it because Sage is upset—it's written all over his face.

I don't want to believe that Quinn is guilty of treason, but she's not family, so I won't trust her. Finding a replacement will be a real bitch though.

"What is it, Quinn?" I ask.

"Clover's trying to reach you." She makes a point of looking at everyone except Savvy. "All of you. She received a...threat at her home."

"What? No." Savvy's hand fists at her chest. I know she's protective of Clover, and though I don't know all the details, I know enough to understand that Clover is more fragile than either Savvy or Madi.

Quinn shrugs, then turns to leave. "That's what she said. They haven't been able to reach you," she calls over her shoulder.

Everyone in the room begins patting their pockets, while Sage hands Savvy hers. How did we all leave our phones, which are typically glued to our hands, in my office?

I'm already pulling my car keys from my pocket when I meet Savvy's gaze and know instantly that something's wrong. Grabbing her by the elbow, I forgo retrieving my own phone, yell for Braxton to grab it for me, and guide her out of the office, into the elevator, and toward my car.

She doesn't speak until I attempt to buckle her into my passenger seat. Swatting my hands away, she blinks as though she's coming out of a trance. "I'm fine, I can do it."

I release her and hurry to my side of the car.

"We'll meet you at Clover's," Braxton calls. Looking up, I see him ushering a shell-shocked Madi into his car with Sage close behind.

Once in the driver's seat, I start the ignition, then turn to Savvy. "What did Clover say?"

She stares at me for a long moment, then shows me the screen.

It takes me a moment to understand what I'm looking at, but once I do, anger fills my every pore.

The photo is of a box containing what appears to be a wedding dress with a knife jammed into the center of it, holding a note in place. The note says: Obsession is forever, and mine is written in the blood of others.

"Send that to me," I say, then put the car in reverse and speed out of the parking garage.

I don't believe in coincidences, and this has DeVane written all over it. They just signed their own death certificates. No one threatens what's mine, and since Savvy is now mine, that means, by proxy, so is Clover.

CHAPTER SEVENTEEN

SAVVY

As soon as Grey brings the car to an abrupt stop, I jump out. Clover and Chief are already on the porch with Pops, who's pacing back and forth.

"Where is it?" I ask, rushing up the steps. Grey's scorching body heat sticks to me like a shadow—inseparable, yet impossible to reach.

Clover pulls her cardigan tightly around herself. It's her coping mechanism, but since she bought all the Taylor Swift versions covered in stars, it makes her look even smaller and younger than she is.

"It was on the porch," she says, pointing to where our mailboxes hang in between our two front doors.

I haven't seen our duplex since the hurricane hit, and while Clover's half looks unaffected, there are windows boarded up on my side.

Cian must have been busy this past week.

Car doors slam behind me as Braxton, Madi, and Sage arrive.

"Who was it addressed to?" Grey asks, flipping the cover over with the toe of his shoe.

"There was no name, so I opened it," Clover whispers. Madi takes the porch steps two at a time and wraps her arms around Clover.

Fear makes my vision blur as I stare at the box on the floor. There's something strangely familiar about it. Something I can't quite put my finger on.

"Clover," Madi says gently. "That quote, on the note, isn't that from one of your books?"

"The fuck?" Grey bellows, causing Clover to shrink in on herself even more.

I elbow him in the gut, willing him with my eyes to calm down before he triggers my poor friend even more.

Clover's shoulders curl in as though she's trying to turn herself into a ball. "Yeah, it's from *My Deadly Vow*."

"Let me get this straight." Grey's foot taps a menacing beat against the wooden planks. "Monroe and I have a possible mole and an ex out to ruin us, and now Clover has a stalker? In Happiness, Georgia?"

"Nice recap there, son. Way to put those big brains of yours to work." Pops chuckles. It's as though he truly can't help riling Grey up.

Grey pinches the bridge of his nose and counts out loud to ten.

"A coincidence?" Braxton asks.

"Bad timing, maybe," I mutter. "What do we do with this thing?"

"Already got the boys in blue on their way to pick it up and take it to the station for forensics," Chief says with his thumbs tucked into the waistband of his jeans. He rocks back on his heels, and you get the full impact of his self-importance.

"Why does it feel like the entire world is trying to suck the happy out of Happiness all of a sudden?" Clover's words are a whisper of a breath. She's physically shaking, and not for the first time, I wish she'd let us in, give us her whole story. But I know better than most that she'll only share when she's ready.

Self-protection is more than a habit for her—it might be the line between fiction and reality.

"The common denominator is us," Grey says. "Braxton and me. Since we came to town, we've brought a whole lot of damage. It's followed me since birth."

"Martyrdom isn't typically your style, Patch. I'm disappointed." My sarcasm is thick.

"It's not martyrdom if it's true," he bites back. His tongue is sharp, but so is mine.

"Moving on," Braxton says, kneeling before the box and poking at the fabric with a stick. Where the hell did he find that? "Regardless of why the sky is falling, I think it's safe to say that it is, or at least someone wants us to believe it is. So there's only one solution for now."

"What's that?" I'm out of suggestions. If he has one, I'm all ears.

"Savvy, your place needs new windows. Grey, yours needs rehab, and Clover, it's just not safe for you to stay here alone, so you'll all move into the Hideaway with us until we get some answers."

Pops whoops with both fists in the air.

Greyson and Madi talk over each other—Grey furious, Madi as animated as a cartoon.

Clover finally collapses onto the nearby porch swing.

Chief nods as though this were his idea.

And me? I'm mentally tallying how many rooms are still available at the inn and know that my day is about to go from *what the fuck?* to *fuck no*. My meddling besties are going to force us to cohabitate again.

Before I can speak, Pops releases an ear-splitting whistle to silence everyone.

"This will be perfect," Madi grins. "Since you and Grey are officially engaged now—"

"What?" Clover jumps to her feet, her own fears pushed aside as she rushes past Braxton and grabs my left hand.

Crap. I'll have to fill her in on the details as soon as possible.

"The ring is being sized," Grey mutters.

"It's what? What ring?" I'm back to glaring at Grey.

"Your ring, my honesty-challenged angel." His tone is so slippery, so dark with hidden promises, that I shiver despite my boiling temper.

"You're engaged? For real?" Clover's words tumble from her mouth with supersonic speed while a crease forms between her brows.

"Yes, Clover. For real." At least Grey drops the attitude when he's talking to my shaken friend. "We've been... secretly seeing each other for a while." The smirk on this man needs a swift slap to knock it away.

"Not so secret, if you ask me." Pops laughs with his whole entire body. "Remember at the Cozy Cup Festival when we saw—"

Madi slaps a hand over his mouth to silence him.

"This past week made us realize that it wasn't hate we were experiencing, but love. Right, angel?"

Oh, the ways I'm going to kill Greyson Reyes.

He leans in and presses his mouth to my ear. "Go along with it, Monroe. We need Pops to believe."

Mother freaking porcupines.

"Yup, Drill Bit," I say through pinched lips. "That's right."

I attempt to put space between Grey and me, but the

asshole grins, and before I can blink, his hand knots in the hair at the back of my head, and he pulls me to him for a bruising kiss I only wish I could be unaffected by.

He kisses like he fucks—hard, dominating, soul-crushing—and my knees wobble as he controls my mouth as though he's the architect of my desire.

No one should be able to cause a reaction like this from a freaking kiss.

Grey finally releases my lips but keeps his so close to mine that we're nearly touching. I'm inhaling his cinnamon scent, and my only saving grace is that his eyes are as murky as mine.

The chemistry of us affects him just as much as it does me.

"I still prefer Patch Daddy." His whispered words heat my already flushed cheeks.

"This wedding will be spectacular," Pops shouts, startling me. "The event of the year, once we get all those dang protesters out of here."

That's enough to douse the butterflies in my stomach, and I push away from Grey.

"What the hell happened to everyone supporting everyone in Happiness?" I murmur. Driving through town, I could feel their wrath like a third-degree sunburn.

"It ain't the whole town," Pop says. "Just a handful who's rallying the outsiders. There are some real green-eyed monsters in the thirties set, ya know."

"Green-eyed monsters?" Grey sounds as though he's hit his limit for bullshit, and for once, we're on the same page.

"Yup, he's right," Chief says. "Bethany Jane's panties are in a real twist over Savvy being named town sweetheart. Then news broke that she snagged the last eligible billionaire, and Bethany damn near lost her noggin. She's probably thinkin' she can get Savvy booted from the court before she's crowned at the town fair."

"The last eligible billionaire? I'm not a slab of beef at a meat auction," Grey grumbles.

"You're really obsessed with those, aren't you?" I ask.

He glares at me for three long beats, but when he first moved here, he was raging about meat auctions too.

"A sign for a literal meat auction was the first thing I saw when I got to Happiness. Of course I checked it out. And news flash, it's fucking disgusting."

"You're just a snob."

"In fairness, it was the first thing I saw too," Braxton says. "Maybe we should look into rearranging some of the signage in town once we get through whatever the hell is happening here."

"Focus, kids." The irony of eighteen-year-old Sage wrangling the wayward adults makes me smirk. "Bethany is being a child and creating an old-school smear campaign against Savvy. Unfortunately, Grey is the CEO of a media empire, therefore national gossip sites are also running with it."

"And someone is feeding them this bullshit," Braxton grumbles under his breath. It wasn't that long ago he and Madi were at the center of a similar storm. "They do put us on a weird pedestal. They all want to marry us, but when we find someone, they're the first to hit the streets in riot gear."

"Champagne problems," Clover whispers, making me smile. But if she tugs her cardigan any more tightly around herself, the threads are sure to snap.

"Bethany will get over herself," Madi says. "But I agree that having us all together at the Hideaway is the way to go. The boys are already heading back to their dorms, so it'll be fine."

Fine. I've been fine my whole life, but suddenly, fine feels like a prison sentence.

A city police car pulls into the driveway, and we all turn to watch as the chief of police steps out. "Afternoon," he drawls.

"Hey, Tim." Braxton shakes the officer's hand.

We form a semicircle around the box as Chief Rigsby slips on some rubber gloves and inspects it.

While he questions Clover, I sneak out to the side of the house to assess the damage to my windows.

It's not as bad as it could have been, but they'll all need to be replaced.

"Are you going to be able to handle this, Monroe?"

Freaking Grey.

"Are you?" I fire back.

"I've never been one to back down from a challenge."

"And what? That's what I am to you? A challenge?"

He nods, but the heat in his expression practically sears my clothing to smithereens.

"Since the day I met you at the Firefly Pub on October twelfth."

Yeah, I'll never forget our first encounter at that bar either, but I don't remember the exact date.

"Stalker much?" The words taste bitter on my tongue. Still, I'd never instantly lusted after and loathed someone in the same breath as I did the moment I laid eyes on Grey.

Some meet-cute we have.

He glides closer as if he's floating on air. "Is that why your handle on the surrogacy website was Firefly12?"

My throat itches as though I've just eaten something I'm allergic to.

"No, Grey. As I said before, I was Firefly12 well before you ever rolled into town."

"Why Firefly then?"

He keeps his distance, but this thing he's doing—communicating as though he cares—is unsettling, because regardless of my actions, I think we're too volatile to ever truly be friends.

"Why ChasingColors?" I counter. Yes, I'm stubborn, but if he thinks he's going to get all my secrets for free, he hasn't been paying attention.

Surprise squeezes my chest when he fully invades my space. "Grey, Violet, and Sage. We were all named after colors, but my life has always been in black-and-white... gray, if you will. The only flashes of life happened in the colorful people around me. Violet, my sister, was full of life and curiosity. Sage, well, you see the calming effect he has on everyone around him. I guess me having a daughter is my way of chasing those colors that are fading as life moves on without me."

It's shockingly honest and raw, and it unsettles me more than his name-calling.

"Why are you telling me this?" I whisper, scanning his face for any signs of deceit, but he's either a much better liar than I gave him credit for or he's telling the truth.

I'm not sure which would be worse.

"Because I've made a decision, and I'm here to offer you a...deal."

My eye roll causes the skin around his left eye to twitch.

"What decision and what kind of deal?"

"First, tell me why Firefly."

In my periphery, I see Chief Rigsby loading the box into his car. That means the family will descend upon us soon.

"I know you're a truth-optional type of person, Monroe, but don't even think about lying to me right now. Trust me,

I'll know." He steps forward, and I retreat, only for my back to hit the side of my house.

Then he leans in.

Cinnamon and blood orange fills my nostrils. It took me a long time to figure out what the citrus scent is that lingers on his skin, but once I did, I laughed out loud. There's nothing more fitting for a man like Grey than smelling like blood anything—he's a shark parading around as a demigod.

"I'm not a liar, and until you can accept that, we have nothing to discuss."

I press my hands to his chest with the intent of pushing him away, but the violent beating of his heart gives me pause.

It matches my own.

"You didn't tell me who you were, Monroe." His thigh presses between my legs, and my mind gets a little hazy. "You allowed me to open up, knowing it was me, and you never said anything."

"I thought I was doing the right thing. You needed a friend. You still need a friend, but you won't let anyone in. I don't regret being there for you."

"Lies spun to gold don't make them true."

"If you're never going to even attempt to see things from my point of view, then what are we doing here? Why this"—I glance at our surroundings—"fake engagement? We're going to end up killing each other."

His large frame presses tightly into mine, and neurons fire in all the wrong directions.

"I have a theory, and I made a decision. But before you get that information, I want to test my theory, and to do that, you need to tell me why you chose Firefly as your name."

My gaze is glued to his neck as he swallows, his Adam's

apple prominent against his tan skin. Then he drops his head and runs his nose along the side of my cheek, his blond hair falling to skim my forehead. "Tell me." It's a demand my body wants to obey even as my mind tells it to stand down while screaming *danger, danger.*

"I..."

He nips the lobe of my ear. It's really freaking hard to focus with him this close.

"Fireflies flash in a pattern to attract their mate," I manage.

"Yes, I did my own research when I left for California. And?"

He...what? "No. It's not an and, it's a but—the adults who glow only live a few short weeks. Like love, their life is fleeting."

He pulls back and stares intently at every inch of my face. As uncomfortable as I am from the attention, I don't back down. If telling him this one truth will make him forgive me, it's worth it.

"Go on." His words work like hypnosis in his deep, silvery voice.

"I'm getting older, and I don't think I would make a very good mother, but growing up, I always imagined myself pregnant and with lots of babies. It makes no sense, since I knew I didn't have a stable upbringing, therefore would have no idea how to offer one, but in all my daydreams, I was a mom."

He encourages me with his eyes but says nothing.

"Now I'm a realist, Grey, and the reality is, kids are probably not in my future. I'm not even sure I deserve the happiness they bring, so I chose Firefly to remember the fleeting moments, the wants that will remain just out of reach."

His hot breath brushes my ear, and it shouldn't be so erotic.

"Becoming a surrogate," I say. "It was my financial insurance policy in case I ever had to defend myself against the DeVanes or the Ashfords again, but it also would have given me a fleeting moment of happiness. I'd get to experience pregnancy without screwing up a kid in the process." I nearly collapse with the confession, but Grey's strong presence and his thigh wedged between my legs keeps me upright.

He doesn't say anything, but his hand has found purchase against my cheek, his thumb slowly stroking back and forth as though he cares.

"Another example of me being selfish, I suppose." I need to break our connection, but I can't seem to gather enough strength to do it.

"For someone who helps other people for a living, you sure are all kinds of fucked-up."

A chuckle bursts out of me. "Most therapists need therapy, didn't you know that?"

He slowly shakes his head. "I do now."

The silence becomes thick, and the urge to flee is overwhelming.

"I showed you mine, now show me yours. What's your theory, and what's your deal?"

Challenging him is safer than whatever is happening between us.

"My theory was that you're a hopeless romantic, but too scared and ashamed of choices you made as a child to allow yourself the pleasure of it as an adult. And my deal is this." He cups my face with both hands, forcing me to look him in the eye.

It's aggressive, demanding even, and it's what finally eases my racing pulse.

When he controls me like this, I feel free for the first time since I was sixteen, and that is why I truly need therapy.

"I want a daughter." The honest rawness in his words rips open the tender skin around all my insecurities, and my blood speeds through my veins like a dolphin chased by a predator.

"G—good luck with that."

"And I'd like her to have a mother."

"I know a great matchmaker—her name's Madi. I'm sure she'd be more than happy to help." I ignore the sharp stab of jealousy that squeezes my chest in a vice.

His grin is devious, delicious, and so damn dangerous to my well-being.

"Who I want is Firefly."

"She doesn't exist."

"She's scared," he counters.

"You hate me."

His long, thick thumb runs along my bottom lip, and his hungry eyes follow it as though he's about to devour me whole.

"Do I though? I thought I did for a long time. But you know what else happens around you?"

"The Grinch in your pants grows ten sizes?"

Said Grinch rubs against my hip bone, and I stifle a sigh that desperately wants to escape.

"That's a welcome side effect, especially since no one else has caught his attention since the first time you yelled at me. But what happens when you're near is a colorful explosion that only you seem to create. Anger, curiosity, lust, fear...it all bubbles to the surface with you, Monroe."

"Why fear?"

"That should be obvious." His goddamn eyes actually sparkle in the sunshine. "My fear is what if, after all these wars, I realize I don't actually hate you at all?"

No. Now he's just messing with my head because he believes I lied to him. He's playing games. He has to be.

Lowering my gaze because I can't take the heat of him a moment longer, I ask, "What's your deal, Grey?"

"Regardless of what happens, I'm bound to protect you because it's my world, my connections that have caused this commotion in your life."

"My past behavior dictates my future. Not everything is about you."

Insufferable, arrogant ass.

"But this is. I feel it in my soul."

I attempt to sidestep him, but he keeps a tight hold on my face.

"You have three seconds to tell me what you're planning, or I'm out of here." My voice is much stronger than I feel.

"The challenge, should you choose to accept it, is this: Don't fight me."

I'm pretty sure my expression morphs into one that can only be read as *Duh.* "What do you mean?"

"We're going to plan this wedding. We'll even put on a show while doing it, but I won't do anything I don't want to do, and you shouldn't either."

"What does that even mean?"

Damn it. I really wish he'd stop stroking my cheek like a lover.

"It means we'll start over. We'll explore this...thing between us without your...betrayal hanging over our heads." His brows draw together, and he bites his lip.

What's he thinking?

He exhales slowly. Almost as though he's resigning himself to something. When his pale blue gaze lands on mine, I hold my breath.

"I'll try to forgive your betrayal, and you'll try to let me in, that's my deal." I've never heard him speak so gently before, and my heart just stops. I'm sure of it. "We'll fight and make up. We'll figure out the push and pull that keeps slamming us together, and we'll do it all with honest intentions and good faith."

He's saying all the right words, but the Greyson I know isn't capable of letting go of a grudge—he's more than proven that over the last week.

"That's not really a deal though." Oh, God. Why do I sound like that? I can't crumble into a needy, wanton submissive around him.

The grin that overtakes his face is predatory.

"If you agree to let down your walls, I'll get you through this mess unscathed. I'll get rid of the DeVanes and the Ashfords in your life once and for all. You'll have a fresh start without any baggage dragging you down."

The sad part is, I know he's capable of doing those things. But the thought of who I'll be without the pressure of fighting for every scrap of my life scares the shit out of me too—I'll be forced to figure out who I am without the weight of bad decisions and self-loathing.

"Can you step back? I can't think when you're mauling me like a demented sex-starved dom."

"Oh, Monroe, you haven't seen anything yet." He takes one step back. There's less than a foot between us, but it feels like a mile.

"And if I...what? Become your good little wifey, what do you get out of it?"

"Wherever our ending takes us, you'll agree to one of two things."

His eyes flash like my own personal red flags.

"What things?"

"You'll either stay my wife for real, or you'll become my surrogate. Either way, we'll both get exactly what we've always wanted."

My mouth drops open. This asshole is seriously going to use my childhood dream to extort me into doing exactly what he wants me to do.

"Whoa. Is this another *I'm getting a baby* type thing?" Madi asks.

Damn. How long has she been standing there?

Greyson doesn't even acknowledge her. His laser focus is still burning a hole through my face. The only indication that he's annoyed is the slight pinch in his jaw.

"You're out of your mind," I say.

He nods, not even bothering to contradict me.

"But...why? You've spent nearly a year hating me, fighting me, discounting me at every step. Why on earth would you want to marry me or have me carry your child?" I lower my voice, knowing it will come out in a hiss of syllables, but not caring anymore. "And did you hear anything I said about not knowing how to be a good mom?"

"Maybe I have more faith in your abilities than you do. Maybe I'm ready to settle down, and since you're the one who makes me feel alive, even if it's with thoughts of murder, it's better than settling for a life with no color."

"Or maybe," Sage says, joining our little circle with Braxton at his side, "you're realizing that you've been avoiding love for so long that you no longer knew where the line between love and hate was until Savvy erased the line completely, one insult at a time, and that terrified you."

"I didn't ask for a fucking family meeting. This is between me and Monroe."

"Grey." Braxton places a hand on Grey's shoulder, and he flinches. "I know you go through life issuing commands that most people follow, but this, a marriage, is different. First you wanted a baby, now a wife. What's going on with you, brother?"

I bite my bottom lip as Grey removes Braxton's hand from his shoulder.

"Monroe and I have a mutual problem. I'm simply fixing it while giving us both what we truly want. End of story, it's not up for discussion." His gaze pierces through me. "You have twenty-four hours to decide, Monroe. I'm going home. I'll meet you at the Hideaway tomorrow, and when I arrive, make sure you have the right decision for me."

He stomps away as though his word is final, as though he has no idea who he's dealing with.

"How dare he make such an outrageous demand?" I attempt to sound offended and fail miserably.

"Is it though?" Clover asks.

I spin to find her leaning against the siding. "Yes. He's lost his damn mind."

"But he's giving you everything you've ever wanted. Freedom—"

"Freedom? He wants to marry me. That's not freedom, that's a chain around my neck."

And an invitation for someone else to let me down.

"He's going to fight the demons who haunt you," Madi says.

"They're not his demons to battle, and Riley's family is actually dangerous."

"So was Greyson's. More so than you'll ever know," Braxton says quietly, as though the admission cost him something. "Grey is more than a name for him—it's the line he's walked since he was old enough to know right from wrong. His heart pulls him into the light, but the weight of his father tethers him to the dark. He spends every waking hour trying to fix shit because he thinks it keeps him on the right side of a moral compass that's always been skewed."

"He'll go even further than Ace to protect you," Sage says. "And he'll do it because he cares more than he knows how to admit."

It's then that I realize every single person I love is looking at me as though they're expecting me to take his deal.

As though it's not completely irrational.

As though it's my only option.

As if it's something Grey truly wants.

"Come on." Madi loops her arm through mine. "I think it's time for some wine and a pros and cons list."

I snort. This will take something stronger than wine to sort out.

Become his wife or his surrogate? How did my life boil down to those two options?

And why is my pulse fluttering like a girl about to be kissed by the boy of her dreams?

Sage hooks my other arm with his. "For what it's worth, I've always known that Uncle Grey doesn't hate you. He may not have known how to categorize his feelings, but it's never been hate."

"Could've fooled me."

"Fireworks, I tell ya," Pops shouts from the porch as we round the corner, startling Clover so much that she trips and falls into Braxton. Thankfully, he's acclimated to her Clover-isms and catches her easily.

"The thing about my uncles is that they'll never let those

they care about fall," Sage whispers at my side. "The fact that Grey is already in fix-it mode with you tells me he cares more than he has about anyone else in a very long time. He may not show it the way most people do, but it's there, Sav. Let that count for something. You both have trauma in your pasts. It would be a shame if it blurred your vision for something that has the potential to be...life-changing."

He kisses my cheek, then takes off toward his car.

It does count for...something. I just wish I knew what that something was.

Either way, Greyson Reyes has just declared my life is about to change. Maybe he's more than the architect of my desire. Maybe he's the puppet master of my whole damn universe.

CHAPTER EIGHTEEN

GREYSON

Okay, in fairness, perhaps I have lost my damn mind.

Marriage? A real, legal marriage? What the hell was I thinking?

Is there a test for witchcraft? The longer I spend in Savvy's presence, the more I believe that she might have cast a spell on me.

The walk up my driveway was faster than when we left. Cian must have put down the plywood that's creating a path and making the hike less treacherous. At least I'm not covered in mud by the time I walk up the front steps.

I'm not even surprised to find Moose sitting on an over-turned bucket, puttering around on the porch with a piece of wood and what looks like a paring knife.

"Grey."

"Moose."

He smirks at my cool tone. It's why I like this old guy so much. He doesn't ramble about nonsense like Pops does.

"Cian was up here a bit ago with an engineer. Structurally, the place is in good shape, but it's got a bit of cosmetic work that needs to be done."

"I figured." The chairs that used to be here are probably swinging from the treetops, so I slide to the floor beside him and watch as he whittles something out of an old piece of wood.

"You and Savvy made quite the entrance in town today."

So much for not using unnecessary words.

"I did not create drama. I gave a solution to a problem that my last name created long before Savvy was even born."

Moose does one of his dramatic head nods in slow motion but says nothing. It's his way of forcing someone to talk, but I don't typically fall for it.

Monroe has me all out of sorts though.

"I didn't have a choice, Moose. She may have made a mistake as a child, but it's chasing her now because of her connection to me and my fucking DNA."

"Hmm." He flicks his knife, and wood shavings fall to the floor. "Have you ever thought about not taking on the past as if it's your burden to bear?" He doesn't look at me when he speaks, and it makes it easier to talk to the guy.

"Isn't it though? Ace may have saved Savvy once and unknowingly put a target on her back, but I'm the one the media has been after since my father went to prison. I'm the one with enough zeros in my bank account to draw attention as if I'm some dark prince with salacious secrets. Savvy's past proves that. She's being dragged through the mud now because my name is attached to her story."

"You know, Greyson, sometimes in life, the only thing we can do is take accountability for our own actions." His words roll off his tongue in a slow, soothing cadence. "You don't owe anyone anything more than that, and by becoming the fixer for everyone who has ever come in contact with the last name Wells, you're only hurting yourself. You have one life, son. Do you really want to live it constantly cleaning up after the devil himself, or do you want to live your life for you? See what your future could be?"

"Not everyone is given a choice in how to live their life, Moose. Some of us are meant to quietly pick up the pieces while eliminating further devastation."

"Is that what you're doing with Savvy?" Thankfully, there's no judgment in his tone. It makes it easier to absorb his words. "Are you rescuing her by actively keeping her in the spotlight this way? Or are you clinging to her because you're finally feeling what it means to be alive?"

My head hits the wall with a thud. Where Savvy's concerned, I don't know anything anymore.

"Go on now, grab your stuff, and get over to the Hideaway. I'm keeping an eye on Cian so he doesn't wreck our sanctuary."

"It's okay. I told them I'd be back tomorrow."

"And I'm telling you." He points at my front door with the sharp tip of his knife. "Get your shit and get over there. You've publicly claimed that girl, now there's no telling what kind of fight you're bringing to her door. If Madi and Braxton's situation taught us anything with those pushy reporters, it's that you can't leave anything up to chance."

I want to argue, but he's right.

"She needs you, Grey. Maybe even more than you need her."

"I don't—"

"Don't you though?"

"There you are," Cian's voice fills the silence. "Grab yer shite, and I'll give ya a ride back into town. Your little Mercedes just sunk into a mud hole."

"Jesus," I mutter, but text Quinn to order me a new SUV. "Can this day get any worse?"

———

I take it back. This day can most definitely get worse, and I'm looking at it the second I walk into the Hideaway with Cian and Moose at my side.

People are everywhere. Fucking everywhere.

A small group of Sage's teammates sit in front of the unlit fireplace, playing Monopoly—a mind-numbing experience I'd never like to have again. Braxton is buzzing around the room with a tray of drinks. Pops sits in his recliner with his hands behind his head and his feet swinging from side to side on the footrest, taking it all in.

Chief paces in front of the bay windows, nodding sagely as he stares into the darkness as if he's the Secret Service. I can hear Sage and two of his football friends, Trevon and Ethan, laughing and talking loudly in the kitchen.

The only ones missing are Savvy and her friends, but the number of people in here is already giving me a headache.

I readjust the cufflinks holding my sleeve closed and inhale deeply. When I first moved to Happiness, I lived at the Hideaway with Braxton, Sage, Madi, and Pops, and that was an exercise in daily self-control.

Add in these extra people, and my entire head is about to explode.

"Uncle Grey, you're back early." Sage stands in the doorway to the kitchen, holding a tray of appetizers.

The room tilts on an axis I'm not equipped for, and I blink, willing myself to focus.

They all move around each other as though they've done it all their life. They're a family with little to no blood relation among them. Uncomfortable tingling sensations dance across my palms.

"Yeah, I…" I don't even know what I want to say, so I don't bother finishing. Instead, I take the stairs two at a time until I reach the landing. Then I open each door systematically in search of…in search of Savvy.

When the hell did she become my touchstone?

When I don't find her on the second floor, I race to the third while wiping my palms on my pant legs.

There are only three bedrooms on the third floor now. One is a primary for Braxton and Madi, and one was being used as storage the last time I checked, so I barrel toward the third door as though I'm shot out of a cannon.

I don't intend to take the door off its hinges, but as it slams open against the wall, I grab it to make sure I don't cause permanent damage.

Madi and Clover sit side by side on the bed, facing me, while Savvy sits cross-legged, giving me her back.

Clover startles at my aggressive entrance, practically jumps out of her skin, and starts to tumble to the floor.

Savvy and Madi grab her before I can reach them and haul her back to the bed with handfuls of sweater and sweatpants.

"Geez, Grey. You're worse than the three-hundred-pound linebacker downstairs," Madi says while smoothing out Clover's clothing.

It's truly unhealthy how easily that woman startles.

"I…apologize." My teeth grind as Savvy continues to give me her back.

"See?" Savvy flicks her thumb in my direction without even looking at me. "Ventriloquist, am I right?"

"Are you drunk?" I feel my lips curl at the corners. That's when I realize my pulse has evened out, my headache has evaporated, and my palms no longer feel clammy.

Clover snickers, then whisper-yells, "Totally a ventriloquist. Did he take lessons?"

"Savvy was just...filling us in." Madi giggles, and the motion sloshes apple juice all over the bedding. She found an odd addiction to juice early in her pregnancy, and now she rests the half-empty cup on her blossoming baby bump.

Longing slashes across my chest as I stare at her protruding belly, but I force it away. There's too much to deal with to focus on getting a baby right now.

Savvy still doesn't look at me, and it stings—I'm not used to rejection. Well, fuck that. For better or worse, we're in this together.

Stomping back down the hall and two flights of stairs, I yell. "Braxton. Sage. Meet me on the third floor. Now."

As a child, I never dared stomp on stairs or slam doors. My father would have punished me, and the sick fucker enjoyed it too much for me to make it easy for him.

But ever since Savvy has inexplicably been woven into the fabric of my life, I'm lashing out in all the ways I've never done before. I can almost understand why teenagers do it now because the noise makes me feel marginally better.

"What's up?" Braxton asks, jogging with much softer footfalls than my own, catching me before I reach the second floor. "Everything okay?"

"No, everything is not okay. I basically bet a woman to marry me, and now she's drunk with two of her best friends on our bed when I need to lay down some ground rules for us."

"Uncle Grey." Sage chuckles my name and makes a wheezing sound. If this kid is actively going to laugh in my face, I might lose my shit. "Are you even listening to yourself? You can't bet someone to marry you. And it's not the

1890s, you don't get to lay down the law." His tone shifts to something more...contemplative, and it has me stopping my march back toward Savvy. "If you don't go at this like a partnership with Savvy, you'll..."

My shoulders tense up around my ears, ratcheting up the ever-present tension headache until I see stars.

"I'll what?"

"You'll lose her," he says simply, then he turns sideways and knocks on the now-open bedroom door. "Hello, ladies. I think my uncle is looking for some privacy with his fiancée but has lost use of his manners. Never fear, Uncle Brax and I are here to escort you to your rooms, because at least some of the Reyes men are still gentlemen."

The little shit.

"Ugh," Savvy scoffs, and when she finally turns, it's with a scrunched nose and fire blazing in her green eyes.

It's her fire that calls to my own. I can see that now, acknowledge it even, I simply don't know what to do with it. We're two meteors headed for a collision that's out of our hands but destined for complete chaos.

What will be left of us when we finally crash into each other for good?

She staggers to her feet, and I move on instinct to her side. One long finger pokes me hard in the chest. "It's ladies' night, you gray devil you." The playfulness of her tone doesn't match the harshness of her expression.

"Gray devil." Clover hiccups as Sage leads her out of the room. "That's funny."

"How much did you ladies drink, hmm?" Wrapping one arm around her waist so she doesn't topple over, I reach for the bottle of wine on the nightstand.

"It was like one and half...glasses." she giggles. Savvy fucking giggles, and I'm transported back to high school.

Not my high school experience because I was busy raising Sage, but what I always secretly envisioned was happening outside of my four walls at the time.

"I like it when you laugh," I whisper.

Braxton is on the other side of the bed, trying to coerce Madi into leaving with him.

"Do you do it too?" Savvy's head falls back against my chest so she can crane her neck to peer up at me. She's a tall woman, but even at five foot eleven, I still have at least four inches on her.

"Do what?" I ask.

Braxton finally lifts Madi into his arms and carries her from the room. Her laughter echoes down the hall as they go.

"Laugh. I need laughter in my life, Patch." Her words are whimsical and light, so unlike the sass and venom I'm used to. I'm drawn to her like the damn fireflies she loves so much as her eyes blink slowly, lazily, dreamily.

"I laugh," I grunt. Gently, I turn her in my arms, then press on her shoulders so she'll sit back on the bed.

Her laughter snorts through her nose, and she sways with the movement. "Yeah, right. You never laugh. You're laugh-a-phobic." Her shoulders shake.

Drunk Savvy is a snort-laugher, and I can't believe I think it's cute.

"Do you ever flirt?"

This question catches me off guard.

Do I flirt?

I'm sure I have, at some point, with someone.

Right?

"Oh my God. You can't flirt. Flirting is fun, Patch. Have some fun." She drags out the word fun and dramatically flops onto her back with her legs dangling off the edge of the bed.

At least she won't fall off now, but her tiny tank top has ridden up high on her ribs that protrude too far for my liking.

My fingers remember how soft that skin is there, but she's had...wait. "Did you say you had a glass of wine? Glass, not bottle?"

I've seen these girls have their ladies' nights. They even have a not-so-secret club name, the Darlings of Disastrous Dating, and I know she doesn't get drunk off a single glass.

Did someone drug her?

I'll kill them. Literally kill them with my bare hands.

I've only ever contemplated murder one other time, and if it hadn't been for a two-day-old Sage needing me, I may have found a way to kill the man who gave me life. But this... this feeling inside me now is stronger than any of the bitter venom I had for Darren Wells. This is all-consuming and wild—it's terrifying because I'm being irrational.

I'm never irrational, yet here I am, wondering if my own goddamn family drugged her.

Get a grip, man.

"Glass," she says, pulling me, at least momentarily, from my rage spiral. "But I haven't eaten in a day...or..." She raises her hand and starts holding up fingers. With each digit she extends, the ferocity of my emotions grows spikes, then blades, then full swords edged with pain.

She settles on four fingers.

"You haven't eaten in four goddamn days? Why?"

That can't be true. I've seen her...fuck. Haven't I seen her eat? She's had plates of food. I've seen her hand move to her mouth. Have I actually seen her eat anything since we played Twister though?

"Savannah, why the hell haven't you eaten in four days?"

"Shh. You don't have to yell." Clover stumbles into the

room. Now she's a lightweight, so I'm not surprised to see her tipsy as hell from one glass of wine, but Savvy? This is... this is something different, and it's settling in my gut like curdled milk. "Here, Sav. Remember, you promised."

I stand to the side, as Clover sways her way over to Savvy and hands her a small package, then goes merrily back the way she came.

That's it. Wine nights are officially banned.

Savvy lifts something in front of her face and squints one eye at the package, then smiles as she attempts to open it.

I survey the scene for exactly ten seconds, then rip the package from her hand. It's...graham crackers. Two to be exact, in packaging like they came straight from a hospital. Two tiny squares.

Is this what she subsists on?

They crush between my fingers as I hold them in the air. "This is what you're going to eat? Two damn crackers that have..." Bringing the package closer to my face, I read the nutritional value. "Sixty calories, Monroe?"

Is she out of her fucking tits?

She makes a grabby motion with her hands. "Mm, yeah. Gimme, gimme."

"Absolutely not. If you won't take care of yourself, then I will."

I lift her easily, too easily. Now that I know what I know, bitter acid gurgles in the back of my throat.

"Ooh, is this how you flirt?" She places her head on my shoulder as I cradle her to my chest and opt for the back stairs that lead straight to the kitchen.

"No," I grunt as my elbow slams into the railing. Fuck, that hurt.

"Ah. Because you don't know how to flirt." The sadness in her words gives me pause. Is she feeling sad...for me?

"No, sweetheart, it's not that I don't know how to flirt. It's because if I flirt with you, I'll be forced to fantasize about your moans without acting on them, and I'm not that noble." I take the rest of the stairs, ensuring I don't slam her into a wall. "The one thing you'll learn about me is that I'm a man of action, and my actions will always speak louder than shallow words filled with empty promises," I say as we step into the kitchen.

"Now yer learning." Pops slams the refrigerator door closed, but he still has a spoonful of Madi's triple berry pie.

"Pops, I know this is your place, but get out of the kitchen before I tell Madi you're the one sneaking in here at night to take bites of her desserts. It's disgusting, by the way —get a fucking slice like everyone else."

He shoves the giant serving spoon into his mouth, then licks it clean before moseying out of the kitchen. The pain in the ass even drops the spoon into his back pocket, and now I'll never be able to eat leftover dessert again.

I gently place Savvy in an island chair, then head to the swinging door Pops just exited and lock it. I bet Madi put this deadbolt on here just to keep him out after he nearly destroyed her kitchen with a soufflé last year.

By the time I get back to Savvy, her arms are crossed on the counter and her head is dead weight on top of them while she snores.

What the hell am I supposed to do now? If I force her to eat something, she might choke, and if she doesn't start eating, she'll die.

My heart pinches in my chest. It's a sensation that used to happen when Sage was young and sick and I didn't know how to help him. That's when I decided I'd never be help-less again.

When my people need me, I will be there, and I will have all the answers.

Watching Savvy sleep with her head on the counter, I know I'm about to learn a whole lot about a subject I'd hoped to never experience again.

And then I'm going to fix her.

CHAPTER NINETEEN

SAVVY

It's blisteringly hot when I open my eyelids. They scrape like sandpaper. It's made worse by my stomach grumbling, reminding me that I've fallen into old habits over the last few days.

Oh, who am I kidding? I've probably been sliding into self-destruct mode for over six months, but I can control it —I always have before.

It's the marching band of monkeys jumping around in my skull that's really ruining my day before it's even started, so I allow my eyes to drift closed.

"Here."

My possum game is strong, and I play dead for a full thirty seconds before opening one eye again.

Grey is fully dressed in a three-piece suit, with his jacket unbuttoned, sitting against the headboard beside me with a plate of something that smells divine, but as I squint at it, my mind falls into old habits.

If you give a mouse a cookie...

That's how I spiral.

One bite craves two, and two turns into everything in the

fridge. One is never enough. If I eat whatever's on that plate, I'll want more, and that will lead to obsessing about something else, until I'm binging and purging and hating myself for being weak.

It's just easier not to eat at all—at least then I can be proud of my self-control instead of loathing my weaknesses.

He narrows his eyes as if he knows exactly what I'm doing.

Fuck, fuckity, fuck.

What happened last night?

That shrew Bethany comes to mind first, and then the floodgates open. Rent-a-womb, the threat against Clover, a decree of marriage, wine, and then...nothing.

Groaning, I sit up. Last night was an anomaly. I don't lose control...ever. But I suppose even ice queens have their limit of shit they can take.

The record scratch in my mind is loud enough that I flinch. I haven't had Riley's voice in my head in years, but he's the only one who ever called me ice queen.

Mental note—call my attorney and confirm that Riley is accounted for. He should have restrictions that keep him in Vegas.

"Monroe, take it." Ah, he's back to being Drill Bit today —half drill sergeant, half pushy asshat forcing himself where he doesn't belong. His gaze, full of pity that I hate, finds mine.

And there's the panic I know so well—the shame and fear that always arrives after the fun of too much alcohol. What the hell did I do to upset him now? I know better than to drink on an empty stomach, but come on.

Yesterday was a lot for anyone.

Apparently, I'm too slow for Drill Bit's liking, because

the next thing I know, a piece of mouth-wateringly deli-cious-smelling bacon bangs against my lips.

"Are you—" He shoves the entire piece of maple-flavored bacon past my lips, then pushes my chin up to close my mouth.

I haven't even begun to chew before he's straddling my hips and staring at me so intently, I break out in goose-bumps all over my neck and chest.

What did I do? Fall out of bed and give myself a black eye?

"Chew."

I do, but only because I don't truly want to hurt myself. Well, not any more, anyway.

Maple bacon is quite possibly the best thing ever created, and a moan escapes after I swallow. There's no way he knew of my slight obsessions with this particular meat. Madi must have had it in the kitchen already. Or, more likely, she cooked, and that's why it smells so good.

Grey's eyes glow like fireflies when he's angry, but they're positively electric when he's turned on. And judging by the Grinch growing against my thigh, I'd say it's the latter.

He holds up a piece of avocado toast, and I swear my eyeballs might roll to the back of my head. It's even topped with fresh watermelon salsa—a pain in the ass to make, but worth every delicious second.

"Why do you have all my fav—"

Again, he feeds me. The first time took me by surprise—now I'm getting suspicious. But as annoyed as I am, Grey looks pissed off, so instead of picking a fight, I aggressively bite off a large piece of the toast.

Shit. *What did I do last night*? I'm sure I'm responsible for his behavior this morning, I usually am, but generally, I know what the hell I did.

I may have perfected the art of playing possum as a small child, but my shame-spiral game is next-level too, and it's taking center stage now.

Holding my hand over my lips, I say, "I can feed myself."

"Can you?"

I frown.

He tilts his head as though he's truly waiting for an answer.

"I'm thirty years old, Grey," I say through a mouthful. "I've been doing a lot of shit on my own for a very long time. Feeding myself is one of them."

The fireflies I love so much narrow as his blue eyes harden like frost. He leans in, his lips ghosting above mine.

"But the question is, will you?" There's venom and possibly fear in his tone that takes me by surprise, and my throat becomes impossibly tight, causing the avocado toast to scratch and tear on its way down.

"Can you move?" I ask. He doesn't. "Please."

Instead, he holds the toast to my lips again, and now that he's thrown down the gauntlet, I clamp my teeth shut tight.

"You promised not to fight me."

I snort. I would never in a million years agree to that, but I know if I open my mouth, he'll feed me again.

"You promised you'd try." My gaze snaps to his. Is that... Did I hurt him somehow?

He sighs heavily and then does the last thing I expect him to do. He places the plate on the bed, then climbs to the floor.

He backed down.

Greyson Reyes backed down—for me.

Oh, God. I did. I hurt him somehow. What the heck did I do?

"No one pays the price for hurting yourself except you,

Savannah." My real name and his words sucker punch all the air from my lungs. "I know that firsthand. Eat the food, and—and I'll be here for you if you want to talk...about anything. In the meantime, I have some fires to put out."

Grey steps forward and leans down as though he's going to kiss my damn forehead, but pulls back at the last second.

"And for the record, in case your memory is a little fuzzy, just because I don't flirt doesn't mean I don't know how."

My jaw flops open like a dead fish, and the asshole takes the opportunity to shove the piece of toast into my mouth. He leaves it hanging when I don't immediately chomp down on it, and I sit there, with avocado dripping down my chin and tiny pieces of watermelon landing on my chest, while he saunters out of my bedroom.

Our. Our bedroom. Our temporary bedroom. Who knew fake engagements came with so many...entanglements.

The unease of guilt and debauchery cause a riotously blinding headache behind my left eye. I know I didn't give him details of how I've punished myself because I've never told another soul, not even my therapist. But I have no idea what I did to cause this reaction from him, and I need to figure it out quickly so I can prepare my counterattack.

Grey and I will always be in a battle of wills...but in the war of me, I'm the only one who can play.

I stare at the door he just vacated, then down at the plate he left me.

How did he even know what my favorites were?

"Clover," I mutter. She has a heart of gold, the courage of a scaredy-cat, and the mouth of Hagrid—she can't keep a secret to save her life—except for her own.

I shouldn't eat the damn toast just to spite him, but the truth is, I'm hungry and slightly hungover, and it's exactly what I need, so I scarf it down as though it's my last meal while thinking about anything but food, then go in search of my mouthy friend.

———

"What time was he down here?" I demand. Clover and Madi sit at the kitchen island, proud as peacocks, and my dread intensifies.

"I came down at six, and he was on his computer at the kitchen table, but slammed his laptop shut the moment I entered the room," Madi says.

"I must have come in shortly after you." Clover reaches for another pump of hand sanitizer, and I reflexively grab the moisturizer Madi keeps above the small desk in the corner, then place it in front of her.

The girl uses so much alcohol-based sanitizer, her skin is constantly cracking.

"Why were you both up so early? What the hell time did we go to bed?"

My best friends look at each other and then at me.

"What?" I ask.

"When Grey made Brax and Sage drag us out of your room, it was...early. I was in bed stuffing pizza into my face by seven thirty," Madi chuckles. "Maybe we're getting old."

I don't remember any of that.

"How did he know my favorite breakfast foods?"

"He kind of seems to...you know." Clover's evading the question...guilty as freaking sin.

"No, I don't know."

"He knows everything about you, Sav." Madi hops down from the stool she's sitting on, and her hand flies to her stomach. "Holy crap. This little potato is like a professional soccer player."

She's about five months along, so I'm not surprised, but I am caught off guard by the tiny sliver of jealousy that lands in my chest. Grey is messing with all the safeguards I put in place for my carefully crafted future.

"Oh my gosh, that's amazing. Can I feel?" Clover jumps down and holds her hands out in front of her.

Madi laughs. "You can try—it's probably too early for you to feel anything though."

Human emotions are a funny thing. Experiencing ecstatic joy for someone else while feeling a little broken and sad for yourself at the same time should be illegal.

"That's wonderful, Madi. Really."

My friend looks at me, really looks, and I hate that flicker of sadness flashing in her eyes as she regards me.

My mask has slipped. It's time to rebuild my fortress.

She nods as though she understands exactly what's happening with my heart right now.

"Now, as for Grey," she says. "He pays attention to details. He sees things most people don't, so it didn't surprise me at all that he already knew your favorite foods. But we did give him your recipe for watermelon salsa."

"Wait," I say as though I was just kicked in the chest. "Are you telling me that he made the breakfast..." I glance around the kitchen, checking for any signs of him, but find none. "Himself?"

"Yeah," Clover laughs. "Apparently, he's the cook in the family. We all know it's not Braxton."

Memories of the mess Brax and Pops made in here not that long ago bring a smile to my face. At the time, I thought it was amazing that Braxton even tried to make Madi something simply because he wanted to help.

Greyson freaking made me breakfast, and not only was it edible, but it was also delicious.

"Hey, y'all." Elle, the fourth friend who makes up our little quad of Darlings, enters the room with baby Keela propped on her hip. "I've been stuck at home for days with no one but Keela for company while she got over her respiratory infection, and now Cian tells me I've missed all the gossip, so get dressed, we're going to lunch."

"I just ate," I say, knowing full well she has no intention of allowing me to back out since I'm probably three-quarters of the gossip she's referring to.

"Listen, Sav. I need adult conversation, and you need to tell me what the hell is going on, so you can sit and hold Keela while I eat because I also have not had a meal in months where grabby little fingers weren't reaching for my food or my nostrils. Fair?"

Elle is a spitfire and nearly impossible to say no to. Especially when she shoves little Keela into my arms.

"Grey made Savvy breakfast in bed this morning." Madi's faux-whisper is embarrassing.

"No. Way." Elle's gasp is comical. Then she loops her arm through my free one and drags me toward the door. "This I have to hear."

———

"Did we have to choose the diner?" I don't whine, but it's a near thing. Everyone and their mother will be here this time of day.

"Yes, we did," Madi calls over her shoulder as she leads the way to a booth in the back, while Elle snags the last highchair from the corner.

It takes a few attempts to actually get Keela to sit in the damn thing though. Who knew babies could make their bodies so stiff they're impossible to bend when they don't want to do something?

I have actual sweat dripping between my breasts by the time I get her in the damn thing.

"See?" Elle says. "It's a good thing she's so stinking cute, because this girl has an attitude the size of a Georgia moon."

She pretends to be annoyed, but the love in her eyes outshines it all as she places a teething biscuit on the table in front of Keela.

But then she turns those eyes on me. "Spill. Cian has told me all the important stuff." She makes a face that indicates she knows about the fake part of our relationship, which makes sense—they're family too. "But I want the juicy details."

"I'm not sure what you want me to say."

"Start with the podcast," Madi says. "Did you know that the clip of the two of you is still going viral? I bet it's part of the reason the whole dang country is interested in your love story now. You could feel the sexual tension in your words. Dang, if he did a live podcast with you..." She fans herself, and my cheeks heat. "Geez, Sav. You'd probably break the internet."

"Hmm." Elle taps her chin, and I immediately scan for all available exits. "That might be a really good idea. A way to get your love story out there on your own terms."

"There's no story," I hiss under my breath. "We're not a love match."

"Maybe not yet," Madi waggles her brows like a perverted old man.

"Not ever."

"But there certainly is chemistry." There's no use arguing with Elle. Grey and I do have chemistry...unfortunately, it's the volatile kind.

"Ugh, she's back," Madi groans.

Slowly, I look up just as Elle and Clover turn in the booth to see who's approaching us.

Bethany has garnered a small posse while I was locked up with Grey. They all look like your typical mean girl, except there's something different about Bethany.

It only takes a second to spot what it is. It's her clothing. She looks put together—nice, even. Her standard uniform of cutoffs and tank tops has been traded in for a perfectly tailored shift dress that makes her stand out in little old Happiness, Georgia.

Why the sudden change?

Old insecurities claw to the surface as I inventory myself. My wardrobe today includes light-wash jeans with holes in the knees and a tank that's about a decade past its prime but is so soft I can't get rid of it. After so many days wearing Grey's clothes, I was thankful to have my own again and chose comfort over style.

I'm falling apart. It's been years since I've fallen victim to self-doubt, and I'm not about to let some bless-her-heart Barbie be the one to bring me down.

Instantly, I feel myself recoil. Since when do I tear other women down? That's not the kind of woman I want to be.

I need to get a grip. Riley is not worth the pain I'm causing myself. Grey isn't... Well, I can't deny that Grey has a hold on me, but no man or woman should ever have this much control over my self-esteem. Period.

"What's your problem, Bethany?" Madi asks. She had her own run-in with this woman at a charity auction when she was bidding on Braxton, and by her tone, it doesn't appear that she's over it yet.

I've never had a problem with Bethany before, but with

three women standing behind her like she's the lead fighter jet, I have to wonder what's changed.

"I'm petitioning the town," Bethany says with a flick of her hair. "Not only should you have to live in Happiness for a minimum of ten years, but you should also uphold the good morals our town prides itself on before you can be crowned town sweetheart."

"Jesus, Bethany. This isn't high school," Elle scoffs.

Madi moved to Happiness when she was ten. Clover and I moved here for college, but Elle was born and raised here, and she's obviously had enough of the dramatics.

We're starting to draw the attention of everyone in the diner, so I stand, then move closer to Bethany. The last thing I need is more attention.

"It's not as though I asked for this. I'm thirty years old, Bethany. I have no interest in childhood theatrics." My voice is low but kind. I'm not looking to make any more enemies today.

"The sweetheart title should never have gone to you in the first place," she hisses. "The town held a vote without all the facts, and you may think it's childish, but it's been a tradition here in Happiness for almost 175 years. It's nearly as important as the Cozy Cup Festival, and they didn't think twice about bestowing it on someone who turned out to be a stripper."

Fucking.

Bitch.

"There are a lot of things I regret, but what I had to do to create a better life for myself will never be one of those things, so take your petty bullshit and ram it up your goddamn ass, you bargain-bin Barbie."

"What? How—how dare you." Her gasp of outrage shows what a piss-poor actress she is.

"You can play dress up in your new designer clothes, which appear to be from last season, by the way, but your soul is still screaming knock-off personality."

She scans me head to toe. "What the hell could Greyson even see in you? You're a bitch with no morals."

"I'll answer that." Grey's voice rumbles like a landslide through the too-quiet diner.

So much for not attracting attention.

But having Patch McGee fight my battles isn't high on my priority list either. He cuts through the women like a knife through room-temperature butter, and I melt.

When did I become such a freaking sucker for this man? He's giving me a Prince Charming kink, and I don't appreciate it.

He doesn't say anything though. His eyes are bright but deadly as he wraps two hands around my head and kisses the living daylights out of me. It's tongue and teeth and desperate, but over before it really begins, and the second he pulls away, he spits fire at my new nemesis.

"You want to know what I see in her... I'm sorry, what was your name? Bargain-bin-Barbie, was it?"

"Bethany," she says through clenched teeth, even though she's still making come-fuck-me eyes at him.

"Right. Barbie, what I see is a woman with fierce loyalty for those she cares about. A woman who doesn't hesitate to stick up for the little guy, even when it puts her in danger. A woman who loves everyone around her so voraciously, she saves very little for herself."

He leans down, so he's eye to eye with her. "And what was it you said about morals? Here's the thing, Barbie. Savvy was born to be a queen, and a queen makes her own rules. Do you want to know how I take care of my queen?"

Bethany swallows, and even I'm flushing hot.

"By getting on my knees to taste her every chance I get. So tell me, are my morals missing too? Or are you just jealous that Savvy is a hundred times the woman you'll ever be and has me wrapped so far around her little finger she'll never begin to untie our connection?" His attention slides to mine. "Even if she wants to." My chin drops to my chest when he returns to Bethany because holy freaking shit. "From where I'm sitting, you're the one looking green."

He kisses the side of my head and begins to turn me back to our friends, but stops. "Oh, and Barbie, the next time you try to intimidate my future wife with your poison pageant posse, you'll have me to answer to."

Grey flicks his wrist as if she's an annoying gnat he has no use for, then guides me back to our booth.

"I—I could have handled that on my own."

"And you did." This time, he does kiss my forehead, and all my friends sigh as if we're in the middle of a rom-com. "But the thing you should understand is that you don't *have* to do it all yourself. Not anymore. Plus," he wrinkles his nose in disgust. "She smells like rotting flowers. I didn't want you to get close enough to bring that stench home to our bed tonight."

"Our." My ass hits the bench seat with the force of an anvil. "Bed."

Grey grins, and I swear he outshines all the bright fluorescent lighting overhead.

"Why are you doing this?"

My friends don't even pretend not to listen. At least it'll save me from attempting to recap this shitshow.

The scent of him attacks my nervous system when he places his cheek to mine, then whispers in my ear, "Because every layer of you that I pull back, the more I learn, the more I crave, the more I want. And I'm done depriving myself of you, sweetheart."

"What did he say?" Clover hisses to my other two best friends.

"I'm not an onion."

He finally pulls back, giving me space to breathe and freaking think.

"No, you're definitely not an onion." He stands to his full height, his attention snagging on Keela, and his entire form softens. "You're more like a rose—simple at first, guarded even, but reveals more as it blooms." His gaze darts to mine like wildfire, and just as dangerous. "It's the perfect name for a daughter too, don't you think?"

He reaches out and pats Keela's head with the gentlest touch, but my lungs have gone up in flames.

"Ladies." He mimes tipping his hat like a jackass before planting a quick kiss on my lips, and then he saunters out of the diner with a to-go bag that Betty hands him, not giving one shit that everyone in the place is staring at him.

"Boundaries," I croak. "We need boundaries."

"Ah, sweetie." Elle grins and Madi bounces in the seat next to me. "I think you're well past boundaries with that man. So let's talk about something fun like, wedding dresses."

"Wedding dresses," I echo with no emotion at all. In fact, the blood pounding in my ears drowns them out completely while I stare at Keela, who might be the only one on my side. She grimaces, turns a troubling shade of purple, then her diaper explodes with a cacophony of very impolite sounds.

"Oops," Elle laughs. "Time for a change."

No shit...or oh shit, I suppose.

"I'll set up an appointment at Blushing Bridal for you." Elle's still talking about wedding dresses, but my mind is focused on one thing—a daddy's girl named Rose.

CHAPTER TWENTY

GREYSON

"Tell me again why we're here?" Brax asks before pulling a nine iron from his golf bag.

It's been two weeks of us living at the Hideaway, and we're no closer to any solutions.

"Press," I grumble.

Truth is, I'm not any happier to be hosting this charity golf tournament or the gala later tonight than he is, but Quinn swears that Kristen, the crisis PR guru she hired, is the best and has insisted on more public-facing appearances to overshadow the news of Savvy's past and my new "elusive billionaire" moniker.

Since we've been unable to prove that Quinn is selling secrets, we're going along with her schemes—for now—and that includes listening to this Kristen woman, all while feeding Quinn purposefully misleading information.

We'll catch the person responsible, even if it's the one person in our company that I trusted almost as much as Braxton to have our backs.

For our golf outing today, two brothers from North

Carolina, Grant and Roman Harrington, round out our foursome.

I recognize their names, and they're likely here because I haven't responded to any of their requests for a meeting.

That's why I hate these things, but the situation called for it. And it'll bring in much-needed money for the Stillwater relief efforts. Brax has taken his daily acts of kindness to whole new heights since working on his Discreet Daily Deeds venture full-time, but this will be next-level, even for him.

As Grant, the oldest Harrington brother, approaches us, Brax mutters under his breath. "I'd rather be one of the drink cart girls with Madi and Sav."

The reminder that Savvy is riding around in a beer cart wearing a tiny fucking golf dress has me tugging on my collar. That wasn't my idea either. If one person even glances at her sideways, I'll probably end up in jail.

"Braxton, Grey. Nice to meet you." Grant holds his hand out to Brax first.

"Finally," Roman growls. Up close, these two could be twins. The Harrington genes are strong.

"Time is money, gentlemen. I'm sure you can appreciate that." These assholes are at the top of the food chain in our social network, but their business dealings are more...varied since their father died.

Instead of focusing solely on the banking industry, they've pivoted their wealth to security of every kind over the last ten years—it's a curious choice, but they've given no statements for their reasoning. Privacy, at least, is something I can admire.

"We drove through the parts of Stillwater that were accessible before coming here," Grant says, steering us to safer topics. "The destruction is truly unthinkable. I'm not sure you can fully comprehend that kind of damage without seeing it with your own eyes."

"It is," Brax agrees. "We'd like to raise a lot of money today. We're hoping to commit to rebuilding 100 homes in 100 days."

When Brax stepped down as CEO of Omni-Reyes, it was so he could focus on what he truly cared about—giving back. We now fully fund Discreet Daily Deeds, a nonprofit, so he can do just that.

The golf tournament falls into his domain, and he's damn good at it. He's much better at shmoozing for money than I am.

I prefer to write a check and walk away.

"We have a check made out for a million dollars," Roman says. He carries an air of impatience with him, and he strikes me as someone who prefers to get his hands dirty rather than play golf. "What do you say we skip the golf and hit the bar?"

It's like he read my damn mind.

Perhaps I judged these men too quickly.

Taking a practice swing with my club, I grunt in agreement. "Trust me, I'd like to. But we have obligations here that require our presence."

"Photo ops," he grumbles.

"Exactly."

Braxton and Grant pair off, leaving me with Roman, and at the moment, I can't say I'm all that upset by it. The thought of getting a hard sell from Grant for the next six hours is enough to make me want to hit myself over the head with my clubs.

"Care to tell me where the media kits are set up?" Roman asks. He's staring through binoculars at the next hole, and he must see the press junket waiting for us.

"All even holes," I grumble, then line up and hit my ball down the fairway.

"All nine of them?" He lowers the binoculars to glare at me. "What the hell kind of shit did you land in, Reyes?"

I wipe off the head of my driver to avoid facing him. Only someone who's been through this would understand the duplicitous nature of doing a good deed in exchange for social proof of goodness.

"Oh, right." He snaps his fingers in a way that tells me he knew all along exactly the PR debacle we're currently in. "You know, DeVane isn't someone you want to get involved with."

My driver lands in my golf bag with so much force it nearly bounces out.

"I'm not getting involved with DeVane. DeVane is part of my fiancée's past." I snap my lips shut. Why am I even telling him this?

"I know," he says cryptically. "It's a shame she's being dragged through this. She seems like a nice girl."

I don't ask him where he met her, even though the question sits on the tip of my tongue with venomous acidity.

"I've got it under control, Harrington."

"If you say so, Reyes."

He takes his sweet time joining me in the golf cart, but the moment his ass touches the seat, I hit the gas and don't speak while I race to the second hole.

When we arrive, Brax and Grant are already in front of cameras. I'm starting to regret not having Braxton as a partner. I feel ill-prepared for these vipers, and it's not something I'm comfortable with.

I'm always prepared.

As soon as Roman and I step up behind our brothers,

the questions start, and the crowd moves closer. Braxton and Grant back away and allow us to take center stage.

Within moments, the civilized reporters turn into raging lunatics, all crushing each other to get as close as possible.

"Greyson, how do you feel about being called 'the elusive billionaire'?"

"Greyson, it's your first scandal since the death of your sister. What do you think she'd have to say about your future bride?"

"Did you meet Savannah in a strip club?"

"Is this a 'Pretty Woman' love story?"

Jesus Christ, these people are idiots.

Roman is the one to step in front of the podium with his hands spread wide, an angry tilt to his lips that can't quite be classified as a smile. "Back up, or we're done here."

"Don't lose yer cool, mate." Cian steps up beside me, and I do a double take.

"What are you doing here, and what the fuck are you wearing?" He's in head-to-toe Hawaiian prints, and his top doesn't even match the bottoms.

"If you think I'm letting Elle roam around in that tiny fecking dress you gave her without me standing guard, then you're a bubbletwit too," he says quietly.

"I didn't give them those dresses. The PR lady did."

"Who's this shite?" Cian nods his head toward Roman.

"Not as bad as I originally thought," I admit.

"All right, then. Keep yer cool. Savvy's keeping hers even with these feckers after her."

"They're not supposed to be heckling her. The press is for golfers only."

"Ya think that matters to these ass goblins? That Quinn person said the same thing, and yet Sav's cart has had a steady stream of oxygen thieves for the past hour."

"Cian." I pinch the bridge of my nose while Roman

answers some generic question about a pop star their security company is charged with guarding. "Your vocabulary never fails to astound me." Lowering my voice, I ask, "Is she okay? How's she handling the pressure?"

"She hasn't punched anyone yet, so better than I'd'a done. Pops is keeping them on their toes, so it's possible he's confusing them enough with his own questions that they haven't hit too hard yet."

"Having her here was a mistake."

"I agree. You sure that Kristen woman's the best at what she does? I wanted to tell her to feck off outta here at least twenty times already."

"Yeah. Quinn sent me her CV." I undo the top button of my golf shirt. "Cian, can you...do me a favor?"

He claps me on the back so hard I'll feel the sting for days. "Already doin' it. Moose and I are taking turns keeping tabs on all four women. Only stepped over here 'cause it looked like you might need a bodyguard." He points to Roman. "Not as good as I'd have done, but better than nothing." He smirks, then retreats to wherever the girls are.

At least they must be close by. This is going to be a long-ass day.

I find Braxton at the second stand with a few old-school reporters patiently waiting their turn, while I'm stuck with the rabid ones of the social media age who wouldn't know how to wait for something if their life depended on it.

With a sigh, I step up next to Roman, who raises his brow at me. I nod, then turn to the spectacle before us.

"I'll only say this once." My voice carries over their heads, and they fall silent, waiting for me to continue. "If one of you disrespects my fiancée, you'll not only be removed from the grounds, but you'll be banned from working with any Omni-Reyes company for life. I expect you to behave like humans instead of leeches and show some respect for the woman I love."

Roman chuckles beside me but then steps in as if he's my press secretary and calls on reporters one at a time.

Obviously, he's done this before.

———

"Here." Roman hands me a flask.

We're only at the ninth hole, and I'm covered in sweat. Not because it's hot, though it is, but because I'm answering the same inane questions on repeat.

Reluctantly, I take a swig and instantly regret it. "What the hell is this, a snow cone soaked in rubbing alcohol?"

"Nah, watermelon moonshine."

It's so unexpected, I laugh. "Didn't take you for a candy-coated paint-thinner-drink kind of guy."

"I'm full of surprises, and this shit will knock you on your ass. That's why I like it. A swig or two is just enough to take the edge off."

"Thanks," I say, shaking my head. The Harringtons are definitely full of surprises.

"Who decided where each reporter, and I use that term loosely, would be stationed?"

It's an odd question to ask, but I take a moment to think about all angles before answering.

"I assume it's the crisis PR agent, Kristen Richardson. Why?"

Roman has a habit of scanning everything around him as if he's the FBI. Is it a work-related habit, or ·is he a para-noid fuck?

"It appears to me the most...aggressive aren't assigned to any particular hole but are chasing down cart girls."

Something hot and uncomfortable rushes in my veins. "How do you know that?"

Roman smiles, and now I can see how easily he can transform into the type of billionaire the tabloids love, except now I know he uses it as a mask.

"I'm in the business of safety, Grey. My clients' and my family's. You think I'd be here if I didn't strategically place my guys all over the course?" He removes something from his ear—it's no bigger than the tip of an eraser—shows it to me, then replaces it. "My intel says the people questioning your fiancée are mostly disgruntled employees you let go when you shut down The Whisperloop."

The Whisperloop was Braxton's adoptive father's media company that spread lies like gasoline on a fire.

I stare at him for a beat longer than necessary, but I can't think of a single reason he'd lie about something like this.

"You want something," I say as I pull my phone from my pocket. "What is it?"

Pulling up Savvy's contact, I type out a text message.

> Me: Are you okay? Do you need more security?

"I simply want you to keep an open mind about my family and keep us at the top of your list should the need ever arise."

"The need for what?" I'm distracted as I wait for those three little dots to appear, telling me Savvy is replying to my message.

"Security," Roman answers without a hint of emotion. "Personal, business, cyber. We do it all. And...we have a vested interest in what happens here in Happiness."

That gets my attention. "Why is that?"

"It's..." He pauses as though he's listening to something I

can't hear. "A family matter, and not my story to tell. But I give you my word, we have no ill will or negativity toward you or your family. We simply need time."

"I don't respond to riddles, Roman."

"I'm not asking you to. I'm freely giving you information to do with what you will, and all I ask is that you keep an open mind and consider our expertise should the need ever arise. Now I know this is your event and all, but I think we should skip the next hole and find cart number four."

I glance up at Brax and Grant giving each other shit at the tee, then back at Roman.

"Fuck it," I say, pressing on the accelerator so our golf cart lurches forward. "Where is she?"

"Grey," Brax shouts as we pass him, but I don't release the pedal. If anything, I will the cart to go faster.

CHAPTER TWENTY-ONE

SAVVY

"THIS IS BULLSHIT," MADI SEETHES. SHE RARELY SWEARS, SO when she does, it's noteworthy.

"This is part of the process." Kristen Richardson is a beautiful woman with a plastic smile and eyes that remind me of deep, bottomless pits.

She's also my own personal devil today. Standing on the golf course with her hands on her hips, wearing a navy Alexander McQueen pantsuit and pale-pink wedge heels, it makes the chasm between us feel that much wider. I roll my eyes hard when I peer down at the golf dress I'm wearing that's half an inch away from being obscene—thanks for that, Greyson.

"They do appear to be more aggressive with them than they are with the men." Quinn has been mostly silent today, but I flash a sliver of gratitude her way when she finally speaks up.

"This is a man's world, Quinn." Kristen manages to sound aloof even when tossing barbs as though they're compliments. "If Savannah can't stand up to them, what chance does she have of tricking the world into thinking that she and Grey are getting married?"

"We are getting married," I say for the third time today.

"Right. I forgot. It's just that it's so...sudden." Kristen's eyes never change, but there's something off about her body language that I can't get a read on.

"They've been together almost as long as me and Brax," Madi says with double her normal amount of sass. "They simply kept it quiet while they figured out where things were going."

"Hmm." Freaking Kristen. I can appreciate that she's good at her job, but I also think she might be a shit human —it's probably what makes her so good at her job. She has no respect for human emotions.

"I did hear they were together at Christmas," Quinn offers, which is strange to me since she was so against us that day in Grey's office.

I can't trust either of these women.

"It's neither here nor there," Kristen says flippantly. "Savannah has a role to play, just as Greyson does. If she can't answer the questions, she really doesn't stand a chance at Greyson's side."

"My question is..." Madi sucks in a breath as though she's actively trying to make herself appear bigger. My poor friend is vertically challenged on a good day. "Why hasn't Savvy been prepped for today? After Braxton and I got together, I went through extensive PR training. You're a crisis PR guru, according to Brax, so why haven't you prepared your client for the onslaught of negative questioning?"

Kristen clicks her tongue, and finally, a spark of...something flickers to life in her dead eyes.

"I was hired to get Omni-Reyes out of a situation they never should have been dragged into—*they* are my client. My expertise does not extend to...significant others." The way she says *significant* tells me she believes I'm anything but.

"Then your expertise is no longer required." Greyson's voice is a deadly storm touching down from the open cooler we're currently refilling. I hadn't even seen him or the stranger at his side approach.

The second he steps into our small circle, it's as though he's siphoned all the air from the entire golf course.

"Don't be rash." Kristen's tone is so condescending, I'm curious to see how Grey will respond.

"Don't be rash," he repeats. His voice is silvery smooth, but his muscles are tightly corded and ready to snap. "Don't be...rash. Hmm."

"I simply mean, I'm the best at what I do, and you're too smart to let something as immature as emotions cloud your judgment. My job is to protect Omni-Reyes and its holdings. I can only do so much when you flat-out refuse to do half of what I'm suggesting."

"I hate to break it to you Ms. Richardson, but I am Omni-Reyes and its holdings, which means I make the decisions, you simply supply options. And as such, I'd like to know why nearly all the paparazzi chasing after my fiancée are people we let go when we dismantled Montgomery Media."

When Grey and Braxton shut down the business Brax's adoptive father had built, a lot of shitty people lost their jobs, but they went out of their way to keep the good ones. Unfortunately for me, none of the good ones seem to be here today.

"What?" Madi is downright feral, but I stay composed, opting to watch Kristen's curious demeanor instead. "After what those leeches did to me, you allowed them back into our lives to go after Savvy?"

"No, I'm sure that's not correct." Quinn quickly flips through documents on her phone.

"I assure you, every person on this property was vetted and invited for a particular purpose." Nothing seems to ruffle Kristen. If I were in any other situation right now, I'd probably even admire her for it.

"Your guest list requires curating." The Drill Bit is out in full form today. "Roman, could you please drive Madi to meet Braxton on the tenth hole? I'll be finishing out the day with my beautiful fiancée while Kristen corrects her mistake before I blacklist her from anyone worth knowing."

The woman actually scoffs. "You could try, Mr. Reyes, but it would never work."

"For your sake, I hope you're able to fix this shit, because otherwise you'll learn very quickly just what I'm capable of." Grey's a walking, talking dark promise, but she's just as turbulent, and it makes the unease grow in my already spinning mind.

"Madi, I'm Roman Harrington. It's nice to meet you." The man offers my best friend a hand. She looks at me as though she's asking permission.

"I'll be fine," I say, waving her off. "Maybe check on Elle and Clover though. I know Cian is probably close by, but I'm not sure Clover can handle this kind of pressure."

Roman frowns, and his long, confident gait missteps. "We'll check on Clover first."

"Elle too," I call out, but he's already guiding Madi toward a golf cart.

"That's...strange."

Kristen snaps her fingers mere inches from my face, and I almost lash out to bite her. Who the hell does she think she is?

"Focus, Ms. Monroe. You have a job to do. People are

counting on you." There's so much vitriol in her words, it takes me by surprise. "You don't want to let anyone down now, do you?"

"Quinn," Grey barks before I can say anything. "Get her away from me before I do something we'll all regret."

Great. Of course Grey would take her side. I've only been out here all day listening to these slimy assholes, but whatever. I roll my eyes. "Don't worry, Grey. I'd rather check on Clover myself anyway."

He moves like my own personal shadow, and his arm sneaks around my waist before I've gotten two steps away. "Not. You. You're mine, and we're about to give those snakes a show."

Confused, I search for Quinn, who's already leading Kristen toward the course.

"What kind of show? I think my body has been on display enough recently, don't you?"

The man's entire chest vibrates. It actually makes noise, a growl that reverberates through his muscles until it finally escapes the back of his throat.

I like it.

"Who the hell picked out these dresses, by the way? It's like you ordered them all from Hussies-R-Us. Newsflash, I need everything in tall, or my ass hangs out."

"I noticed. And I didn't approve them. This was all done by Kristen and Quinn."

"She's a bitch." It slips from my mouth, and I instantly regret it. Tearing other women down is not who I want to be. It just proves again how out of sorts I am.

"Which one?" He chuckles.

Both. But Quinn, oddly, did stick up for me just now. "Mostly Kristen." Jesus. I sound like I've been sucking on lemons all day.

"Agreed. Now, tell me what we need to do."

"Well, first you need to get your Grinch out of my ass and release me."

He does so slowly, lifting one finger at a time, before stepping back.

"Thank you. We're almost done restocking. I was just about to add the last case of High Noon when Kristen showed up."

Grey walks to the shed door and pulls out a pallet of High Noons, then places them in the beverage cooler.

"Ready to head to the next hole?" he asks, slipping into the driver's seat.

"Hey, I'm driving."

"No."

"What are you even doing here? Aren't you supposed to be playing golf?"

"Change of plans." His gaze falls to my bare thighs when I sit next to him. The 'Omni-Reyes Happiness' dress is obscene when I'm standing. Sitting is like being in a bathing suit. "The logo looks good."

"Again, could've fooled me that you didn't order the damn things." A giant smiling sunshine spreads across my breasts, with Omni-Reyes above and Happiness below.

"I'm not someone who shares, sweetheart. So, the very last thing I would have put you in is a cocktease of an outfit. That"—he meets my stare with so much heat I'll feel the burn for days—"is for my eyes only. But here we are."

"Yeah." I swallow hard. "So, what's the plan?"

His real smile knocks the air from my lungs. Not the one he uses professionally. Not the one that scares people away, but the one that makes him appear younger and not so jaded and eases the tension in his face.

"The plan? We're going to sell some beer, answer some

questions, and make damn sure the world falls in love with us—the real us—not the version people think they know."

Sarcasm is my default, and my ensuing laugh is its soundtrack. "Grey, we couldn't even fool our best friends into believing we were friends for one day while they got married. You sincerely think we can trick the world into believing we're in love?"

His hand falls to my upper thigh, and my lungs rattle in my ribcage.

"I know we can."

"What exactly is your plan here?"

"To show them who the fuck we are."

"And you're so confident that who we are is what they want to see?"

"No, I don't care about what they want to see. I only care that we give them the truth."

"What truth?"

There's that damn sun-blinding smile again.

"You're fire, sweetheart, and I'm the accelerant. We've been tempting and teasing each other, too afraid of the flames, but from destruction, new life will always bloom. Instead of fighting our natural inclination, it's time to give them a taste of it, show them what it means to be engulfed by..." He waits until I face him head-on. "Love."

"You want to burn them with the intensity of our hatred for each other."

He laughs, and I feel it deep in my gut. "Love and hate are as fickle as flipping a coin. No one side is right, but how it lands dictates your path forward."

The cart stops at the next hole, and we're immediately surrounded by people, but this time, his friend Roman and three other men with more muscles than good sense push the crowd back while we reopen the drink coolers.

"What's his deal?" I ask, indicating Roman.

Grey frowns for half a second, then it's as though he makes a decision, and the lines of his face relax. "A new friend, I think."

"Huh. I thought you were allergic to those."

"I am. Or..." That line is back between his brows, and guilt licks at my spine for teasing him. "Maybe I was. We grow and adapt, or we die, and my time isn't up yet. You ready for this?" He opens the windows to the bar cart and expertly arranges cans.

"As ready as I c—" Greyson's lips devour mine, and cameras click like crickets on a silent night. I attempt to pull away, but he tugs me closer on a groan I feel all the way to my core.

"Let me in, Monroe." His words ghost atop my lips, and when I suck in a breath, he tastes me like a starving man. With tongue and teeth colliding, he masters my mouth as if he's truly in control of the universe. And by the time he sets me back on my feet, my cheeks are red, my lungs are heaving, and my head is a mess of contradictions.

Turning to the crowd, he displays a dazzling grin. "My fiancée and I are a bit competitive, so we've decided to turn this into a game—for charity, of course."

"What are you doing?" I hiss.

"We'll answer a question for every beverage purchased."

"Grey." I tug on the back of his shirt, and he simply reaches around to take my hand in his.

"We'll be keeping score. We'll get a point for every question answered, and we lose a point for each one we skip."

"Grey." I squeeze his hand with all my strength, and it barely fazes him. "This is a terrible idea."

"The winner of our friendly competition will donate one million dollars to today's event."

That smug bastard. I barely have four thousand dollars in the bank, and he likely knows this, but it kicks off a line of questioning I'm sure he was expecting.

"Do you have a million dollars, Savannah?"

"It's Savvy," I grumble.

"What's mine is hers, so yes, she does. Oh, would you look at that? Point for me."

Quinn pushes through the crowd, producing an A-frame whiteboard with Grey's name in black and mine in red. She draws a single line under his name.

I knew she wasn't on my side.

"What did you do? Text her?"

"I'm always prepared, sweetheart." He leans in and wraps me in a hug. To our audience, it's a loving embrace, but then he whispers in my ear, and I know I'm going to regret this entire day. "How about a...private wager?" I don't respond, so he continues. "If I win, you'll get on your knees for me like the sexy little submissive I know you to be."

"And when I win?" Did I just growl?

"If you win—"

"*When* I win, you'll do whatever I say."

"In the bedroom," he's quick to add.

"Deal."

"Jesus Christ. You two are trouble." His new friend Roman grins.

Ugh, did he just hear that entire conversation?

He winks, and my face goes up in flames. Guess that answers my question.

"N—next," I say to the crowd. A twenty-something with long, greasy hair and the worst excuse for golf attire I've ever seen steps forward.

Roman glares at him but nods for him to continue. When did Roman become master of ceremonies?

The kid hands Grey a twenty-dollar bill. Grey makes change and hands him a root beer.

"How old were you when you first met Riley DeVane?" the kid asks, and my world tilts in a barrage of colors I'm unprepared for.

"She was underage, and therefore unable to speak to anything that may be considered a crime or is currently sealed in court documents." Grey turns to me with a predatory smile. "Point for me."

Motherfucker. He's got me two to zilch.

"You." Roman points to a woman with pink hair.

"How did you two get together?" she asks, shoving a credit card into Grey's hand.

"That's an easy one," I say, giving myself time to come up with something because saying we stripped each other naked after a knock-down, drag-out fight is probably not the story we want to spread. "From the moment Grey stepped into Happiness, he hasn't been able to keep his hands off me." I flash the man in question my most dazzling smile. "Shocking, right? Greyson isn't known to be overly demonstrative, but he saw me and wasn't backing down until he got me. Of course, I hated him at first. He's arrogant and pushy."

He flinches, and guilt sinks it's claws back into my throat.

"But he's also kind and...loyal. It just took peeling back a few layers to see that at first."

The side of my face burns with the heat of his stare. When our eyes connect, the inferno of us licks like blue flames in his irises.

"All true," he says. "Point for Savvy."

"Next," Roman calls out, interrupting our moment. "You have to buy a drink to ask a question."

Focusing on what's happening in front of us, I pull my shoulders back when I recognize the next guy as someone who harassed Madi when we were young adults—Jackson Witherby. He's a weaselly little shit and always has been.

The weasel slips money into my palm, and its damp, as though even his hands are overly sweaty. Gross.

"Rumor has it the Wells family and the DeVane family have a sordid past—"

"We don't answer to rumors," I say, interrupting him. "Nor do we answer questions that don't pertain to us. Next."

Grey raises his brow in my direction but says nothing.

"Hey, I paid for my drink."

Greyson hands him a Budweiser, the least expensive option we carry, but otherwise ignores him.

"I didn't get to ask my question," he whines.

"Time is money, Mr. Witherby," I say. "I suggest next go around, you ask an actual question without a lead-in shrouded in rumor." Dang, that felt good.

"Point for Savvy." Grey looks...proud.

"Savvy, Sunshine Studios has tanked in recent weeks. Are you concerned about your past hurting Greyson's new business venture?"

"Savvy's podcast is still number one on the charts. We aren't concerned about anything there," Grey says smoothly.

But my skin itches.

A middle-aged man wearing a light pink polo raises his hand, then steps forward when Roman calls on him. He's vaguely familiar, but I can't place him. He hands Grey some money but refuses a beverage. "How do you think the victim of your poor choices feels, watching you parade your life in front of the cameras while she sits in her childhood bedroom, dreaming of what could have been?"

Camera flashes blind me. It's as though every person here has suddenly turned their camera on me, and Grey slips his hand into mine.

"As I said," Grey's voice is a rumble, but I squeeze his hand to cut him off.

Elle's advice to get ahead of my story sings in my head.

Swallowing hard, I don't hide the emotion on my face.

"I will always regret the choices I made as a young girl." My voice is steady and smooth, but my insides tremble violently. "I haven't been able to see my childhood friend since the accident, though I've tried."

I make eye contact with as many people as I can. "You want a headline, but the truth is, I trusted the wrong person when I was no more than a child, and I lost one of the most important people in my life. But don't think for one moment that she doesn't exist in my heart every single day. I'm the one who was forced into that car without my consent. I wasn't the one driving, but I will always carry the guilt of what being my friend cost Paige."

The man opens his mouth for a follow-up question, but Grey interrupts him. "We need to move to the next hole."

With my hand securely in his, he leads me to the passenger seat while Roman secures the beverages.

A moment later, Grey slips in beside me, holds my hand in his, and whisks me away.

"You won that game," he says calmly.

My head swivels toward him, but he stares straight ahead.

"I can't wait to see what you do to me." Dark promises linger on every syllable he speaks.

I try to pull my hand from his, but he squeezes harder.

"I thought you said we were done with the physical aspect of our...whatever this is," I challenge.

A smile tugs at his lips. "I said it was over when we were enemies. Now you're to be my wife, so we have new rules to set. I still possess willpower that you don't. However, you won, and I don't go back on my word. Plus." He lifts our joined hands and kisses the inside of my wrist. "I'm curious to see what you'll come up with."

Sitting back in my seat, I bite my cheek. Anything I say now would give him the upper hand. I'm pretty sure this jerk just cheated his way back into my panties.

CHAPTER TWENTY-TWO

GREYSON

"THIS IS RIDICULOUS," SAVVY COMPLAINS THROUGH THE bathroom door.

"I agree," I say from our bed at the inn. I miss the solitude of my house, but I lie back and cross my arms behind my head, replaying everything that happened during the golf tournament today.

"I don't understand how any of this is going to solve anything." She's been hiding in there for a very long time.

"It probably won't, but it will bring in more money for Stillwater, and that's what's important right now."

Her grumbled curses behind the closed door make me smile, even as I try to work out what was off about today.

It keeps coming back to Kristen, and that rips the smile from my face.

I haven't been able to find a single connection between Kristen and me or Savvy, so it wouldn't make any sense that she's attempting to sabotage us, but that's what my gut is telling me.

It also means that Braxton was probably right, and I can no longer trust Quinn either.

The bathroom door slides open, and my jaw drops as Savvy steps over the threshold. "How the hell is spending thousands of dollars to attend a gala helping people who lost everything?"

She stands before me in a form-fitting rose-gold silk dress that makes her skin appear to shimmer.

"Grey?"

Blinking rapidly, I force my focus on her words. "What did you say?"

"How is this"—she scans her curves with her open palms—"supposed to help people who lost everything?"

Goddamn. She has no idea how gorgeous she is.

"Rich people like to get dressed up and flaunt their wealth. It's a dog and pony show, but we do it because in the end, they donate money we can give directly to those affected by Hurricane Isolde." My voice is pinched, and I'm beginning to sweat.

"Why can't they just donate the money? Do you have any idea how much this dress cost?"

I nod, knowing exactly how much it cost because I chose it myself. Madi offered to help, because fuck knows I've never purchased women's clothing before, but I know Savvy's silhouette, and I knew exactly what I wanted to see her in.

Now I regret my decision because every person in attendance will see what I do—perfectly welded broken bits that create a beautiful masterpiece. She's stained glass in human form.

"You look—"

But she holds up her hand to quiet me.

"Grey, this isn't a date. You don't have to placate me with empty words."

My eyes narrow as I stand to my full height.

"I don't say things I don't mean."

"This isn't real. You don't have to play pretend when no one's watching."

"I'm watching." I speak harshly, tired of the bullshit. "Against all odds, I find myself wanting you, Savvy. We made a deal, and the deal is very real."

Her eyes widen a fraction before she slips on a mask. She wants to hide from me, but I'm done playing these games.

"You want to fix me, Patch. That's not the same thing."

She's trying to rile me up—it's what we've always done. Push and pull. Fight and fuck. Well, she's about to learn that there's a whole other side of me that's been created just for her.

I step closer, breathing through my nose to keep the irritation from bleeding into my tone. "If the roles were reversed and I dared tell you how you felt, what would you say right now?"

"I'd tell you to fuck off, that this thing between us is complicated enough. You're in your savior era, and you see a damsel in distress, but the bogeymen don't scare me anymore."

She begins to squirm under my stare when I don't reply.

I do want to fix her. I also want to fuck her, even though I said that would never happen again. I want to hold her, and I'm not a cuddler. I want her near me even though she irritates the living hell out of me.

I want to love her even though I'm not entirely sure I know how.

Despite all the contradicting statements in my mind, I want her because her messy colors make me feel more alive than I've been in—ever.

I don't bend for anyone, yet I'm turning into a contortionist for her.

"Fine."

"Fine?" she mimics. "What's fine?"

"We'll have to do this the old-fashioned way if you insist on being stubborn and not sticking to my plan."

She takes a step back, and I move in tandem. She smells like seduction, and I know she tastes even better.

"What are you talking about now?"

My Firefly's eyes glow as she scans every inch of the room. Is she searching for an escape? My cock twitches. I like the idea of chasing her.

I'm fucked.

Lowering my voice, I say, "You asked me if I know how to flirt."

Recognition shines in her eyes before her cheeks flame hot.

"And if you won't honor our agreement to try, then I'll just make you fall in love with me."

She snort-laughs, and images of her and us fill in the future I wasn't sure I'd have.

One where she antagonizes me in the kitchen and I fuck her in the pantry. One where she sighs into my side while watching a movie and I carry her to bed after she's fallen asleep. One where I tuck my body around hers as she sleeps every night for the rest of our lives.

Holy shit. I already fell in love with my enemy.

Savvy must see something in my face because her mouth opens but no words come out, and that lovely shade of blush careens down her neck.

"You're serious," she gasps.

"Deadly."

Savannah Monroe is my future, even if she doesn't know it yet.

"Don't be ridiculous, Grey. This is all for show. It's too... Honestly." Her arms fly into the air. "I don't even remember what the hell we're doing this for anymore. It's never made sense. None of it. Why you went from hating me to protecting me in the blink of an eye. Why you declared we're getting married when we've never even been on a date. It's stupid to think people will ever believe that you're with me, Grey. Don't you get that?"

No, honestly, I don't. "I was a coward." Brutal honesty appears to be my strategy with her, and the wild beat of my heart agrees.

Her lashes flutter, and she drops her chin to her heaving chest. "What?" she whispers.

"I've wanted you since the moment you pressed your chest into mine and told me to back the fuck up."

Brows furrowed, she bites on her bottom lip while staring up at me through long, thick lashes. "At the pub, your first night in town?"

I nod in agreement. "And every time you've challenged me since."

Her sigh reverberates through her like the last ripples of a wave on a stilling lake. "Just because you want to fuck me doesn't mean you want me, all of me. We can't make it through a wedding without fighting—that can't be the kind of life you want."

"There you go again, making assumptions about what I want." I ache to reach out and touch her, but the arch of her spine reminds me of a feral cat, so I give her space. "I like fighting with you. I love making up with you. I enjoy that you challenge me, even if it irritates the hell out of me. What's so wrong about that?"

"Are you a masochist?" she fires back, still retreating.

"Only for you."

"Did someone hit you in the head with a golf club and not tell me?" She scans the room, clocking the exits.

I smile, big and predatory. "No, but I do like taking care of you."

"Why?" Her thumb makes its way to her teeth. She's going to chew on that disgusting nail again, but I refrain from tugging it from her lips...this time.

"Why do I like taking care of you?"

She nods.

"Because I don't think you let anyone else do it."

"So you like the challenge?"

"I like you."

"You're giving me whiplash, Patch." She's using that stupid nickname as a shield, but it's growing on me, and my skin buzzes with warmth every time I hear it. "How can you go from hating me a month ago to liking me today?"

"That's just it, sweetheart." I move in, pressing my torso into hers, cupping her chin in my hand, and tilting it up until her gaze finds mine. "It didn't happen overnight. It happened with each sharp lash of your tongue. With every stolen moment when our friends were in the other room. It happened between barbed-wire-laced words and gentle caresses."

"What did?" Her voice rattles as though she's trying to suppress a tsunami of emotion.

"Us. I can't pinpoint the exact moment we went from you and me to us, but we did, and it happened when all those fine lines between love and hate built a bridge from me to you."

"You..." Her lip trembles, and I wrap my arms around her, holding her tightly against my bare chest.

"I'm going to tell you something I've never told another soul." God, this is going to hurt.

She stiffens in my arms. It's as though I can feel her walls rebuilding brick by brick.

"My biggest fear is ending up alone." Blood rushes in my ears as I admit that.

Savvy's arms are locked around my waist, and she squeezes me hard. Almost as though she can't believe what I just admitted.

Truthfully, I can't either.

"Why—why did you tell me that?"

"Because I realized something else today. You might be the only person I know who has more trust issues than I do, and I'm afraid if I don't take the first step, you'll never open the door to your heart. Luckily for both of us, I'm okay with being a pushy bastard and breaking the lock you hold so tightly."

She frowns up at me. "Are you sure you didn't hit your head?"

Laughter bubbles out of me. "I'm sure. But I will also try to be patient while you wrap your head around us."

"You? Patient?" Her scoff lights my fire.

There is nothing I love more than bantering with this woman.

"Yes, I'll *try* to be patient," I reply.

There's so much confusion floating in her eyes, I almost feel guilty.

"I think we should slow down. I—I don't even know if I want kids, and you desperately do."

I nod. "I do. In time, but if I'm being fully transparent here, since the hurricane hit, I haven't really thought about babies or surrogacy. I've been too consumed by...you, so that tells me that maybe I need to reevaluate my plans. I wanted a baby because they inherently love you unconditionally. Love any other way has never been on the table for me before." I shrug. "I'm asking for time, with you, to figure all that out. In the meantime, we have a lot of other shit to figure out."

"You mean the DeVanes?" she guesses.

I scan her too-thin figure. *And getting you healthy.* But my latest research showed I shouldn't force that conversation on her. She has to want to talk to me about it.

"Among other things," I say. My attention catches on the ring box I placed by the bed, and I move to retrieve it.

"This isn't...well, this is the ring I could get on short notice." A jeweler in London is working on the real one, but I think that will freak her out too much. Before she can respond, I slip the single oval solitaire diamond ring with a pavé band onto her finger. It's too loose, but once she's healthy again, it'll fit perfectly.

"Jesus, Greyson. This is all moving too fast." She pulls away, and I watch her go, feeling a sense of pride when she stares at the ring on her hand.

"I know. But now you know where I stand, and I'm about to put my flirting skills to work to win you over."

"Who the hell are you, and what have you done with Drill Bit Grey?"

"Back to Drill Bit, huh?"

"It's better than asshole."

My bark of laughter sounds loudly in the silent room. It's a rusty sound I'll have to work on.

"That's very true." I hold my hand out to her. "Shall we go? Braxton and Madi are probably waiting for us downstairs."

She mumbles something about a lobotomy but takes my hand.

Perhaps my directness has thrown her, but once I've made a decision, I rarely go backward, and now it's full steam ahead to get her to agree to everything Happiness has to offer...with me.

CHAPTER TWENTY-THREE

SAVVY

"Is this for real?" I wobble slightly in my too-tall heels as we step into the glittering foyer of the new Omni-Reyes headquarters. I don't even want to know how they transformed this building in such a short amount of time.

If this is what they're working with here in Georgia, what the hell did their California offices look like? It's all so shiny, so pristine, like a hurricane didn't nearly destroy a town a few miles away.

The contrast stings. We're standing in opulence, while others still search for pieces of their lives. The chasm between the haves and the have-nots hits harder when you've always been on the side of the outcasts.

The entire first floor of their newly constructed office building has been converted into an elegant gala, complete with open bars, tall floral arrangements that reach for the sky like geysers, and blackjack tables that are supposed to encourage generosity. I don't know whether to gag or grab a cocktail.

"This is another world... Such a waste of money," I mutter under my breath.

Grey responds coolly, "Unfortunately, this is just the way it works in some circles."

My stomach betrays me with a loud, low grumble. I don't even respond—just shrug. I can fake it till I make it with the best of them, but Grey throws me off kilter.

Unfortunately, the man doesn't miss a damn thing. "Hungry?" His tone is clipped, almost irritated, which makes me straighten my spine, but I don't answer.

He grabs my elbow and guides me toward the side room where catering is prepping trays. Before I can even blink, he's flagged down a waiter and is studying the hors d'oeuvres like it's his job.

"See anything you like?" His gruffness grates my nerves like the roughest sandpaper.

"I'm too nervous to eat." It's a lie, and I know instantly that he's caught it.

He snorts and starts plucking pastries and finger foods onto a plate. "Sweet. Little. Liar."

Heat floods my face, and my defenses rise. "Care to elaborate? What, exactly, am I lying about now?"

"I know you, Monroe. I've watched you. You don't let nerves stop you. You bulldoze through them. It's who you are."

I want to argue, but I can't. Not really.

"What could you possibly be nervous about here?" he asks, all push and no pause.

"Oh, I don't know... maybe the fact that my life feels like it was swept up in a hurricane that hasn't spit me out yet? I can't tell which way is up, and now I'm in a $4,000 dress that could've fed 1,500 people. I know because I looked it up. I'm wearing the equivalent of 1,500 emergency meals, and I can't even think about the cost of this ring."

He studies me for a long moment, his silence saying

more than our squabbles ever could. "Did you worry about food as a child?"

"What?" I blink. Heart racing. Palms sweating. Blood rushing. How the hell did he get that from our conversation?

"Did you have food insecurity growing up?"

I hesitate. "Sometimes." Lying would do me no good, since he's a human lie detector that seems to have a direct connection to my conscience, so I supply a sliver of truth instead. "But that has nothing to do with this."

It does, but there's no reason he needs that information.

My stomach rumbles again, and Grey's face hardens into furious lines. "Did you eat today?"

"Why are you so obsessed with my food intake?" I snap.

"Because someone has to be." His tone is sharper now. "Pick. Something."

He pushes the plate toward me. When I narrow my eyes, he softens. "Please."

Ugh. Fine. I grab the mushroom puff and bite into it, then try not to moan when it hits my deprived taste buds.

He watches me like I'm performing magic. Like chewing is an intimate act.

"I may have grown up in a different world than you," he starts, "but I'm insensitive, not ignorant. Braxton and I paid for this event, and the foundation is matching our costs in donations to Stillwater. These events bring in bigger donors. It's a game. One we play to help others."

I glance at the food when he inches it closer to me, then grab an oyster. He grins as though I just agreed to sink to my knees for him right here.

I allow myself a moment to savor the salty flavors that burst along my tongue. I am hungry, and I do need to get control of myself.

He offers me one more bite of something unidentifiable,

and I decline. He pops it in his mouth... then immediately regrets it. Do I take satisfaction in his grimace? Yes, yes, I do.

"Want anything else?" he asks, swallowing so hard it's audible.

"No," I sigh, hand over my stomach. "There's dinner at this thing, right?"

He nods, but his expression carries a shadow, a secret I don't understand.

"Let's get this over with," I say.

He slips my arm through his, and irritation prickles my spine when his touch centers me, reminds me who I am—that I can do anything.

"Try to have fun, sweetheart. I'm on your side here."

My breath catches. I don't respond, but I can't let it go either. When we're standing on opposite sides of the same line, things make sense. I can handle whatever he throws at me. Side by side, fighting together, is a game I don't know how to win.

As we move through the crowd and find our table, his touch grounds me, tethering me tighter to him with each step.

The rest of our party is already seated. Madi is next to Braxton, and Grant, who I met this morning, is next to him. On Grant's other side is Grey's nephew Sage, followed by Clover, then Grant's brother Roman. Sitting in such close proximity, I notice the similarities between the brothers—I'd think they were twins if I hadn't overheard Grant introduce himself as the oldest brother earlier in the day.

Grey pulls out the chair next to Madi, and I quietly slip into it. Who knew he could be such a gentleman? Then he sits next to me, his hand finding its home on my thigh like we've done this a thousand times before.

I flinch at the pressure, but Madi catches my attention before I can react further.

Grey's thumb draws slow circles on my leg through the slit in my dress, and even though my brain is in overdrive, my muscles start to relax. I allow myself to sink into the moment, trying to pretend that just for tonight, this could be real.

Conversations buzz around us. Clover is curled in on herself but speaking rapidly to Roman about her latest thriller novel. It's adorable, honestly. When he replies, she reaches into her purse and grabs a tiny pen and notepad before scribbling down something about gun safety and security protocols.

"New career opportunity?" Grey asks, being a smartass. He doesn't typically gravitate toward people so quickly, but he and Roman seem to be kindred spirits.

"No." Roman is as gruff as Greyson is. Perhaps that's why they're getting along. "She has some...technical questions and inconsistencies with security and weapons handling. I'm simply offering my expertise."

"How...magnanimous of you," Grey says.

"Not particularly. I'm a fan of her work," he says as though he's commenting on the weather.

"You—you are?" Poor Clover's face burns brighter than the sun.

"Yes," Roman says, pointing to Grant. "Our entire family enjoys your work."

I narrow my eyes while Braxton and Grey also sit up straighter.

"Relax." Roman rolls his eyes. "Our mother was a voracious reader. It's the one thing she instilled in all her boys. There's nothing nefarious in our appreciation of literature... or your friend here."

The hand on my thigh squeezes, drawing my attention to its owner. Grey scowls at Roman before dragging the same expression to Grant, and I feel as though I've missed something.

The brothers stare at Clover with interest. I wouldn't say it's sexual or predatory, but there's a curiosity there, and Grey obviously finds it bothersome. I just don't understand why.

Clover's nervous chatter only pauses when synchronized servers arrive with plates in hand, setting them down in unison.

"That is so cool," she whispers, the awe showcased in her wide eyes and innocent smile.

"This is the kind of shit our mother loved," Grant says softly, and Grey shifts in his seat. "She passed away last year. We're all missing her."

My stomach clenches in sympathy. Grey offers his condolences, then promptly eats left-handed so he can keep his right hand on me. The gesture shouldn't make my chest flutter, but it does.

It's awkward to watch, and Braxton's muffled laughter has Grey tightening his grip on my thigh before slowly dragging it away.

After cutting into my steak, I slowly slide it to the edge of my plate. Madi will think it's because it's too rare for me. That's what I want her to think.

I know I need to get a handle on my life. It's a slippery slope, it always is, but there are too many unknowns right now. Knowing I have a problem and understanding that I'll wrestle it into submission the moment I have an ounce of energy to spare makes dealing with it a little easier.

The control makes me feel safe, even if it's only a figment of my imagination.

It's only a problem if I can't manage it, and right now, I've got this.

Switching to the lobster tail, I bite into a buttery sliver of heaven. Grey grunts beside me, but I ignore him—it's become an art form of mine.

But then the jerk reaches over my plate, stabs my filet, and places it on his own plate. Huh. Well, that solves that—damn it. Before I can stop him, he delivers his own lobster tail to my plate.

"What are you doing?" I whisper, attempting to keep the attention off us.

"I didn't like the lobster, and you weren't touching the steak," he says.

My nostrils flare, but I say nothing.

"Grey, that's..." Madi flashes her sunshiny grin my way. "It's very sweet that you know Savvy doesn't like her steak so rare."

He nods but doesn't comment. Instead, he wraps his arm around my chair and leans in to kiss the side of my head before whispering, "Eat."

Asshole.

With his heated gaze on mine, I take another bite of lobster and nearly moan. Something that looks like a lobster should not taste so damn good.

Across the table, Roman's attention on Clover becomes even more focused. The shift in his demeanor is subtle, but my pulse spikes.

"Have you had stalkers before?" Roman's tone sends a chill racing through my bloodstream, and suddenly Grey's hand is back on my thigh.

"No." Clover's laugh is uncomfortable at best. "Honestly, I do my best to blend in. Most people wouldn't recognize me if I walked around with a sign over my head."

Roman's shoulders are wound tightly, and his knuckles are white around his utensils. "Not even after the *Deathly Vows* movie adaption a few years ago?"

He must really be a fan if he knows about that.

Roman shifts his focus to Grey and shrugs. I can tell he's forcing his muscles to relax because Grey does the same thing. "It's my job to know everything about everyone we do business with, and that extends to their family."

That seems suspicious, but I let it go. For now.

Clover instantly keys into the rising tension and rushes to defuse it. "Oh gosh, no. I was so nervous, I never even made it to the red carpet for the movie premiere, and I didn't do any interviews or anything. It's not really my thing."

"Is there anyone in your life who makes you uncomfortable?" Grant asks.

"No. I love everyone," she says quietly. "I have a great, quiet life."

The Harrington brothers' questions are beginning to feel like an interrogation, and my poor friend is about to have a panic attack.

"But it is weird that Valen has suddenly started replying to your letters," I offer, taking the pressure off Clover, but voicing a concern both Madi and I have had since his random sonnets started arriving last year.

Roman drops his fork to his plate with a clatter. On the other side of the table, Grant leans forward too.

"What letters?" Grant asks.

Grey and I make eye contact but say nothing.

"Oh, Lord. It's nothing." Clover shrinks in on herself. "Valen is just...he was a childhood friend I lost touch with. I've..." Her brown eyes flick nervously around the table. "It's really stupid and beyond embarrassing." If the poor girl flushes any harder, she might pass out. "But I've written him letters for years."

"And he's been…" Roman cuts a look to his brother that I can't decipher before quickly focusing on Clover. "Responding?"

She shrugs. "Last year, he wrote back with a sonnet, which completely threw me for a loop. A few months later, a poem."

"It's weird as hell," I mutter under my breath.

"Why didn't you tell me any of this?" Grey asks so low I'm the only one who hears.

"That is…strange," Grant says stiffly, saving me from having to reply, and I'm thankful because I'm not in the habit of sharing my best friend's secrets. "We'd be happy to look into it, if you'd like." He's looking at Grey, but Clover answers.

"Oh, no. No, no, no. It's okay. I've been writing to him since I was a teenager. It's obvious he doesn't want anything to do with me." She shrugs sheepishly, but her pain slices through me. I know how much this asshole's silence kills her. "It's become a habit now, I think. I should probably just stop writing him. It's pathetic."

"No," Madi says. "It's not. You two have shared…history. You do what you need to do. If he didn't want you writing him, he would have said so or returned your letters."

"If he knew about them." At least, that's what I think Roman muttered. I can't be sure, and his expression gives nothing away, but Grey is throwing a murderous expression his way too.

"Maybe," Clover says as she slips back into the shawl she brought with her and ties it tightly around herself. The fact that she removed it at all tells me she had been at least a little comfortable with Roman, and that rarely happens.

Grey nods toward Clover, and I follow his line of vision to find Grant studying him closely. "Perhaps it is time to set up a meeting."

Grant nods, and I shiver, not from cold, but from the feeling that things are about to change—for us all.

CHAPTER TWENTY-FOUR

GREYSON

SAVVY ROLLS OVER, AND IT SOUNDS LIKE WATER SLOSHING around in a half-empty bottle.

"How much water do you drink?"

"What?" She sounds as pissed off as I do.

She shifts in the bed again. We might as well be on a cruise ship for the ocean-sized waves moving around in her belly. I swear to God, if she filled up on water so she wouldn't have to eat, I might strangle her myself.

Instead of bickering with me, she laughs. The sound hits me hard in the chest—it always does—and knocks the air out of my ire. All I have left is a heavy sigh.

"I didn't drink enough today, so I chugged a few glasses before bed. I guess it hasn't settled yet."

The moonlight slips in through the cracks of the curtains, highlighting her face.

I don't bother with the pillow wall anymore. I want her next to me.

Lifting the covers, I slide all the way across the bed and then take it a step further until I'm hovering over her. With my weight resting on my forearms, I stare down at her, loving that I've caught her off guard. Loving how her chest heaves. Loving how she licks her lips and arches her spine—subconsciously pressing her chest into mine—right where it belongs.

"What are you doing, Grey?"

I shake my head because I don't fucking know.

"You said our physical relationship was over, that you had more restraint than me."

Leave it to her to continually call me out on my bullshit, even after sleeping together nearly every night for the last two weeks.

"And then you went and begged." My words skim across her cheek. If I just lowered my lips a little more...

She smiles, but there's a sadness to it that guts me.

"I say a lot of really dumb shit, Monroe. Haven't you figured that out yet?"

"You do," she says, her voice low and throaty but distant, as though her mind is a million miles from here.

I lower my hips to hers, slowly enough that she can push me away if that's what she wants. Her lashes flutter, but she doesn't look away, and she doesn't try to move.

"But maybe you were right," she says. "This is already too complicated."

My mouth inches closer to hers. "Or maybe I'm just an idiot."

"Finally," she whispers, and my cock jumps in relief. "Something we can agree on."

Such a ballbuster. But I laugh, and her smile presses her cheek to mine.

A rumble like thunder works through her belly, and we both freeze.

"Tell me," I plead.

"Tell you what?" She's no longer soft and pliant beneath me. She's shoring up her walls again.

I know she should come to me on her own. I know what all the research says—it's not about me. But I'm an asshole who's silently falling into madness because I don't know how to help, so I ask the one thing I definitely shouldn't.

"Why are you starving yourself?"

With my weight holding her down and lying cheek to cheek, I feel the instant she stops breathing.

Pushing her isn't the right step. I've read every article I could find on disordered eating.

I fucked up. Again.

"Move." The fear and anger in that one word lights a fire in my chest.

I don't move.

"Greyson." My name sounds like gravel on her lips. "Move."

Using my forearms, I lift my weight off her, then stare down into a sea of green.

"More." She blinks slowly and stares at my ear, my nose, my throat—anything to avoid my eyes.

"My sister did it for control when she had none."

I'm sorry for sharing your secrets, Violet. I hope you understand why I am.

Savvy's body locks beneath me again, nervous green eyes slowly dragging to mine, and I nod. "I pay attention, Sav. But I also recognize some of the signs."

Moisture pools in her left eye, and she turns her head to hide it from me. My shoulder burns from the odd plank position I'm holding myself in, so I shift back to sit on my heels between her thighs and give her some space.

"I'm not starving myself," she whispers into the silent night. The rest of the inn has been in bed for a while now.

"Then what are you doing? I know exactly what you've eaten for the last two weeks, and it's not enough to sustain you, Sav."

"It's not what you think," she bites back.

"Then help me understand."

She finally turns her tortured expression my way. "You have to stop trying to fix me."

My shoulders sag. I know that's what she thinks. And for the most part, she's right. I am a fixer. I have been for as long as I can remember, but with her, it's different.

"It's not you I want to fix, sweetheart. It's your demons and the shadows that haunt you that I want to destroy."

I hold perfectly still as she drags herself up to sit against the headboard.

"You're so confusing, you know that, right?"

A smirk tugs at my lips. "Confusing is the least problematic thing you've ever called me."

She playfully shoots a bare foot out to push me away, but I grab it in midair and hold it to my chest, right above my heart.

My thumb drags over her tiny tattoo of a cartoon firefly. I really should have caught on sooner that she was both Savvy and my Firefly.

"I'm serious, Patch." She's trying to put space between us again.

"I know." Dropping her foot to the bed, I follow her soft skin up her shins, then plant my fists on the bed beside her, crawling as I go until I'm straddling her hips, and cup her face in my hands. "I spent all that time avoiding you, or telling you how much I hate you, and now you don't know how to believe anything I say. I get it."

Her gaze flicks back and forth between my eyes. I know

she's searching for inconsistencies and partial truths, but I'm being as honest as I know how to be.

Please see that, Savvy—see me.

"It was easier to hate you than to admit I needed you." It's an effort to keep my tone even when my heart is pulsating with all the emotions I try to lock away. "I pushed you away because if I didn't, I'd have to acknowledge how lonely I was. And I know you won't just take my word for it because I don't open up like this to anyone. Braxton pulls shit from me sometimes, but I've never voluntarily given information, and even though I want to with you, it still feels like a razor is being ripped from my asshole with every single truth I lay at your feet."

"That's...very descriptive."

I huff out a chuckle. "What I'm saying is that I'm trying here, Sav. Will you do the same?"

She bites her bottom lip and looks away. It's long moments with my hands cupping her face, and the longer she keeps her eyes off me, the more painfully my chest riots.

"I'm not starving myself," she whispers. Her stomach growls loudly, contradicting her statement. "I'm not." She meets my stare. "Not really. I have...before. I don't know how to explain this."

Her focus flicks to a point on my neck, but I don't release her.

"Try." For a man who never begs, she's turned me into a mendicant.

Her shoulders shudder, and everything in my soul is screaming to hold her close, but I'm afraid any movement will have her shutting down again, so I remain still.

"It's not something that ever goes away." She meets my eye for half a second before finding something more interesting to stare at. "It's not something I've ever talked about with anyone either."

Pride and hope flare in my chest. I'll be her first.

"You've never gotten help?"

She tries to shake her head, but it's clasped between my palms.

"When I was younger, I—I took pills. Laxatives." She winces, but I keep all judgment out of my expression. "There was also this herbal tea that made my stomach cramp so badly I didn't want to eat."

What the fuck was in that? I don't ask though. I'm not sure I really want to know.

"What made you stop taking that shit?"

Something flickers in her eyes, something that haunts her, something I want to chase away.

"I didn't want to die."

"A—and now?" My voice cracks, but I don't hide it from her. I'm done hiding, I just hope she can be done too.

"I'm not trying to..."

"What?"

"Nothing. I don't want to die. I'm not taking any pills or laxatives or anything like that."

"But you've lost weight you couldn't afford to lose, Sav. I know your body better than I know my own. I see the fatigue even if no one else can. I hear the girls saying how good you look, I hear strangers praise, but I see your pain even if they don't."

She swallows, and I feel it against my palms.

"If you're not trying to hurt yourself, then what the hell is going on?"

"I didn't say that," she snaps, and I recoil. "It's more complicated than that, Greyson. It's not like I can just give you an answer like, I wanted to lose fifteen pounds, so I starved myself. It doesn't work that way—at least not for me."

Things become clear in a flash of snapshots, and guilt seeps into my soul. "You're punishing yourself."

"It's not a conscience decision I made. It just...happens sometimes, until I get a handle on it."

"When did this start?"

"When I turned sixteen, but after Paige's accident is when it was the worst." There's no hesitation. So she started punishing herself when her life felt out of control, but especially after her friend was hurt.

She was fine when I met her, wasn't she?

Nausea swirls in my gut.

"What was the trigger this time?" I ask.

She quickly stares at a point behind me. "I'm not sure."

It's a lie, and we both know it.

"Don't lie, Savvy. Not about this." It's nearly impossible to keep my tone light, and I hear a catch in the words. I'm sure she caught it too.

"It wasn't just one thing, Grey. I just...I felt out of control. Too many things were broken—I couldn't catch up."

A memory of a teenage Violet begging me to be quiet so our dad wouldn't find me hits me hard. She was always trying to control things too. I didn't understand it was her way of keeping us safe until it was too late.

"Was I one of the things that made you feel out of control?"

She won't meet my eye.

"Savannah, at the risk of sounding like a narcissistic fucking asshole, did my behavior contribute in any way to you punishing yourself?"

She brings her arms up to break the hold I have on her

face, then she pushes me away and stands. "You're right, you sound like a narcissistic asshole."

"Answer me, Sav. Please."

"I don't know, okay?" Her voice is a broken scream that has no power behind it. "Is that what you want to hear? I. Don't. Know. Riley was released from prison, work pressure was intense, things here were...complicated. Then when you left, it felt like a piece of me broke, and it's so ridiculous because we didn't even like each other. How could I miss someone who was actively recruiting me as his enemy?"

She stomps to the window and presses her forehead to the glass while I attempt to control my breathing.

I was too weak to admit to myself that I was hurt by her —that I needed her—and she ended up harming herself.

"We're idiots, Sav."

She sniffs—it's a fragmented laugh with no sound.

"You can't take this on, Grey. I was damaged long before I met you. I know you'll want to fix this, fix me, but it's not your place and it's not your responsibility. I'll always carry this with me."

Little clouds of condensation form on the window from her puffs of air.

"Some years will be better than others." She sounds so tired. I want to demolish anything and everything that makes her feel like less than the perfect mess she was meant to be.

"But I don't believe it's something that will ever be cured." Sadness rolls off her in waves. "Yes, there are coping mechanisms, and new systems I can learn, but I'm the only one who can do anything about it. If you're only here because you need to fix someone, then we should stop whatever this is now before we ruin any chance of friend-ship between us."

I slip out of bed. "Oh, sweetheart. We're already so much more than friends. I'm just biding my time until you see it."

"That's not—"

"I told you. I don't want to fix you, just your demons. You're more than what haunts you, Sav. You're not broken, but like all of us, our past is full of wounds that never healed properly. Is it really so bad that I want to be the medicine that cures some of those cuts?"

"It's not your job," she growls, and it punches me in feelings I didn't know I possessed.

"Was it Braxton's job to teach Madi how to trust in love again?"

"That wasn't the same thing, and you know it."

"What I know is she was hurting, and he found a way to make her feel better. That's all I want." I step behind her and tug her back to my front. "I just want to make you feel better."

"You give me whiplash." She relaxes into my hold.

"Let me make you feel better." I insert so much innuendo into my tone that it comes across cheesy, but she laughs, and it's worth the slight humiliation.

"When did everything get so...intense?" Slowly, her shoulders unwind, her fists unclench, and her breathing evens out.

"Well, we started hate-fucking, met on a surrogacy app, got stuck together in a hurricane, hate-fucked again, realized maybe it wasn't ever really hate-fucking, had some asshole try to blow up our lives in the media, got fake engaged, decided to have a real relationship, admitted some really hard truths, and now here we are."

Her chuckle loosens a knot in my chest.

"We did things all out of order," I say.

"What happened to meet-cutes and dating? We went straight to the reality-TV version of romance."

Resting my chin on top of her head, I hold her more tightly around the waist. "I have no idea what a meet-cute is, but dating I can do something about. Come on."

I hold my hand out to hers, palm up, silently praying she'll meet me halfway.

When her hand slides into mine, another one of my walls comes crumbling down, and I lead her from our room.

"Grey, it's late," she whispers when I gently nudge her onto a stool at the kitchen island. "We're going to wake everyone up."

"Then I suggest you be quiet." Moving through the kitchen, I quickly grab what I need to make blueberry pancakes and bacon, then set it all on the counter.

Savvy sighs, and I can feel her irritation from across the room. "Is this going to be your thing now? Trying to feed me? Do you have a note on your phone about all the calories I've consumed?"

My stomach chooses that moment to shut her up with a loud growl. "I happen to be starving, so can you just sit back and try to enjoy our first official date?"

"A, you never asked me on a date. And B? It's one in the freaking morning, Patch. This isn't a date."

I shrug. "I beg to differ." I slip a plate of bacon into the microwave and set it for three minutes, then dump the pancake ingredients into a mixing bowl.

"This is your kind of date?" Her arms are crossed as she studies me.

"Actually." I pause and really think about it. "Yeah, dating for me in the past has been a means to an end. Dinner, drinks, fuck."

"So romantic."

I whisk harder, then add a dash of cinnamon and vanilla before spraying a pan and dropping a ladleful of batter in.

"That's the thing," I say. My back is to her as I scatter blueberries through the half-cooked batter. "Romance never had anything to do with it."

"And it does now?" This is the feisty woman who gave me no choice but to fall in love with her.

"You're wearing my ring, Savannah. The only thing that matters is romance."

Glancing over my shoulder, I catch how her thumb swings the diamond around her finger.

"So you're an expert on romance now?"

It's my turn to scoff. "Far from it. Before Braxton and Madi, the only healthy, loving relationships I'd ever seen were between a bunch of dudes and a kid. Ace, Brax, Sage, and I? Yeah, that's unbreakable love, but romance? I'd never seen it in action until the moment I walked into that bar and saw Madi lose her ever-loving shit over my brother being auctioned off for charity."

A wide grin spreads across her face. "That wasn't love, Grey. That was jealousy, pure and simple."

"Sure," I say with a shrug, then flip the pancake over. "But that kind of jealousy stems from love—I saw it in both their faces. And it intrigued me enough that I spent the next few months watching their interactions. Somewhere between fucking you in pantries and carrying you through mud piles, I realized that's what I wanted, not the mind-numbing meaningless dinner dates and unfulfilling fucks. But late-night pancakes and pillow walls that never stood a chance."

"I think I liked you better when you grunted answers. This talkative side of you is unnerving," she grumbles.

I place two pancakes on a plate and remove the bacon from the microwave.

From the cupboard, I grab the real maple syrup Madi hides from Pops—that old menace would probably drink the stuff straight from the bottle if she didn't—and place it on the counter.

My palms spread flat against the cool granite, and I lean over the top of the plate I placed in the center.

"Now, the real question is, are you a dipper or a soaker?"

Savvy frowns. "What are you talking about?"

"There are two kinds of pancake eaters. Do you dip, or do you soak them in syrup?"

"Why does it matter?"

"Oh, it matters. Think of it this way. Dipping is like having nice, boring, vanilla sex. Soaking every inch of the cake is like the messiest, dirtiest, most hardcore fucking there is. And I already know how you like to fuck, so I'm wondering...do you dip, or do you soak?"

"You're equating how I eat maple syrup as the basis for how I like sex?"

"Yes."

"Why?"

I can't see my face, but I know the moment she catches the wickedness shining in my eyes. Her breath hitches, and the pulse in her neck flutters erratically.

I hold her gaze as I lift the plate and the syrup. "Because it's time you made some new memories to eradicate your false belief system around food. Grab a glass of milk and silverware, then meet me in front of the fireplace."

"Patch," she grumbles.

Ignoring her, I walk out of the kitchen, knowing that I only have a few minutes to prepare for our first date.

CHAPTER TWENTY-FIVE

SAVVY

Nerves make my hands shake as I hover in the doorway of the den. Greyson stands, shirtless, in the center of the room with a tablecloth laid out at his feet.

"Come in." His confidence has me stepping into the room.

With the grace of a predator, he slips behind me to close the pocket doors. The snick of the lock engaging causes goosebumps to sweep my exposed skin.

His hand gently wraps around my elbow, and he guides me to the tablecloth, where he sits on the floor, motioning for me to do the same.

"What's going on, Grey? It's the middle of the night, and people are sleeping all around us."

"Makes it that much more exciting, doesn't it?"

"Makes what exciting?" I whisper. "Getting caught doing something stupid in our best friends' home?"

"Our first date." He leans over the plate and, with the utensils he removes from my hands, cuts the pancakes into bite-sized pieces. Then he dumps a shitload of maple syrup all over them. "It could get messy though."

I narrow my eyes as he inches closer. He has a sick fascination with food and sex. Grey stabs a piece of blueberry pancake, swirls it around the syrup, and before I can complain, he lifts it to my lips.

Syrup drips in a heavy, sticky glob to the inside of my thigh and his gaze darkens as I open my mouth, allowing him to feed me.

"Tell me something I don't know about you." His voice is husky, and my breath catches in my throat when he leans over and licks the syrup from the inside of my thigh.

"Ah…" The second swipe of his tongue has my stomach coiling with need. "When I was ten years old, I wanted to be a librarian."

His tongue pauses against the soft skin leading to my core, his breath adding sensations to my stimulation and nearly short-circuiting my brain.

"You'd have been one sexy librarian, Sav." He places an open-mouthed kiss halfway up my thigh, then pulls away.

I know without a mirror that my pupils are blown wide. "This is an…unusual first date."

"Fitting, don't you think?" He hands me the fork. "Since we've done everything ass-backward, I didn't think taking you to the diner for meatloaf was going to cut it. Plus, I didn't want to take ten steps back and then have to wait for sex with you."

"If this is our first date, then sex is definitely off the table," I lie. "I'm not that kind of girl."

"We'll see. Your turn. Feed me, Monroe."

Jesus, why is his commanding tone the ringmaster of intense desire?

Scooping up a piece of pancake with as much syrup as I can, I slowly lift it to his mouth, watching as a line of syrup falls from the fork to his abdomen before the bite reaches his lips.

"Did you think of me when you ran back to California?" I'm still whispering, but now it's more about fearing answers than waking our temporary roommates.

Before he can respond, I crawl two feet closer to him, then force him to lean back on his palms while I clean up his stomach with tiny kisses.

His groan makes my kisses hungrier, more eager.

"Night and day, Monroe. You were a sickness and there was no cure. You had already embedded yourself in my DNA, and no matter how far I ran or how hard I tried to block the memory of you, you were here." He slaps his chest. "And fucking with me here." He taps his temple.

I continue kissing the ripples and indents of his stomach until my tongue is branded with the taste of him and syrup.

His cock bobs in his shorts, and he finally pushes me away with a gentle hand on my shoulder.

"My turn." He takes the fork from my hand. But now I'm beside him, and before he lifts the syrup-covered bite, he motions for me to lean back on my elbows.

As soon as I do, he holds the fork over my right nipple, waiting as a slow string of syrup creates a messy circle on my tank top.

"That's going to stain," I grumble. He shuts me up by slipping the pancake past my lips. Sweet blueberries explode in my mouth when I bite down, and I moan.

The fork hits the plate with a clatter, and then his mouth wraps around my syrup-covered nipple. He sucks on the fabric of my tank top with long pulls that send contractions through my core.

The man laps, licks, and sucks until my entire nipple is soaked and I'm a panting mess.

"You play dirty."

The smile that Grey shoots my way says more than words ever will.

It says: I'm just getting started.

It says: Endgame.

His eyes darken as he stares up at me, then he bares his teeth, biting my nipple and pulling at the same time.

"Fuck." It's a moan that's pulled from the deepest corners of my soul. His ministrations throb everywhere in me.

"Your turn." He hands me the fork, and I blink three times to get my brain to work.

I can play dirty too though. Knowing he won't end this game until all the food is gone, I place three pieces on the fork, then swirl it around until I've soaked up as much syrup as I can.

He growls when I hold the fork over his cock, and moans when I tip it sideways, watching the line of syrup that falls from the pancake onto his hard length.

"I love this game." His words are tortured but honest, and I feed him the giant bite.

Then I use my tongue to lap at the fallen syrup. I close my lips around his fabric-covered cock and suck. Hard, long, deep pulls. My scalp prickles when he fists my hair, holding me in position as though I have anywhere else to be.

"Too. Many. Clothes." His hips jerk as I run my open mouth along his length, soaking the shiny cotton of his shorts. "You'll pay for this, Monroe."

I look up to find him staring at me with so much heat, I'm shocked the room isn't engulfed in flames. Lowering my chin, I stare up at him through thick lashes and add pressure to his cock with my tongue.

"Get up here." His jaw is clamped so tightly, the muscles in his neck pulse in time with his heartbeat.

Easing off his cock with a smirk, I sit back and rest my palms flat on the floor behind me.

He dives for the plate of pancakes, and as he works to load up the fork, nerves settle in my chest.

The one thing I can count on with Greyson Reyes is that he'll always come back harder, more determined than before. He stalks me now with one thing on his mind—taking control and helping me free my mind.

My eyes widen at the size of the bite he expects me to eat. There has to be at least five pieces of pancake on it. Syrup drips from the fork to my thigh, then—as if he's located my clit with GPS—he dribbles a little pool of syrup onto my shorts. The heat of it instantly warms the tingling bundle of nerves.

A piece of pancake falls into my lap, and he grins. "Dinner and dessert."

I open my mouth to tell him I can't take that bite, but he uses the opportunity to feed me. He holds eye contact, daring me to contradict him as he scrapes the food into my mouth by sliding the fork along my teeth.

Asshole.

My mouth is too full to complain, and he takes advantage of that too by dropping between my thighs, eating the piece of pancake, and then attacking my clit with ruthless precision right through the fabric of my clothes.

"Oh." It's the only sound I can manage as I scramble to chew and swallow.

"I can smell how much you want me, Sav. Do you have any idea how much that turns me on? Nothing has ever been as sweet as you, salty as you, goddamn incredible as you."

He bypasses my sleep shorts, going straight up the leg hole to clamp his lips over my clit through my sheer panties, and stars fill my vision.

A long, low moan escapes my lips, and without breaking contact with my core, Grey somehow manages to grab a piece of bacon and then shove the entire thing into my mouth.

It's heavenly, and my only fear is that he's creating a new kink, a Pavlovian response to bacon and his dick. Every time I smell bacon for the rest of my life, I'll remember how his sinfully skilled tongue tasted me.

"Have you touched yourself to thoughts of me, Sav?" I cry out when his finger slips under the band of my panties. His knuckle grazes my seam over and over again as sparks light up my entire nervous system.

"Yes." There's no point in lying. He knows I struggled when he left. That says more about my feelings for him than any words ever could.

He grabs the fork again, this time lifting my tank and bringing a bite of his creation to my belly, rubbing the sticky sweetness all over my skin. His free hand drags my shorts and panties down to my thighs, and I gasp as the syrup trail dips lower, over my clit, across my lips, and back up to my other hip before he lifts the fork to my mouth.

"Taste how sweet you are, Sav."

I don't even hesitate to open my mouth, but the only thing I taste is syrup and blueberries. He's created a huge mess on my skin and wastes no time cleaning it up with his tongue, his lips, his entire mouth.

His dark gaze darts from my pussy to the plate, and I whine in protest.

"No more pancakes, Grey. Please. Please just touch me."

His expression turns feral, and I know I've got him.

"Do you have any idea what hearing you beg does to me? I could come in my fucking underwear just hearing you beg for me." He lowers his shorts, and his fist wraps around his thick, pulsing cock, but his gaze darts back to the plate of food.

"You have an unhealthy food kink, you know that?"

He ignores me as he finishes removing my clothes, but his smile shines in his eyes. "I don't have a food kink."

I scoff, but it dies on my lips when he uses his thumbs to open my pussy lips to him. "What would you call it then?"

His mouth clamps down over my clit, and I keen like a cat in heat. Fuck. He's too good at this. I'm so lost in sensation that he's flipped me to my hands and knees before I even realize I'm moving.

His cock nudging my entrance causes me to arch my back and push against him.

"I'd call it a Savannah kink." He leans over my back, bringing his mouth to my ear. His hand darts out to grab my chin, twisting my neck until he can meet my eyes. "But if having a food kink is what it takes to keep you by my side, then I'll happily fuck you while feeding you any food your heart desires."

It's simultaneously the sweetest and most fucked-up thing anyone has ever said to me.

But that's what we are together, right? Sweet, fucked-up, combustible, insatiable, inevitable.

"No more food, Grey. I'm not a game you can play and win. You either want me for me and all my messed-up scars, or you let me go and we move forward as friends."

He rams his giant cock into me in one go with no warning, and a shocked cry pulls from deep in my chest.

His hand instantly covers my mouth to muffle the sound.

"Does this feel like a game to you?" He growls. His

thrusts border on punishing, and I love every second of it. "You think you need to punish yourself for shit, but that's not going to happen anymore."

Greyson fucks me as if the end of the world is coming and the only thing that will save us is an orgasm so intense we convince the universe to hold its breath. He's hard and unforgiving. The sound of skin against skin, his groans and grunts, my moans that go on into infinity fill the air, adding to the soundtrack of us.

We shouldn't work.

We fight and annoy the hell out of one another. We push buttons just to see reactions.

But the way we make up? The moments in between the push and pull?

It's magical.

"Grey. Grey. Grey." I chant his name into his palm as though he truly is my savior, my other half. I chant his name until my voice is hoarse and barely audible. I chant his name until his fingers slide around my hip to pinch my clit.

And then he commands me with one single word. "Come."

I detonate around him. My arms give out, and my face would have smashed to the floor, but as though he sensed my weakness, he hauled my back to his front right before I would have face-planted into the hardwood.

But he doesn't stop fucking me. He thrusts up from the floor, hitting a new spot so deep inside me that it steals my breath. And his fingers continue to stroke and thrum against my overly sensitive clit.

Tears leak from the corners of my eyes. My lungs burn from lack of oxygen, and maple syrup still coats my tongue.

I'm in sensory overload, and then he presses his mouth tightly to my ear.

"I'm going to imprint myself on every inch of you, so the next time you try to hurt yourself, I'll feel it with every fiber of my being. From here on out, you're mine and I'm yours. If you punish yourself, you'll also be punishing me, and I won't allow that. If you need an outlet..." He groans, and his thrusts lose their manic tempo. "If you need an outlet, a sounding board, someone to take your pain, then you come to me. To. Me. Do you understand?"

He slaps my pussy with his open palm, and my core tightens around him.

"Answer me, Savannah."

"Yes. Yes."

"Now you're going to come again, and when you do, I want you to choke my cock with your tight little cunt. I want you to mold your walls around me. Memorize the feel of me. And know that when you're a hundred years old, I was the one who knew you, loved you, and understood you from the inside out."

My head thrashes against his shoulder. I hear his words, but I'm so far gone I can't begin to comprehend them.

"Come, Monroe. Give me your orgasm, and give me your fucking heart."

I lose touch with my senses the instant my muscles clench around him. He roars louder than a lion, but I'm no longer scared of his bite.

He's a predator in every aspect of his life. But somewhere along the line, I stopped being his prey.

Now I'm just his, and I need to figure out how to reconcile that with the rest of my life.

"Are you okay?" He's holding me with such confidence, I willingly go slack in his arms, and he gently lays me out on the floor. Grey stares down at me with a youthful, boyish glow I've never seen on him before, but I still can't form words.

I just had an orgasm that transcended life, my body, my soul, and I'm not sure how all my pieces fit back together again just yet.

Unable to answer, I shake my head, and his features soften.

"Hold tight. Let me clean this up, and then I'll carry you to bed."

I'm nearly six feet tall. The idea of a man carrying me anywhere has always been laughable, but this man keeps proving all my theories wrong.

Moments later, I'm covered in a tablecloth and cradled in his arms as he takes the stairs, moving quietly as though we didn't just wake the entire house with the most intense sex of my life.

"Did you mean what you said?" I whisper. I don't even know what I want him to clarify, I just know he said a lot of things that nearly put me into cardiac arrest, and I need to know what's real and what was lust-induced.

"I said a lot of shit, Monroe, but I can tell you, from the moment I said I wanted to marry you, I have meant every goddamn thing I've said, and I'll never lie to you. Whatever's making you question what just happened down there, pack it away. I know trust doesn't come easy to either of us, but we have to start somewhere, and I vote for starting together. When you fall, I'll be there to pick you up, and you need to do the same for me. That's what this partnership is all about."

Nothing about our story has been conventional. Nothing about us will ever be easy—we're too stubborn for our own good.

But as I study the sincerity in his eyes, I know I want to try—with him, I want to try for it all.

"Partners," I murmur.

"By partners, I mean marriage, Monroe." He opens our bedroom door, then silently closes it behind us before gently setting me on the bed. "I never wanted the happily ever after, but for the first time in my life, I'm seeing the outline of one—with you."

"What if I turn out to be the evil stepsister?"

His frown changes his entire face, but he bites his bottom lip, and I can see his mind working behind his jumpy eyes.

"That's not even a possibility, but if, by chance, it happens, then we'll find the balance of good and evil together."

I want to argue. I want to fight him—it's what we do best —but then he presses a devastatingly sweet kiss to my lips. It envelops all the goodness he possesses, and he transfers it to me with the confidence of a hero in a romance novel.

It hits me then... That's who Grey is—the wounded protector archetype who has no problem ruining anyone who gets in the way of his family, but underneath that protective layer is just a man who wants to love and be loved.

We're more alike than I could have ever imagined.

"Go to sleep, Monroe. Our story is just beginning."

He's my own personal Mr. Darcy, and he's willingly playing the part.

CHAPTER TWENTY-SIX

GREYSON

"It doesn't have to be perfect—I just need it inhabitable," I say.

I had to wait two weeks for new windows to arrive because of a supply issue, but I'm more than ready to bring Savvy home—to our home.

Braxton chuckles beside me. "You know, you don't have to rise to the occasion every time Pops pushes your buttons."

That crazy old fuck is the reason Savvy isn't by my side today. He all but insinuated I couldn't take care of my fiancée because I couldn't even get my house in order.

So instead of being with her and ensuring the bitch brigade leaves her alone in town, I'm here, at our house, installing new windows.

I swear, if bargain-bin Barbie so much as looks at Savvy funny, I'll ruin that woman's miserable existence.

Jesus Christ. I've turned into exactly what I used to ridicule—obsessive and a pussy for the one woman who drives me up the wall. I must make a face to go along with my erratic thoughts because Braxton chuckles.

"She's fine, Grey." His hand lands on my shoulder, and I

can't contain the snarl that crawls up my throat faster than a blowtorch. He snickers but removes his hands, holding them palms up, as if that will defuse my irritation.

"Pops pushes 'cause sometimes you need a push," Moose says to my left. We're holding up a window frame while Cian nails it in place from the inside.

"He pushes because he has no boundaries and thinks everyone's business is meant for him," I grumble back.

"Got it," Cian calls through the window. "Brax, need ya in here."

Braxton nods, claps me on the back, then walks away.

Moose heads in the other direction and sits on a cooler full of snacks that Pops has already eaten most of.

"Ya know, Gilly hated me at first." Moose chuckles as though he's lost in a memory. "Hit me in the head with a shovel the first time I showed up to ask her for a date."

"Jesus. What did you do?" I lean against the side of my house and cross my ankles.

"I was so caught up in what I thought were my responsibilities that I forgot she had thoughts and feelings of her own. Our pas were business partners. They died in a car wreck when I was eighteen, Gilly was sixteen."

"I'm sorry to hear that." And I am. Moose seems to be one of the lucky ones who actually loved his father.

He nods, the motion thoughtful and silent. "We'd always joked we'd end up together. Got along well, liked each other enough. But after the accident, I was left with two households to provide for. I was so consumed by duty that I became a robot, mechanical in my thinking and stubborn to a fault. When the company was in trouble and I needed my inheritance to make ends meet, I told her to marry me."

I wince. An image of me demanding the same thing of Savvy crosses my mind.

"How'd she take that?"

He points to his temple. "She gave me a concussion with a shovel."

I could easily see Savvy doing the same thing. "What did you do?"

A rare smile tugs at the corner of his lips. "Pops had been with Maisie a few years by then. Childhood sweethearts and all. For the amount of trouble that man caused, he had an uncanny ability to heal fractured hearts."

I scoff, but Moose just lifts his brow to me in question. "You think he doesn't know exactly what he's doing every time he pushes you closer to Savvy? You think he didn't know exactly what he was doing, playing matchmaker with your grandfather? Pops is a meddler, no doubt about that, but he's rooting for you, son. Nothing makes him happier than seeing those he loves in love."

I'm not convinced that Pops has any planning abilities whatsoever, so I focus on his story. "How'd you get Gilly to fall for you?"

He shrugs. "I just kept showing up. One day, one moment at a time until the fabric of her life wound so tightly through mine there was no beginning and no end, just us."

"I'm showing up for Savvy."

"Mm-hmm. But showing up with a bulldozer and showing up with a shovel are two very different things. Go at that girl with a bulldozer, and she'll piss in your gas tank just to leave you all alone, seizing in the hot sun."

"You want me to hit her with a shovel?" My head hurts from this conversation.

"I want you to meet her halfway with a shovel and then slowly chip away at the cement that girl's got clinging to her shoes."

"You think she's drowning." It's the same fear I've had since I returned to Happiness.

"I think she's been treading water so long she doesn't remember how to ask for a hand." His voice is rough with age and wisdom I can't begin to fathom. "She needs a life preserver, not a rescue. You keep bulldozing your way into her problems like you are, and she's likely to go under just to spite you. But hold her life preserver while she finds her feet and you just might find a way to keep her."

"I..."

"You're a good man, Greyson. You hide behind bitterness and a cold demeanor, but even all your ice can't hide the heart of you. Trust those you love with it. You might be surprised what you uncover about yourself and them."

"I can't just sit by and do nothing when there's a problem I can fix."

"No, I don't expect you can. But let me ask you this. When Sage was learning to walk and fell, as toddlers do, did you hold his hand all the time, or did you allow him to figure it out, even with the risk of him getting hurt?"

An image of baby Sage brings a smile to my face. Braxton was always better about letting him cry things out than I was. I tried to use a baby harness so I could yank Sage upright every time he started to fall.

Fuck. That was a disaster.

"I can see it on your face, son. You wanted to protect him, but in the end, you knew all you could do was be there to comfort him after he fell or he'd never learn. Life isn't about living with no pain, Greyson. It's about how we move on from the pain and who's holding our hand when we do."

"So, what, you just want me to allow her to hurt while she figures it out?" Even as the words leave my mouth, I know I can't do it. I won't.

"No, I don't think you have it in you to allow anyone pain if you can help it, but I do think you can learn to be a team player. What Savvy girl needs is someone to protect her blind side while she makes the play."

"You want me to be her O-line." Jesus, now Moose is giving me advice on Savvy in football metaphors.

He chuckles, a raspy sound that starts in his rounded belly. "That's one way to look at it. Savvy needs to be the quarterback in her story. She has a job to do, and she can do it well, but not while the opposition is constantly attacking her. Be that line of defense she needs to be her own hero. Help her make the play of her life. She needs that control."

I flip my lucky coin through my fingers while Moose watches. What he said makes sense, but the idea of letting Savvy feel any pain sticks in my stomach like a thousand swords. But if I control the threats, the moves she'll make will inherently be less painful, right?

"That makes sense," I finally concede.

"The best thing Gilly ever taught me was that life is not a game of chess. The moment you try to think three steps ahead in matters of the heart is the moment you lose. Love is about action and reaction, with each player having equal power. You can't plan Savvy's life for her, but you can react to her choices with love and compassion. See her as your equal in every matter, and you'll be years ahead of most of us."

Savvy is my equal. I've always known that, even if I refused to admit it.

But does she?

"Grey?"

I push off the wall just as Brax and Pops round the corner. Pops is muttering curse words under his breath, while Braxton's face is marred in worry lines.

"What's wrong?"

"Riley DeVane just tried to check into the Hideaway."

"He's here?" My head swims as though I've been deprived of oxygen, and my muscles seize for control.

Braxton nods. "The reservation was booked through a business account, but Madi's been cyberstalking that asshole since Savvy told her everything. She recognized him immediately and told him there was an issue with the booking."

"Where is he now?"

"Sitting in the den at the Hideaway." Braxton doesn't have a temper the same way I do, but anyone looking on now would be hard-pressed to believe it. The vein in his forehead is bulging, and his tone is vicious.

"He's just sitting there?"

Braxton nods, then heads toward the driveaway.

"Mads told him she'd have to speak to the owner and asked him to come back," Pops grumbles.

"The fucker said he'd wait," Braxton blurts.

"Where's Savvy?" I ask, already pulling out my phone. I should've put a tracker on her.

"Madi said she was still at the fairgrounds with Elle and Blissy, setting up the Blissful Beans & Leaves booth. I tried calling them all, but it went straight to voicemail."

"Reception's shite at the fairgrounds," Cian says, dusting his hands off on his jeans. "Let's go. I'm driving."

"I have an SUV. Why are we all going to cram into your truck?" I hate those things. I feel like a toddler wedged into a car seat every time there's more than two people.

"'Cause Moose and Pops are taking your car to the inn. We're going to raise hell until we get our girls back, and your suburban mom truck ain't going to cut it at the fairgrounds."

Suburban mom truck, my ass. "It's an Escalade."

"Prissmobile. Only an asshole spends that much money on a vehicle for one person. Now give Moose the keys so he can get to the inn and keep that wanker confused until we get our girls."

"You're not going to Madi?" I ask Brax.

"Sage is on his way over with some of the football team. She wants me to go with you."

"Will she..."

"Sage has the entire offensive line arriving at the inn in about five minutes. If I don't go with you, Madi will have my head."

"You two, in the bed," Cian calls while opening the passenger door and letting out a whistle that could wake the dead.

What the fuck?

A bear of a dog comes barreling out of the woods with its tongue hanging out the side of its mouth. It's easily a hundred-pound beast, and it's headed straight at us.

"What the hell is that?" I ask before lifting myself into the bed of the truck like some TV cowboy.

"That," Cian grumbles, "is Elle's impression of a good idea. She dropped him off about twenty minutes ago."

"But what the hell is it?"

"Wrecks, come." Cian whistles again, and the beast changes directions in midair, tumbling over giant paws in a somersault when it lands, only to get back up and charge the truck.

"Holy shit." Brax jumps in the back with me, which is stupid, because we're sitting ducks in here.

"Rex? You named that thing Rex? Like 'king'?"

The dog leaps from ten feet away and slides into the passenger seat like he's stealing home plate.

"W-R-E-C-K-S," Cian spells. "Because the fecking thing

has separation anxiety and wrecks the shite out of everything."

"And why is he coming with us?"

"Because if you thought the hurricane caused some damage, it'll be nothing to what he'll do if we leave him here alone."

"Why isn't he sitting in the back?" Braxton asks. At least he's as confused as I am.

"Wrecks won't stay back there, and we'll end up chasing him all over Happiness. Trust me, it's better if he's contained."

"Nothing in this town ever makes sense," I mutter.

Peering through the glass partition separating us from the cab of the truck, I find Wrecks gnawing on the dashboard.

"That something you want to happen in your prissmobile?"

I wince as Wrecks's teeth sink into the dashboard a second time.

"Fuck no."

"That's what I thought. Now let's go."

Cian shifts the truck into gear and presses a little too heavily on the gas. Braxton and I are thrown to the tailgate and land with a thud in a pile of limbs.

"He did that on purpose," Braxton mutters.

"Why the hell—"

"You wore a fecking suit to hang windows, Grey." Cian chuckles darkly. "Are you even trying to fit in here?"

Disentangling myself from my brother, I cautiously make my way over to the wheel well and take a seat, then use both arms to hang on to the side of the truck.

"I don't need to fit in." My words are lost to the wind whipping around my face, but Brax hears them just fine.

"But don't you want to?" he asks. "Don't you want to be part of the family we're creating here?" His voice is raised, but I'm not sure if he's angry or just making sure he's heard.

Do I want to? I want to be where he and Sage are, yes. I want to be where Savvy is, even if it pisses me off in every way. I want to see Braxton's child grow up. I want to be there for Sage as he enters each new phase of life. I even want to watch Madi become a mother because I happen to know she'll be an excellent one.

But do I want all these other...complications that come with the newfound big, messy family?

A car horn interrupts my internal war. Braxton and I both glance up to find Moose behind the wheel of my SUV, fighting off Pops, who appears to be leaning over, attempting to beep the horn.

"He's going to get them killed."

"Pops must have really enjoyed his teen years." Braxton chuckles.

"What?"

He waves toward Pops, who's now sitting back in his own seat with his arms crossed over his chest. Is he...pouting? "That man is seventeen going on seventy-five."

Cian slows to a stop at a four-way intersection, and Pops rolls down his window and raises his fingers in a peace sign. "Go get our girls." He lowers his index finger so now he's flashing the universal *fuck you* sign. "We'll scare off the boogeyman."

"Jesus," I mutter. "Is this the best plan we've got?"

Cian steps on the gas again, causing Braxton and me to readjust our grips so we don't topple over. We go straight, while Moose turns right to head to the inn.

"Any idea what the hell Riley would be doing here?" Braxton asks.

"There's only one reason he'd be in Happiness—to fuck with Savvy." And that option fills me with murderous aggression I don't know how to control.

The truck hits a dirt road that slams my ass against the metal of the wheel well.

"Dammit, Cian. That's going to hurt tomorrow," Braxton says.

Dust swirls all around us. It gets into my nostrils and my ears, and my suit is instantly ruined.

Fucking small towns. This would never happen in LA.

And look how miserable you were there.

Cian takes a corner without slowing down, and my left leg is airborne in an attempt to stay upright. Across from me, Braxton is in a similar predicament.

"This is why seatbelts were invented," I shout. We hit a bump in the road, and it tosses us to the center of the truck bed.

"Jesus, Cian. Cut the shit," Braxton bellows, but there's a smile on his face I don't understand. Is he...enjoying himself?

For fuck's sake. He's gone hillbilly billionaire on me.

The truck stops with a lurch that has my lunch revisiting my throat. Cian's out before my head has even stopped spinning, and the wildebeest of a dog follows him.

"Elle," Cian shouts, drawing more than a few curious stares.

We're parked behind a bunch of...shacks? I don't even know what to call these stands that are set up all in a row.

Elle pokes her head out of one on the end, and Wrecks takes off in her direction with Cian shouting curses behind him.

"Stay. Sit. Heel," Elle shouts, but Wrecks ignores them all.

Cian moves faster than I've ever seen him, and he tackles Wrecks right before he launches himself at Elle.

"How the hell is that safe?" I ask, running to help Cian.

"Don't get me fecking started," Cian grumbles while wrestling, physically wresting, with Wrecks until he finally gets ahold of the dog's collar.

Elle stands in the doorway, laughing so hard she has tears falling down her face.

"This is funny?" I ask.

"You should see your faces," she wheezes. "Wrecks would never hurt me, but Cian hasn't figured that out yet."

"Elle." I stare at her in utter disbelief. "He was about to take you out. He would have flattened you like a pancake."

She waves a dismissive hand my way. "What are y'all doing here?"

Savvy steps out next with baby Keela on her hip, and my chest collapses.

I want to capture the scene before me in oil paints and pictures.

She's magnificent, and strong, and so damn perfect I can't breathe.

"We've, ah…" Braxton steps forward, tugging on the back of his neck and staring at the ground. "We've got a problem at the inn."

"What?" Savvy and Elle both gasp.

"Is Madi okay? The baby?" Sav is already making her way down the rickety stairs.

"They're both fine." Brax's soothing tone does nothing to erase the worry lines from either of their faces. "But there's a guest waiting to check in… Someone who shouldn't be there."

As if on auto-pilot, Savvy hands Keela off to Elle.

"Who?" With every step she takes toward us, I see her

walls building around her limbs like a magical string tightening her armor.

"Riley," I say, ensuring her focus is on me when she gets this news. I'm the one who will take her shock, her fear, her anger. I'm the one who will absorb it, control it, and spit it back out at anyone who tries to tear her down.

I don't know when the change happened. When I went from lusting for her body to craving her connection, willingly burning the world to the ground for her, but there's no denying that's where I am.

I am her protector, her partner, hers.

Her steps falter, and the flash of fear in her eyes cuts me to my core, but she recovers faster than I'd like. I hate that she doesn't allow herself time to come to terms with bad news—she just reacts and puts plans into motion.

She's playing chess too...except she hasn't realized that I will always protect my queen.

"Did he say what he wants?" Her voice is devoid of emotion, and I want to rip out Riley's heart for turning her into this version of herself.

"No. We're heading there now."

Another flash of fear. "Madi's there." She picks up her pace as she heads for Cian's truck.

"Moose, Clover, and Pops are with her," Braxton says.

"And Sage is there with some of his teammates. Madi's safe."

Her gaze cuts to mine with harsh lines of anger and vulnerability.

"No one is safe around Riley, Patch." She steps onto the bumper, then lifts one long leg over the tailgate.

"You're not sitting back here." I catch her by her other ankle before she can lift it over the edge.

She kicks me free. "Watch me."

She doesn't need a rescue—she needs a life raft.

With a heavy sigh, I haul myself over the tailgate and sit next to her. Braxton follows next, while Elle squishes in between Cian and Wrecks in the front.

"Hang on," Cian calls over his shoulder. At least he gave Savvy a warning. She adjusts her grip on the edge.

"What do you think he wants?" Her voice is low, sad, despondent. I only hear her because I've pressed myself tightly into her side to hold her steady.

"I don't know, sweetheart. But I can say for sure we're not going to like whatever it is, but we'll get through it together."

I twine my fingers through hers, give them a gentle squeeze, and my chest warms instantly as I stare at our joined palms. This, us, together, is stronger than she knows, and I'll do everything in my power to prove that to her.

CHAPTER TWENTY-SEVEN

SAVVY

We pull up to the Hideaway like the cavalry, but instead of weapons, we have solidarity. It's a strange thing to face off with Riley with an entire team behind me.

What would it have been like if just one person had been on my side when I was a teenager?

Would it have made a difference?

Would I have still lost everyone I loved?

Would I be who I am today?

This one deranged man and his equally unstable family are the catalyst for who I am today. Everything good and everything broken that I am came from the shattered pieces of the girl that two families want to blame for their misfortune, and until now, they've had the power to do just that.

"We've got you," Elle says as I climb down from the truck bed. She looks like a rodeo clown as she straddles Wrecks while holding onto his collar. If that damn dog wanted to bolt at any second, she wouldn't stand a chance.

The sight makes me smile despite the rising tension in the air.

Grey jumps down and secures my hand in his. "Can everyone give us a moment, please?"

Cian's eyes bug out of his head. He's probably never heard Grey ask for anything nicely, but Brax pats him on the back and heads up the porch steps with everyone else following closely behind.

"I just want you to know—" Grey doesn't finish his sentence. I think he's waiting for me to look up at him, but I'm scared of what I'll find when I do. When he grows impatient, he hooks his finger under my chin and tilts it up. "I understand what it feels like to not have people believe you. So, I want you to know, I do. I believe you, and I believe in you, and so do they." He nods with his head toward the crew that's patiently waiting on the porch for us. "We have your back, regardless of what DeVane came here to say."

Damn him. All the tension that had previously been sitting on my shoulders now lodges in my throat.

"If you need anything while you're in there, just squeeze my hand, and I'll take over."

Really? I fully expected him to commandeer this entire thing, and his smirk tells me he knows it.

"I said I believe you, but more importantly, I believe in you. I know you can fight your own battles—I simply want you to understand that you no longer have to. Are you ready?"

My heart claps against my ribs like an inmate waiting for the jailbreak. Greyson Reyes is breaking me out of the prison I've lived in for years, and I'm helpless to stop him.

"I'm ready." But my wobbly voice betrays me.

Thankfully, he doesn't comment on it. He simply steps to the side and allows me to lead us to the porch.

As soon as I take the last step, the front door bursts open, and a pissed-off Madi scans all the faces until she lands on mine. "Let's kick some ass." She's five foot nothing of pissed-off mama bear, but she's using every last inch of her size to her benefit.

She's going to be an amazing mom.

With a breath that keeps lodging painfully in my side, I nod, then enter the inn, dragging Grey behind me like a silent sentry I didn't know I deserved.

We find Riley in the den, sitting on the sofa with his arms and legs spread wide, as though he's the king of this kingdom, and my stomach twists violently as I read every thought in his mind. It's why he always lost at poker—he lacks the control it takes to mask his emotions.

His dark sneer screams only one word: mine.

Sage and some of his teammates sit across the room, glaring at him, with Clover sandwiched between them. Nervous energy pours out of her, but she too appears to be attempting murder with her stare.

I nod at them in appreciation. This is what it feels like to have a family, and Riley won't take that from me. Widening my stance, I face him.

"Riley." My tone is arctic and decidedly unfriendly. "What do you want?"

"Sin." The word slips past his lips, hissing his serpent-coated lies. Even Wrecks growls, low and dangerous. I smile when Riley sits up straighter.

When the dog trots over to sit on Clover's feet, I nearly laugh as fear shines in Riley's expression.

"Savannah is the only name I respond to. I'll ask you one more time, what do you want?"

He leans back again, as if to show me he's just getting comfortable, and slowly studies the people at my back.

"You've amassed a motley little crew, haven't you?" He makes no move, but it feels like he threw the first punch.

Grey's chest presses into my back, but he doesn't say anything, just silently lends me his strength, and that one small action is enough to erase all the bullshit he's put me through. Grey is on my side, and I can't believe I ever doubted it.

Riley expects me to fold first. After all, intimidation is how he always got his way when I was a kid, but I'm not that teenager anymore. Even without the support at my back, I'm not the same girl I once was, so I hold my glare and wait for him to get to his point.

Even Pops stands silently in the corner, but he bounces on his toes—his need to release energy preventing him from staying still.

"Have you told them the truth?" Riley's voice is oily and slick. It's hardened with age, but it's as repulsive as it is in my nightmares.

Wrecks growls in his direction but doesn't leave Clover's side—almost as if he knows she needs his protection more than anyone else.

Wrecks and his loyalty give me strength. "I have nothing to hide."

"So you lied to them," he counters.

"On the contrary. I told them every sordid detail of my past, Riley. Something you can't comprehend because you've built your stories on lies."

"It's strange, don't you think?" He glances to my left, and he must be staring at Elle because Cian rumbles behind me.

"What's strange?" Elle sasses.

"The story she's undoubtedly told you all. If that were the truth, do you think her own family would turn on her as they have? Her parents, her brother, even her best friends? Her sugar-coated version of the truth has always skated over her actions that led us all here."

"Her family is a piece of shit that never cared about her. That's not Savvy's fault." Grey's a solid wall of muscle behind me. He's so close that I feel every intake of breath and the words that rumble through his chest.

"Savvy," Riley hisses. "That's what you go by now? Sweet, isn't it?"

My clenched fists ache at my sides. "I have nothing to say to you, Riley, so unless you'd like to get to your point, it's time for you to leave."

He jumps to his feet with more agility than I thought his paunchy belly capable of. Grey instantly shifts to my side, making Riley's grin turn positively menacing.

"My point. You want to know my fucking point?"

Grey slides a hand around my waist, attempting to push me behind him, but I don't move as Riley stalks close enough that I can see the veins in his neck and temple that give away the poison rotting his insides.

"I'll get to my point when you call off your guard dogs. We have things to discuss—in private."

"Not happening." Grey's tone is cold and final, but I know Riley. He won't leave until he gets what he wants.

"I'll speak to you in the kitchen, but I won't ask anyone to leave."

Grey snaps his head to me. "Are you kidding me? No way, Monroe. Not happening."

I press my hand to the center of his chest, silently reminding him to trust me. The sooner I deal with this asshole, the sooner I can get him out of Madi's inn.

Whatever Grey reads in my expression has his jaw clenching shut and the muscles in his neck pulsing rapidly. "Ten minutes, and then I'm coming in."

It's the best concession I'll get out of him, so I nod my head. At least he's trying to let me lead this.

"Savvy, are you...are you sure?" Clover asks before chewing on her bottom lip.

"I'm sure. Thank you."

"Leave the door open." Grey's voice is as rough as coarse gravel. "I mean it, Monroe. Keep it open."

"This way, Riley." I lead him into the kitchen, then hook the swinging door open. In my periphery, Grey has angled himself to have me in his sights.

It gives me the confidence I need. Stepping around Riley to the opposite side of the island, I keep the large slab of granite between us. From this vantage point, Grey appears over the top of Riley's shoulder, only a room away.

"You have ten minutes to tell me why you're here, and the clock is ticking, so again, I suggest you get to your point."

"My point," Riley says through clenched teeth, "is that Paige lost the use of her legs. I lost years of my life, Austin lost his sister, and what did you lose?" The dark, destructive edge in his voice nearly has me calling for Grey, but I stand firm.

I can do this.

I've lost more than he'll ever understand—I lost myself, and it's time I found her again.

"Nothing," he spits. "You lost nothing."

Cian and Brax step closer to Grey—an army ready to step in, but I gently tell them no with a tiny shake of my head.

Riley's glare continues to burn holes through my soul.

"Say what it is you think I owe you before my friends come in here and escort you out." I'm only giving him this courtesy to try and save the people I love from any of his retaliation tactics that I know are coming.

He reaches behind his back. Grey instantly calls out and lurches forward, but when Riley retrieves a piece of paper from his back pocket, Brax and Cian hold him back. Riley stares at the paper for a long moment—long enough for sweat to trickle down my spine, unease snaking around my ribcage.

Then he tosses it onto the island, and when it lands, the air in my lungs cuts like shards of glass.

I'm reaching for the paper as my eyes burn with unshed tears.

It's a save-the-date card for Paige and my brother's wedding.

Pain slashes through my chest. You'd think after a lifetime of betrayal, I'd be stronger or more resilient, but this proves the walls I've built are made of straw. "I—I don't understand."

"It would be a shame if Austin were ousted as a dirty cop and Paige was once again left broken and alone, don't you think?"

"Are you threatening me?" I hate how small my voice sounds.

"Call it a premonition."

"A—Austin isn't dirty." I know that in my soul. He may not have believed me, sided with, or stood by me, but he's not dirty.

Riley shrugs. "Hypothetically speaking." He glances behind himself at my loved ones, crowded together to keep an eye on me. "Money speaks louder than actions. Everyone in this house knows that."

He continues to stare at someone, and when Clover shrinks behind Cian, I know it's her. My hands clench at my sides with every painful accusation I want to hurl at Riley.

"I heard poor, delicate Clover had some...unexpected gifts," Riley says, and fire burns through my system, roaring and racing to cut him off from my friends—my family.

"What did you do?" I seethe.

"Who? Me?" His fake innocence makes my head explode. "Nothing, Sin. Clover writes some pretty fucked-up thrillers that have a, shall we call them, obsessive fanbase, and your little town here likes to spread gossip like melted butter. But I will say this, *whoever* doxxed her information must have known this was a...possibility." I can tell by his smug expression that it was him. "Shame about Madison's ex too, though I'm too late to enjoy his particular brand of...love. So much...pain in this little town of Happiness, don't you think? It does always amaze me how easily people are willing to give up information if the price is right."

He's bribing someone for information on me and my friends. I know it. It's how he works, but I can't give him any kind of reaction, or he'll pounce.

"I've heard enough," I say.

He slaps both hands onto the island. "You haven't heard anything yet. You are mine, you slutty little sea witch. You've always been mine, and you will always be mine. Mine to ruin. Mine to shame. Mine to destroy."

He stands to his full height, but Grey is shifting his weight from foot to foot behind him, and I know he'll only hold out a few more moments before he barges in here.

"But, Sin, I've grown." God, his voice takes on a slithery edge, and goosebumps erupt on my arms. "I've had plenty of time to think and plan, so I'll give you a choice."

An indelicate scoff escapes me, and he narrows his eyes as though he's already thinking of punishments for the infraction.

"You can either come home to Vegas and be my mine, or I'll stay here and ruin everyone and everything you love."

That's not a choice—it's a death sentence.

"Why did you show me Austin and Paige's save the date?"

His snarl curls into a cruel smirk. "Because Austin wants you to finally step up and take accountability. He wants you at the wedding, but only if you can make amends for your wrongdoing. Paige's family, of course, wants nothing to do with you, but as his best man, I've promised to keep you in line."

"Best man?"

His mask slips, and I'm face-to-face with the demon he holds inside. "Didn't you know? Austin felt so guilty over your lies that he's come to visit me every week. Over ten years, we've formed an unbreakable friendship."

"You've manipulated him into a friendship, you mean."

"Now you're learning. People will always do what I want them to do—even you. The sooner you learn that, the less pain I'll inflict on those assholes behind me."

"It's time for you to go," Grey says, charging into the room.

Riley taps the save the date I've placed face up on the island. "The only problems they have in their relationship are because of you. You've ruined lives, Sin. Not just mine, but theirs. You deserve to pay for what you've done, and they deserve closure."

The closer Grey gets, the stronger I become.

"The only thing I did was make the mistake of trusting you when I was a child," I hiss. "Everything spiraled because you were a spoiled little rich boy who couldn't take no for an answer." My voice cracks, and I focus all my energy into controlling it. "If they're happy and in love, then I'm happy for them. I've tried to make peace with them both over the years, but I can't force anyone to believe something they don't want to see."

I step forward, and Grey's hand catches my hip, as though he's going to physically restrain me from moving, then with a gentle squeeze, he lets me go.

"Yes, it hurts me to not be part of their lives anymore, but I have zero regrets about the actions I took after you forced me into that car. I have zero regrets about ensuring you stay out of my life. And that's the truth. So, if you're here to make threats or issue commands, I don't care to hear them. You, Riley DeVane, are nothing to me."

"Maybe not now, but I will be, Sin. I've had ten years to think of all the ways you should be punished. But after seeing this"—he points to every person I love—"I know what will hurt you the most, so you can be sure you'll see me around because I'm not going anywhere. I will haunt your life until you've paid for your crimes."

"And what crime would that be?" Grey demands. He's a loaded cannon ready to fire. I'm actually impressed that he's held it together as long as he has.

"She's the reason my car crashed into the tree. She's the reason Paige will never walk again. It's all her fault." Riley's devilish grin sends a chill down my spine.

In that instant, I know he means what he says—he has no intention of ever leaving me alone.

A flash of a memory steals my breath. The ugliness in his expression right before we crashed into the tree. He'd looked at me with unseeing eyes and made a promise my subconscious had done everything in its power to block out: *You are mine, Sin. Till death do us part, you are mine.*

Then he drove straight into that tree, and everything that came after was pain and heartache.

CHAPTER TWENTY-EIGHT

GREYSON

BRAXTON ESCORTS DEVANE OFF THE PROPERTY WITH WRECKS barking at his heels while my mind swirls with so much anger and fear, I know it'll all come tumbling out when I open my mouth.

"What were you thinking?" I finally hiss. Whirling around to face Savvy, I attempt to rein in my vitriol when I see how pale she is.

She shudders, and I bite back a curse, then stomp toward the fridge, where I pull out all the ingredients for a sandwich. I need to keep my hands busy, and she needs to eat.

"Why would you agree to speak to him in private?" I toss the bread on the counter. "What did he say?" The drawer rattles when I paw around for a knife. "What does he want? How can I fix this if I don't know what the hell is going on?"

She's silent as I slap together the sandwich, then slam it onto the counter in front of her.

"Eat," I demand.

"I—I can't. I think I might be sick." I hate how small her

voice is. This isn't Savvy. This is someone retreating into the wounded version of herself, and I want to murder that fucker for sucking her back in time.

"Hey, mate. Take a step back." Cian is wound just as tightly as I am, but he's able to maintain his composure enough to keep his voice gentle.

"I—I know Riley," she says. "If I didn't hear him out, he would've just made things worse."

"You know him?" I sound slightly unhinged, so I do take a step back, fill my lungs with air, and try again. "Well, do you know me, Monroe? Have I not shown you that I'll do whatever it takes to keep you safe?"

Okay, so perhaps Cian's right. I need to calm down.

"I just wanted him away from all of you. I did what I thought was right."

"No," I say, proud of myself for finding my composure this time. I slide the plate closer to her. "You did what you've always done—you placated him because it's always been you against the world. Well, guess what, Monroe?"

She shakes her head with dazed eyes.

"You're not alone anymore. You're not his, you never have been."

"That's not what he thinks." Her palms slap down on the island with a snap. "He's delusional and scarily manipulative, Grey."

"It doesn't matter what he thinks, Sav. You could never have been his when you were always meant to be mine."

Her chest expands on a sharp hiss of breath.

A chorus of *aws* break out as Elle, Madi, and Clover join Savvy at the island.

"Ooh, can I get one of those too?" Madi asks with a hand resting on her belly.

With an aggravated sigh, I set about making them all sandwiches.

"What are you doing?" Clover asks as I set the ham in the frying pan.

"Madi can't eat deli meat unless it's cooked until it's steaming, or she runs the risk of listeria," I mutter.

When silence hangs in the room like a wet blanket, I turn to stare at the women. Even Cian is smirking in my direction.

"Why do you know that?" Savvy asks.

I shrug and get back to work. "I read a lot." And it's true. But I also planned to have a child of my own, so I needed to know what the hell I was doing.

Braxton enters the kitchen with Pops and Moose. "He's going to be a problem."

"I know." Savvy sounds so dejected, I want to shake her.

"Monroe." I place fried ham onto Madi's sandwich and then hand it to her. "I need you to tell us everything he said, and then I need you to promise that you'll accept our help."

"But I—"

"No buts," I say roughly. "You're not alone anymore, and nothing he can say or do will change that." I meet the eye of everyone in the room, happy to find them all nodding in agreement. "So while you eat, tell us what he said, and then together, we'll make a plan."

She scowls at me but picks at the bread and finally spews the bullshit demands DeVane has made of her.

"Sav?" Madi asks cautiously. "Do you think you should at least try to talk to your brother? Get his side of...this, before you make any decisions?"

"No way," I blurt. "All he's done is hurt her for years. He doesn't deserve her."

"Respectfully, Mr. Slightly Unhinged, this is not your decision," Madi huffs. "Savvy?"

Is she irritated...with me? What the hell? We're on the same team here.

My gaze snaps to Savvy's. The pain her idiot sibling causes is not far from the surface, and it drains what little color she had left in her cheeks. "I've tried to talk to him over the years, but he's always said the same thing—until I take accountability for what I did, he wants nothing to do with me."

"He sounds fecking brainwashed," Cian mutters.

"Riley has always been...persuasive," she says. "And Austin wanted so desperately to be accepted in that circle. I wouldn't say he's brainwashed, but possibly willfully coerced. After the accident, he only saw what he wanted to see. It made the most sense to him that I, the wild child, the problematic one, was to blame."

"But what about Paige? You said she wasn't like her family," Clover says quietly.

"She wasn't." A sad smile sits hesitantly on her lips. "When we were younger, she was wearing designer clothes before we even knew what a designer was, while I wore Walmart daily deals and socks from the dollar store, and she couldn't have cared less. But I have no idea what her life has been like since the accident because her parents wouldn't let me have any contact with her. For all I know, she believes the same thing Austin does, or she's just been in survival mode and agrees with whatever her parents say because it's easier. I can't blame her either way. Her life was irreparably damaged because of Riley's actions."

"So essentially, you've got two wealthy families wanting you to be the scapegoat for their children's poor choices,"

Moose says as if commenting on the weather. I forgot he and Pops were even here.

Savvy flinches, and my chest thumps painfully.

Her pain has a connection to my own.

"I made poor choices too, Moose. It isn't entirely on them."

Her heartbreak is my heartbreak.

"No," Moose says before I can. "You had some choices taken away from you, and you were too young to know how to get away."

"Agreed," Cian says, crossing his arms over his chest with Wrecks panting at his feet. "Twatgobblin chose to get in that car all fecked up. Paige chose to get in that car with you, knowing that he wasn't of sound mind."

"Cian's right," I say, frowning at the mess she's made of the bread of her sandwich—she's plucking it like a chicken. "You're the only one who didn't choose to get in that car that night." She opens her mouth to argue, but I silence her with a gentle kiss that leaves the entire room silent.

My lips hover above hers. "I understand the guilt, Monroe. The guilt of surviving. The guilt of thriving. The guilt of coming away physically unscathed, but no matter how much you punish yourself, you will never be responsible for the actions they chose to make."

"He won't just go away." She shudders as she speaks, and I wrap my arms around her.

"No, he won't," I say reluctantly.

How do we protect her from a madman?

"Okay, so our problems are multifaceted right now," Braxton says. "Let's plot them out and go from there."

Madi hops off the stool and pulls out a notebook and pen, then slides it across the island to me.

My brain is already making a list, so I put it to paper.

1. Keep Savvy safe.
2. Confirm Sage's protection in the dorms.
3. Get control of Clover's doxing issue.
4. DeVanes. Ashfords. Austin.
5. Find out who the town snitch is.
6. Mole?
7. Brainstorm any ways Twatgobblin could mess with Madi or Elle.

"Ha, knew Twatgobblin was a catchy one." Cian chuckles to himself, but I ignore him.

8. Create good press for Sunshine Studios.
9. Remind everyone who the fuck Omni-Reyes Media is.

"Am I missing anything?" I ask.

Savvy leans into my space, her scent enveloping me in gentle calmness.

"Jesus," she mutters. "That's quite the list. Where do we even start?"

Looking up, I find Braxton and Cian already staring at me. A silent conversation carries between us. It says: We'll do whatever it takes.

"I can't believe I'm about to say this." I slip my hand into the pocket of my pants and squeeze my lucky coin. "But I think we should call in the Harrington brothers. At least get their take on it and see what they suggest."

"Good call." Braxton hums. "That should cover items one through three on your list, and potentially four, five, and six too."

I stare down at the numbers he recited and nod.

"Number five is obvious," Madi scoffs.

"But why would she do it?" Clover asks.

Savvy shifts beside me. "I think she's made it clear her reasoning capabilities recently are severely lacking."

"Bargain-bin Barbie." I can't believe that name has come out of my mouth more than once already.

Savvy shrugs. "She suddenly shows up in designer clothes, acting like queen bee? It's almost too obvious."

"How would Riley have known to go to her though? If he was digging around Happiness for any amount of time, someone would have spoken up." Moose says, sitting thoughtfully in the corner, but I can tell how much this upsets him.

Happiness is a community, a family, and in Happiness, Georgia, no one screws around with family.

"Knowing what I know now of Happiness, Moose is right," Brax says. "If they'd been nosing around, searching for someone to turn, people would've gotten suspicious."

"Unless they already had someone close by. Someone who's been watching from the sidelines and already knew the weakest players." Madi's lips purse as she stares at me as though she expects me to come to the same conclusion she obviously has.

Madi has always gotten a weird vibe from Quinn. Braxton's words smack me in the face.

Quinn has been coming here for almost a year, helping the transition of our company from California to Georgia go smoothly. She's the most likely culprit, but why?

"You think it's Quinn," I say. The corner of Madi's eye twitches as the words leave my lips.

"Or someone she's been working closely with." Madi's a spitfire who doesn't back down from a fight. The expression she flashes my way tells me she'll fight for Savvy the same way I'd fight for Braxton. "I refuse to believe it's a coincidence that all the shitty reporters were assigned to Savvy at the golf tournament. That was deliberate, and you all know it."

"Kristen." Her name slips through clenched teeth like a curse. "She's been working for Omni-Reyes since before your wedding."

"If I were writing this mystery..." Clover speaks up. When she finds all our eyes on her, she shrinks in on herself and lowers her voice. "The villain would be Kristen, trying to frame Quinn. What I would have to figure out though, is how Kristen is tied to Savvy's past."

"I've never met her before," Savvy says.

"Maybe not," Elle says. She's frowning at Savvy's plate too. Is this the first time she's noticed that one of her best friends has a worrying relationship with food? "But that doesn't mean she doesn't know you...or someone who wants to hurt you."

"Maybe numbers four, five, and six are connected, then," Braxton mumbles, staring at the list. "Savvy's past, the snitch, and/or the mole."

Could Kristen have a connection to the DeVanes or the Ashfords? Could Quinn?

"How good are the Harringtons at their job?" Pops asks. He's been unusually quiet.

"They're the best," Braxton says, still staring at the list. "Easily top two in the entire world when it comes to private protection and global security. They can find a shadow in the dark at this point."

"You've been quiet, Pops." It sounds as though I'm picking a fight, but for once, I'm not. Pops has never been so silent in all the time I've known him, and something feels off.

"*Mea lux,*" he whispers, and I follow his line of sight. He's staring at Savvy's firefly tattoo on the inside of her heel that I've never given enough attention to.

But I look closer now, with his words in my head, and my skin heats as I narrow my focus, not on the firefly but the line of text that trails behind it, making it appear to glow, and it causes my brain to short-circuit.

The text is a delicate thread, so it's easy to miss.

It's just two little words—*mea lux*. My hand fists the same two words on my lucky coin so tightly, the ribbed edges of it cut into my palm.

"What did you just say?" I ask.

His murky gaze meets mine. "Mea lux."

My light.

"Where did you hear that?" My breathing is labored.

"What does it mean?" Elle asks.

"It's Latin," Clover says, staring wide-eyed at Savvy. "It means 'my light.'"

"It's also what's carved into the coin that Ace gave Grey." Braxton's worried expression is focused on the hand in my pocket that might now be bleeding.

"Where did you hear that?" I repeat, fairly confident that Pops wouldn't have pronounced it correctly on his own.

"The last time Ace visited," Pops says with a heavy sigh. "He was muttering it and mentioning you and Savvy."

My finger reaches out and traces Savvy's tattoo. She gasps and pulls away, but I had to confirm it was real.

"Geez, Pops. The last time you pulled out an old Ace story, you gave half my inn away to a near stranger." Madi's tone is laced with frustration, but the curve of her lips contradicts it.

Sure, Pops and Ace pulled a shady deal that could have potentially cost Madi her inn, but it all worked out in the end.

"Ace wasn't a fortune teller. There's no way he could've foreseen these events." I'll be the voice of reason if no one else will.

"But he likely knew that when he rescued Savvy in Vegas, he unwittingly put an even bigger target on her back," Braxton muses, rubbing Madi's stiff shoulders.

"When did you get the tattoo?" My question draws curious glances, and soon, everyone is peering down at Savvy's heel.

"After..." She crosses her leg and unconsciously presses her middle finger to her firefly. "On the way home from Vegas. Ace said I needed to always remember to be my own light." She shrugs, but I can tell she holds the memory close to her heart. "We made a stop, and I came home with this."

"Did you choose it? My light?"

Savvy shakes her head. "Ace did."

I'm glad she had Ace, but I'm irritated that even her best friends never inquired more about her inscription. I'm more irritated with myself for never looking closely enough.

Clover obviously knew what it meant, and I know what it means, but none of us bothered to ask what it meant to Savvy.

She gives, and gives, and gives until she has nothing left for herself. She needed to mark her skin to remember not to burn herself out.

How many times in this woman's life have people let her down?

"That was around the time Ace gave Greyson his coin to replace the one he lost from his sister," Braxton says.

Loudmouth can take his show-and-tell and fuck off with it.

It's obvious that Ace was leaving a trail of breadcrumbs, but we've already eaten the candy and jumped into the fire.

Whatever his intention was, it's my future I'm fighting for now.

"I'll call the Harringtons," I say, my voice gruff as I wrangle with the untethered emotions crawling up my throat. We need to get back on track. "Let's also step up our game and offer Kristen and Quinn different information we know the mole won't keep secret to catch them in the act of treason. We'll need to fill in our attorney while we wait for all the pieces to come together."

I attempt to maintain eye contact with Braxton, but my gaze keeps drifting to Savvy's foot.

"If this were a story I was writing..." Clover has taken the notebook I wrote my list on and is scribbling so fast she's smudging the ink with the side of her hand. "I'd probably have the hero and the heroine carrying on as though nothing were amiss. Let the town see you in love. Show the world how well you work together."

"That's your plan?" Disdain drips from my words, and I immediately feel like a rotten dick. Even Wrecks wraps himself around her legs and growls in my direction.

Clover might be the most gentle human on the planet, and I just shat all over her.

When Savvy elbows me in the gut, I know I'm right.

"Sorry, Clover. That was...rude. I'm on edge, and I apologize for taking it out on you."

Savvy reaches over and places the back of her hand on my forehead.

"Oh, for fuck's sake, Monroe. I'm not sick. I'm also not a monster."

"To anyone but me," she mumbles.

I lean into her space until my lips press against her ear. "I didn't hear any complaints about my monster cock taking care of you last night, Monroe. Is that the monster you're referring to?"

Color rises high on her cheeks, and I pull back with a smirk.

"Okay," Elle says. "So, you call the Harringtons to do their thing, and in the meantime, we focus on the fair. Everyone in town will be there—it's as good a place as any to put on a show." She smirks, and Cian rolls his eyes.

Savvy yawns, and she sways with exhaustion on her stool. I place my hand on her back and rub small circles there, pleased when she doesn't push me away.

"How about we call it a night and reconvene in the morning," Madi suggests. "The fair is going to take a lot out of Savvy and Grey, and we'll have a lot of work to get them ready for it."

Jesus. What now?

"I agree," Braxton says. "Let's meet here at nine, and we can fill Grey in on all his...duties." He smirks, and I know instantly that I'm going to hate everything about this.

"I'll do whatever I need to do," I say, then take Savvy's hand in mine. My gut wants me to force her to eat the sandwich, but my heart tells me she needs a break—even from me. "Come on, Monroe. Let's get you to bed."

No one stops us as I lead my future wife out of the room and up the stairs.

Neither of us speak as we climb into bed, and I hold her to my chest to ease the fears that have settled there.

I don't know what the future will hold, but I do know that happiness will only come for me if Savvy is by my side.

"Goodnight, Monroe."

"Goodnight, Patch."

Savvy falls asleep the second she closes her eyes. Sleep doesn't come so easily for me, but I do lie still, counting her breaths like sheep and savoring the calm that only comes when she's in my arms until the sun comes up.

———

I GROAN WHEN I ENTER THE KITCHEN TO FIND EVERYONE'S already here. It's not even seven yet.

"Trouble sleeping too?" Braxton asks.

I nod and head straight for the espresso machine.

"Any word from Riley?" he asks. I finally take in his appearance, then glance around the room. Everyone looks like hell. "We're all just as worried as you are, Grey."

"She was mine long before she was yours," Madi jokes, then removes a quiche from the oven.

"She's not yours," I mutter under my breath.

Braxton chuckles, and I go back to my espresso.

"We might as well get started on the fair," Madi says just as Savvy enters the kitchen, grumbling about caffeine.

"Is the fair anything like the Cozy Cup Festival?" I ask. It's too early for this shit. Everyone's awake and nodding as if they're excited for another damn festival, but there's a heaviness to the air that doesn't belong here in Happiness.

Apparently, Riley's sudden appearance has everyone on edge—hence the family meet and greet at the crack of dawn.

Mornings are for silent workouts and planning sessions, not crowded kitchen clusterfucks. But the more they speak, the faster my mind works out all the ways that Savvy and I could annihilate a competition.

"The Cozy Cup is about bringing everyone together with friendly competition. The town fair is about..." Clover bites her lip, and I swallow down a groan. "Celebrating love."

"Celebrating. Love," I repeat as though I can't compute the two words. "Celebrating what about love, exactly?"

"Just shoot me," Savvy grumbles right before her head hits the kitchen island with a dull thud. I've never met anyone who despises mornings more than Monroe. I slide her my espresso, then turn to make another.

"Well..." Madi already sounds too cheery for my liking.

"Town fair is where we showcase the new town sweetheart," Pops says with an irritating whistle to his words.

"You...showcase the town sweetheart." I glare at each person in the room, understanding dawning and not liking it one bit. "How does Happiness showcase their sweetheart?"

"This has disaster written all over it." Savvy groans again. She's picking at the quiche Madi made, but I'm the only one paying attention.

Braxton chuckles, and Cian purposefully stares at a blank spot on the ceiling while swaying with Keela fast asleep on his shoulder and attempting not to laugh.

I linger on the serenity of the sleeping baby for a moment.

"She's a night owl," Elle says, catching me staring. "Her internal clock is all screwed up."

"Showcasing the sweetheart is a time-honored tradition." How the hell is Madi so damn chipper?

"Madi." The warning in my tone hits a brick wall. "How do you showcase sweethearts?"

"You're not going to like this." Cian chuckles, a full, belly-shaking laugh that has Keela stirring, but nothing seems to wake her.

How I long to sleep with the security of a baby surrounded by love.

"Explain," I demand, forcing my gaze away from the tiny ball of pink once again.

"Well." Elle stands and begins talking with her hands. "It starts with naming the most eligible bachelor. Then it's the Sweetheart Crowning Ceremony."

"Most eligible bachelor," I scoff. "You've got to be kidding me."

"Nope," Elle laughs. "And he has to put his best foot forward to win that title, and then the rest of the weekend, other bachelors have the opportunity to—"

"To what?" I interrupt when my hand fists my mug so tightly, I'm afraid it will crack.

Pops loses his shit, and I'm certain he'll be on the floor, rolling around in laughter at my expense soon.

"The other bachelors have the opportunity to woo her away." Cian's laughter gets the better of him, and he swipes at his eyes, then hands Keela over to Braxton.

"The entire weekend is dedicated to Savvy?" Is that pride in my tone?

"Sort of," Madi says. "She's more like the face of the festival. In reality, everyone is showing off for everyone else—like the last hurrah of the summer."

"In the old days, it was a way to arrange proper marriages," Pops says.

Fucking perfect.

"But times change," Madi says. "We're not dealing in dowries anymore. Now, a bachelor or bachelorette might compete in one of the challenges, but they could be showing off for the sweetheart, someone in the crowd, or just to win the prize. But the vibe of the fair is really all about love. Finding it, spreading it, experiencing it."

My heart gallops in my chest. All I heard was competition—no one is competing for my girl but me. "What sort of challenges?"

"My favorite is Cupid cowboy." Pops hoots with laughter, and I'm already regretting this particular life choice. "All the bachelors in town line up for shirtless line dancing. You should see how it makes all the ladies swoon. That's how I got my Maisie, you know?"

"You've been doing this shit for that long?"

"Next year will be the 175th anniversary," Moose says proudly.

"Shirtless line dancing. Shoot me now. Isn't that...sexist or something?"

"We don't make anyone disrobe. It just...happens some-times when the competition gets fierce." Clover giggles.

"Fine. What else?"

"There will be a Savvy trivia time," Madi says. "You know, like how well do you know Savvy?"

I stare straight through Miss Monroe. "Easy." My confi-dence in this challenge isn't inflated. I doubt anyone knows her as well as I do.

"Remember, Savvy's just the face. Everyone's in it for the prizes or bragging rights." Madi pats Keela's back and then takes her from Braxton.

They keep passing her around the room, but I'm not even itching to hold her. My mind is completely filled with thoughts of Monroe.

"Then there's the bachelor bake-off," Elle says, calling my attention back to this small-town rite of passage. "How are your baking skills, Grey?"

"Fine," I mutter.

"Oh," Clover chirps in. "Don't forget the matchmaker mamas, where all the mamas get to showcase their boys, but that's really more for the younger generations. Oh, who wants to woo—game-show style is a fun one."

"My favorite is the build-a-date," Elle says. "You have to build something that would showcase Savvy's perfect date out of whatever supplies they have in the booth at the time of the competition."

"Chili for charity is my personal favorite. Won that one six years running," Moose says.

Sorry, old man. I might like you more than most, but you're going down.

"Lots of competitions, got it. What are the prizes for each of these idiotic games?" I shouldn't have used the word idiotic. As soon as it leaves my mouth, I see hurt flash on all the ladies' faces.

Why am I such an asshole sometimes?

"Each competition wins time with Savvy," Braxton blurts, and I narrow my eyes.

"Wait. Madi was a sweetheart. Did you have to do all this stuff?"

Madi's cheeks flush crimson.

"It happened before I arrived," Brax says bitterly.

"What kind of time do they win with her?" I ask.

"Dates, events, that kind of thing. The person who wins can either take Savvy, or they can excuse themselves from the running and use the prize with someone else."

"Does that happen often?"

I didn't think it was possible, but Madi's cheeks glow even hotter. "Not usually."

"So you're telling me, my fiancée could potentially go on multiple dates with multiple assholes?"

Savvy sighs heavily. "It's not like this is re—"

Spinning on her, I lower my voice to an octave I'm not

sure should exist in human nature. "Finish that sentence, and I'll show you just how real we are, Monroe."

"Okay, okay," Moose says, clapping his hands. "Everyone, calm down. It's really very simple, Grey. If you don't want to share, then you're forced to win."

"Simple?" I scoff. I've never line danced a day in my life. But something tells me I'm about to throw my whole back into it because no one's going to steal time with my girl.

The first thing on my list is ensuring that I'm named the most eligible bachelor of Happiness. Here's to hoping I can write a check for it.

CHAPTER TWENTY-NINE

SAVVY

"Savvy?" Elle shouts as if she's trying to blow the entire inn down.

"I'm packing," I yell back. Freaking Grey is demanding we return to his house today. I'm not sure why I agreed to it other than I know Riley is lurking around town, and Grey, the giant pain in the ass, makes me feel safe.

"Save it for later." Her feet pound on the stairs as she runs up two flights to find me. She barrels through the door as though she's top-heavy and can't quite stop the forward motion. "We have to go."

Spikes of panic flare to life. They start in my gut and find their way into my veins before spreading to every limb. "Is it —did Riley do something?"

"Oh," she pulls up short. "Crap. No. Sorry. We have to get to Happiness U's practice field, pronto. Madi and Clover are meeting us there."

She tugs on my hand and manages to get me to my feet.

"Why? What's going on?"

"Grey is working with the football team again but cut

338

conditioning short today and demanded the boys teach him how to line dance."

An image of his face when he learned about Cupid cowboy sears itself on my retinas.

"No. There's no... Are you serious?"

"Yes!" She's so gleeful her cheeks are painful to look at. She'll be sore later from all that smiling. "Come on. They're about to start, and we cannot miss this—I got a babysitter and everything."

"How'd you even know?" I ask, allowing her to drag me to the hallway and down the stairs.

"Sage texted Madi." She laughs. "But if Grey finds out, you didn't hear that from me."

"Oh my God. It's payback for the time they spied on Sage when he was trying out for the team."

"It totally is." She claps her hands together. You'd think she was seeing the ocean for the first time with how excited she is.

"If we get caught, Grey will be pissed."

"Mm-hmm," she hums. "Come on. Hurry up."

We race out of the inn to her idling car. If Grey is seriously learning how to line dance, this is an opportunity I can't pass up.

Ten minutes later, we're parked on the far side of the football field and tiptoeing along the fence that will lead us to a break in the chain link and straight to the bleachers while Cole Swindel plays through the loudspeaker.

"Where are Madi and Clover?" I whisper.

Elle points to the backside of the bleachers, and sure enough, Madi, Clover, and Braxton are belly-down in the dirt, spying on something.

This is going to be a disaster, I can feel it.

With the entire team facing the visitors' goalpost, we're

able to slide under the bleachers without being seen, but the idea of dropping to my belly where there's 100 percent certainty that beer is the number one ingredient in the dirt is not something I'm super excited to do.

"Get down here," Madi whispers. She tugs on my hand, and I drop to my knees.

The amount of germs and DNA under here is enough to make me dry heave.

"Look," Clover whispers on Madi's other side. At least she was smart and brought a blanket to sit on.

I don't get as close as them because the last thing I want to do is lie face down in someone's backwash, but I'm close enough to peer out between the metal slats.

I track line after line of white football pants before I finally land on a pair of gray slacks.

Greyson Reyes has never followed the rules. Not when Coach B. coerced him into helping out with the quarterbacks, not when the assistant coach roped him into working on special teams, and not now, when the boys should be running and pushing sleds across the field.

Instead, Grey stands in gray suit pants that cost more than my monthly mortgage and a white undershirt that clings to every muscle.

Ethan, a local kid and starting lineman, stands in front of them all, counting the beat like a maestro while demonstrating each move.

And holy hell. I think we just found the one thing Greyson Reyes isn't the master of—the man has two left feet.

The team sways to the right, but Grey slides left and slams into a running back.

Then the team twirls with two stomps while Grey swings the wrong way and gets his foot clobbered by our center.

"Ow," Braxton moans with sympathy pains. "That had to hurt."

"H—how is he so bad at this?" My wide-eyed gaze can't break away from poor Grey, who's clearly agitated but refusing to give up.

"They've already been at it for an hour," Clover whispers.

Five rows of football players move forward. The center lineman scoops up Grey so he doesn't knock him over because Grey is the only one moving backward.

The snickers from under the bleachers grow louder, and although I'm smiling, I don't like anyone else making fun of him.

"Shh." I feel all eyes on me, but I don't give them my attention.

Poor Grey.

Ethan blows a whistle, and all the football players look to Grey, presumably to see what he'll do next. Grey is known for requiring perfection, and on more than one occasion has made the entire team run many miles after a less-than-stellar performance.

"Okay, let's try this a different way." Ethan is a giant kid, and his voice booms across the field. "Ever seen the movie *Dirty Dancing*?"

Braxton rolls over and bites his arm to keep from howling.

Greyson must voice some kind of opinion because the players around him all take a step back.

"Well, do you want to figure this out or not?" Ethan fires back.

"Uncle Grey," Sage says, pushing his way to the front.

"Coach," Greyson demands like an asshole.

"Coach." Sage's smirk could light up the entire town on

Christmas morning. "You're the king of unorthodox methods, and you're running out of time to figure this out. I've been to the Firefly with Ethan. He's the best line dancer we've got."

"How are you getting into Firefly? You're only eighteen." Of course that's what Grey would focus on.

"Wednesday and Sunday are eighteen and over. Now focus, please?" Sage is loving this a little too much.

"Fine." That word holds all his frustration. "What do you suggest? But keep in mind, Ethan, if you make a fool out of me, you'll be running doubles during hell week."

I'm pretty sure Ethan rolls his eyes. At least, I would've.

"Here." Madi nudges my leg, and I glance down to find her offering me a tiny pair of binoculars.

"Where the hell did these come from?"

"They come in handy around here, so now I keep a pair in my car." She shrugs as if it's normal.

It's not normal, but since I really want to see Grey's face, I don't say anything. It takes me a moment to bring his features into focus, but when I do, I gasp.

"See?" Madi says smugly.

Determination lines Grey's face—his bright red and slightly angry face—while Ethan stands facing him. Behind him, Trevon places his hands on Grey's hips—his movements slow and jerky, as if he's waiting for Grey to lash out at him.

"They're not—"

"Remaking the dance tutorial scene?" Madi is gasping for air. "They are. They really, really are."

"Okay," Ethan says over the music. "Tre is going to make sure your body moves in step with mine. Relax, Coach. If you're all tight, you'll never move correctly."

"Just do it." I can almost feel the rumble of Grey's words.

"No. Way." Clover gasps while Braxton slides his phone into position to record.

I lean over and snatch his phone away.

"Hey." Brax stares at me, and whatever he sees has him holding up his hands in surrender. "This is gold. I'll never get this type of chance again. You don't understand. Grey doesn't make a fool of himself. Ever."

I slip his phone into my back pocket.

"Anyone else want to try me?" I whisper-yell.

Madi, Clover, and Elle all shake their heads but give me shit-eating grins, and I return my attention to Grey.

Oh. My. God. Trevon is moving Grey's body with his own. When they step forward, Trevon uses his left leg to push Grey's left leg forward. When they slide to the right, he moves Grey with his hands that are still on his hips.

They make it through four rounds before Grey finally starts to catch on, and Trevon gives him a little more space.

By the time they've done the same four moves thirty-six times, Grey has almost got it.

When the next song comes on, Ethan instructs all the guys to get back in line and start over.

Grey immediately bumbles and stumbles through every move.

Oh, Grey.

"Fuck." Grey curses before kicking at the ground. "Go again." He makes a circular motion with his pointer finger, and everyone awkwardly steps back into lines.

He misses the second step, and Trevon slides in behind him again.

"Why is he putting himself through this humiliation?" I mutter. "It's so hard to watch."

"I thought you knew Grey better than that, Sav." Braxton's tone catches me off guard, but when I look at him, a giant lump forms in my throat. "He'd do anything and everything for those he loves. He's doing this for you."

His words blow me over, literally. My ass hits the dirt so fast I can't catch myself, and my foot shoots upward, kicking him in the chin.

Braxton howls, and chaos ensues.

Madi rolls over my legs to check on Braxton. Elle tugs on my shoulders to pull me into a sitting position, which only results in me whacking my head on a metal support beam. Clover jumps at the sound of my head meeting metal, and her limbs tangle with mine until Clover, Elle, and I are flailing like the arms of an octopus, but no one is in control of our extremities.

"What the hell are you doing?" Grey's voice rattles around in my brain.

It must hit the others too because we all freeze.

Laughter drowns out any thoughts I might be trying to formulate.

"Have we got to give you kids a name now?" Coach B. asks from somewhere behind me. "Y'all obviously didn't learn your lesson the last time I caught y'all under here."

"How about the Bleacher Creatures," someone suggests, and I groan.

Grey is going to be so pissed.

"Pigskin Peepers." Oh, God. The whole team is getting in on this.

"The Sideline Sleuths."

"Get out from under there. Now." It doesn't seem to matter if Grey is angry or turned on, his rumbly Drill Bit voice just does it for me because I respond to his command without thought or question.

"Goal-Line Gossips."

"That's enough." Coach B. doesn't raise his voice, but

everyone hears him. "If y'all keep getting into the stadium undetected, who's to say our competition can't do the same thing?"

"Well, Coach." I groan as I crawl out to a place where I can stand. It's so freaking filthy down here. "I dated a guy in college who taught me how to sneak in here. He worked with the grounds crew. I don't think just anyone could get past the gate unless they knew where the faulty chain link is, so I think you're safe from the competition."

"Five full ladders, then hit the locker room," Grey shouts, using his coaching voice. Even that is sexy as hell.

A chorus of groans hits my ears, but I slowly spin to face Grey's tumultuous gaze.

"What are you all doing here?" He's barely holding on to his control.

"Ah, Uncle Grey. We're just worried about you. You remember how that goes?" Sage is taunting his uncle, and he knows it.

Grey's jaw clenches so hard I can practically hear the squeak of his teeth grinding together.

"I was under there to make sure you were safe." Grey's mouth barely moves, but we hear every word.

"And they were under there to show support, since you seem incapable of asking for help from those who actually know what the hell they're doing." Sage wraps his uncle in a hug, then lines up to run ladders with the rest of his team.

Coach B. chuckles, then walks away, leaving Grey on one side of the white line, with me, Brax, Madi, Clover and Elle on the other, but Grey is only staring at me.

The longer he stares, the more intense my desire to laugh. I don't even know why. It's not kind to laugh in someone's face, but this entire situation is out of control.

Madi sniffs next to me, and it's the crack that splits me

wide open. I laugh. Hard. Tears stream down the sides of my cheeks as I gasp for air through the full-belly giggle-fit.

Grey stands and watches it all for long moments while Madi reaches into my back pocket to remove Braxton's phone—I'd forgotten I still had it.

"This is funny to you?" he finally says.

"It's funny to us all," Braxton howls.

Grey ignores him, waiting for me to answer.

My stomach cramps with my effort to contain my delight. "It." Gasp. "Is." Gasp. "Come on, Grey. Did you see yourself?"

I swear, the left corner of his lip twitches.

"They *Dirty Dancing*ed you." A new round of laughter fills the air around us.

This time, I know his lip twitched.

"You—you looked soooo uncomfortable."

One tooth separates his pressed lips, then two. I've almost got him.

"I kept expecting Ethan to put his hands on your shoulders and make a Greyson sandwich while 'Hungry Eyes' played overhead."

His shoulders bounce, and he flashes two more teeth.

"No one puts Greyson in the corner though, Monroe. Not even for you."

"Did you—" I look to Braxton on my right, but he's doubled over laughing. "Did he just make a joke...about himself?"

When I glance back at Grey, he's wearing a large, genuine smile that makes my chest ache.

And then...he laughs. It's a sound that fills in all the cracks in my soul that not even superglue and denial could fix. His face relaxes into the happiness. He's so carefree in this moment, I want to bottle it up and spray him with it the next time he's carrying the world on his shoulders.

I want to see him like this forever.

A whistle blows on the field, but Grey's attention is on me—on the happiness that leaked from my eyes while watching him, on the way my chest rises and falls too rapidly, on the smile I can't seem to wipe from my face even as my cheeks heat under his intense perusal.

"Are you laughing at me, Monroe?" Each word he speaks is expelled on a step closer to me.

I nod, feeling the pressure on my cheeks and knowing I'm exerting muscles that have remained dormant for too long.

"Well, with you," I say. "You obviously have a sense of humor about yourself."

He steps into my space, wrapping his arms around my waist and pressing our hips together in a way that's not even close to a PG rating.

"I love your laugh." He's so quiet, so earnest when he says it that the rolling laughter catches in my chest. "You don't do it enough."

"We'll, ah...just see you later." Elle's stage whisper is so ridiculous, I bury my face in Grey's chest.

"I laugh," I say when they're out of earshot.

He shakes his head, never breaking eye contact. "Not enough."

My shoulders droop. "What are you doing out here, Patch?"

Soft lips press against my forehead. "I studied the list of challenges at the fair, made a plan of action, and then implemented steps to learn what I didn't know."

"But...why? Why go to all this trouble?" I'm scared of his

answer, and I want it more desperately than I've wanted anything in a very long time.

"It's simple, Sav. You're mine, and I'm yours. If you think I'll allow anyone else to win, even momentarily, what's mine, then you're out of your goddamn mind. Say it."

"Say what?" Tension finds its home between my shoulder blades.

"That you're mine."

The eye roll is automatic. "I'm yours...for now. Nothing lasts forever, Grey, you know that."

"Stubborn, sexy ass." I'm not even sure if I was supposed to hear those words, but I feel them in the intensity with which he stares at me.

"You're mine, end of story. I have the bachelor bake-off in the bag. Savvy trivia? Easy. Chili for charity, I can do in my sleep. Build-a-date, I'll figure out as I go. But Cupid cowboy and who wants to woo the sweetheart are my sticky points. I've never wooed anyone in my entire life. Line dancing feels cult-like. But I'll figure out how to win both, even if I have to make myself a fool to do it."

He laces his hand through mine and leads me toward the parking lot.

"Until then, we've got some speed dating to get through."

It takes a moment for his words to register, and when they do, I dig in my heels.

"Speed dating? What are you talking about?"

"Exactly what it sounds like. Madi and Clover will be at our house in an hour to help."

Traitors. Neither of them said anything to me.

"Help with what?"

Grey holds open the passenger door of his brand-new SUV. "I'm going to learn how to woo you, and to do that, I need to know every fantasy rolling around in that big head of yours. The girls are coming over to facilitate a practice run of who wants to woo."

"That's cheating." I huff but slide into his passenger seat. "Madi is a cohost at the live event. She can't give you the questions ahead of time."

"I'm not asking for the questions ahead of time, I'm asking them to prepare me for anything and everything they think I should know to win."

"That's still chea—"

The asshole slams the door before I can finish my sentence.

"It's not cheating," he says when he gets behind the wheel. "It's a cram session."

"Oh my God. It's the same freaking thing."

His hand lands on my upper thigh, and the fight drains out of me.

For better or worse, Greyson is taking a crash course in all things me.

And part of me hopes he's still here after the final exam.

CHAPTER THIRTY

GREYSON

"Jesus, Grey. What did you do? Threaten Cian and make him work around the clock to fix your house faster than anyone else's?"

She always thinks the worst of me.

"No, smartass. It's called money. If you're willing to pay enough, you can make anything happen. *And* I'm paying him double for finishing ours. *And* I called in a company from Maryland to rebuild my garage and apartment for me so I don't monopolize all of Cian's time. *And* as soon as the new company is done on my rebuild, I'll pay them to help Cian catch up over in Stillwater. Any other questions that have your devious little mind hell-bent on painting me the bad guy?"

"I don't have a *little* mind." She's cute when she pouts.

The doorbell rings right before the door opens, and Madi walks in with Clover close behind. I forgot to lock it.

"Hey, guys." Madi's smile is radiant. I swear, all these women love seeing me uncomfortable.

"Hi." I don't elaborate because if I do, she'll engage me

for much longer than necessary. Instead, I head to the kitchen to pull out the takeout containers while the three of them speak in hushed tones not meant to reach my ears.

Is it normal to want to keep Savvy all to myself? Probably not, but the idea of sharing her makes my skin itch.

"Come get plates." Fuck. I try again without my organic hostility. "Dinner's ready."

Madi and Clover are the first around the corner, but Savvy drags along at a much slower pace.

"I figured we could make plates and then sit in the dining room so we can get started. I have my MacBook set up in there to take notes. Does that work?" I don't make eye contact while piling my plate with California rolls and tempura because that's what I've seen Savvy eat in the past.

"Sounds good," Madi singsongs, almost like she's daring me to look at her, so I do. Her perma-grin has got to go.

"You're taking this all very seriously." Clover's voice is always just a touch above a whisper. Has she ever yelled at anyone?

I realize a moment too late that everyone is staring at me expectantly.

Oh, right. Clover said something.

"I take everything seriously. I'll meet you in the dining room."

The whispers of gossip bubble up as I exit the room. Then I'm left pacing the length of the table for another ten minutes before anyone joins me.

Savvy enters first, and the talons of impatience embedded in my chest retract their claws.

"Monroe, you can sit here," I say, pointing to the chair I have a death grip on. "Clover and Madi, you sit across from us."

"You have assigned seats?" Savvy's question drips with sarcasm, and I control my breath in response.

"Yes. I need to study everyone's reactions to the questions, so I'll know how to respond at go-time."

"Go-time?" she snorts. "Grey, this isn't a covert operation. You're not a Navy SEAL. It's a small-town fair."

"It's *our* small town's second biggest event of the year. And it only comes in second to the Cozy Cup Festival because in January, everyone's all strung out from the holidays and needs an excuse to get drunk and happy without all the pressure."

I feel Madi and Clover's gaze on me, but I ignore them. "I saw how intensely everyone took the Cozy Cup Festival, and I worked tirelessly to ensure Madi won for Braxton's sake. Did you think I wouldn't put in the same amount of effort when it's you and me on the line?"

Savvy's eyes are wide and watering. "You— You're unhinged, you know that, right?"

I wave her off. "Yes, yes I know." Adopting an annoying female tone, I say, "How can you go from hating me to loving me in the blink of an eye? How can you fight me every step of the way, yet say you want me forever? How can—"

"Don't be an asshole," Savvy snarls.

"My point is." I ensure my tone is dark and demanding. "I don't know how it all works, it just does. I want what I want, and if you'd stop fighting me for two seconds, you'd realize it's everything you want too."

A chair slides into place across the room. A quick glance tells me Clover is intensely uncomfortable because if she pulls her cardigan any tighter around herself, she's sure to collapse a lung.

"Now," I say as gently as I'm capable. "Can we please get

on with this so I can learn everything I need to know to win?"

"This isn't how normal people go about dating, you understand that, right?"

I feel my face pull into a smile. "Yes, I understand, Monroe. I understand it all. And after I learn what makes you tick, I'll ensure you have the fairy tale you dream of yet don't dare to reach for."

"That's not—"

"Swoon," Clover says, fanning her face. "Seriously, swoon. Can I use that line in a book? Can you imagine if a stalker said that to his next victim?"

My jaw drops while she reaches into a bag at her side for a small notebook. "Clover, in no way, place, or time, would a stalker be the Prince Charming in that scenario."

"Oh, Grey," Clover gasps as though I'm out of line. "You're out of the loop. Stalker thrillers and stalker romance are hot commodities right now."

I blink three times before I can shift her train of thought from my consciousness.

I also add *find Clover a therapist* to my list of shit to do.

"Okay. Well, no stalking, but I would like to know what I'm up against with this game. I..." My palms sweat, and my stomach hollows out.

What the hell is that?

Holy shit.

I think I'm insecure. Wiping my hands on my pant legs, I inhale deeply through my nose because screw that. I don't allow insecurities.

"I don't know how to woo," I say. "I can fake a pleasant date. I can pretend to listen and care. I can fuck—"

"Jesus, Grey." Savvy slaps a hand over my mouth. "Just... stop. What you're trying to say, I believe, is 'please help me. I don't know how to woo someone, and I refuse to lose any of the competitions so please, help me.'"

Tugging her hand down to my chin, I nod. "Not anyone though, Savvy. You. I want to know how to woo you."

"You're...impossible." She drops her hand and her face, but not before I see a lovely flash of red creeping across her features.

I love it when she blushes.

"Let's just get this over with," she grumbles.

"Okay," Madi says while bouncing in her chair. "Clover and I thought the best way to do this was with a version of twenty questions."

While I listen, I pick up a California roll, dip it in soy sauce, then place it on Savvy's plate since she's left hers mostly empty.

"How will that help?" I ask, staring at Savvy. Finally, she picks up her damn chopsticks.

"Well, we'll ask Savvy a bunch of questions. Your job is to listen. Then, after we've asked her the questions, we'll turn to you and ask you how you would respond to certain things based on her answers."

That sounds... It's not terrible.

"Okay." In my periphery, I see Savvy's jaw working. A quick glance at her plate tells me the California roll I prepared for her is now gone.

Pride fills my chest until I'm nearly combusting.

"Let's do it." I'm feeling more confident now and transfer a piece of tempura from my plate to hers.

This time, she swats my hand away, but not before I drop it, and when she stabs at it with her chopstick, I smile.

Madi catches my attention. She's wearing a frown as she stares from my plate to Savvy's as though pieces of a puzzle are finally clicking into place.

Yeah, you guys are good friends, but I'm better. Savvy will never harm herself under my watch. I'll ensure she has everything she needs to get herself healthy again.

"Madi?" I lift a brow at her dazed confusion.

She shakes her head and then nods. "Yeah. Okay. Ready, Sav?"

Savvy wipes her mouth, then sets her napkin down as though dinner's over.

I roll my eyes but focus my attention on what they're saying while I lift another California roll to Savvy's lips.

She accepts it from me while shooting daggers at my chest with her glare.

"Enough," she hisses. "I can feed myself."

I slide my plate so it rests between us. "Then do it."

"I'm sorry. Can we pause this for just a second? I'm going to get myself some more food." Savvy's gone before anyone can respond.

I follow closely behind.

The moment she hits the kitchen, she spins as though she knew I'd follow. "You can't do this, Grey. This, you, embarrassing me and feeding me in front of my friends? It's not going to help me. Don't you get that? I'm not starving myself."

I scoff.

"I'm not," she insists. "I had a minor setback with all the stress. But I wasn't actively trying to harm myself."

"It's the inactive harm I'm worried about, Sav. You didn't even realize you'd slipped into old patterns, did you?"

She swallows and breaks eye contact. "Not at first, no," she admits as though it pains her. "But now I'm aware, and I'm working on it. Don't pull that shit out there with me again. I mean it."

Anger settles into the frown she shoots my way. Her

hand covers her mouth, and she shakes her head as though I've betrayed her. "Oh my God. That's...that's what all these games have been about. You've been trying to trick me into eating."

I busy myself with takeout containers.

"Screw you, Grey." My head snaps up. "No." She waves her hands in front of her. "Seriously, just screw you. You don't get to do this. You don't get to be the mastermind pulling strings in my life. If you see something you don't like, then you talk to me like a normal human being. You don't use my body and my attraction for you against me. Jesus, Grey. *Fuck*," she yells. "How could I have been so stupid? How did I not see what you were doing this whole time?"

Helplessness settles into my shoulders. I don't know how to talk my way out of this one. I didn't want to upset her—I just need her healthy.

She steps into my space, a fiery ball of indignation. "I'll only say this once, Greyson. Once. Are you listening?"

I nod.

"If you *ever* try this Machiavellian bullshit to play with my head instead of talking to me again, no amount of your self-control will matter. We'll be done. I'll burn every bridge from me to you with so much gasoline, the fire will burn long after we're dead. Do I make myself clear?"

"I..." I what? What can I say to that? "I'm just worried. That's all. I'm scared for you."

The lines around her eyes soften fractionally. "I understand that, but I also cannot take on your feelings about my life. I'm doing the best I can to handle my own shit, okay? I promise you though, I'm working on myself. You either have to accept that or leave me the hell alone."

She doesn't wait for me to answer, and it's a good thing

because anything I say now will end in a fight I don't want to have with her. Leaving Savvy now would shred all the pieces of my heart that's only just begun blooming for her.

And now I sound like a fucking Heartmark card.

I want to take care of her, and because of that, I will accept a hell of a lot—there's simply no other choice.

With a silent curse, I join the girls at the table.

"Sorry," I mutter. It's the best I can do. "Let's get to the questions, okay?"

Madi nods, but the lines between her eyebrows are more prominent than they were when she first sat down.

Clover is the only one smiling, which makes me wonder how much she already knew about Savvy. It's the quiet observers who cause the most trouble sometimes.

Savvy sits in silence, eating—slowly, but eating.

"Yeah," Madi agrees. "We'll do rapid-style questions, Savvy. Just give the first answer that pops into your mind."

Savvy nods, and I pull my MacBook closer.

"Crowded or intimate?" Madi asks.

"Intimate." There's no hesitation in Savvy's reply. It has me leaning in closer, craving this vulnerability, the unfiltered version of her.

"Night or day?"

"Night."

"Dinner or coffee?"

Savvy's gaze lands on mine—a missile hitting its target. "Dinner."

"Fancy or casual?"

"Casual."

Madi's smile widens. "Beach or mountain?"

"Beach."

"Indoor or outdoor?"

"Outdoor."

"Sailboat or rollercoaster?"

Savvy taps her chin with her pointer finger. "Sailboat."

"Hot or cold?"

"Hot."

The sound of my fingers hitting keys fills the silence until I finish typing Savvy's final response.

"Okay, Grey. Your turn. Close your eyes," Clover says.

I scowl at her for three long seconds, then begrudgingly follow her command.

"Picture yourself and Savvy together."

That's easy. Every damn time I close my eyes, visions of her rise like smoke.

"Now," Madi says. "Build the perfect date in your mind and tell us what it looks like."

Salt air.

Ocean breezes.

Private chef.

"The perfect date would be at a small private bungalow on the beach." My voice is low, hesitant. It's a weakness I force out with a cough. "The ocean would be calm and crystal clear, with a slight breeze that sways the empty hammock."

The muscles in my neck release the vicious hold they always have on me as I fall deeper into the fantasy. It's so real, I can almost taste the salt air on my lips.

"We'd have a private chef make us dinner. Lobster thermidor for Sav, surf and turf for me. He's serving us at a table for two right on the beach that has sheer netting to keep any bugs away from Savvy—mosquitoes especially like her."

My lips split into a smile. "We're sitting on a raised platform, and all around us is decorated with those stupid twinkly lights and flameless candles so the breeze doesn't extinguish them, but we aren't across from each other. We're side by side so I can hold her hand as we stare out at the ocean. She's on my right because she can't eat with her left hand, but I make do."

Somehow, I conjure the sound of a pop and woosh in my mind—muscle memory kicks in, and it's as though the bubbles are bursting on my tongue. "Our waiter opens the champagne and offers Savvy the first taste. It's a very pale shade of pink because she prefers the slight sweetness of it. It's...peaceful."

I tilt my head down as my mind spins the tale in a dirty direction, and I pop my eyes open before it can get out of hand. The last thing I need is to sprout a boner with Savvy's best friends in view.

Across the table, Madi's eyes are wide and glassy. Clover's chewing on her bottom lip, and when I drag my gaze to Savvy, she's pale and trembling.

"Shit." I snap my attention back to Madi. Seeing Savvy this way cuts deeply. It's a knife to the gut that just keeps twisting and turning. "What did I do wrong? What did I say?"

Madi covers her mouth with a shaky hand. "Nothing. You didn't say anything wrong."

My neck cracks as I spin and turn from one face to the next. "Then why are you all staring at me as if I just kicked a goddamn puppy?"

Savvy's chair screeches beside me, and she stands before I can stop her. "Sorry," she mumbles. "Just...excuse me for a second."

The short red skirt she's wearing flows behind her as she rushes from the room.

"What just happened?" I press a fist into my lower belly, hoping the pressure will stop the bleed.

"Well, Greyson Reyes." Clover's voice is more confident

than I've ever heard her. "What happened is that you just described Savvy's perfect date, right down to the 'pale-pink champagne' and hammock."

"What?" I frown as a headache grows behind my eyes.

"We've known Savvy a long time," Madi says. "We've done a lot of dreaming together over the years. Right down to our perfect dates, perfect first kisses, and our perfect happily ever afters. You, my friend, just described her fairy tale."

My ribs fall into the back of the chair, jump-kicking my lungs into action as though they forgot their only purpose was to pump oxygen to my limbs.

"You know her, Grey." Clover's smile is kind and genuine. It makes me hate whatever happened in her past to make her feel as though she has to guard every piece of herself even more than I already did.

"I agree," Madi says with a small frown. When she looks at me, I find guilt swimming in her irises. "You might know her better than anyone."

"I want to," I say. I want to be the man she deserves, and I'm beginning to realize that Moose was right. I can't do this on my own. "Will you help me?" My focus shifts to the door Savvy walked through—away from me.

Asking for help isn't easy for me. I don't even remember the last time I did it, but then again, I don't remember a time when anything felt as important to my future as Savvy Monroe does.

"Yes," Clover says.

"What do you need?" Madi is more cautious, but I don't blame her.

"You said you know all her perfect firsts? Dates, kisses, happily ever after? Tell me how to make them all come true."

"Mr. Fix-It has a Prince Charming complex too. Who would've thunk it?" Slowly, a smile spreads on Madi's face.

"Not me, that's for damn sure." I can't tear my attention away from the door. "But here I am, at your mercy to get the girl."

CHAPTER THIRTY-ONE

SAVVY

"Can you believe she has both of them fighting over her? Her, of all people. She's not even that pretty, and she's damn sure not special."

Why are public restrooms breeding grounds for mean girl shit? Someday women will learn to eradicate this nasty cliché.

Flushing the toilet, I step out of the stall and come face-to-face with Bethany and her crony, Amelie.

Amelie immediately stares at the floor and fidgets with the strap of her purse. "So, um. I'll see y'all around." She spins and nearly sprints out of the restroom of Blissful Beans & Leaves.

I just wanted a freaking coffee. Is that too much to ask for?

Without saying a word, I cross the small space to wash my hands while Bethany glares at me. Today she's wearing a Gucci shift dress from last summer's collection. One thing growing up as the poor girl surrounded by unimaginable wealth taught me was how to spot a deal so I could fit in. This dress has giant G's interconnecting across the cornflower-blue fabric, and I've seen this particular style on resale threads for almost six months.

"What do they even see in you?" She spits. Actually spits. Spittle flies from her lips, and her eyes are crazed. She reminds me of a less macabre version of a zombie…maybe a vampire…some kind of monster anyway.

I sigh obnoxiously loudly. "You'll have to be more specific, Bethany. I know a lot of people."

"Slut." Her scoff reeks of jealousy.

Waving my hand in front of the machine, I wait patiently for the paper towel to dispense, then do it again before ripping it off and turning to face her.

"I'm a lot of things, Bethy, but a slut is not one of them. I'm also a girl's girl. That means I put women before men, always." She stares blankly at me. "Let me rephrase that more clearly—I support women. I would never tear someone down because their beliefs don't align with my own. That, apparently, is one of our many differences. Now, is there anything else you'd like to hurl my way, or are you done? I'm sure Riley's waiting for you to do his dirty work somewhere, so I wouldn't want to keep you from your underhanded bullshit." I plaster on a saccharine smile that only irritates her more.

"Riley who?" Her left eye twitches.

"Don't ever play poker, Bethany. You can't lie for shit."

"What do they see in you?" Her whine is nearing desperation.

"So you're not denying that you're on Riley's payroll?"

She crosses her arms to hide the tremor in her hands. "I don't know what you're talking about."

"Again with the lies." Another well-timed dramatic sigh from me has her scratching her neck as though she's having trouble breathing. "Fine, Bethany. Here's how I know you're lying. That dress you're wearing cost $3,700 when it released. Now, you can get it on resale for, I don't know, maybe $1,000? You work at the local preschool. You can't afford a $1,000 dress on your salary. But you know who would pay good money for information on your neighbor? Riley."

"You're delusional."

"Am I?" I cross the restroom as if I own it and toss my paper towel into the trash can. Fake it till you make it and all. I open the door and press my foot against the bottom, holding it open. "I wonder what our town would think if I told them my suspicions. I mean, you do remember what happened with Madi's ex, right? How the good people of Happiness took to having a traitor in their midst?"

"You have no proof."

"In the court of public opinion, the only thing you need is doubt. And I'm not the only one who has noticed your new wardrobe, Bethy."

"Are you threatening me?"

"That's funny." I laugh. "Considering you're taking bribes from a convicted criminal who's only back in town to hurt me, how could I possibly be threatening you?"

"What do you mean, hurt you?" She truly has no idea who she's working with. "He doesn't want to hurt you—he's in love with you. They're both in love with you. Why? Why you?" She's so loud, she's drawing attention in the coffee shop. Madi's caught on to my current situation and is headed toward us.

"Riley is not in love with me, Bethany."

"He is. He told me he is." She slaps a hand over her mouth the second the words hit the air.

Of course he did.

"He's a pathological liar. Would someone who loves me

come here and open old wounds about my brother? A brother I looked up to my entire childhood. A brother who chose everyone else in the world but me. No, Bethany. He came here to hurt me. To make me pay for his crimes because he's a narcissist who didn't get his way. And you played right into his hands. Every comment, every line you fed him, he'll use to hurt me."

Madi pushes past me and attempts to stand guard, but I'm a foot taller than she is, and I can still see Bethany over her head.

"Are you proud of yourself, Bethany?" Madi is a wildfire, waiting for a spark.

"No. That's not— He said—"

"What?" I ask. "Did he tell you if you help him get me back, he'll pave the way to Greyson for you?"

She pales, and I know it's the truth.

"Say that isn't true, Bethany." There's a pleading tone to Madi's words. She doesn't want to believe what's right in front of us.

Honestly, I don't either. Deep down, I know Bethany isn't a villain—she's lonely, and loneliness can make even the kindest soul do despicable things.

Isn't that why I was with Riley in the first place? Soul-crushing loneliness.

"Are you freaking kidding me? Bethany, what the heck?" Madi's pregnancy hormones hang onto a fuse these days, and she's about to light the place up.

Pressing a hand to her shoulder, I gently pull her to my side.

"He said he loved you." There's a hollowness to Bethany's tone and an expression that calls to the broken pieces of me. As she stares from me to Madi, another piece of her breaks before our eyes.

"He's a master manipulator," I tell her gently, allowing the door to slowly swing shut. "I've lived it, I know how convincing he can be. But I promise you, it isn't love he feels when he looks at me, it's pure hatred. He doesn't want to take accountability for his actions when I was a teenager, and that means he has to place the blame on someone else. I'm the easy target. I always was."

"I just... I thought... Grey and I had such great conversations during the Cozy Cup, a...connection. I just..."

Oh, Bethany. I get it. I really, really do.

"You just thought what?" Madi's face is bright red—a newfound mean streak flaring to life. Mama bear instincts must grow with pregnancy too. "That he was going to fall head over heels for you because you talked about the stinking weather?"

"Madi..." I infuse as much warning as I can, but she's on a roll.

"Newsflash, Bethany. Grey has never loved anyone but his family. He's never allowed himself to. He was never going to fall for you simply because he wouldn't allow it. Savvy took him by surprise. She challenged him. Forced him to open up. Made him feel. She's the only one who could've gotten to him because they're endgame. They're meant to be together, so you slithering in and attempting to break them up says so much more about your crappy morals than it would ever say about them. I gave you the benefit of doubt after you tried to bid on Braxton, but this? Actively working against happiness is a step too far. I can't even look at you."

My best friend stomps out of the restroom. Two seconds later, she reopens the door. "Savvy. Let's go." She's still figuring out how to control her protective instincts while her personality screams scared-first-time teacher on the first day of school, and it all comes from a place of pure, unfiltered love.

As bad as I feel for Bethany, she made a decision, and now she'll have to live with the consequences of her actions.

"There is always a way to right a wrong, Bethany. Admitting you're wrong and trying to change shows more about your character than an old Gucci dress ever will."

Tears fill her eyes, but I leave her and her decisions in the bathroom that smells like disinfectant.

"Can you believe the nerve on that girl?" Madi is fired up and ready for a fight. Maybe she's having a boy—all that extra testosterone would account for her feistiness lately.

All I feel is overwhelming sadness because this is what Riley does—he infiltrates happiness and infects it with his poison. You hit rock bottom before you ever feel his bite.

"It's not all her fault, Madi. Riley is a snake dressed up like the Easter Bunny. I don't believe she intended to hurt anyone."

"You're a better woman than I am," she grumbles. Her eyes narrow as she glares over my shoulder, and I know Bethany just exited the restroom.

"Leave her alone, Mads. I know what it's like to be in her shoes."

"You're nothing like her."

"Maybe not now. But when I was a kid? I was so desperate for love, I was willing to go against every red flag my intuition threw at me. Riley has a way of making you feel safe, loved, and heard. Then he uses it against you the first time you step out of line."

"So you're just going to let her get away with it?"

I catch sight of Bethany's slumped shoulders as she weaves her way out of Blissy's. "Sometimes the greatest punishment is our own conscience."

Madi grumbles unintelligibly, so I step in line to order. "Where's Brax?" We need a change of subject, and Madi can talk about her husband for hours.

"He and Grey are setting up a Discreet Daily Deeds booth at the fairgrounds. They're going to let everyone submit some wishes, and they'll grant as many as they can."

Freaking Braxton could not be a nicer guy. The man spends millions of dollars every year doling out anonymous good deeds.

"That's really nice of him," I say.

"Them. It's really nice of them." She smiles, and it's her mischievous one that reminds me of her grandfather. "They're also working on recipes for the bake-off and the chili for charity events, while campaigning for most eligible bachelor votes."

Good Lord. "Being named the elusive billionaire in the national news wasn't enough for Grey?"

"Not when you're on the line, it's not. Sav, do you know that while he's campaigning, he's also asking everyone in town for their favorite memories with you? The guy is cramming like this is a final exam for a class he never attended. He's all in."

"He's just a sore loser. He'd—"

"If you're about to say he'd be this way no matter who the sweetheart was, I'm going to stop you right there because I know Grey well enough to know that he wouldn't be anywhere near this event if it weren't for you. The guy lives for work, and yet he's spent all week learning the story of Savvy Monroe."

"He—"

"Loves you."

"You really need to stop interrupting me. That new habit of yours is really annoying."

The line moves forward, and I greet Blissy with a hug before ordering a coffee and one of her specialty tea bags to go for later.

When I first moved to Happiness, I thought the town-wide battle of coffee versus tea was a myth. After living here for ten years, I've yet to pick a definitive side because I'm not looking to make any enemies and someone is always watching.

I don't need to give anyone ammunition to use against me come January's festival.

"Did you hear me?" Madi asks, touching my arm.

No, I was lost in thought about a stupid feud that keeps the town running through the coldest months of the year.

It's one of the many reasons that it was so easy for Happiness to feel like home to me—we simply accept everyone's quirks here. In fact, it's what endears the residents of Happiness to each other.

We're a family.

One that will kill me to lose if it comes to that.

Madi's nails dig into my arm, cutting little crescent shapes into my skin and dragging me from the conflicts in my mind.

The atmosphere in Blissy's has changed, making me shiver.

I glance over my shoulder, and ice spreads through my veins.

Riley has entered the café with a calculating smile and cold, dead eyes trained on me.

The buzz that typically fills the space is eerily quiet, but the only one unaffected by it is Riley.

Since Betty learned she'd accidentally given the wrong person too much information about me at the diner, everyone's been on high alert around strangers, and the tension rolling off my neighbors makes the air too thick to breathe.

All eyes follow him as he walks straight toward Madi and me.

His hands land on my upper arms, and he pulls me in for an air-kiss to both cheeks. I'm too stunned to move, plus, Madi is still breaking skin on my forearm.

"So good to see you, Sav. Can I get you a coffee?" he asks, projecting his voice for all to hear.

"Already taken care of," Blissy shouts like a curse. "Her fiancé ran a tab for all her needs."

Riley's eye twitches, much like Bethany's had earlier, and his hands grip my biceps hard enough to make me flinch. "Isn't. That. Nice."

I shrug out of his hold, and after another painful squeeze, he releases me.

"We have a lot of history, Sav. I don't want to just throw that all away. Not when we have so much..." He flashes the room a predatory smile I think is meant to put people at ease but has the exact opposite effect. "...to look forward to. I mean, your brother is getting married. It practically makes us family again. You know how close my mom and Paige's mom are. They'd do...*anything* for their children."

It's a thinly veiled threat that hits me hard, but I don't show any outward emotion at all.

"I wish my brother and Paige a lifetime of happiness," I say in a flat tone. "But they chose not to have me in their lives, and I will honor that request. You and I have nothing to discuss."

He lashes out quickly—a lightning strike with no warning. His hands wrap around my biceps again as he steps into my space, lowering his mouth to my ear. It snaps Madi out of her daze, and she attempts to wedge herself between us, but Riley's hold on me is too strong.

"This is your only warning, Sin. Don't fuck with me. Give me what I want, or I will destroy this embarrassment of a town. Then I'll follow you from place to place, ruining everything you touch until the day you die."

It all happens in less than fifteen seconds, but it's all it takes to get my Happiness family moving. Moose appears on my left while Blissy rounds the counter, holding a broom like a baseball bat.

"Touch her again, and I'll break every finger in your dirty paws. Ya hear me, kid?" Moose towers over Riley's weathered six-foot frame.

Riley glares up at Moose, but his stupidity outweighs common sense, and he doesn't release my arms. Instead, he squeezes harder while glaring at Moose.

"Are you threatening me, you big ogre?" Riley never did learn to think before he spoke.

"Nah, kid. That's a promise."

"You're threatening me in a room full of witnesses. Is there a brain in that giant body of yours, or are you as stupid as you are big?"

Moose laughs. It's not his normal laugh either. This sound is terrifying and has Madi taking a step back.

"Anyone hear a threat?" Moose asks the room.

"Yup." Chief stands up, flashing a badge he should no longer have. "Heard this out-of-towner threatening our new sweetheart. Heard him threaten Madi too. Pops won't like that one bit. Also heard him threaten the whole dang town of Happiness. Sounds like a terrorist to me."

Riley instantly loses his swagger as panic swims in his wild eyes. He's on probation. Making threats would certainly send him right back to prison. His hands squeeze me so tightly I can no longer fight the wince when my skin pinches between his fingers.

"That's not even close to what happened," Riley seethes, wrenching me to his side as though he forgot he was still holding onto me. "What the hell's going on here?"

"Let her go." Moose glares at the point of contact on my arms as though he has X-ray vision.

"I heard him make threats against the town and others like it," Blissy says, ready to take a swing at Riley the first chance she gets.

"Same here." Marty from the hardware store steps forward, followed by Betty from the diner.

"Would you like to file an official complaint?" Chief asks with his thumbs tucked into his front pockets.

"If you don't, I will," Moose says calmly.

My gaze snaps up to the gentle giant who's been Grey's sounding board for months now.

"We protect our own, Savvy." Gone is the menacing tone he used with Riley, and in its place is a grandfather full of love and compassion. "This guy threatened not only you but everyone here. We won't let that slide."

My lip begins to sweat as the seriousness of the situation weighs on me.

If I speak to the police, the real police, not Chief, there's a very good chance that Riley will be sent back to prison. But if I do that, the DeVanes will most certainly come after me.

Madi holds up her phone and snaps some photos of Riley grasping my arms. It sets him into a spiral, and just when I think he's going to lunge for her, I twist my shoulder, causing his fingers to dig deeper into my skin, but I'm able to face him head-on.

"Already got the whole thing recorded, Madi. No

worries." It sounds like Betty, but I don't dare look away from Riley to confirm.

"You won't get away with this." He whispers low and deadly, but it lands as intended.

"Neither will you." I wiggle my left arm, but he doesn't release me. "I'm not the same little girl you could bend to your will, Riley. You killed that girl the day you stole Paige's freedom. And the difference is, now I have an army to stand at my back. All you have is..." I lower my voice. I'm not sure why I want to protect Bethany, but I do. "A woman you manipulated and hurt simply because you could."

"My family. Paige's fucking family," he rants.

My torso jerks with his angry flailing, and Moose growls beside me, but I plead to him with my eyes to stand down. So long as no one intervenes, he'll only hurt me.

"Yes. You have them," I concede through the pain radiating up my arm, wondering if it's possible to break a bone by simply squeezing it. "I also suspect you truly do have my brother too. That's a loss I'll feel until my dying day, but all losses heal with time. And I have the Reyes family on my side now. I have Happiness on my side. But most importantly, I have myself." I step forward, forcing him back a step, and he finally drops my aching arm.

"And I'm stronger than you've ever given me credit for. I'm smart, and I'm powerful. You, Riley, will always be a scared little boy begging for mommy's approval. So go home. Go home and make mommy happy because you will not get what you came for here. You'll never get me."

I back him up another step, then another, as a sense of strength rushes through my system. He appears to be caught off guard by my words and my actions. It fuels the confidence that I've desperately needed.

We make it to the front door, and he finally digs in his

heels. "Remember, Savannah. There's more than one way to ruin your life. And I'm going to exhaust every single one of them."

I toss my arms into the air. Nothing I say even puts a dent in his giant ego, and I've hit my breaking point. He will come after me. He will make good on his threats. But I don't have to willingly lie at his feet. "Bring it on, you big crybaby. Bring. It. On. I'm not scared of you anymore. There's nothing you can do to me that I haven't already done to myself. So go ahead, you goddamn bag of shit. We'll see who lands behind bars first. But I guarantee I won't be the one in the orange jumpsuit."

I poke him hard in the chest. It shocks him, and I feel another odd sense of empowerment. He's always been stronger than me, but this time, I'll fight back with every-thing I have.

"You just made the biggest mistake of your life," he hisses.

"Ha." I pause, opting for dramatics. "Oh, you're serious?" He hates being mocked, so I do it intentionally. "Sorry to burst your tiny-brain bubble, but I already made that mistake the day I agreed to go out with you when I was a teenager."

His eyes fall flat, the rage rippling off him like heat on the asphalt, but I don't back down now—I can't. I have to protect the family that found me, took me in, and showed me what love should look like, even if all it does is take the target off their back and doubles the size of my own.

"And by the way." I fill my lungs as though it's liquid courage and push on. "The age of consent may be sixteen in the state of Nevada, but that pesky little court of public opinion that matters so much to mommy dearest would probably have a different opinion, considering when I was sixteen, you were twenty-two. And I kept receipts, Riley."

I lower my voice—quieter, more lethal, a dangerous whisper. "I have every message you ever sent me, and I have no problem asking my fiancé to blast those messages on every channel that Omni-Reyes owns."

"In case you don't know," Madi says, attaching herself to my side. "Omni-Reyes is the largest media conglomerate in the United States. Hell, I might have my husband blast that crap everywhere just because you're a disgusting predator."

Riley's breaths come in short, desperate pants as though he's drowning on dry land. "You have no idea what kind of war you're starting here, Sin. But I promise you, it's one the DeVane's are ready and willing to win."

I shoo him away because he'll hate being dismissed.

"I have no doubt you believe your lies, Riley." My insides quiver as the bravado I'm wielding attempts to give out. "It's what makes your manipulation so hard to decipher. But your web of narcissism has been lifted, and never again will I bow to your demands. Get the hell out of here before I let Blissy take a swing."

He glances over my shoulder, and whatever Blissy does has him blanching before he scurries out of the shop like the rodent he is.

His tantrum can be heard for half a block, and the second his voice fades, I crumple into a nearby chair as the adrenaline wears off, and I begin to convulse with withdrawal-like strength.

What the hell have I done?

CHAPTER THIRTY-TWO

GREYSON

"Have you ever made chili before?" Sage asks. He and his friend Ethan are painting the back wall of our Discreet Daily Deeds booth in a calming green color while I scour recipes, pulling out what I like to create my own.

"I have two days to perfect it," I say.

"Not to...cast doubt," Ethan says. He's the only one of us who actually grew up in Happiness, so his intel is key. "But in the South, we start making chili with our dads as soon as we're old enough to stir a pot. Same with grilling and making secret rubs."

"What the hell is a secret rub?" Braxton asks.

"It's usually a blend of spices, maybe some brown sugar, that you mix together and then rub all over whatever meat you're cooking." Ethan is older than Sage, but the two of them instantly bonded over football.

"Hmm." A secret rub. I could work with that. "Interesting."

"What about the bake-off? Do you honestly think you can win every event?" Sage asks.

"You doubt me? I'm crushed."

"Well, Uncle, this isn't a boardroom. If we were acquiring a new company, I know you could do it. But here you are, at the fairgrounds, wearing a $10,000 suit in 100-degree heat while quizzing everyone around you about their likes and dislikes and grilling them for every Savvy-related detail they're willing to share."

"Your point is?"

"My point is, this is out of character. Have you even slept?"

"I think what Sage is trying to say..." Braxton finishes screwing in the latch on the treasure chest he built to store everyone's wishes. "Is that we're concerned."

"About you and Savvy," Sage says.

Her name has a direct line to my heart, and it races as my mind conjures all the ways she could be in trouble. "Savvy? Why are you worried about Savvy?"

Sage and Braxton share an uneasy expression while Ethan ducks out behind the booth.

"You're fixated, Grey," Brax says. "We just... We know you're seeing similarities between Violet and Savvy. We just want to make sure that..."

"That what?" Sweat trickles down my spine, and my jaw tightens with tension.

"We just want to make sure you're in this for the right reasons." Sage is choosing his words carefully, and it makes me uneasy. The three of us don't censor ourselves around each other. Ever. "I know you've always carried guilt over my mom's death." His words butterfly my chest open, and the knife lodges painfully in a rib. "We just want to be sure that you aren't projecting those feelings of guilt onto Savvy because if that's the basis for your relationship with her, she'll end up hurt again."

"Grey." Braxton gentles his tone, but I can't look at him.

I'm angry and confused. If I face him, he'll feel the wrath of my confusion.

"We're not saying that's the case, but if roles were reversed, you'd point it out. That's all we're doing. It's just a conversation."

I know it's the truth. I was a dick when Braxton got engaged, but I was being selfish. They're coming at this from a place of love, I know they are.

"Maybe at first," I admit. "Fixing things has been my coping mechanism since I was twelve years old, and Savvy, well, she needs me even if she won't admit it."

"You can't fix her, Uncle Grey—only Savvy can do that."

Braxton's phone rings. He glances at it, then sends the caller to voicemail.

"I know. And somewhere along the way, I went from wanting to fix her... No, that's a lie." I drag my hand through my hair and collect my thoughts. "I still want to fix her, but how I go about it has changed. I don't want to change her. I don't want to make her do things she's not ready for. I just want to be there for her, by her side, holding her hand while she figures things out. We work. Together, we work."

"I think you do too," Braxton says.

"You want to be her partner." Sage's eyes glisten with emotion. He used to wear eyeliner to hide from people, but he stopped that shortly after moving to Happiness, where everyone accepted him just as he is—a sensitive genius who happens to be a gifted kicker on a football team.

Could they accept all of me too?

"I do," I say. "I want her to be mine. Not like Riley wants her—I don't want to own her, but because she wants to be mine and she wants me to be hers."

Braxton's phone rings again, and he frowns. "Hold on, it's Madi again. Let me just make sure everything's okay." He steps to the side of the booth while Sage and I watch on. "Hello? Wait, Madi. Slow down. What happened?"

I step around the booth and study Braxton's face. His expression contorts, and I turn to stone.

Something's wrong.

"When? What did he say?" Braxton looks to me, and I feel it in my bones—something happened to Savvy. "We'll be right there. Did someone call the police? Not Chief, but the station."

My mind summons all the ways Savvy could be hurt, and I'm blinded by guilt so powerful, my vision blurs.

Why didn't I insist the Harringtons come immediately?

Sage pats my back. "Breathe, Uncle."

His words act as a defibrillator, and I greedily inhale but force myself to release the breath slowly.

This is my fault. I should have stayed with her. My fault.

"She's okay," Brax says. "But Riley threatened her at Blissy's, and she..."

"She what?" I don't recognize the sound of my own voice.

"She has some bruising on her upper arms."

"He put his hands on her?" Each word comes out louder and harsher than the one before as I follow Braxton to the parking lot. "What happened? How did it happen?"

"Madi was pretty upset. I don't have all the details, but Moose is there with her, and Chief Rigsby is on his way to Blissy's now."

We reach the car, and Sage holds out his hand at the driver's side door. "You're too upset to drive. Let me."

I toss them to him because if I don't, we'll waste precious time fighting over it. I slip into the back seat to give myself time to clear my head. I love my brother and my nephew, but right now, the only thought in my head is that I didn't protect Savvy—again.

Ten minutes later, Sage double-parks in front of Blissy's. I jump out, but my mind is no clearer. There's only one thing driving me forward, and it's an overwhelming urgency to see Savvy.

The bell above the door rings loudly as I enter. I scan left to right until I land on Savvy, sitting in the corner, facing the door, with Chief Rigsby sitting in front of her, while Madi and Moose flank her on either side.

Moose has his hand on her shoulder in a protective, fatherly gesture I appreciate more than I ever could have imagined.

This is why Braxton and Sage love this town so much. Even when they're not around, they know there are people who will protect those they love in their absence.

We've never had anything like that before.

Savvy lifts her head, and our gazes lock, solidify, band us to one stream of consciousness, and my chest nearly explodes.

She isn't a replacement for the loss of my sister. She isn't a new outlet for my grief. She isn't a vessel to carry my child.

She's the piece of me that's been missing—the faith to my skepticism, the light to my dark, the matter that fills the void of me.

Simply put, she's the best parts of myself I forgot existed, and when she stood before me as my own personal reflection, I fought her every day because I was scared of what I had blocked out. That stops now.

Moose nods, then slips back to allow me access to my girl. In my periphery, Sage and Braxton surround Madi. The three of them sit silently, allowing me to stand guard over my future—Savannah Monroe.

"Are you okay?" I scan every inch of her face, her neck, shoulders, belly, all the way to her toes, then repeat the process in reverse.

"I'm fine, Grey." Her voice wavers. She's putting on a brave face for everyone around her.

"Savvy, we'll need to take pictures of the bruising," Chief Rigsby says. "Would you like to do that here, or somewhere more private?"

I glance around the space, seeing it for the first time since I entered to find it nearly empty.

"Blissy sent everyone home," Moose says behind me. Regardless of blood, this man is family.

"Here's fine." Savvy only focuses on my face, as if she's pulling strength from my proximity, and it fucks me up seven ways to Sunday, but I will stay strong for her.

She's staring at me as though she's pleading with me for something, but I can't interpret what she needs, so I gently take her left hand in mine, squeezing it lightly, hoping it gives her whatever she's searching for.

As her palm slips into mine, I feel her nervous energy flowing into my veins. I keep my breathing even, calm, relaxed, and eventually she mimics my cadence.

With her right hand, she slowly lifts the sleeve of her T-shirt over her shoulder. I don't want to look, but I need to see what he's done to her.

Another squeeze to her hand. Another shot of confidence I don't feel. Another subliminal message that I'm here for her.

Then I look lower and fight back a gag.

Deep-purple fingerprints have already formed on her thin arms. That fucker squeezed so hard that welts have formed where his fingers pressed her skin between them.

"Grey?" She's close to breaking. I hear it in the way she says my name—unsure, scared, and too timid.

I glare at the marks on her arm, blink as though my lashes are the shutter of a camera, and burn this image into my mind for eternity, then vow that it will never happen again.

Another slow blink of my damp lashes, and I wrangle my self-control into submission, then lift my gaze to her haunted one.

"This will never happen again," I whisper.

She nods, and a single tear lands in the crease of her eye. Using my free hand, I wipe it away before it has the chance to fall.

"Don't cry, baby. He isn't worth your tears."

"Th—they're not for him."

I frown but actively work at keeping my body language open and loose for her. "I'll always carry your pain, Sav. I'll dry your tears and kiss them away."

"They're not for me either." Another one rolls down her cheek, and I catch it with a gentle kiss.

"Then why are you crying?" My voice cracks, and I realize that seeing her in pain is more than I can bear.

"For you."

I jolt backward. "For me? I'm not the one hurt, sweetheart. Don't ever cry for me."

"Okay, Savvy. Can you show me the other side?" Chief Rigsby asks.

She nods but doesn't look away from me as she releases my hand to lift her other sleeve.

This time I don't look. I've seen enough, and I'll remember it for the rest of my life.

Another tear. Another stabbing pain through my heart.

"Don't cry. Please, Sav."

"You don't understand."

Chief Rigsby's camera flashes.

"Then explain, and I'll fix whatever's causing them."

She smiles. It's wobbly and full of overwhelming emotion. "It's just that I...I realized something."

"What's that?"

She lowers her shirtsleeve when Rigsby sits back in front of us, and I immediately take her hand in mine again.

"You love me. Despite our history, regardless of my past, in spite of the chaos I bring to your life. You love me."

My lungs expel all the trapped air in a loud whoosh that blows her hair around her face. "Finally. I've been telling you that for weeks now. I'm glad you're finally listening."

"Savvy," Chief Rigsby interrupts. Again. "Are there any more marks we should photograph?"

My stomach drops into my feet.

"No."

Thank God. If there were, I'd end up in jail for murdering the piece of shit.

"Okay," he says. "Well, the good news is that I ran Riley's name on the way over. He's missed a check-in with his parole officer, so there's a warrant out for his arrest already."

"What?" All the practiced calm I've been faking for Savvy's sake goes up in flames.

"It appears that no one knew he left Vegas or where he went," Chief Rigsby says. "I've alerted his parole officer of his whereabouts, and we've called in a local bounty hunter. But the bad news is now he'll know we're looking for him. When suspects are backed into a corner, they can become more dangerous." He says this last part to me, but I've already read between the lines.

"You think he's going to attack Savvy again."

Chief Rigsby is the youngest chief of police Happiness

has ever had, but he's proven himself time and time again to be reliable and trustworthy. He's a helper, and he takes care of his residents.

He drags a hand through his hair. "I do. I'm bringing in some help from Wayfair County since I'm working with a skeleton crew due to the hurricane. We'll do everything we can to keep you safe."

"I have the Harringtons coming in a few days," I say, but he stares at me blankly. "They own Harrington Bank and Trust as well as one of the best security companies in the world. I'll call and see if they can come sooner. I want Savvy protected at all costs."

I screwed up by not demanding their attention immediately.

"Grey." Savvy squeezes my hand, and I hold hers firm because this is not a negotiation.

"I've heard of them." The way Rigsby says it makes me believe he knows of their uncle, but the brothers are nothing like that piece of shit.

I've done my research, contacted colleagues, and most importantly, they've proved themselves to me with the information they've shared freely since the golf tournament.

"Having more eyes on her is probably a good idea," he finally concedes.

"I'm right here," Savvy says, finding some of the sass she's known for.

"We know," I say. "But please, for me, don't fight me on this. If Riley is out here with a vendetta and forgoing the stipulations of release, it means he's detached from reality. He isn't thinking about the consequences of his actions. I need all the help I can get to keep you safe until he's back behind bars."

The bell over the door jingles again, and we all look up

to see an ashen-faced Bethany. Jesus Christ. At least she isn't dressed like bargain-bin Barbie today. The cutoff shorts and red Coca-Cola T-shirt feel more authentic.

"What is she doing here?" Madi growls, surprising me.

I glance around the room and know I've missed something important because Bethany is obviously enemy number two right now.

"Sorry, Bethany," Blissy says, stepping forward. "We're closed for the afternoon."

"I—I know." She stares at Savvy. "Is it true? Did he hurt you?"

"You need to leave," Blissy tries again.

"Is it true?" Bethany asks again, her voice breaking in multiple places.

Beside me, Savvy lifts the sleeve of her T-shirt to show the bruising.

"Oh, God." Bethany's hand flies to her mouth as she shakes her head. "I—I didn't know. Savvy, I didn't know. I'm so sorry."

I'm out of my chair as though her words have electrocuted me. "What are you talking about?"

Savvy reaches for my hand. The moment her skin touches mine, the panic stops boiling over.

"Thank you, Bethany," she says. "I'm glad that you believe me, but your words don't hold a lot of weight right now. I hope, for your sake, you can make some changes."

What the hell is she talking about?

Bethany sniffles. "That's why I'm here. I honestly didn't know. Riley told me he loved you, and I believed him."

"Get. Out," I growl.

Savvy tugs on my hand, and reluctantly, I take a seat at her side.

Bethany has gone from ashen to ghostly white. I'm surprised she's still standing.

"That's...that's why I'm here. I don't have much to tell you. Riley never, like, confided in me or anything."

"Un-fucking-believable." I didn't think my jaw could get any tighter, but this witch just proved me wrong.

"What is it, Bethany?" Savvy asks quietly.

Why the hell is Monroe being so nice to this woman?

Bethany wrings her hands together and shifts her weight from foot to foot. Her face is free of makeup, and paired with her casual clothing, it's a stark contrast to the last few times I've seen her.

"Well, I don't know who it is, but Riley did mention once that he had a 'pulse' at Omni-Reyes. I never understood what that meant, even when he said it, but I figured it might mean something to you." Her shoulders are curled so far in, her spine is bent forward.

"What was the context?" Braxton asks, his normally friendly demeanor now brusque.

"He—" She glances at Savvy and winces. "He wanted information from me about your relationship. But he said he had a pulse at Omni-Reyes, someone who would always be loyal to him no matter what."

"The mole," Braxton hisses.

"I can't believe you sold Savvy out for a few new dresses. You're more than pathetic—" Madi balls her hands into fists, but it's Savvy who places her palm over them to calm her.

"And you gave him information about us?" Savvy is calm. Too calm.

Bethany nods, and disgruntled noises fill the air all around us.

"What did you say?" If Savvy doesn't show some

emotion soon, I'm going to rip her out of here and take her to the hospital because obviously she's in shock.

"I told him how you seemed to hate each other but couldn't stay away from each other either. How—how Greyson looked at you like you held all his secrets, but you always had a wall up."

I scoff, but Braxton rolls his eyes. "She's right," he says.

"Anything else?" I'm not as kind as Savvy is.

"Just that it didn't make sense. You're always fighting. It's like you had him under a spell I couldn't figure out."

"So, you didn't give him any information that he wouldn't have seen with his own eyes?" Sage asks. Of course he's as nice as Savvy is. My nephew is incapable of being an ass.

"I...I told him that..."

"Told him what?" I roar. My patience is long gone.

She flinches, but I don't feel an ounce of remorse. This woman was actively working against my fiancée, and that's unacceptable.

"I told him that Clover was your weakness, and that you would always drop everything to be by her side, and then the very next day her private information was all over the internet."

I'm across the room, ripping the door open before she even blinks. "Get. Out."

"Greyson." Savvy stands and wobbles on her feet.

Fuck this.

"Bethany, I don't know what you thought coming here would do. It doesn't absolve you. It doesn't make what you did right."

"Grey. Enough, please. This is between Bethany and me. We've talked, she knows she was wrong." Empathy bleeds from Savvy's tone. Luckily, I don't suffer from that same affliction. "She's here because she wants to help. Beating her down now won't do anything but break her beyond repair, and I refuse to do that to anyone. Not when I'm living proof of the damage it can cause."

Just like that, she slams her truth into me like a wrecking ball.

I nod once in acknowledgment of her words.

"Is there anything else you'd like to share, Bethany?" Savvy sounds as though a good strong wind would knock her over.

"No. I'm—" Her broken sob echoes across the room. "I am truly sorry, Savvy. If there's anything I can do—"

"You've done enough," Madi growls, and I mentally high-five my sister-in-law. Braxton married well.

"Thank you for telling us, Bethany." Savvy sinks back into her chair.

I rattle the bell above the door to indicate it's time for Bethany to go.

She takes the hint and leaves without making eye contact with anyone.

Then I cross the room and crouch down in front of Savvy. My palms rest on her thighs as I stare into her weary eyes.

"Rigsby, is there anything else you need from us right now?" I ask.

"No," he says. "Not from Savannah. If the rest of you could come down to the station to give your statements, I'd appreciate it though."

"We'll be there," Moose says.

"Is Savvy free to go?" I ask.

"She is, but—"

"She's staying with me."

"Good," Rigsby says. "I'll come out to check on you both tomorrow."

As soon as he's given the all-clear, I scoop Savvy up in my arms. Sage drops my keys into her lap, and Blissy opens the door. Without another word, I carry her out to the car.

By the time we make it home, she's curled into a ball, leaning on the passenger door, fast asleep.

I've never seen my future so clearly, and for once, it's filled with happiness. It's filled with Savannah Monroe, and I'll burn the world to the ground before I allow some shithead like Riley DeVane to take that from me.

CHAPTER THIRTY-THREE

SAVVY

"I'm not staying cooped up in the house, Grey. I won't give him that kind of control. Happiness has worked hard on the fair, and for whatever reason, they made me a big part of that. There's not a chance in hell I'm going to skip it because Riley *might* do something."

"It's not a question of if, Monroe, it's when. *When* he'll do something. To you." Grey's frustration makes his tone harsh and demanding, but this isn't a corporate office where he's the dictator—it's my life.

"I won't hide from this fight anymore, Patch." I square my shoulders, putting space between us. "I can't do it. I don't want to be the woman who hides from life anymore."

"Is that what you think you've been doing?" He tilts his head as though I'm an exotic zoo animal. "Because that's not what I see. I see a woman who picked herself up when tons of shit fell on her. I see a woman who rebuilt herself bigger and stronger than before. But we're not dealing with a handsy bartender here. We're talking about a potential stalker, someone with nothing left to lose. Someone who will attempt to hurt you—someone who already has."

"And you really think that he'll get through the entire freaking town? Come on, Grey. You're not thinking logically. The opening ceremony is tomorrow. I'll be surrounded by hundreds of people. I'm going. End of story."

"What if the Harringtons say it's too dangerous?" He's so damn stubborn.

"They're on your payroll, so I'm sure they'll say it's too dangerous because that's what you'll tell them to say."

God, I'm tired. We haven't been in the house for more than five minutes, and he's already pushing my buttons.

"If I tell them you're in charge, that you make the final call, do you promise to do what they say?"

After Grey set me down at the kitchen island and made me avocado toast with a fried egg, he pulled his lucky coin from his pocket.

Over and over again, it weaves through his fingers while I think.

"I won't interfere," he says. "If you do everything they say, I won't override your decisions."

"Fine. I'll listen to them, but missing the fair is out of the question."

Horns blare, and before I can explain, Grey has a large kitchen knife in his hand, and he's standing between me and the door.

"Put that away before you hurt someone. Jesus."

He doesn't move. "What the hell is going on?"

I drop the last half of my toast to the plate and stand. "That will be the homecoming court from the high school."

Grey lowers his arm but doesn't release the knife. "Come again?"

Leaning over him, I grab the knife and set it on the counter. "Come on, I'll show you. No need for a knife, Sirius Black."

He frowns at the reference. "I thought Sirius was a bad guy?"

My jaw drops open. "Did you not read the books? Sirius was Harry's godfather. He protected him."

Grey's face breaks out into a beautiful smile.

"What now?" I groan. His carefree, happy smile makes me uneasy.

"At least you acknowledge that I'm trying to protect you."

"You're a mess. Let's go. The kids will be looking for you," I say.

He flinches, and it makes me laugh as I drag him through his home and open the front door.

Cars fill his long, somewhat disfigured driveway as last year's homecoming king and queen walk up the steps arm in arm.

"What the hell is going on?"

"It's a whole thing," I say. "This is their last act as outgoing king and queen. They get to crown you before the sweetheart ceremony."

"The entire town is in on this?"

"Yup."

Cora and Mike stand in front of us, dressed ready for a prom.

"Doesn't the town have any other form of entertainment?" Grey mutters under his breath.

"Just us," I say with a smile. "Hi, Cora. Hi, Mike."

"Hi, Miss Savvy. Mr. Greyson, are you ready and willing to take on the role of most eligible bachelor?" Mike asks.

"I am," Grey says seriously.

"And do you promise to make the fair your top priority?" Cora smiles up at him. Girl, I get it.

"Ah, sure."

"Do you promise to do whatever necessary to ensure

that Miss Savvy feels like a queen this weekend?" Mike was captain of the lacrosse team last year. He's a good kid with a good heart, but he eyes Grey as though he's suspicious of him, and I smile.

This town has my back.

Grey grabs hold of my hand. "Always."

"Do you promise to uphold the traditions and responsibilities that come with this title?" Cora might actually swoon at Grey's feet soon.

"Of course."

I can't believe Grey is taking this all so seriously, especially when these kids are just trying to get this over with so they can get to the good part of their evening.

"Then by the power gifted to me by the royal court of Happiness, I now pronounce you Happiness' most eligible bachelor." Mike places the crown onto Grey's head as all the kids in the driveway pop confetti poppers.

Silly string, paper string, anything that sparkles and shines flies into the air.

"It's like a wedding." Grey chuckles.

"You may kiss your sweetheart." Cora claps her hands and bounces on her toes.

"Hey! That's not part of the ceremony—"

Grey tugs me into his arms, cutting off my words. His lips collide with mine. The kiss is demanding and hard, just like the man himself. It's a promise of all the things Grey agreed to.

The kids on his disaster of a front lawn all laugh and cheer with a few wolf whistles, reminding me that we have an audience.

"Is that the entire ceremony?" Grey asks. His lips ghosting over mine.

"That's it."

He turns to the kids, who are already antsy to get to their after-party. "Thanks, everyone. We'll see you at the fair." Then he scoops me up in his arms and carries me inside to even louder cheers. The entire town will know about this before morning.

Grey doesn't set me down until we've reached his room and the attached bathroom.

"What are you doing?" I ask as he leans over the large tub and turns on the water.

He opens the cabinet beneath the sink and digs around for something. He doesn't answer me until he stands with a bottle of expensive-looking bubble bath in his hands.

"You're tired," he whispers. "But he put his hands on you, Monroe. I want to throw you in the shower and scrub your skin raw to remove his filthy germs from your body, but I don't want to hurt you. So instead, we're going to get in this tub so I can clean you, and then I'll put you to bed."

"Greyson."

"Please." His voice is pitched low, and I realize he needs this. His hands tremble as he tips the bubble bath upside down and squeezes the light pink liquid into the stream of water. The scent of roses floods my nostrils. "Let me take care of you, at least for tonight."

He doesn't look at me, opting instead to watch the bubbles form in the water. "I know you can handle yourself, sweetheart. Hell, if you can handle me, you can handle anything, but I can't get the image of your bruised arms out of my mind. I need to take care of you tonight. I need to feel your body and know that while he marred your skin, he didn't break you."

I'm overcome with emotion. His raw honesty, the guilt he's taking on as though it's his cross to bear, is more than I know what to do with.

"Please, Savvy."

"Okay." It's the only word I can form, and his shoulders relax with my acceptance.

I track his movements as his hands lift my T-shirt over my head, his fingers trailing along the outline of my bra before he removes that too. His eyes flash when he skims over the bruising on my right arm before reaching for the button of my skirt and slowly lowering it down my legs.

He falls to his knees and gently lifts one leg, then the other, and tosses the skirt to the side, but his thumb hovers over my tattoo.

The intimacy of the moment causes my knees to tremble. He sees it—he sees everything—and he holds me steady with both hands.

"Do you want to talk about it?" I ask.

He leans forward and presses a whisper of a kiss over the tattoo. "Ace always knew what he was doing. He cared about you, Savvy. And I've finally gotten my head out of my ass to see why."

"Are you upset? About your coin and my tattoo?" I whisper.

"No." It spills from his lips like a wish. "The purpose of my coin is to ground me. He knew what he was doing grounding me to you."

"He was a good man. I'm grateful I got to know him."

Grey swallows hard. "Me too." He lifts his gaze away from my tattoo and meets my eye. "Do you want to leave your panties on?" I've never heard him this gentle, this... shattered. I honestly didn't know he had it in him.

"Leave them...on? In the bath?"

He's staring intently at my face, studying my reaction, waiting for my consent.

"Yes, Sav. He abused you today. If you're more comfortable leaving your panties on, I support that."

"Riley overpowered me today, Grey, don't get it twisted. He didn't abuse me because I'm not a victim." I slip my fingers into the tiny strings at my hips and push them down my thighs until they pool at my feet.

Grey doesn't break eye contact as he stands. When we're chest to chest, he takes me by the hand and helps me into the hot water. The scent of roses will forever be a direct link to this memory for me—the day he laid all his weapons at my feet and offered me his hand—a symbolic gesture of teamwork. He doesn't release my hand until I'm seated, then he shuts off the faucet and smiles.

"Relax." He could work in a spa using this new tone of his. "I'll be right back."

The walls shrink in around me. "I—I thought you were getting in?" I curl my knees up and wrap my arms around them.

Why is he leaving? Why don't I want to be alone?

I said I wasn't a victim, and I'm not—not anymore. But sometimes vulnerability breeds fragility, and Greyson is the kryptonite to all my protective layers.

"I am, sweetheart. Just give me a moment to collect some things. Lie back and relax. I'll be back in less than five minutes."

Being vulnerable has always made me feel weak in the past, and I've hated every second of it. But somehow, here with Grey, it's not hitting like a weakness. Instead, it heals like a stitch in the fabric of my story, and he's the one holding the needle.

"Okay." My chin falls to my knees, and I inhale the calming scent of the bubbles. His footsteps retreat, and the events of the day all crash into me at once. It's as though he'd been warding off the negative energy, and with some separation, it dares attack.

Focus on breathing, Sav. In for four, hold for four, out for four, repeat.

A pop has me jolting, causing water to slosh around in the tub. "Sorry, sweetheart. Did you fall asleep?"

Shit. Had I?

Concern is written in his furrowed brow as he scans every inch of skin visible to him. "I was only gone a couple of minutes."

"I don't know. Maybe?"

He holds up a bottle of champagne wedged into an ice bucket and a plate of strawberries.

"Is this my *Pretty Woman* moment?"

Grey's laughter wraps around my shoulders with the comfort of the best kind of hug.

"While I'd very much like to see you in nothing but a tie, I was thinking that it might help you relax so you can sleep. The strawberries are simply what I had in the fridge, and I"—he stares at the plate in his hand—"like feeding you."

His admission presses against my most tender pieces.

This isn't like the other times he tried to trick me into eating. Tonight, it's how he's showing his love language—he's caring for me because this is how love makes sense to him.

"You're vexing," I sigh.

"Well, Monroe, I hate to break it to you, but you're the only problem I never want to solve."

"Why?"

He smirks, then sets the champagne, glasses, and the plate of fruit on a tray that he clips over the edges of the tub.

"Because you challenge me. You push me and demand the best of me without ever saying a word. You make me better because I want to be someone you deserve." As he speaks, he quickly undresses.

He's built like a Greek god, all carved muscle and veins that roll and pulse under his skin.

His long legs slip into place on either side of mine, and he leans over to grab a glass and a berry. He hands me the champagne and waits while I take a sip, then another, before he takes it from me and sips the crisp drink himself.

Then, as promised, he feeds me the juiciest strawberry I've ever eaten. I don't know where he gets his groceries from, but these taste unlike anything I've ever had before.

Leaning into my back, he drops the berry stem onto the tray and grabs another. When he reclines into the tub, he pulls me with him. I relax into his chest, and my eyes drift closed.

Cool glass touches my lips, and I open for him. He tips the champagne flute, and the bubbly liquid fills my mouth. I swallow, and he removes it.

His warmth presses into me as he leans forward, but I keep my eyes closed and listen as ice clinks against crystal.

Here, in his arms, I'm safe enough to relax, and I'm finally allowing myself to enjoy it.

The shock of ice against the bruising on my left arm causes me to gasp, and my lashes pop open as I watch him gently trace the injuries.

"I'm sorry," he says so quietly I'm not even positive the words are meant for me. "I underestimated him. He should have never been able to get to you like this."

"What did I say about playing the martyr?"

His chin is pressed to the top of my head as he shakes it left to right.

"Blissy's was full of people, Grey. There were over ten witnesses. Even I had no idea he'd go this far in public."

"I should've anticipated it though." The ice has melted, so he reaches over the edge of the tub and retrieves another piece. Angling my head to the side, I see he's placed the bucket of ice on the shelf beside us, along with the glass we'd shared.

He presses another piece of ice to my right arm, and once again follows the deep, angry marks.

"Can we please not talk about him tonight?" I plead. "I know what he's capable of, Grey. I also know that I won't allow him to win, so for tonight, I just want to pretend that I'm...normal."

Grey kisses the side of my head—a silent acknowledgment of my request, I think.

"Unfortunately, you'll never be normal, Monroe. You can't be." I stiffen in his arms, then lift my legs back up, ready to curl into a ball again. "You can't be normal because you were created for the extraordinary. You were made to stand out, to shine, so never settle for normal. You're too valuable for that."

My insides quiver, like the first crack of thunder before a storm. Emotions are building, ready to strike and cause damage.

No one has ever thought me valuable before—possibly not even myself.

It might be the nicest thing anyone has ever said to me, and I don't know how to release the overwhelming sensations that are boiling my insides.

Strong arms band around my chest, holding me tightly. His fingertips are cold, but his palms are warm.

My hands fall to his forearm, gently stroking his skin beneath my fingers.

"Thank you, Greyson. For seeing me. For...everything."

His cock thickens at my back, and a spike of arousal attempts to pull me from exhaustion.

Water sloshes in the tub as he attempts to put space between his cock and my ass, but I push back against him.

"You never thank someone for caring—that's not how relationships work." His words are stunted. I'm pushing him when he's trying so damn hard to be a gentleman.

I arch my spine, pressing my backside into his groin. The need for him to take control of my body is as essential as air. I can't explain it—except I'm craving the freedom submission brings me.

I'm so tired of fighting for everything I have. Tired of treating every decision as if one wrong move will be the one to sink me. Tired of being alone.

"You're an expert on relationships now?" I meant to tease, but my words are so breathy, it's possible I'm only torturing myself.

"Not on all relationships." His hand grips my hip beneath the water, holding me still. "Only on the one that matters."

"What one matters?" I attempt to roll my hips, but he's already taken control of them. A long, pained sigh escapes my lips as I melt into his touch.

"This one." His husky tone has my pussy clenching for release. "What are you doing, Sav? Tonight is about taking care of you. It's not about sex."

"Please." I whimper—it's a sound that has never left my mouth before, and he tenses beneath me.

"Please what?" His words are strained. The hot air he expels lands against the sensitive skin of my neck, and I shiver.

"Please," I say again. "I need you to..."

"Words, sweetheart. Use them. Someone hurt you today, and I'm not going to take advantage of that."

My head thrashes on his chest. He's going to make me say it—he needs me to say it.

He's unlike any man I've ever been with.

"You're not taking advantage," I whisper. "I—I need you to touch me. To help me forget. I just want to feel, Grey, without guilt, sadness, and regrets tethering me to a life I had no control over."

"Fuck, Monroe." His arm bands tighter around my shoulders, and I feel his forehead drop to the back of my skull. "You need to sleep—I'm trying to do the right thing here."

"That's just it." I pull on his arm, and he drops it to the side of the tub, allowing me to move forward, then turn to face him. I bring my knees to my chest and wrap my arms around them. "I think, all this time, you've been the right thing...for me...and I've been too stubborn to admit it."

There's sadness in his eyes, but he smiles, and I realize maybe it isn't sadness at all but hard-earned acceptance.

He reaches for my ankles, then pulls them to either side of his waist, meeting me in the middle of the tub before wrapping them around his back.

We're nose to nose, chest to chest, and he cups my face on both sides.

"I love you, Savannah Monroe."

Oh, God. I'm having a heart attack.

"I know that terrifies the hell out of you, but I. Love. You."

"T—thank you?" Holy shit. Why the hell did I say thank you? Who says thank you when the sexiest man alive says they love you?

Me. That's who. The hot mess express train to blabber's bluff.

Grey barks with laughter, his cinnamon scent splashing me in the face with every exhale.

"You're welcome, my honesty-challenged angel. Tell me what you need." The kindness in his eyes obliterates my embarrassment.

He truly does love me.

I slip my hand between us and wrap my fingers around his thick cock. "I want you to hold my power safe so I can let go because I know you won't try to take it from me forever— just for a little while so I can breathe—so I can be free."

There's a hint of sadness in his expression again, but he blinks it away before I can read too much into it.

"You are free, baby, always. Giving up your control doesn't mean you lose yourself. It means you trust me enough to take care of you while acknowledging that you've always held your own power. It means you trust me to hold you together so you can let go. You never have to face life alone again, Sav. Never again."

"Never again," I whisper.

"Never." He kisses the corner of my mouth. "Again." Then kisses the opposite side. "You can always trust me. I swear to you."

"I do." My words are cut off with a gentle press of his lips to mine. "I do trust you," I mumble as his tongue seeks entrance.

Grey pulls back to stare into my eyes. "You will never regret trusting me."

But will you regret trusting me? It seems to be a pattern of mine. I tend to break everything good and kind in my life.

Before I can ask him, his hand slides down my back,

then he brings it forward to cup my pussy, and all thoughts escape me.

"I'm going to ask one time, and I want an honest answer. Are you sure you're up for this?" His finger taps against my entrance, and I moan.

"Yes. Yes, I want this. I want you."

"You have me, baby. You probably always have."

With one thrust, we become one...as though it's how we were always meant to be.

CHAPTER THIRTY-FOUR

GREYSON

"Fuck," I hiss when I'm sheathed in her warmth.

Savvy's forehead falls to my shoulder, and her teeth sink into my skin. She's never been a biter, but that jolt of pain sends white-hot lust coursing through my cock. It thickens inside her.

She's so exhausted, she can barely keep her head up. But I can't deny her even when I know she needs sleep because I believed her when she said she needed to let go.

"This is going to be fast, sweetheart. And hard."

My right arm hooks on the edge of the tub. I use it as leverage to pound up and into her core.

"Yes," she mewls, rocking her pelvis against mine. God, she's so sexy.

I band my left arm around her, holding her to me as I thrust up, and up, and up. Water sloshes over the edge of the tub, but I couldn't care less about the mess.

She groans, but it sounds frustrated, and I pull her up so I can see her face.

"What's wrong?"

Tears fill her eyes, but she doesn't allow them to fall. "I— I can't."

I freeze. Everything stops. I start to pull out, and she cries as if in agony.

"What is it, Savvy? What's wrong?"

"I'm so close. So, so close. But I— My mind—I can't focus. It's too...muddy."

I smile sadly. "Then that's my fault, baby. It means I'm not doing enough to distract you."

She shakes her head, but I cut her off with sharp, stabby thrusts.

I use one hand to hold her down, then spread my long fingers until one lands on her swollen clit.

"Argh," she whines. It's a pleading sound that goes straight to my balls.

"Jesus, Monroe. Your sexy fucking cunt was made for me." Two sharp thrusts. "You swell so beautifully around me, gripping, squeezing, swallowing my cock like it's starving."

Her moans grow louder.

"You like it hard, don't you? You love it when our skin slaps together. Do you hear it? Do you feel how you gush around me every time I punch into you?"

"Yes. Yes. Yes." She's chanting as though she's lost all control of her verbal skills.

"I dream of waking you up with my cock buried so deep in your core that you'll gasp awake, begging me to fuck you harder."

"Oh God. Yes."

"You'd let me fuck you wherever I want, wouldn't you?"

She squeezes my dick so hard, I see stars and lose control of my breath.

Savannah Monroe gets off on dirty talk. She couldn't be more perfect for me.

I know the moment she falls back into her worried mind, but that's not happening tonight. Tomorrow is for worrying. Tonight is about feeling free.

I pick up my pace on her clit, then drag my free hand down her spine. The moment I thrust up, I breach the entrance to her asshole with my thumb.

She screams out as a spasm courses through her body.

"Are you going to let me fuck this tight little hole too? Hmm?" Her ring of muscles clenches then relaxes as I swirl my thumb and press it in deeper.

Another guttural moan spurs me on as she clings to my arms, my shoulders, anything she can latch onto.

I pound into her pussy and her ass in tandem, whispering in her ear every dirty thought that pops into my head.

"Grey. Grey, please."

I'll never tire of hearing her this way.

Three more thrusts, and she screams so loudly that if we had neighbors, the police would surely be called.

Her inner muscles spasm, milking my cock. Lightning sparks in my balls right before I shoot my load deep inside her, but I don't stop. I keep thrusting, pushing in and out, up and down until she collapses against me.

"Thank you," she mumbles. She winces as I remove my thumb, and then she passes out cold with her cheek pressed tightly to my chest.

I sit there for long minutes, holding her close, then I quickly wash her body, lift her from the tub, and put her to bed, where I wrap myself around her and vow to make us last forever.

———

"YOU WANT ME TO SHUT DOWN CORPORATE?" I ASK. I'M SURE I heard him wrong.

All four Harrington brothers sit at my dining room table, and it's disconcerting as hell. Roman, Sterling, and Chase are identical triplets, but they look like a carbon copy of Grant, the oldest.

I don't even know who I'm talking to.

"Just the headquarters, and only for a week. Give your employees a paid vacation while we sort this out." I think it's Sterling talking, but who the hell knows.

"There's a shit ton to unpack here." Okay, this guy is Roman. I appreciate his direct approach and no-bullshit attitude. "You think the leak is coming from Quinn or Kristen, but we don't know which one because neither has taken the recent bait you've given them. I'm not convinced that the packages to Clover are related beyond DeVane doxing her private information, so that needs to be handled separately."

"I don't care if he sent them himself, he put out her private information, knowing this would happen. It is his fault," I snarl.

"That's all true, but we'll talk more about Clover and the packages in a moment," Grant says. I only know it's him because he has a few more lines around his eyes. "There are some...complications we'll need to discuss first."

"Wait. Packages? As in plural?" I ask, glancing toward the stairs, thankful that Savvy hasn't come down yet.

The Harringtons speak in a silent conversation before Grant finally nods. "She received another one late last night at the inn. Whoever delivered it knew where the cameras were and evaded all of them."

"Fucking hell. DeVane has been loitering around town,

and he could have scoped out the cameras when he tried to check into the inn."

"It's possible, but let's stick to Omni-Reyes first," Roman barks. I appreciate that he appears to have one tone and it's similar to my own. "We'll have a forensic team scan the entire building while your employees are out. If there's a connection between either woman and Riley DeVane, we'll find it. That's the easy part. What we're concerned about is the escalation of DeVane's behavior with Savannah."

"Me too," I admit. It tastes bitter leaving my mouth, but I'm not too prideful to ask for help, not when it comes to Savvy.

"We'll have a team on her at all times," one of the triplets says. "We'll also have a team on Clover, Elle, and Madison. If he can't get to Savvy, they'd be his next target."

"We're also working with the bounty hunters to bring him in before anything else happens," Sterling—or maybe it's Chase—says. They should wear name tags.

"Good. Okay." It sounds as though they're taking all the precautions I'd ask for. "Savvy insists on attending the fair." I study Roman's face as his mouth falls into a grim line. At least he thinks it's a terrible idea too. "She'll fight us if we don't make it happen, and she's stubborn enough to go with or without us."

"He'll be expecting it though," Roman says.

"Then we need to be three steps ahead of him because I can't convince her to hide out. She's...tenacious." A smile plays on my lips even though there's nothing funny about this conversation.

Roman chuckles. He's met Savvy, and he undoubtedly remembers how relentless she can be when she has her mind set on something.

"We'll get a team on the fairgrounds within the hour," Grant says.

Noise on the staircase draws our attention, and I watch as Savvy's legs come into view. Step by step, she appears, but when I see her eyes, I'm out of my chair so fast it scatters to the ground.

Wood scraping the floor tells me the Harrington brothers have risen as well, but they give me space to approach Savvy.

"What happened?" I ask the moment I reach her. My hands scan her body for injuries while I study her face.

She shakes her head, looking so damn lost, I want to murder someone.

"Savvy, what is it? What happened?" I ask again.

"A—Austin called." Austin. Austin, her shithead brother.

"Okay." I hold her hand and lead her to the sofa, then gently push her to a seating position while I crouch in front of her. "What did he say?"

"He said..." The floorboards creak, and she looks to the left, where the four copies of the same man stand in a militant line.

I hook her chin with my finger and drag her attention back to me while simultaneously shooing the Harringtons toward the door.

"We'll wait for you at Omni-Reyes," Grant says. "We need to discuss Clover's team as soon as possible. There are—"

"I'll call you," I say, cutting him off. The last thing I need is to pile one more worry onto Savvy's shoulders.

"Clover's team?"

Asshole Harrington.

"Don't worry about that. We're putting teams on you,

Madi, Elle, and Clover until we find Riley, that's all. He needs some more details about Clover."

The front door clicks shut.

"Wait," she calls out, but they're already outside. "We should do that first. Clover…"

"Will be fine. I promise. First tell me why you're so shaken."

That's all it takes for her eyes to lose focus again. What the hell happened?

"Sav, I need you to tell me what happened."

"He just… He still doesn't believe me. Riley's mom got a call from his parole officer, letting her know that a warrant was issued for him, and that he'd attacked me here in Georgia."

"A place he shouldn't have been," I remind her.

"Austin didn't…didn't believe me. He said I was making it all up. Again."

That asshole is done.

"He said I was ruining Paige's life all over again because now everyone is distraught over Riley when they should be focused on her wedding. He said…he said that Riley's trying to start over. He said that Riley is getting…married. He said Paige thinks I'm jealous that everyone has moved on while I'll always be alone, so I'm doing what I always did, hurting them."

"Sweetheart." She blinks vacant eyes. "Monroe," I try again. "I'm sorry to tell you this, but it doesn't sound like Paige was ever your friend, and as far as your brother goes, he sounds like he only cares about himself. Riley getting married is disconcerting, but we'll look into it. Do not allow them into your head. They don't deserve you, Sav, so don't allow them space in your precious heart either."

She nods. Words are easy, but I know firsthand how hard it can be to lose family.

"I just...I always held out hope that Paige cut me off because her family demanded it. This proves...it proves that she never even tried to stand up for me. I— She's probably made me the villain in her story, and everyone believes it."

I hate that she's right. I hate that they've done this to her over and over again.

I'll find a way to make them pay for the pain they continue to cause what's mine.

"But you're not the villain, and you're no one's scapegoat. You're the hero in this story, and in our story, they're only a footnote in our lives if you allow them to be."

"I've always loved them." The sadness in her tone shreds my lungs to bits.

"And because you're all things good—stubborn, but good—you probably always will. It's up to you if you allow them to use your love against you though. If I get a vote, I say you shelve them and cling to the family who loves you for you. Because we know how amazing you are, Sav. And we'll always fight for you too."

She surges forward, nearly knocking me on my ass as she wraps her arms around my shoulders.

I hug her back as we tumble to the floor, and I squeeze her tight. I don't think either of us has had enough affection in our lives, and I'll be the one to change that for us both.

———

"Immediate paid leave message is sent."

Roman sits beside me, making notes of his own. "Good. We'll start sweeps of the executive offices as soon as the last person has left the building."

"No one is going to believe that a brand-new building is having a plumbing emergency," I say. I wouldn't believe it.

"It doesn't matter what they think, but no one will question free vacation time, trust me. Especially not PTO. You should also know because of who you are, we're keeping my internal team very small."

I open my mouth to argue because I was hoping for a goddamn army, but he holds up a hand to stop me.

"Small but mighty, my friend." My shoulders tense. I appear to be collecting friends like Pops these days. "We pulled the best from each division to be here—you're our top priority—but you also require privacy, so we're taking that very seriously. We'll begin in your office and work our way out. The entire building will be scoped out in twenty-four hours. If anyone is transmitting information from here, we'll know it."

I lean back in my chair and focus on my lucky coin. I've studied every inch of this thing for years, but now I see it with new eyes. The sage and violet sticking out of a vase. The Latin word, *Domus*, etched into the placard—home, unity.

But it's the tiny little bug that always reminded me of a storm cloud—all this time, I thought that the storm represented me. Once again, Ace was ten steps ahead. It's a lightning bug, a firefly, and it represents Savvy.

I don't believe he thought we'd be where we are today, but I do think he had every intention of helping his three boys find their home here. Savvy, like me, needed a family to call home.

Ace was a sneaky shit, and his reach extends far beyond the grave.

"We have teams in place for Madi and Elle. Clover's team is having trouble with someone named Chief, who appears to be under the impression that he's running the operation."

My chuckle has him lifting his head from his computer screen. "Word of advice, work with Chief, not against him, and things will go a lot smoother."

Roman's expression remains impassive. He's got one hell of a poker face. "I appreciate the feedback, but I can't have anyone interfering. Not when she's already had a threat made against her."

I hold up my hands in surrender. "Your call. But good luck getting rid of him."

Roman pecks away at his computer with his pointer fingers. "We have a new team leader coming in for Clover's team. He's finishing up another job but..." There's a catch, a slight hitch in his tone that wasn't there before. "He's our cousin. He won't have any trouble handling an old man. He's our chief strategist—this company was actually his brainchild."

"Chief will meet Chief," I chuckle. "I'd pay good money to be a fly on that wall."

"Yes." Roman clears his throat. "We should talk about that—"

A knock at the door has me dropping the coin in my pocket, then looking up.

Quinn stands at the threshold, and the temperature in the room drops by twenty degrees.

Everyone here knows she might be the traitor—the person actively trying to hurt my family.

By her rigid posture and watery eyes, I'd say even she is aware of what will happen next.

"Yes, Quinn?"

Carla's voice from HR rings in my mind about lawsuits and firing anyone too quickly, so I keep my tone even, dead.

"Mr. Reyes, I know you believe it's possible that I've turned on you."

Well, I wasn't expecting her to come right out with it. Roman sits up straighter next to me with renewed interest.

She crosses the room, removes a single piece of paper from her file folder, and places it on the conference room table between us. "This is my resignation letter."

Convenient.

"I've worked for you since you were in college. I've worked nights, weekends, and most holidays. I've never complained, and I've always been on your side."

"You've been an exemplary employee," I agree.

"When Braxton ran off and left you to run Omni-Reyes after Ace died, I was by your side. When Braxton dragged you here, even though you hated it, I was by your side. I took on the job as your confidant, your adviser, and your friend when no one else would." Her voice is like steel, but her gaze is watery, and I'm still not convinced she's who we're looking for.

"I spoke up about Ms. Monroe because I believed we had built a level of professionalism where my opinion was valued. I was mistaken. However, I will not have my integrity called into question this way."

"No one has made any accusations—"

"Don't insult my intelligence. In lieu of my two weeks' notice, I offer you this." She slides an entire folder across the table to me. "I hired Ms. Richardson because she's the best at what she does and has been for nearly a decade. Her references were excellent—her track record speaks for itself."

I open the folder while she's speaking, and my leg starts bouncing as I slide it over to Roman.

"I based my opinions of Ms. Monroe on information Ms.

Richardson had given me. But then I witnessed the golf tournament."

Roman flips over grainy photos of my PR guru sitting in a parked car with Riley, their heads together in what appears to be a heated argument.

"Those were taken two days ago in the parking lot. You'd given me a migraine, Mr. Reyes, and I was lying down in my car during my lunch break. I'll provide a doctor's note should you need one."

"You took these photos?" Roman asks.

"I happened to sit up just as she got into the car. I was unsure of what was happening, but she appeared nervous, so." She shrugs. "What can I say, you've made me paranoid, so I took a photo. Now, having confirmed the other party in those photos, I had HR send me her background check again. I've included it in the back of that folder."

Anything I say right now could land me in hot water, so I need to choose my words carefully. Roman doesn't have the same approach.

"Some could find the timing of this—" he says.

"Suspicious, yes, I'm aware." I've never heard Quinn so cold. "Trust me, had I known I'd be in a position of having to defend myself, I would have started compiling alibis long ago." She drops another folder onto the table. "Luckily for me, I care about my honor more than this job, and when pushed into a corner, I'm a scrappy bitch."

Using one red painted nail, she slides the final folder to me. "People should never underestimate a woman who has fought hard for the career she earned."

This folder contains screenshots of social media posts ranging in date from ten to fifteen years ago—all of them are of a younger Kristen at various events, and they're all with the Ashfords and the DeVanes, but she has a different last name in all of them—back then she went by Kristen Crawly.

"She's connected to them," I mutter. "But how?"

"That's beyond my pay grade, Mr. Reyes. Luckily you have the big fancy IT team to figure it out for you."

Fuck. I think I owe Quinn an apology.

Roman scribbles something and slides it over to me. He's written: Are you sure she's innocent?

Am I?

Braxton and Savvy don't think so, but I know Quinn better than anyone, and I don't think I'm wrong. If it ends up biting me in the ass, I'll take the blame then.

"Quinn," I say, standing.

"Unless you're going to tell me about my severance package, I don't need to hear anything else," she says.

I nod, and she sighs heavily.

"Can I be honest with you?" she asks.

"Please."

"I hate it here in Georgia. You're an asshole. Completely unbearable to work for, and I'm tired. When you sent out the notice about shutting down the office, I realized I haven't taken a vacation in the entire time I've worked for you. That's over ten years, Mr. Reyes. Ten. Years. And while you compensate more than fairly, this whole fiasco was a wakeup call for me. I want a life, and I can't have that working for a man who's married to his job because my job is you. So please just give me a big fat check and call it a day."

She spins on her pointy heel, then pauses at the door. "For what it's worth, I think Ms. Monroe will be good for you, and I hope that information on Ms. Richardson gives you what you need to get this company in order. Ace was a good man, and he'd be proud of how you guys are running it today."

Quinn's gone before I can formulate a response.

"Well, if she is innocent, seems like this will be best for everyone," Roman says. "I have my team mining the internet for the connection between Kristen and Riley. We'll have it soon."

I drop back into my chair. "I'm a shitty boss."

"Sounds like it." Roman cracks a smile, and I don't feel like pummeling him.

Perhaps that's called growth.

CHAPTER THIRTY-FIVE

SAVVY

"When you're in a crowd, say at a concert, what are you looking for when you scan for a threat?" Clover asks her bodyguard, Rip.

"Miss Clover, my job is to remain hidden and out of sight. You should go about your day as if I'm not here," Rip replies.

I don't know the last time I've seen Clover this excited about anything. You would think all the extra men trying and failing miserably to fit into a town fair would send her into panic city, but it appears to be doing the opposite.

"You're not blendin' in very well," Chief says. "In my day..." I tune him out, knowing it will be a one-man pissing contest until Clover moves on to her next line of questioning.

The truth is, Grey kept his word, and for the most part, our security is out of sight, and they've allowed me to move freely about the fairgrounds.

I should feel safe, but internally, I'm a mess. The local police have listed Kristen as a person of interest but haven't been able to locate her, and Riley is still...somewhere. My brain glazed over when Grey was trying to explain why the FBI was involved in locating Kristen. Something about insider secrets and corporate blah, blah, blah.

I just want life to go back to normal.

Well, maybe not completely normal. The Grey not hating me part is pretty great, but waiting for the next shoe to drop is exhausting.

"There you are." Madi waves with both hands, and it sways her entire body. Her baby bump has become her new center of gravity.

That twinge in my chest flares to life, watching her. Do all expectant mothers naturally hold their belly, or is that learned behavior?

It's probably because they have to pee all the time. If I stick with this line of thinking, perhaps the butterfly in my chest will settle.

"Are you ready? You look gorgeous." She whirls her finger, and I oblige by spinning in place so the thin fabric of my sundress swirls around my knees. Not that she's paying attention while she wraps Clover in a hug.

"I don't know if I'm ready, but I'm here."

"I'm so glad you went with the red dress. It looks hot. Look at your boobs." She reaches in as though she's going to weigh them, and I finally laugh. They do look great in this dress—a square neckline always flatters. "Hey, Carson."

My new bodyguard groans a begrudging hello.

"Hi, Rip. Hi, Chief." Madi continues making the rounds until she's hugged everyone.

"Miss Monroe," Carson says under his breath.

"I know, I know. They're not supposed to talk to you. They've all been warned, but have you ever been in a small town, Carson? I'm doing the best I can, okay?"

He smirks, but he never takes his eyes off the crowd.

"Yes, ma'am. I grew up in a tiny town called Burke Hollow, so I know them well."

Inwardly, I cringe. When did I hit the ma'am era? "Then can ya cut me some slack?"

"I'll see what I can do. Are you ready to head over to the main stage?" he asks.

"Elle's meeting us over there," Madi says. "The guys are already warming up."

"Warming... Who's warming up?"

"Grey's getting some last-minute pointers from, well, from everyone." Clover giggles. Glancing down, I see she's already gotten into Blissy's Happy Juice.

Blissy gets a special license to sell alcohol once a year, and every year we say we need to regulate it better. Happy Juice is a town-wide hangover waiting to happen.

"Let's go put Grey out of his misery."

"Firefly green," Carson says into an earpiece I can't see.

Rolling my eyes because this is over the top, I step forward, and I swear two more guys move with us.

Taking three more steps, I side-eye the movements and then stop suddenly.

The human wall puts on the brakes, but when I peer around at our surroundings, strangers are in conversations, people are laughing, kids crying, bells ringing.

I'm losing my mind—paranoia has never been so visceral before.

"Everything okay, Miss Monroe?" Carson is half a step behind me.

"Call me Savvy, Carson. Everything's fine." I hook Madi's arm on my right and Clover's on my left and angle us toward the main stage. I will not allow Riley to ruin one more thing for me.

"Carson," I call over my shoulder.

"Er, yes, ma'a—ah, Savvy?"

"We agreed to three guards."

"We did, yes."

I drag my friends another ten steps, and swear I can feel eyes on us from every direction.

"Then tell me why it feels like so many more?" I ask. "Did Greyson approve more?"

I almost feel bad for Carson right now.

He holds up his hands. "I'm only in charge of your team, and there are three of us here today. I stay with you—Jack moves ahead of us, and Mark bats cleanup."

"We had a plan," I grumble, pushing through the crowd toward the main stage. "If Grey went back on his word..."

Stay calm, Savvy. What's the saying? Paranoia will destroy ya?

Cutting through the concession stands, I take a right at ring toss and another right at the house of mirrors, then stop in my tracks when I come out at the front of the main stage.

The first thing my brain registers is that Grey is shirtless. The second thing is that he's laughing. Really laughing. His head is tipped back, showcasing his Adam's apple and day-old scruff along his jaw.

Greyson has day-old scruff.

And he's wearing jeans.

Jeans that hang low on his hips, and all his tanned California skin glistens under the midday sun.

Cian claps him on the back. They're too far away to hear what they're saying, but their mannerisms are loose and comfortable.

Grey could pass for a regular guy in this moment—it's a shock to my system but not unwelcome. This is Grey unguarded, and I might like this version of him as much as

I like the protective asshole who pushes my buttons for fun.

All the guys are here. Braxton, Sage, Moose, Pops, even the football team has circled around Grey. They're all here —for him.

Roman leans into Grey's space, then nods in my direction. I'm sure Carson alerted him to our arrival, and Grey scopes me out as though he'd been waiting for me.

It hurts to breathe.

This moment feels poignant, like I've been running my entire life to get to him, and here he is, standing in a crowd of people that fades into nothingness as though it's just him and me on the precipice of something great.

He waves, never losing his smile, then parts the sea of people to come to me.

I feel high, drugged on the happy pheromones he's exuding.

"Hey," he says when he's close enough to touch. "Sorry, I'm all sweaty."

His smile never wavers.

"I—I'm mad at you."

"You are." His eyes dance—two pale blue irises bouncing with delight. "What did I do now?"

I think I might be floating.

What the hell is happening to me right now?

Smiling like an idiot is my answer.

"I don't remember," I say.

"Please, please let the rest of our arguments for the rest of our lives go like this one." His lips meet mine. It's gentle and sweet.

Nothing like the blisteringly desperate kisses we normally share.

But no less consuming.

"I've missed you this morning," he says quietly, but I can see questions lingering behind his eyes.

"It looks like you've been busy," I say. Behind him, the boys chuckle.

"Are you hungry?" he asks, and there's the question he really wants to ask.

"Grey, we talked about this."

He holds up both his hands in surrender. "I'm just asking, sweetheart. I didn't finish my sandwich, so I saved it for you in case you were busy this morning too."

"No, I'm good." And I am. I really am this time.

I can see the fight in him, still wanting to push, still wanting to ensure my safety, but he nods and lets it go.

"Good, I'm glad." He smiles, and it fills me with love.

He wants to fight for me, but he's trusting me to do it myself.

It's progress.

"I think I figured out how to win this thing," he says, wrapping an arm around my shoulder and leading me toward the stage.

"Oh yeah, how's that?" I ask, leaning my head against him, soaking in the comfort he gives.

He pulls me in closer to his side. I'm not even angry about the sweat. We're in the middle of an active threat, and I'm...content.

"The bigger fool I make of myself, the more people cheer for me." His dimples are both on display.

"That's your strategy?" My laughter rises right along with his.

"I need an edge, and since I don't seem to be picking up line dancing very well, I'm going to play to my strengths."

"Your strengths. In line dancing."

He takes my hand and tugs me to the stage stairs.

"Hell no. If I never line dance again after tonight, I'll be happy. But I know how to work a crowd."

Carson catches my eye.

"Oh, I remember why I was mad."

Grey leads me up the steps with humor shining in his eyes. "What is it now, sweetheart?"

"Did you approve about a hundred more guards than the three we discussed?"

The curtain is still lowered on the stage, so it's a little dark back here, but he leads me effortlessly to the chair that's built to look like a throne.

"Well, a hundred seems a little excessive," he says dryly. "You agreed to follow Harrington's plan."

Carson slides into the shadows off to my right.

"Roman said there would be three, Grey. Three."

He leans in and kisses my nose. "I can confirm there are three guards on you and one on each of the girls. Whatever else Roman put into place is on him, but no, I'm not aware of any others." He frowns. "Why, did you see something suspicious?"

Did I?

I shake my head. "I think I'm just anxious."

"Are you sure?" Apprehension clouds his features.

"Yeah, sorry. Ignore me. Now, are you ready to win this thing?"

His cocky smirk is back in play. "Cian and Sage are betting against me, but Braxton and Moose are going double or nothing in my favor."

"I... What about... Why..."

"I'm going to win by whatever means necessary." He will too. It's right there in his eyes the color of a summer sky.

I scan the length of his body as he replaces his T-shirt, and holy shit.

"Are you wearing cowboy boots?" Jesus, are they what's making his ass look so good in those jeans?

He clicks his heels, and I drop my head back to the throne.

"Moose got them for me. They look good right?"

"Who are you, and what have you done with Drill Bit?"

Greyson doesn't have any right to move as quickly as he does, but he's on me in a millisecond, his scruffy chin rubbing against my cheek, and his warm breath sliding down my neck.

"Oh, Monroe." He groans, then nips at the sensitive skin beneath my earlobe. "Drill Bit is still in control, I'm just letting you have the fantasy of being in charge. This is your thing, but tonight, at home, I'll really show you what I can do with these hips." His lips press to mine, but it's too chaste. "I might have learned a few tricks today."

My jaw drops as he swivels his hips in a move that would make Magic Mike proud.

I squirm in my seat while he slowly lowers himself into his.

At some point, Moose joined us on stage. As master of ceremonies, he's apparently in for a show we won't soon forget.

"Ready, kids?"

"Where did Moose get a top hat from?" I whisper.

"Ready," Grey calls back, then to me he whispers, "Pops insisted."

"Of course he did."

The curtains rise, and so does my temperature.

"Oh shit." It slips through my lips as I scan every single face as far as I can see.

"What? What's wrong?" Grey snatches my hand and tugs until I face him.

The stage isn't huge, but most of the town is here, and my happy little bubble of a moment ago bursts.

"Sav?"

"I'm fine. I just...I guess I never pictured this part of it." Moose is speaking to the crowd, but Grey has a way of sucking you into his orbit and drowning out everything else. "I'm center stage. He could...he could be..."

Worry lines form deep between his brows. "Yes, he could. But we have everything in place. You're safe here, even if you're on display. Roman has taken care of everything."

"Can Greyson prove he's worthy of our sweetheart, or will another prince prove victorious?" Moose's voice is amplified through the sound speaker.

"Oh, God. What if Riley wins?"

Grey's face is ferocious. "That will never happen."

"Right. Right, of course." *Get your shit together, girl.*

"Greyson Reyes and Savvy Sweetheart." Moose calls out our names, and Grey uses his grasp on my hand to help me rise.

I feel a little like royalty as our friends and neighbors clap, cheer, and whistle. It's easy to fall back into the safety of home-field advantage.

Grey squeezes my hand, then lifts our joined palms to the air.

"They love you," I say when the cheers get louder.

"Nah, I'm just arm candy. You're the sweetheart they're rooting for."

"Are we ready to crown this year's sweetheart?" Moose asks the crowd.

Madi, Clover, and Elle account for at least thirty percent of the noise as they begin chanting my name.

Not going to lie, it's kind of good for the old ego.

Moose hands Grey the microphone.

Shit. How did I forget this part?

"I've been told it's my duty and my honor to introduce this year's sweetheart, Savannah Monroe."

Bricks start stacking in my throat.

"A few months ago, I bet none of you would have thought I'd be the one delivering this speech. But a few months ago, I was an idiot."

The crowd laughs, and a brick is dislodged. This is his superpower. This is how he'll win...he simply won't give them any option but to fall in love with him.

"Have you ever met someone who was your equal and from the very first words out of their mouth, you knew you were either going to kill them or marry them?" Geez, he really does play well to a crowd. "Well, that was me, except I was too stubborn to admit the truth. The moment I met Savvy, I thought for sure we were going to ruin each other."

He turns back to me, and his face softens.

"And we did." He's talking to the crowd, but it feels like his words are meant just for me. "In the best way possible, we tore down walls and childhood trauma. We shoved, kicked, and pushed each other through uncomfortable situations, and we came out on the other side, stronger, healthier, and...in love."

Come on, Grey. Now it's time for you to get your shit together. This isn't how the introductions are supposed to go.

"I can honestly say there's only one woman strong enough, kind enough, smart enough, and stubborn enough to carry the baggage I came to Happiness with." His voice is as smooth as melted chocolate. "But she held it over her head as though it weighed nothing, then tossed it onto the highway where she ran over it a few hundred times until the load was something I could bear.

"That's why she's your sweetheart. Because she has a capacity to love that is so pure, so true, so...perfect." He smiles a smile he reserves just for me, and my knees wobble. "*She's perfect*. And she's the perfect representation of everything good here in Happiness. To our sweetheart, Savvy Monroe!"

He holds out the microphone to Moose, then pulls it back at the last second. "Oh, any prizes I win, I'll be raffling off over at the Discreet Daily Deeds booth—except time with Savvy, that's all mine. All you have to do to enter is drop a wish in our treasure chest."

A chorus of oohs and aahs fills the air as he finally hands over the microphone to Moose, then uses his thumbs to swipe under my eyes.

"What the hell, Drill Bit? That's not how this was supposed to go."

"I improvised."

Moose hands him a crown I've never seen before.

Grey lowers it so I can see.

My stomach drops into my toes.

"What did you do?" I whisper.

"I improvised." He winks. Greyson Reyes freaking winks. "Moose told me they go missing every year, so Clover and Madi helped me source one just for you. I would have done it myself, but it turns out I'm not that crafty." He holds up his forearm, where a small half-inch burn sits. "Turns out hot glue guns are fucking hot."

Tears blur my vision as he spins a crown made of light pink silk roses, adorned with sprigs of violet and sage. But it's the wire spires that appear to float around it with tiny glowing fireflies dangling from the ends that makes my nose tingle.

"I couldn't find a way to make the bugs glow forever." He

lifts it and places it on top of my head. I know people are cheering, but I can't hear anything but my pulse beating in my ears. Then he leans in, presses a kiss to my cheek, and whispers, "Since they only glow for thirty days, I bought a lifetime supply."

Before I can respond to that, he kisses my lips. "Showtime, Monroe. It's time to win your heart." He points to my crown. "How's that for wooing you, huh?"

He jumps off the edge of the stage and takes his position in the front line. With his family and friends surrounding him, he rips his shirt over his head and twirls it around in the air.

Dear God, he's all in.

CHAPTER THIRTY-SIX

GREYSON

I'm feeling ten feet tall when I jump off that stage. I knew I could woo her.

Line dancing? Not so sure.

"What exactly is your game plan here?" Braxton asks after I toss my shirt on stage.

"Full and complete humiliation. If I can't win by following the moves, I'm hoping to make them feel bad enough for me that they vote for me anyway."

"You'll get an A for effort." Sage hoots louder than Pops on my other side.

"Exactly."

"You've got this, Greyson."

Peering to my left, I grin at Madi and Clover, who are climbing the stage stairs while giving me two thumbs up.

Fuck yes, I've got this.

"How many times did you watch those videos last night?" Braxton raises his voice as the music starts.

Too many. That's how many. I may have also incorporated some old-school male stripper moves too.

Please God, do not let me pull my groin.

The music picks up, and I step forward, out of the line, giving myself plenty of room.

And so I don't unintentionally hurt anyone.

Being crowned most eligible bachelor meant I got to choose the music. Clover was all too happy to suggest "Country Girl" by Luke Bryan. My only hope is to shake my ass every time he sings about it.

"Go, Grey, go." It sounds like Elle, and I laugh as I begin to move.

I'm much better at this than I thought I'd be. All that practice last night must have finally paid off. Either that, or it's the swig of moonshine Roman gave me a half hour ago.

Jumping to the left, I stumble when I realize everyone else is facing away from me.

Okay, so perhaps not as good as I thought.

The song blares all around me until it's vibrating through me. I become one with this damn song, and I pull out a move that hopefully won't scar any small children. Thrusting my hips forward, I grind against air, and the catcalls begin.

That must be a good sign.

If this makes it to the tabloids, we'll need to revamp our in-house PR consultants.

Savvy catches my eye, and I trip over my feet at the smile she graces me with. She's biting her bottom lip like she doesn't want to laugh, so I do it for her.

Lifting both hands, I flash her the universal *who the fuck knows* gesture.

I can't hear her laughter over the music, but it washes over me just the same.

I'm sweating more than I did playing football.

How long can this song possibly go on for?

Reaching into the recesses of my vast three-day-old

dancing knowledge, I pull out another award-winning move and drop to the ground. Using one hand to prop myself up, I roll my hips.

Dirty? Yes. Appropriate? Probably not. A hit? Fuck yeah, it is. Everyone cheers.

Braxton's laughing so hard he falls over just as the song finally ends. Sage, the little shit, has his phone pointed at me in my one-handed plank position.

Cian's doubled over, hands on his knees, Elle pounding on his back.

Slowly, I lift myself to stand, almost too afraid to make eye contact with anyone else as I dust off my hands.

As long as I win this damn competition, it doesn't matter what kind of fool I've made of myself.

"Well, folks." Moose is struggling to contain his laughter, so I feel like that should be bonus points. "I can't say we've ever had a competition quite like that."

"You were a cross between Napoleon Dynamite and Jenna Ortega's version of Wednesday Addams." Braxton is still wheezing on the ground.

It wasn't *that* bad.

When I finally look up to Savvy, she's standing on the edge of the stage with both hands covering her mouth and eyes full of mirth.

Fine, maybe it was worse than bad, but I'd do it all over again if it put that joyful shine in her eyes.

"Can we have all the contestants line up on stage?" Moose says. "We'll announce a winner by applause."

"Fuck me, that's how they do it?" I mutter, which makes Braxton laugh even harder.

I line up like cattle and walk on stage but bypass half the other assholes so I can stand behind Savvy. When guys line up on either side of her, I wrap my arm around her shoulders too, just to be clear about where my priorities are.

"Hi." She grins up at me.

"Hi."

"Drill Bit's back, I see." Her shoulders shake beneath my grip.

Lowering my arms to her waist, I tug her into me and smirk when I nestle my length into her ass. "Never left, sweetheart."

Moose walks down the line, hovering a hand over each jackass up on stage. A roar of applause has me straightening my spine, then leaning back to see who the asshole is.

"That's Eddie," Savvy whispers.

"Why do you know that?" I think the town fair is giving me lockjaw.

"Because he won the last three years but has no interest in settling down. Word on the street is his hips don't lie, if you know what I mean."

"Stop. Talking."

Her belly shakes beneath my palm, and all I want to do is toss her over my shoulder and drag her ass home.

"Stop scowling, Grey." She giggles, and I frown harder, hoping to hear it again. "You're supposed to be putting on a show."

"You're enjoying this entirely too much."

She shrugs. "I mean, you're not wrong."

"Braxton said I looked like Napoleon Dynamite and Wednesday Addams had a baby." When did I succumb to pouting?

This town is ruining me.

Savvy gasps and chokes, then gurgles on her laughter. I stand with a grimace plastered on my face while Moose holds his hand above the guy on my right, and then the guy on my left.

What the actual hell is going on? "Did he just skip right over me?"

I glare down the line of contestants and huff out a small tantrum.

There's no way I was worse than Chief—even he got applause.

I scan all available exits in case I need a quick escape. Roman leans against the railing, obviously suffering some kind of secondhand embarrassment. He shakes his head in disgust, but I swear I saw his lip quirk up when I dropped it like it was hot.

"And we have one more contestant," Moose says, walking back toward center stage.

Holy shit, I'm nervous. I've never been chosen last for anything in my entire goddamn life.

Is that what's happening now?

I move to a small town for my family, meet a woman who drives me up the damn wall, fall in love with the maniac, then lose my mojo too?

"Greyson," Moose calls, and for one painfully horrifying moment, it's dead silent, and my lungs seize in my chest, but then just as quickly, I feel like a goddamn rock star when the deafening cheers hit the stage.

Existential crisis, my ass. I've still got it, motherfuckers.

I throw my arms up in the air and yell like I just won the Super Bowl, then I do what I wanted to do earlier—I toss Savvy over my shoulder and haul her away.

———

"Roman." He stops a few feet ahead of us. "You can send your guys home." I glance down at Savvy. I've felt her exhaustion for the last hour. "We're all heading home, so I've got it from here."

"I'm starving," Madi says to our left. "Can we please hit up the food trucks on our way out? They're right by the parking lot."

"Grey, I think we should stay." Roman looks from me to Carson, who also nods. "Just because we haven't seen Riley doesn't mean he isn't here."

The fact that he thinks I can't protect my wife instantly puts me on the defensive, but logically, I understand he's just doing his job.

"Brax," I say. "We'll meet you by the picnic tables, okay?"

His gaze darts between Roman and me like he wants to say something, but then silently guides Madi toward the exit.

"It's fifteen minutes, tops, Roman. I'm not going to leave her side. I've got this."

He steps forward, and I regret having Savvy between us now.

"And I disagree. If I pull my guys, this would be the perfect time for Riley to strike."

"You said yourself you haven't seen him tonight. I appreciate your expertise, but I'm perfectly capable of getting Savvy home."

Roman drops his head back and looks to the stars. I'm fairly certain he mutters "arrogant prick" to the night sky.

"This is my case, Grey," he says. "I'm not sending my guys home unless you fire us. I will, however, have them pull back and do a perimeter sweep until you leave. It's the best I can do. I'm not willing to sacrifice my reputation because you want to play hero."

"Play her—"

"That's fine," Savvy says, cutting me off. "Thanks, Roman. I'm really tired, so as soon as we get Madi all her snacks, we'll head home."

He nods, then speaks into his earpiece with a pissed-off scowl tossed my way.

Roman will have to learn not to underestimate me if he wants to continue working together.

"You hired him because he's the best," Savvy says when we're out of earshot. "You should probably listen to him."

"Monroe, you've been on edge and uncomfortable with them around since you arrived. I can keep you safe for five minutes so you can relax with your friends before we call it a night."

She shrugs at the same time a yawn swallows her face.

We find Clover, Braxton, and Madi sitting at a picnic table with every type of fried food you can imagine spread out over the top. You really can't fight a pregnant woman's cravings, but I've never seen it displayed so...gluttonously before either.

They must have hit every food vendor before commandeering this lonely picnic table and stuffing their faces with sugar in every form of confection.

I don't hate it.

I especially don't hate how Savvy curls into my sprawled legs when I straddle the bench seat.

"I don't think anyone will ever beat Grey's...inspired performance today," Clover says earnestly.

"Inspired by what? Satan?" Braxton will never let me live this down.

"I won the first competition, didn't I?" I see no reason to hide my smug pride as I reach over Savvy for a piece of fried dough covered in powdered sugar. "Tell me again how this is any different than a donut?"

Clover gasps as though I've said something blasphemous.

It's a fucking donut.

"It's fried dough, completely different." Clover might add me to her hit list for this offense.

Savvy expels a small gasp as her phone screen lights up her face. I wait for her to say something, and when she doesn't, I squeeze her side while the friendly banter of our friends washes over us.

I could get used to this. Maybe not at a dirty picnic table, but the easy comradery and conversations.

"Grey, you have to try the fried plantains," Madi says, shoving a small brown turd-shaped thing in my face. Glancing at my watch, I realize we've already been sitting here for half an hour. "Ah, I'll pass. We should really—"

"Shit." Roman's curse cuts me off. He's walking toward us at a clipped pace with a hand to his ear, so I wave him over, still trying to get Savvy's attention. I should have taken her home fifteen minutes ago.

"Any sign of them?" I ask when Roman is close enough.

"No," he says, and the tension in my neck recedes. "My guys are heading to the east field now. No one's been on any of your properties today either. But I wanted to talk to you about Clover's detail, if you have a moment."

Savvy stiffens in my arms, but her head is down.

"I'm here." The gruff voice is unfamiliar, and I twist on the bench to see the man standing behind me. He's oddly familiar.

"Clover?" Braxton asks. I scan the group to find Clover blinking rapidly, but all the color has drained from her face.

"Clove?" Savvy asks, finally lifting her head.

In a tangle of limbs, Clover falls all over herself as she tries to escape the picnic table.

"Shit." Roman sighs. "I tried to get here before he did."

Savvy is out of my arms and around the table a moment later, while Madi attempts to balance with one leg still stuck under the table. Who knew picnic tables were so hazardous?

Roman rounds the bench to stand beside the newcomer, and now I can see the familial resemblance between them—it's the shape of their eyes, and their dark, nearly black hair.

"What's going on?" I ask. The tension in the air takes on an acrid scent.

Clover's staring at Roman's friend like she saw a ghost, and then she starts hyperventilating.

"Get him out of here," I say, still unsure what the hell is happening.

"Clover? Are you okay?" Savvy's asking on the other side of the table. The poor girl's mouth is still popping like a blowfish.

The guy standing next to Roman is staring at Clover, but his expression is completely blank.

"What the hell happened?" I ask, more aggressively this time, and instantly regret it because Clover squeaks like a goddam cat toy.

"I—I." Nothing else comes out of her mouth.

"I wanted to discuss this with you in private," Roman says, gesturing toward the guy at his side. "This is my cousin."

"Valen. M—my Valen," Clover says just before she faints. Savvy barely latches onto her arm before she hits the ground.

What the hell is it with these two and fainting?

"For fuck's sake." Before the words are even out of my

mouth, Valen has reached Clover and is lying her on her back, checking her pulse, and then all hell breaks loose.

Again.

"What do you mean, that's Valen?" Madi starts plucking at the elastic on her wrist and pacing in a circle around Clover.

"Your cousin? You've known that Clover's *Valen* is your cousin this entire time?" Savvy's words are lethal.

"He doesn't know that he's Clover's Valen," Roman says.

Everyone stares at Roman while Valen pulls something from his pocket and wafts it beneath Clover's nose.

"He's missing most of his childhood memories. He doesn't remember anything before he was sixteen," Roman says. "We've been looking for a ghost for years. That led us here. Valen runs Styx and Stone Security."

Clover Styx—she changed her last name to Danforth when she entered the foster care system at fourteen. Glancing around the table, I don't find any indication that anyone else knows that bit of information. I'm only privy to it because I ran thorough background checks on everyone when Braxton first moved here.

Clover stirs, stares up at Valen, screams, and then passes out again—this is worse than the reality TV Savvy's been making me watch.

Valen sighs, then lifts Clover into his arms and starts walking off without saying a word.

"Where the hell are you taking her?" Savvy demands, keeping pace with him.

I'm not far behind. "You have some explaining to do, Roman, you prick."

"I always do." He sighs, and I get the impression whatever is happening with Valen has weighed heavily on him for years.

Behind us, feet are shuffling to keep up.

"Stop pulling on my arm, you're jostling her head," the enigma known as Valen growls at Savvy.

"You'd better watch your fucking tone," I say, but remove Savvy's hand from his arm because he's right.

"Birdie team, take flight." As soon as Roman speaks, he removes his hand from his ear.

"Where are you taking her?" Savvy demands.

Lights flash on a black van straight ahead.

"Oh, no. You're not stuffing my best friend in the back of a van." Savvy runs ahead, spreading her arms wide. As if that's going to stop him.

He walks around her and opens the sliding door with a push of a button. She scrambles to block him again, but in a tone that sounds like he's been gargling with wood chips, he says, "Move."

Behind him is what appears to be the workings of an ambulance, so before she can lay into him, I pull her to my side.

"Hey." I spin her so she can see what I'm seeing just as Valen lays Clover on a gurney. We all crowd around as he opens another set of smelling salts.

Clover blinks her eyes open, dreamily, peacefully. Then they widen, and she goes full rigor mortis. "Am I dead?" Only her pupils move from side to side as though she's terrified of any movement at all.

Valen's laughter is unexpected but warm. "No, Honeybee. You just passed out."

"Honeybee?" Madi asks. "Where the heck did that come from?"

Valen frowns. "Beats the hell out of me. You good, lady?" He stares down at Clover, and if heartbreak had a photo, she would be the poster child.

"Valen?" Clover's body vibrates.

"Roman, you'd better have a really good explanation for this. What the hell, man?" Braxton says as he shoves his way to the front, trying to get his hands on Madi, who is attempting to wrap herself around Clover.

Clover appears to be in shock.

"Get him out of here, Roman. Let us get Clover home, and then we can talk. But to be clear, this feels like an ambush, and I'm not impressed," I snap.

"It's not," he says with such determination I stop in my tracks. "It's family." There's something in his eyes I recognize, something that makes me want to punch him just a little less, something like loyalty. "Valen was supposed to arrive in the morning."

"We'll talk." I lean in closer to Clover. "Clove? Are you okay?"

"How? How?" she says in response.

"We should get everyone home," Braxton says at my side. "We've been out here too long without guards close by. With Riley on the loose..."

I nod. "You're right."

"Clover?" Madi tries again.

I find a blanket hanging on the wall and wrap it around Clover's shoulders. She flinches away from my touch, and my gut sinks.

Braxton meets my eye, and we both know there's more to this story than anyone is privy to.

"Let's take her back to the Hideaway," Braxton says. "I'll see what info I can get from Madi, and then we'll get a doctor or...someone to talk to her." Neither of us can take our eyes off our girls' best friend.

Clover calls that man a friend, but if this is what

happens when she sees him, we need to seriously reconsider her definition.

I inch closer to Clover with my hands held high. After close to a minute, she still doesn't focus on me, so I move slowly toward her. "Clover? I'm going to lift you out of here, okay?"

She doesn't say anything, her blank stare focused on where Valen had previously stood. This isn't good. "Sav?"

Braxton backs away, and I lean out of the van.

"Savvy?" I spin in a circle, then run to the back of the van, where Valen squats with his head in his hands, but no Savvy, so I sprint to the front. "Where the fuck is Savvy?"

My heartbeat pounds in my chest.

Thump. *Find her.*

Thump. *Where the hell is she?*

Thump. *I can't lose her now.*

"She was just—" Madi's voice cuts off as she too spins in place.

"Get back here. Firefly's missing. I repeat, Firefly is missing." Roman climbs to the top of the van, which startles Clover, who then begins rocking in place.

This is a nightmare.

"Where is she, Roman?" I can't breathe. My pulse pounds violently in my ears.

This is my fault.

Why didn't I listen to Roman?

Fuck.

He warned me, and I didn't listen.

He stands on top of the van, scanning the dark street with a pair of binoculars that appear to glow as he spins in a circle.

Feet pound on the pavement as Valen steps into view and three of their guys race toward us.

"Monroe!" Her name is ripped from my lungs as though it has spikes and talons attached to every syllable.

I race to the end of the street.

Look both ways.

Run back.

Whatever has happened to her is on me.

"Where is she?"

Madi stays with Clover while Braxton backtracks to the concession stand.

Her name is called over and over again.

Savvy?

Sav?

Savannah?

"Monroe!" My knees tremble. I'm stumbling through the empty street.

Where the hell is she?

What have I done?

"We were all right here," I say, returning to the van. "Right here. Right. Here!" My voice echoes off the metal walls of the van.

I didn't listen. Roman's right—I am an arrogant prick. Me and my fucking need to do things myself might have just cost me another life I couldn't afford to lose.

It's my sister all over again, except this time I had the help. I had them right here, and I sent them away.

I double over with my hands on my knees and vomit. It's an exorcism of guilt that's building like a tidal wave.

Reaching into the van, I wipe my mouth with the corner of a sheet.

Someone moved Clover. Madi's no longer here either.

How long has it been?

Where the fuck is my wife?

"We'll find her." I don't know who says that. I don't care.

"He took her." The words are so low, no one hears me. "He. Took. Her." I roar.

"I've got her," someone shouts. "Her phone is moving on the other side of the fairgrounds."

I follow the voice.

"Let me see."

Braxton stands at my side as Roman ushers me closer to Valen. "She's here." He lifts his gaze from his screen, spins forty-five degrees, then points. "She's headed that way."

I don't hear anything else they say because I take off at a dead sprint.

I'm coming, Monroe.

I should have accepted help.

I'm coming.

I'm so fucking sorry.

Please don't let it be too late.

CHAPTER THIRTY-SEVEN

SAVVY

"Monroe, stop!"

I almost trip over my feet when I look back. Grey is sprinting toward me with Roman right beside him.

No, no, no, no, no. My chest explodes with pain. It's how I suspect being shot feels.

The red light appears in the center of Grey's forehead again, and a sob that starts deep in my belly rings out through the open field.

"Make them stop, or I'll kill him now." Riley's completely unhinged. I know he'll do it too.

"Stop," I scream with everything I have. It's wrenched from my belly, devastating in sound, soul-crushing in execution. "Don't come any closer."

Grey halts, his winding arms reminding me of a cartoon character running straight for the edge a ravine, then he slowly inches closer. Even from thirty yards away, I can see the fear in his eyes.

"I'll kill him, Sin, and his blood will be on your hands." When Riley texted me at the picnic table, I didn't want to believe he was serious.

Then, as soon as Clover was in the ambulance, the red dot appeared on Grey's back.

I had no choice but to run when Riley said to, and now it might be for nothing.

I didn't even get to say goodbye.

"Grey, don't move. Stay there."

"What the fuck is going on, Monroe?"

"Start walking backward, Sin. I'll tell you when to stop. If they so much as breathe wrong, I'll shoot them between the eyes."

This is how my soul dies—with the lies I know I must tell to save the only man who ever loved me and all my jagged edges.

"I—I can't do this with you. Just let me go."

His fist clenches above his heart, and his hard body appears to stand taller. He'll never forgive me for this. No matter what happens next, Grey and I will never have a chance.

Not after I lied to him about the surrogacy app. Riley will either kill him, or Grey will hate me until eternity for lying to him again.

There is no happy ending here. There's only death or a lifetime of pain—and both options will kill me.

"I don't believe you," he calls back.

Slowly I take one step away, then another, but Grey moves in tandem, and I see the red light appear on his chest.

"No!" I taste blood in the back of my throat. "Stop. Please. Stop. Don't come closer."

Roman holds a hand to his ear, then says something to Grey—the harsh consonants of words reaching my ears in a cacophony of mismatched sounds.

"Where is he, Savvy?" Grey has lost the edge in his voice,

but it's replaced with sheer determination that scares the living hell out of me.

I shrug with my phone in the air.

"Get rid of them, Sin. Last warning." I've never wished death on someone until this very moment. If Riley disappeared, I would never mourn him.

"What do you want me to do?" I cry. I don't know if I'm talking to Riley, Grey, or some higher power, but I feel more helpless now than I ever have before.

"Move your fucking ass," Riley hisses. My legs comply, even though every step I take away from Grey cuts me open with a self-inflicted wound I'll never be able to heal.

"You don't have to do this, Savvy." Grey's pleading with me while also listening intently to whatever it is Roman is saying at his side.

The bright red light appears on Grey's forehead again, and I stumble back a few more steps while pure terror is ripped from my chest in a horrifying scream.

"You have one minute to get to me before I start putting holes through that asshole."

"Savvy, I'm going to come and get you—"

"No. God no, Grey. Listen to me. P—p—please." I take a step, and so does he. "I hate you."

I'm sorry.

"I hate everything about you."

I love you.

"I hate how awful you were to me. I hate that you saw my insecurities and used them for your own benefit." I'm hysterical. My words are a run-on sentence full of mucus and shame. Each lie sets my heart on fire.

"I know you do, baby." Why is he still creeping forward?

"Thirty seconds, Sin. Ticktock."

I startle and walk backward a little faster.

"I'm not your sister." I scream so loudly, my words echo off the empty pasture that will host a petting zoo tomorrow.

Grey's steps falter.

I'm sorry.

"I'm not a replacement or a plan B." I choke on the hurtful words. "One day, you'll wake up and realize I was never yours to save."

He takes one slow step forward. "I love you, Monroe." The tightness in his tone tells me although he's saying the words, he's struggling to believe them.

That's good. I need him to hate me, wish he'd never met me, loathe me. It's the only way to keep him safe.

"You don't love me though—you just want to fix me. But here's the truth, Grey, I was never going to stay. Not with you because I don't love you."

"You do." He doesn't sound mad, or even irritated, just… scared. I keep inching away from him.

"You're not a hero, Grey. You're just another man looking for a win."

"In our story, I am your hero. Just keep talking to me, sweetheart."

What?

Roman is speaking quietly, but I don't think it's to Grey.

"Is he on the phone?" Grey asks.

I nod, and another soul-aching sob escapes.

"You have to leave, Patch, please. Please turn around and leave." My knees tremble. I'm not sure how much longer I can hold myself up as I creep toward the devil himself.

"I'm not leaving you, Savvy. If you run, I'll follow. If you hide, I'll seek. If you panic, I'll soothe. If you break, I'll be your glue."

"He has a gun," I shout when Grey attempts to come closer. "Don't move. He has a gun, and he will shoot you."

"Did you see the gun, sweetheart? Have you seen it?"

How is he so calm?

"I have to move, Grey. He gave me one minute."

"Did you see the gun?" he barks.

"He has the laser trained on you. He's going to shoot. Please, please just go." Blood rushes in my ears.

"Can you mute your phone, Sav?"

I'm too scared to ask any more questions. I put it on mute, hoping Riley doesn't notice.

"The laser is a paw print, Savvy. It's a goddamn cat toy."

My head is shaking, but I don't understand what he's saying.

"No, what? No. I saw it land on your chest and your forehead. He said...he said—"

"Did. You. See. A. Gun?"

Did I? Not today, but I know Riley had guns when we were younger.

"I... Not today, but he knows how to use them."

"Now, Sin. I'm not messing around here, you insolent little slut."

The viciousness in Riley's tone makes my hands shake so much I bobble my phone, wasting precious moments.

"Once again, you didn't trust me, Monroe." Grey inches closer, but he still feels so far away. "You ran instead of coming to me for help. I'm really starting to get a complex, and you know how bad my trust issues run already." He takes a step forward, and I take two back. "He just got out of prison, so we're playing his game on the off chance he does have a gun, but you should have trusted me."

"I'm going to kill him, Sin. I swear to fucking God." Any semblance of control that Riley had left has gone out the window. He's going to kill us all.

"Just twenty more seconds, baby. Hold it together.

Roman's team is circling around the back of him now. We just need him to believe that we're following his directions. It's almost over."

No. No, he can't mean that. And even if he does, he'll never trust me again. Riley wins either way.

"Fuck," Roman shouts. "He saw my guy."

An engine roars, tires squeal, and my night erupts into madness.

"Run, Savvy. Run." Grey's terrified expression penetrates my panic, but so does Riley's shouted threats.

"Time's up, Bitch. I warned you. I told you what would happen if you weren't mine."

What the hell is happening?

Grey rockets toward me like a bullet while Riley roars nonsense into the air.

An engine is getting closer, so I turn and run.

"No, Savvy! No..."

I look up.

There's nothing human in Riley's gaze as he drives a giant pickup truck straight for me.

He's laughing. Manically. His shouted curses, threats, and promises of violence pierce what should be a silent night.

I always wondered how my life would end. For a few years, I fooled myself into thinking I could have a normal life here in Happiness.

But my past was always going to collide with my future. I just didn't know it would happen quite so literally.

Time slows in these last precious moments of my life. I'm still running, zigging and zagging, fighting for my right at happiness, but then the time comes, and I know he'll hit me no matter where I go.

I have just enough time to look over at Grey one more time.

It's his face, his scent, his love that I'll take with me to heaven—or hell, depending on who gets the final say.

He's my hero, my knight in shining armor, and I never got to tell him how much his determination, how much his loyalty has meant to me. This will hurt him, break him. I just hope my death doesn't destroy him.

I'm almost glad my end will be quick because I know I couldn't carry the weight of his guilt that hits me when his gaze connects with mine.

"I lied," I cry, hoping he knows I mean about everything.

I lied to protect him. I lied to keep him away from Riley.

Braxton and Sage will be able to explain it to him, right?

They'll let him know why I said horrible, unforgiveable things in my final moments of life.

Right?

Thump.

Crunch.

Glass rains down—it's not unlike the night of the hurricane, except this time, I know I won't make it out in one piece.

A crack of bone.

I'm weightless—airborne.

Then I'm hit again, and I feel myself contort in ways that shouldn't be possible.

Something crushes my lungs.

Another bone snaps.

People are yelling.

My body is shutting down. I know it is. Everything should hurt, but I can't feel...anything.

Greyson? Is that Greyson?

He's crying.

Don't cry, Patch.

I did this for you.

I'm your hero this time.

He needs a hero too.

I love you, Grey.

And I'm so, so sorry you had the misfortune of falling in love with me.

I'm so sorry.

I'm so, so...

CHAPTER THIRTY-EIGHT

GREYSON

"I think you've proved your point, Monroe. The silent treatment is losing its effectiveness, don't you think?"

Not even an eye flutter.

"Come on, Monroe. You win, okay? You're the biggest, baddest badass around. Want me to take out a billboard?"

Just talk to me, please.

"I need you, okay? No one will fight with me right now. Not even when I get up in Braxton's face. Not when I slammed Roman into the wall for not telling me he told me so. They're all walking on eggshells around me, and I can't stand it."

Her only response is the constant beep, beep, beep that's my only soundtrack now.

"Please don't do this to me, Monroe." There's nothing left to my voice, so it comes out as a hoarse whisper.

"Grey?"

My head is pounding, but I lift it from Savvy's hospital bed when Braxton and Madi enter.

"Why are you wearing scrubs? Is the baby okay?" I ask her.

She offers a sad smile. "Yeah, I was trying to blend in so no one questioned me getting in here today. You know, only two visitors at a time. Yesterday, they wouldn't let Clover in."

I hate this place. I'll buy the fucking hospital if they don't start catering to Savvy's needs better.

"Grey." Madi's voice breaks, but she swallows it down, shaking her head as though that will help. They're all doing that now—hiding their feelings, sheltering me.

It's not what I want. I want to rage with them. I want to lose my fucking shit. I want to purge all the acid in my throat and scream until she wakes up, but they don't...so I remain here, stoic, silent, dying.

"Have you slept at all?" she asks.

I scratch my chin. I've never had a full beard before, but I can't bring myself to care. I'm also in a rotation of sweatpants and whatever shit Sage or Braxton bring me every couple of days. I only shower at five in the morning if one of the nurses is here with Savvy because she hates mornings. When she wakes up, I'm certain it won't be at five a.m.

Most days I don't shower at all—I can't take the risk.

Eventually, someone nags at me until I cave.

Everyone nags these days.

It's been two weeks since that asshole tried to take Savvy from me.

Some people would say he succeeded, but they're full of shit and they don't know her like I do.

She's still in there, I know she is, and I'll wait however long it takes.

It'll be any day now, I know it. They only started reversing the medically induced coma four days ago, for Christ's sake.

Braxton thumbs through the makeshift desk I've turned

Savvy's hospital tray into, not that I've done much work. He's been keeping the company afloat, I suppose.

"Quinn can handle this stuff, Grey." Braxton is checking my work, and I can't blame him. My mind isn't in anything except getting Savvy better. I spend more time researching head injuries, broken bones, and coma facts than I do on Omni-Reyes business these days.

"After how we treated her, I'm surprised she was willing to come back," I say, knowing I still owe Quinn an apology.

"These are not normal circumstances, Grey. And she would've been an idiot to turn down the six-figure bonus I gave her."

I shrug. "It's the least we can do. We were horrible to her."

"We were," he agrees with a heavy sigh I know carries a ton of guilt because I feel it too. "And we'll make it up to her another time. She cares about you, Grey. I'm sorry I didn't see it for what it was sooner."

Madi fusses over Savvy's hair, and I focus on not squeezing the hell out of Savvy's hand in frustration. She comes every day to brush it and runs some essential oil diffuser I don't understand.

It's annoying as hell.

I brush Savvy's hair every damn morning, I don't need Madi to do it. I wash her and help with physical therapy and turning her so she doesn't get bed sores. I even painted her nails her favorite coral color before the nurses scolded me— some bullshit about being able to see the color of her nailbeds.

I don't want them here, but I know Savvy needs them almost as much as she needs me, so I do my best not to snap every time she fucks up something I've just done.

We're doing just fine, and when Savvy wakes up, I'll be

the one here for her. I have to be. I'm the reason she's lying here this way. I was too stubborn to listen to Roman.

Why didn't I listen to Roman?

"You haven't left her side at all, Grey." I know Braxton's concerned, but he would be doing the same exact thing if it were Madi lying here so he can just fuck off.

"And I won't."

He doesn't bother responding to that.

I will not leave this room until Savvy does.

"Did her parents call you back?" Madi asks while fussing over the blanket I just adjusted.

Stop messing up my system!

"Yes." It's a guttural sound that has Madi's face falling.

"What did they say?"

"They said that they're not responsible for her medical bills." Useless pieces of shit.

"And her brother?" Braxton asks as Roman slips into the room. He's my own personal grim reaper—a physical reminder of the guilt that taints my soul.

My nostrils flare. He won't make eye contact with me, but he doesn't get to take my guilt from me. I did this, not him.

"I asked Roman to come in," Braxton says. "We have some things to discuss, but first, tell us what Savvy's brother said."

"He didn't say anything." My teeth gnash together. "He asked about her assets. Her fucking assets, as though she's an ATM, so I hung up on him."

"I've confirmed through...*other* channels, that Austin Monroe has been calling twice a week to 'see if she's dead,'" Roman says quietly.

The asshole isn't even asking if she's alive. She's worth

more to him dead, but the entire world will collapse if that happens, and he'll be the first to feel my wrath.

I close my eyes and count to ten. "It's okay, Monroe. You don't need people like that in your life. I'm your family now."

"Do you..." Madi loses her composure, and I stare at her.

Is this when we break?

My heart rate speeds up, ready for this outlet. Is this when we scream and threaten the entire universe to bring Savvy back to me?

Please let this be when we break.

"Do you talk to her a lot?"

Disappointing.

I think Monroe would love it if we had a communal melt down.

Jesus, maybe I'm losing it.

"Yes. The doctor said it was good to talk to her."

"Grey, you're Savvy's fiancé, but unfortunately, that doesn't automatically make you her next of kin." Roman is a big guy, but he backs himself into the wall now because he likely knows I'm one whistle away from blowing my kettle. "Austin has filled out paperwork to become her medical power of attorney."

I stand so quickly, the metal chair legs scrape against the linoleum floor as it slides to the wall behind me.

"Over my dead body." Oh God. I think I broke a lung. I can't get a full breath of air. Panting gives way to gasps for oxygen that won't come.

I slam my fist into my chest, trying to jumpstart something into working properly, and then Braxton is on one side, Roman on my other.

Madi stands directly in front of me, wearing an expression of pity that I despise.

"Slow down your breathing, Grey." Braxton sounds like he's underwater.

Roman slams me back into my chair, then forcefully shoves my head between my legs.

Fuck me.

I've done this for Savvy.

"You've got this, Grey. Deep breath in, then out. Slowly." Madi's running her palm over my back, but it isn't her touch I crave.

I don't know how long we continue on this path, but I'm covered in sweat by the time I sit tall again.

Roman is down on one knee at my side, his concerned stare taking in every inch of my face.

I never got the chance to get down on one knee for Savvy. I should have. I should have done everything differently.

"I can fix this, Grey. It won't be legal, but I can get a post-dated marriage license in your hands in two hours." If I looked at Roman closely enough, I would probably admit that he's also completely torn up about Savvy being in this bed.

Unfortunately for him, I only have enough room to handle my own fucked-up emotions over the situation right now.

"Do it." I laugh, then lean down and kiss Savvy's hand. "Oh, Monroe. You're going to really hate me when you wake up, but I promise, we'll do another wedding any way you want. Whatever you want." Turning back to Roman, I nod. "Get it done, and make sure it can't be contested."

"It won't be," Madi says. "You had lots of witnesses at your wedding last month. Me, Clover, and Elle were all in the wedding party. Braxton, Cian, Sage, and even Roman were all there too."

Something cracks in my chest then. When I look to Braxton, he nods in agreement, and a tear settles in the corner of my eye.

"I'll do it now," Roman says, standing.

"Any word on Kristen?" I ask, when he's almost to the door.

He turns back to me. "Her credit card was used at a Hilton this morning in Rhode Island. I have a team en route now."

That bitch has eluded us for weeks. It's not enough to have Riley back in prison for attempted murder. I want to destroy everyone associated with him, and Kristen is the top of my list.

Madi's gaze darts between Roman and Brax. "You have to tell him."

"Tell me what?" My vision is blurry again, but I prepare myself for another hit.

Roman stands on the threshold, obviously warring with something in his mind.

"From what we've uncovered, it seems as though Kristen was scheduled for an arranged marriage with Riley right before he went to prison last time," he says with a deep sigh. "Their families wouldn't let her out of it, even though he would be behind bars for ten plus years. My best guess is she's been fucked up by his decisions too, but I'll make sure to get answers out of her before we turn her over to authorities."

He faces the bed. "Savvy," he says gently. "If you can hear us, I hope you'll wake up soon. Grey needs you." He walks out the door without a glance back.

He's not wrong. I do need her.

The room falls into an uncomfortable silence, and a sense of foreboding washes over me.

"What?" I ask when the unease threatens what's left of my patience.

"Do you think, maybe," Braxton is hesitating, and I brace for impact. "Grey, it's been two weeks. Do you think that maybe we need to prepare for the possibility that she won't wake up?"

My fist clenches the front of his shirt. I don't even remember moving. "That's not going to happen, and if that's your line of thinking, you can leave and not bother coming back."

"We're not your enemy, Grey." The sadness in Madi's words claws at my chest—it's an infestation of fire ants, and I want to douse myself in boiling water to get rid of the sensation.

"So that's it?" I hurl the words in accusation. "You've just given up?"

"That's not what we're saying." Braxton keeps his tone light and his body language open and relaxed. Who knew he was such a showman.

"It sure as fuck sounds like it to me."

"I'm just saying we've spoken to the doctors—"

"Shut up." It bellows out of me as though I'm possessed. "Just shut up or get the hell out of here. Savvy needs positivity and love. If you can't give her those two things, just those two things." A sob chokes me up. "Then, then get out."

"We love her too, Grey." Madi's shaking, but my emotional intelligence is reserved for Savvy. Braxton will comfort her later. "Okay. Okay, Grey. You're right. Maybe I'll just sit and watch her favorite movie with her. How's that? Maybe you could shower, or get something to eat while it's on?"

"*How to Lose a Guy in 10 Days*?" I ask.

Madi's smile is fragile and close to breaking, but she nods with watery eyes.

"I'm sure Savvy will appreciate that, but I'm not going anywhere. I only shower at five in the morning when a nurse is around because Savvy would never wake up that early."

Madi's jaw drops, and she stares from me to Braxton.

"Have you slept, Grey?" Braxton's frowning, and he's wearing the same expression he wore when Sage broke his collarbone in the fourth grade.

"I sleep enough. Put on the movie, Madi, but I'm not giving up my seat, so you'll have to see if you can con a nurse into giving you another one."

"I'll go get one," Braxton murmurs. I stop making eye contact with him because I don't appreciate the way he's looking at me—as though I'm damaged, broken, lost.

Madi signs in to a streaming service, but I ignore her and instead fix Savvy's bedding the way it should be done. I hate the way Madi tucked her in. Savvy will be much more comfortable if I fix the corners so they're not suffocating her.

I need to be able to breathe, Patch. No more prison corners on the sheets," she'd said to me once. After that, I learned how to make the bed to her specifications, but of course I never told her that.

I do now. "Remember when you told me no prison corners?" I wait in case she responds. She doesn't. "Well, I watched you untuck all the edges that morning, and then from that day on, I made the bed the way you liked it."

Walking around the bed, I start on the other side.

"It took me an entire week to get used to your loosey goosey bed sheets, but honestly, it didn't really matter because we always ended up tangled in each other anyway."

When she's tucked in the way she prefers, I cradle her face in both of my hands.

"I'll learn all your ways, Monroe, if you just wake up for me, okay? Come on, sweetheart. That's a deal even you can't refuse."

A wet, garbled noise has me lifting her eyelids. Is this it? Is she waking up?

"G—Grey," Madi sobs.

My name from Madi's lips steals my hope—the damn grim reaper coming for my soul.

Hope is a dangerous thing. When hope dies, so does joy. And when joy dies…

"What?" I ask.

"A—are you okay?"

"I will be, just as soon as Savvy wakes up."

She makes more wet, raspy sounds. I know she's crying, but crying feels like giving up. I'll rage with her. I'll beg with her. I'll do a fucking rain dance with her. But I will not cry with her.

"Savvy's ready for the movie," I say.

Madi hiccups and presses play.

Braxton enters a few moments later with a chair that he places by Savvy's bed. Madi sits opposite me and takes Savvy's hand.

I fight the urge to rip it away from her. I have no good reason to do it, and it would only lead to problems. Rationally, I know Savvy belongs to them too, but with so little of her to spare right now, I'm finding it really painful to share.

Braxton sits on the floor along the wall and stares blankly at the television screen.

They're sitting vigil, but me? I'm still praying for a miracle.

With Matthew McConaughey's voice in the background,

I rest my head on Savvy's bed, as close to her heart as I can get, and close my eyes.

She just needs a little more time.

————

I WAKE TO THE SOUND OF WHISPERS. THE S-SOUNDS HISSING and harsh Cs and Ks somehow softer.

They weave through my dreams and conscious mind like a bad trip.

"Is it legal though? Will Austin be able to fight it?"

My head snaps up at the mention of Austin. His mother definitely should have swallowed him.

"Fight what?" My voice is rough with sleep, and my head feels as though it's floating.

Perhaps I do need more rest, but that will come when she wakes up.

I blink the blurriness from my eyes.

Either everyone is sneaking in, or the CEO of the hospital finally got my message because Madi, Braxton, Sage, Moose, Pops, Clover, Roman, and even Valen are crowded in like sardines.

And no one seems to mind.

There are folding chairs lined up under the windows for Braxton, Sage, Pops, and Moose.

Madi and Clover huddle together opposite me at Savvy's bedside.

Sage is sitting on the floor next to me while Valen hovers behind Clover, and Roman stands guard at the door.

What the hell?

My frown deepens as I scan the room.

"Elle and Cian are in the cafeteria feeding Keela," Madi says. "They're taking turns coming in."

They're not why I'm so disoriented though. Where the hell are Savvy's doctors? The clock on the wall says they should have been in to see her an hour ago.

"We submitted your marriage license to the hospital," Roman says, wiping all other thoughts from my mind. The edge that drew me to him in the first place is absent though. Is that because he's taking on my guilt over Savvy?

It's not his fault. I'm the one who insisted on sending the men home.

"And we have our attorney, Mr. Coop, notifying her family." Braxton has the confidence I'm lacking these days. "If they try to fight anything, he'll take care of it."

"I had no idea her family was so...horrid." Clover's voice is barely more than a whisper, but I notice that Valen moves as if on autopilot to squeeze her shoulder.

"What's he doing here?" I ask her.

I haven't even finished my sentence before she's tugging a navy-blue cardigan with white stars more tightly around her middle.

"Clover received another package three days ago," Braxton says. "He's...ah, staying in a camper van outside her house because we didn't think you'd want anyone in Savvy's side of the duplex."

"I don't want him in there with her stuff, but she's not going back there, so if you move all her shit to our house, then I don't care what he does with the space." Turning to Clover, I frown. "Are *you* sure you want him that close?"

Clover bites her lip but nods.

I turn to study Valen. "Does that mean you remember who she is?"

His jaw twitches, and his eyes glaze over. It's as though he just shut down the ounce of humanity he had in himself, and then he shakes his head in jerky movements that appear unnatural to me.

Moose stands and hands me a coffee. "Not scalding hot anymore, but it's warm. It'll help ya wake up."

"Thanks."

"The marriage license. It's legit?" I ask.

Roman nearly smirks. "It's legal, and as legit as a forgery can be. But our guy is so good not even the CIA could tell the difference."

"So, Savvy and I are married. She's mine?"

"I'm not a dog. I don't belong to anyone." Her words are muffled around the feeding tube, but they're there.

I drop the coffee to the floor and cup Savvy's face in my hands as I scan every inch of her.

Why aren't her eyes open?

"You heard that right?" I've lost control of my emotions. The floodgates are opening, and there's not a damn thing I can do about it. "Right?" I shout. "Please tell me someone else heard her. Savvy, please. Please open your eyes."

Madi jumps out of her chair. I can feel her hands sliding all along the bed, and in my periphery, I see her pulling a red emergency cord.

"Did you hear her, Madi?" Each word is a plea exhaled on a painful sob. "Someone fucking tell me they heard her too."

"We heard, Grey." Madi has tears cascading down her face, and this time, I succumb to them as well. I shudder and shake as hope fills in the cracks of my damaged heart.

"Why won't she open her eyes?" I'm pleading, begging, for answers. I thought I felt fear when I saw her fly into the air. But this is almost worse. "Monroe, open your goddamn eyes."

The door bursts open, and the nurse pauses to take in the number of people disobeying their two-visitor rule.

"Forget about them, get over here," I yell. "She spoke. Two whole sentences. We heard her. We all heard her."

The door opens again, and three doctors barrel into the room.

"Everyone out. Clear the room," one of them shouts.

"I'm not going anywhere." The vehemence in my tone startles him, and he swallows thickly before nodding.

"We need everyone else out then, give us some room to work," the doctor I recognize says.

"Out. Everyone out," I bark.

"Easy, Grey." Two words spoken by an angel. My angel.

"See?" I can't control the hysteria in my tone, and I don't have the bandwidth to try.

As our family filters out of the room, Savvy's eyes flutter open for less than three seconds.

But it was enough to see her, to know she's in there, awake, and coming back to me.

The doctors crowd the bed, but I keep hold of her hand and drop to my knees.

She came back to me.

She didn't leave.

She kept her promise.

CHAPTER THIRTY-NINE

SAVVY

IT FEELS LIKE A LIFETIME OF BEING POKED, PRODDED, AND SENT for test after test before I'm finally wheeled back into my room, where apparently Grey has been pacing a rut into the flooring for the last six hours.

His eyes are red and puffy.

He's sporting a freaking beard, and I don't hate it.

But it's the vacancy in his eyes that burns like a branding.

I put those shadows there with my callous words and lies.

The nurse engages the lock on my bed, then checks my vitals for the fourth time this hour. We won't know the extent of my injuries until more tests are run, but cognitively, they believe I'll make a full recovery.

A recovery no one but Grey thought would happen.

While the nurses took me for tests, they told me how stubborn and bossy Grey has been.

He hasn't left my side. Not once.

When the doctors told him my chances of waking up

were essentially nonexistent, he told them to get out and brought in new doctors.

He's been my advocate, my caregiver, my protector, even when all evidence told him he should prepare to move on.

The nurse wheels over a table with a plastic cup of ice water, then leaves the room.

Grey stands sentinel in the corner, almost as if he's afraid to make any sudden movements. I'm so tired, but I have so much I need to say.

"I'm sorry," I say. The weight of releasing those two words attempts to lull me to sleep.

"Stop. We don't have to do this."

I flinch as though he struck me. His words are so similar to the ones he uttered when he learned I was Firefly, and it sends panic racing through me.

I knew this would happen, right? I knew that lying to him a second time would be the final nail in our coffin.

Without making eye contact, I lift my hand to keep him from speaking. I have to get this out before he leaves.

"I didn't mean any of it. I swear I didn't. I don't hate you. I don't hate anything about you."

He crosses the room with three long strides.

"I know you don't think of me as a replacement for your sister. I know that you want to fix my demons, not me. I know that you loved me, and I'm so sorry I lied to you again. I'm so sorry I broke us."

Greedily, I gulp for air. "You are my hero, Grey. You're the hero in my story, and I'm sorry I said words I knew would hurt you. I'm so sorry."

He leans down and presses a kiss to my forehead. "Are you done now?"

Feebly, I shake my head no. "I have so many other apologies to make, but everything hurts, so I'll have to make a full apology tour at a later date if you'll let me. But I need you to know one thing."

His thumb gently caresses my cheek. "What's that, Monroe?"

"I love you. With my whole heart, body, and soul, I love you." The heaviness in my chest squeezes a little more tightly.

"I know. That's why I'm here. My love isn't past tense, sweetheart, it's here, now, alive and thriving. I saw through your plan the moment you ran. I knew you were choosing words as the most painful weapons in your arsenal, but I understood what you were doing. And even if I didn't know how you felt about me, I know you would have never left Clover in that condition if you had any other choice."

Clover. What happened to Clover?

My unasked question must show on my face because he frowns. "Do you remember Clover passing out when Valen showed up?"

"Valen?" I attempt to sit up too quickly, and it feels as though I'm being electrocuted by a million live wires.

"What do you remember, sweetheart?"

"The line dancing and the fair. I remember Madi being hungry. Then...then yelling really horrible things at you. But I don't..." I search the room as though it will fill in the blanks for me. "I'm missing things, Grey. Like a hole in my memory." Tears slide down my face in a constant stream of emotion. "Will this, what if I can't remember? How will I testify to put Riley in jail? Oh, God—"

"Hey, hey." Grey runs his palms over my biceps, careful to avoid the fracture at my elbow that has apparently already had surgery. "That won't matter. There were enough of us there that witnessed everything..." He chokes on a sob.

His chin quivers, and the torment is written all over his expression.

"We saw it happen, baby. There are enough witnesses, plus your phone records and what happened at Blissy's. You won't even have to testify if you don't want to. He won't be getting out this time. I'll make sure of it."

He slides into a chair at the side of my bed—the nurses told me this is where he's spent the last two weeks, and we cry together.

It's messy and incoherent. It's blubbering and sobbing words of love and fear.

It's cathartic.

It's healing.

It's teamwork.

When I start to fade into sleep, he speaks again. "When he hurt you the first time, you were all alone. I don't think any of us truly understood just how isolated you were until this happened, but you won't ever be alone again."

He twirls the engagement ring he placed back on my finger before they wheeled me off for testing.

"After Violet died, I felt so alone, even though I had Braxton, Ace, and baby Sage. Nothing was ever about me again. I wouldn't allow it to be. I put all my energy into being the kind of parent Sage would need, the kind of grandson Ace would want, the kind of friend and brother that Braxton would choose."

"Oh, Grey."

"I was safeguarding my heart, but really what I was doing was making myself an island that no one could get to. Somehow, you airdropped into my remote way of living and you blew it up spectacularly."

I'd laugh, but it hurts. Four broken ribs are pure hell. "I do have a way of blowing up people's lives."

"But that's it. Before you, I wasn't living. I was existing and experiencing life secondhand through my brother and my nephew. You showed me what it means to live, and I refused to spend one minute living without you, so I sat here, swimming in the guilt because when it comes down to it, I was the one who sent Roman's men away. I'm just as responsible for you being in this bed as Riley is."

"No. Absolutely not, Grey. You don't get to carry this guilt around your neck."

He stares at me with so much pain in his eyes that I know he doesn't believe me—he thinks this is all his fault.

"I prayed," he whispers. "I begged. I pleaded and bargained for you to come back to me."

"And I did." My eyelids droop, and it's harder to open them this time. The pain meds are starting to kick in.

"You did. And I've never been more thankful for anything in my entire life. I made you a deal a while ago, but I'm ready to renegotiate."

I smile even as my eyes flutter closed.

"Legally, we're married, and while I don't regret doing it this way, I do want to do it again, the right way, for you."

Someday soon I'll yell at him about marrying me this way but today is not that day. Not when he wants a big fancy party just so he can declare me as his for all to see.

Honestly, that's sounding really good to me too.

"Sleep, sweetheart. I'll be right here when you wake up."

And I know he will be. The innocence I lost as a little girl raising herself throws up a giant two-handed fist pump.

Greyson Reyes has healed a childhood wound I thought could only be patched up and boarded over.

That little girl who sits in the corner of my soul, sobbing into her folded knees, wipes her tears and smiles.

I'm going to be okay.

Grey and I are going to be okay.

We'll be better than okay, because we have forever to get there.

———

"You're going home today. Are you excited?" Madi moves about my hospital room, packing up cards and gifts that have accumulated over my two-month-long stay.

I am excited, but also nervous, though I don't tell her that. I still have to use a walker—my broken hip on the right and broken leg on the left caused so much damage. It's been a painful recovery.

And we're still not sure if I'll ever walk without some kind of limp again.

"I tested out the elevator Grey put into your house." She means his house. I'm still struggling to come to terms with it being ours since I didn't buy a damn thing for it. "It's going to make it so much easier to get around."

"I told him he didn't have to do that." I'm bitter today, and I don't know why.

"Sav. I think that man would build you a 50,000-square-foot castle, complete with a moat and private gardens, if that's what would make you happy."

Maybe that's the problem. I haven't done anything to deserve his devotion. If I'm completely honest, I've done everything possible to push him away time and time again.

The hurtful words I hurled at him the night Riley hit me with a truck take up so much real estate in my mind—the intrusive thoughts filling my every waking moment—and I don't know how to silence them.

"What's wrong, Savvy?" Madi drops into Grey's chair. With only five days left until her due date, she's swollen everywhere, but she's scary enough that Grey finally went to check on the house and left me in her care.

"I'm struggling," I admit.

Madi's easy smile and kind eyes do little to ease my worries. But I love her for trying. "You've been through a lot."

"I guess."

"Can I...ask you something?" Her hesitancy puts me even more on edge because it hits home what a shitty friend I've been.

"Always," I say, meaning it.

"Why didn't you talk to us? Me and Clover, at least. We've known you since we were nineteen."

Emotion saws at my throat with a rusty serrated knife.

"If you're not ready to talk, I understand," she says gently. "But you were my rock when Braxton's family attacked me. You've been Clover's emotional support person for eleven years. You're the friend that stepped up and protected us anytime we couldn't do it ourselves, but we never got the chance to be that person for you."

She grabs a tissue and dabs at her eyes.

"Were we so self-absorbed that we completely missed the signs? I feel like we failed you in every way."

Oh, God. Is that what they think?

"No, Madi. No."

"Grey has alluded to you having an eating disorder, and Clover said she had suspicions. Then all this stuff with Riley, but most importantly with your family, Sav. We had no idea they were so terrible to you. You never mentioned them, and when you did, you glossed over what it was really like. The way they treated you, God, Sav. I'm so sorry."

My shame spiral burrows deep into my chest.

I think I'm going to be sick. It's almost thirty years of

shame bubbling to the surface, wanting an escape I've never allowed.

"I'm sorry," Madi says. "This can wait until you're feeling better." She stands, but I grasp her wrist before she can move away.

This conversation has been a long time coming.

"I think I was six when I started parenting myself...and to some extent, my parents too." I can't meet Madi's eyes. I know she had a shitty childhood with her own parents that led to her moving in with Pops when she was ten, but at least she was brave enough to talk about it.

I hid behind a facade I created to make myself feel better.

"By the time I was thirteen, I was angry. Angry at my parents, angry at my circumstances, angry at every adult who had ever let me down, so I rebelled. I started going to parties, stealing stupid shit one day, food the next, meeting the wrong people."

Madi reaches out and clasps my hand in hers.

"I met Riley when I was fifteen at a party Paige got us into. By the time I was sixteen, we were dating, and I liked that he was so much older than me. At first, he made me feel safe. He took control, and I didn't have to worry about where my next meal would come from."

"He groomed you, Sav."

I nod, still unsure if that's what actually happened or if I was just so desperate to be loved that I ignored the signs.

"About a year before the accident where Paige lost use of her legs, I felt like I'd lost control of my entire life, and I found it by controlling what I consumed. I would starve myself, then binge and purge. At one point, I was taking upward of twelve laxatives a day."

"Oh, Savvy." Madi squeezes my hand, and I take strength from it.

"Sometimes, I'd get hungry and talk myself out of eating because I knew I'd make myself throw up and hated that weakness. But I had this mantra—If I give Savvy a cookie, she's going to want a Big Mac. It's how it always worked. If I ate a plate of lettuce, it would feed my hunger just enough to turn it into a monster, and then I'd eat anything in sight."

She sniffles, but I keep my focus on our hands.

"It was just easier not to eat. It got easier when I met you and Clover, and slowly, over the years, I got better. Until Grey left and Riley was released, I hadn't even thought about what I was eating or not eating in years."

"I wish you'd talked to us about any of this, Savvy. We would have helped."

"I—I was embarrassed. I'm the friend who has it all together. I'm the one you come to when things are falling apart. I'm the rock. I like being the rock. It makes me feel... useful and needed. I don't know who I am if I'm not the person you all count on."

"Geez, Savvy. You will always be that person to us. It's who you are, but even rocks can be bowled over in a tsunami. You can't be anything for us if you're not there for yourself first. You know, you can't pour from an empty cup and all."

Finally, I make eye contact and find the truth I was afraid didn't exist.

"I think somewhere along the way, I learned that no one could love me as much as I loved them, so I created this mask. I became someone you guys needed but never shared the darkness I hid beneath. I didn't want to give you a reason to push me away."

"I understand that you were protecting yourself, Sav.

Everyone you've ever counted on has left you more broken than the last, but I appreciate you telling me. Hopefully, now we'll be able to prove to you that we'll never leave you alone, we'll never push you away. You're our family, the way family should be, and we won't ever let you down."

My phone beeps as Madi's buzzes.

Clover.

"Can you believe Valen calls her Honeybee and has no idea why?" she squeals, diving for her purse on the floor to retrieve her phone.

> Clover: Upstate New York. Wouldn't this place make a great murder hotel?

> Clover: Photo sent.

"Oh, gross. A murder has definitely taken place there," Madi laughs while texting back.

> Madi: Absolutely. Please tell me you're not staying there.

A couple of weeks ago, Clover received yet another threat. Riley opened the door to Clover's hell when he put out her private information on the dark web, so the Harrington family made a suggestion: Take a road trip with Valen to retrieve all the letters she's mailed him over the years.

She only said no because I was in the hospital, but after a week of back and forth and a lot of reassurance that she couldn't do anything for me, I convinced her that if this was something she wanted to do, she should.

I got the biggest shock of my life when she left the next day with him but also brought Chief and Elle's dog, Wrecks, along for the ride.

My scaredy-cat friend who's afraid of her own shadow packed up to go on an extended road trip with a man she hasn't seen since she was fourteen, a seventy-year-old man whose self-importance is a matter of national security, and a dog who eats tires for fun.

It's the man who doesn't remember her that makes me the most nervous—a stranger whose heart may remember hers, but whose mind can't recall a single fact about her.

Clover had absolutely no reservations about jumping into a car with him, so who were we to keep her from this adventure?

We did insist that she and Chief check in with us eight times a day, and at least three of them had to be video calls—we couldn't just take Valen's word that they'd be safe. We also joined a family plan on Life360 and track her every move.

I still don't know if it was the right call, encouraging her to go, but I'd also never seen her so...alive before.

"Do you think he's ever going to remember her?" I ask.

Madi freezes with her thumbs on her phone. "I don't know, but no matter how it plays out, she's finally getting closure, and that's more than I ever thought she'd get."

"True. I just don't want to see her get hurt."

"If it's any consolation, after watching them together, I don't think she'll get so much as a hangnail with Valen around. He's too...protective. Her heart might be another issue, but we have to let her write her own story."

I laugh. "As long as her story doesn't have any murder attempts, serial killers, or stalkers, I'm all for it."

My hospital room door opens, and Grey walks in as though he owns the place. And based on the threats Elle told me he made, he just might.

"You ready?" he asks. He's not wearing a suit, and he hasn't the entire time I've been in here.

The dark denim and light blue button-down are a stark contrast to the Greyson Reyes I first met.

He appears almost relaxed.

"The nurses are dragging their feet, but I'm done with this hellhole, and I'm taking you home."

Okay, maybe not relaxed, but a work in progress.

"I'm ready," I say. "But I'm a little afraid of what I'll be walking into."

Grey rolls his eyes. Rolls his freaking eyes like a teenager. I'm not hating this new and improved version of him.

"You'll be walking into your new and improved home, Monroe. Don't turn this into a thing. You're my wife—"

"Allegedly, and illegally, I might add."

"The ink is dry, sweetheart. You are mine, and I am yours, so I—" He tugs on his collar as though he's uncomfortable. "I made a few minor adjustments to our home so you'd be comfortable. Now, do you want to sit here talking about it all day, or do you want to go see what me and Elle have been up to?"

Elle is a fabulous interior decorator. Hell, she decorated my entire duplex, but the fact that he hired her makes my palms itchy.

It's the fear of the unknown, I realize, when he pushes a wheelchair into the room.

"I'm ready but..." I chew on my thumb nail until he looks up at me. "I still need help with day-to-day tasks, Grey. I can't even pee without help to the toilet. Don't you think it would be better for me to go into a rehab center?"

He scoffs as though that's the most ridiculous thing he's ever heard. We've already had this argument so many times, I can practically here his reply before he says it.

"Monroe, I think I've been waiting my whole life to take care of my wife. Do you really think I'm going to allow someone else to do it now that I have you?"

Ugh. He's really wearing out the wife moniker.

"Fine, *husband*. Let's go."

He's on me before I can even pull back the blankets. His hands cradle my face, and the intensity of his stare sends shivers coursing over my skin. "Say it again."

Good Lord. This really is going to be a thing, I can feel it.

"Husband," I say with as much attitude as I can muster.

My tone doesn't even faze him. His lips press to mine in a demanding kiss that tastes of power and control, but also patience, love, and cinnamon.

I melt. I freaking melt right into his hands. I'm the M&M's in the palm of a toddler's hand who fell asleep with them in their grasp. Ooey, gooey, melted.

"Y'all are so stinking cute. But let's get this show on the road. Braxton and Cian have the grill going at your house, and everyone's ready to celebrate your homecoming." Madi bounces with happiness.

"What the hell? I wanted to take her home alone. I've got...stuff to do. Who said you could all just show up—"

"Grey," I cut him off. I know sharing is a new concept for him, but I feel like I need this. I need them—the family who found me and made me whole again.

"Fine," he grumbles. "But everyone had better be off the property by eight at the latest. Six would be better."

"Grey." Madi laughs. "It's already four o'clock."

"Five would be preferable," he says. His head is lowered while he helps me out of the bed, but I saw the smirk on his face.

"It's fine, Madi," I say. "I'm looking forward to seeing everyone."

"It'll be the best welcome-home party this town has ever seen," she says, tossing a bag over her shoulder. I just hope she doesn't go into labor before the night is over.

I've lived in many places over my lifetime, but none of them have ever truly felt like home.

Perhaps Madi's right though. Maybe this time, I've finally found where I belong and that's all I need to create a home.

CHAPTER FORTY

GREYSON

I'm so damn nervous that I've sweated through the light cotton button-down I'm wearing. It's November, but Mother Nature doesn't appear to work on a regular calendar because it's still hotter than a preacher's collar at a strip club.

Unbelievable. Now I'm sounding like Pops. I need to stop spending so much time with him.

I'm also pissed because I had a whole plan, and now the fucking town is going to ruin it.

We pull up to the front of the house, and Savvy gasps.

"Greyson, what the hell did you do?" She's gaping at the wheelchair ramp Cian built to the front door.

That's just the tip of the iceberg though. If she gets pissed about that, what the hell is she going to say about... everything else?

"It was necessary," I say, then jump out of the car before she can respond.

Braxton meets me at the front of the car as though he was waiting for us. Knowing Madi, she probably texted him as soon as we were close.

"Hey," he says, looking tired but happy. Madi is due any day now, and I can see the fear etched in the lines around his eyes.

"Hey. I saw what you had set up—"

I slap a hand over his mouth, and his damn eyes twinkle while I spin to make sure Savvy didn't hear anything.

"Do not say a word."

He nods, and I lower my hand.

"I was only going to say that we...improved on it. It's all set and ready to go when the sun goes down."

Meddlers. They're all a bunch of nosy do-gooding meddlers.

I don't get a chance to ask him how the hell he improved on my plan because Madi opens Savvy's door, and I sprint to cut her off.

That's my job, damn it.

"I've got this, Madi."

She smirks as though she did it on purpose, then steps out of my way.

I squat beside the car. "Do you want the wheelchair or the walker?" She already had physical therapy today, and sometimes she's in a lot of pain after.

She winces, and I have my answer. She wants to use the walker but needs to use the chair.

"Never mind. I've got it." I hustle to the back of the SUV and pull out her wheelchair, then I set it beside the passenger door and help her out of the car.

She flinches in pain when I lower her to the seat. "Sorry, baby. We'll get better at this."

"What if—what if it's always this way?" she whispers.

I overheard her talking to the doctor. I know that her biggest fear is that her injuries have caused permanent damage, especially the nerve damage in her spine, but the reality is, it's too early to know what her new normal will be.

Regardless of what happens, I'll be here for her. If our family only ever looks like me and Savvy, I'll be okay with that too because she's who and what I need to feel whole.

I chose Savvy, and I'll continue to choose her through each stage of our lives. "It won't be."

She opens her mouth to argue, but I cut her off. "But if it is, we'll figure it out together. I'm in this, Monroe. You're not going to scare me off with your doomsday fears. Now, are you ready to go see our new and improved home?"

I haven't abated her fears—a shadow lurks behind her sad eyes—but hopefully the changes Elle and I have made will show her how serious I am.

"I'm ready." She pouts. She's so damn cute when she pouts.

"Then let's welcome you home, sweetheart." I push her chair up the newly paved driveway, up the ramp, and through our front door.

"Holy shit," she gasps the moment I get her over the threshold.

Elle has redecorated the entire space to fit the coastal vibe Savvy had at her condo.

Slowly, I push her chair into the family room so she can take it all in.

The couches are a shade of light grayish-green I can't remember the name of, but they're huge and make you want to sink into them and never get up. The coffee table is made of old driftwood that Cian pulled from the bay that Moose transformed into a statement piece for the room.

"Everyone helped," I tell her. I'm thankful that even though I can hear what sounds like a herd of elephants outside, they're giving us the privacy of this moment.

"You changed your entire house."

I chuckle. "I did because it's not my house anymore, it's ours, and I wanted you to be comfortable here."

"But you have to live here too. What about what you want?"

"That's easy. There's only one thing I want, one thing that can make me happy, and that's you. The rest of this is just...jewelry."

"Grey." It's a half sob, half gasp as I turn her chair to head to the kitchen. She holds up her hands, silently asking me to wait.

On the far wall are framed photos. Photos of us as children, photos of us together, photos of our friends who have become our family. They're all positioned at the ends of branches of an iron tree that's been hung against the wall.

"It's our family tree. Our family, Monroe, the way we create it. Elle and I had it made, and sourcing some of the photos wasn't easy because your friends are a nosy bunch of asses, and it was supposed to be a surprise, but I..." I pinch the back of my neck. "Well, I thought it was important. This, here, these people, this is our life—our family, and it's beautiful because we chose it."

"Geez, Grey. I wasn't prepared for this. It's...it is beautiful and so meaningful. Thank you."

"We're not done yet. Want to see the kitchen? We put the elevator back there too."

She nods, and I wheel her through the house.

"Holy shit," she blurts when we enter the kitchen. It used to be all dark wood and—Elle said—very masculine-feeling. Now it's white, and bright, and straight out of a magazine. "Grey, what did you do, completely gut the place? What about Moose? Isn't he upset?"

"No, he actually helped with almost everything. He

wants this to be a family home. He wants us to be happy here. I should also mention that Cian finished the apartment above the new garage, and I'd like Moose to move in there eventually, if that's okay with you. He isn't doing so well on his own anymore."

"Yes," she forces out. "Of course." Her emotions are getting the better of her. "You shouldn't have done all this though. Not for me."

I whirl her chair around, and she makes a startled sound.

"Always for you, Savannah. Always. The sooner you learn that, the better off we'll both be. You're not going to come in second anymore. You're not going to be last on the list, even if that list is your own. You, sweetheart, deserve the world."

"But." Tears well in her eyes. "I'm still so fucked-up, Grey."

"So am I. We'll be fucked-up together."

"No, what I mean is, I have a lot of trauma that I still need to work through. A lot of ghosts I need help burying. It isn't fair for me to ask you to wait while I figure out who I am."

"Still so stubborn," I whisper. "You're not asking me to do anything. I'm here because it's where I want to be, end of story. And I'm so glad you want to talk with someone. I have a list of the best therapists in the state, but if you don't like any of them, we'll keep looking until you find someone you're comfortable with. Sage told me that the most important thing is that you're comfortable."

"You..." She frowns, and I feel like I'm messing something up. "You looked into therapy for me?"

Shit. "Just to have in case you wanted to. The doctors suggested it, so I took the initiative, but you're definitely in the driver's seat. You choose whoever you think is best. I'm just here to support you. And…" I release a heavy sigh that slows my racing heart. "I've been looking for someone for me to talk to as well. I want us to work, and I want us to be the best versions of ourselves for that to happen."

"You want to go to therapy too?"

I shrug. "I know I'm not perfect. Close, but not quite there. If someone can help with that point five percent of myself that's damaged, it's worth a try."

"Humble. Always so humble."

"I try. Now, the elevator is over here," I press a button hidden in a panel on the wall, and a moment later, the doors slide open.

"I didn't even see that there."

"That's the point. I wanted it to blend in. Now, do you want to see what we did upstairs, or do you want to go say hi to everyone?"

"Grey?"

"Yes, sweetheart." I bend at the waist and press my lips gently to hers.

"Thank you…for all of this. It's completely over-the-top and unnecessary, but I appreciate the effort you put into making this feel like…our home."

"You will always be worth the effort."

I kiss her again, and someone clears their throat. I'm about to curse them out when Sage walks into the room.

"Welcome home, Savvy," he says. "Your visitors are getting anxious to see you. Most of them weren't allowed to visit you in the hospital because *someone* was playing bouncer and gave your room a guestlist." He raises his brows at me, but I simply shrug and look away.

"She was trying to heal."

"Why am I not surprised?" Her laughter is a balm to my weary soul.

"Because you love me?" There's no masking the hope in my tone. I sound like a love-starved six-year-old.

"Yes, Grey. Because I love you."

A loud whoop echoes in the kitchen, and then I realize the sound came from me.

What can I say? I'm a man in love, and I needed to hear her say that more than I realized.

"Now." She raises a brow in my direction. "Let's go say hi to our friends."

"Acquaintances," I correct. "If they're not on the wall, they're acquaintances."

"Oh my God, Scrooge. Lighten up," Savvy admonishes. "Everyone in Happiness is a friend."

They can be friends when they've proved themselves worthy. But I know better than to voice that opinion. The way Sage is laughing makes me think he might be a mind reader though.

"Fine," I grumble. "Let's go say hi to our *friends*."

I squeeze the handlebars of her wheelchair, and she reaches around to press her fingers into mine. "I don't know if I can ever thank you enough for everything you've done, but I do love you, Grey. I'm in love with you, and I think I probably have been since the night we met."

Lowering myself, I kiss the top of her head. "Me too, Monroe. From first fight to first kiss, and everything in between, you are my true north, and I promise to love you until my last breath."

She squeezes my fingers again, and then I push her outside to start the first day of the rest of our lives...as one.

CHAPTER FORTY-ONE

SAVVY

"I can't believe you put in a freaking pool, Grey."

He shrugs in his rocking chair next to mine. "Your physical therapist said it was good for your recovery."

I simply smile. If I've learned anything about this man, it's that he will always harness the stars whenever possible.

"How long is everyone going to be here?" he grumbles, checking his watch again. "They're just hanging around for the free food and booze."

I laugh. "That's not true, Patch. They're here because they love us."

"Who the hell is Quinn talking to?"

I follow his line of sight and laugh again. "That's Eddie."

"Eddie," he grumbles.

"Remember? He won Cupid cowboy three years running." I study his face as recognition dawns.

"Shit."

"Hey, she deserves a little fun." He nods, but I sense the guilt he's carrying still. "Did you talk with her?"

"I did." He leans his head back against the rocking chair that Moose carved his name into. "She said she accepted my apology and will stay on with Omni-Reyes if she can do it from California with more...boundaries, and a fuck ton in bonuses. Apparently, I'm a shitty boss."

"It was extraordinary circumstances, Grey. If she accepted your apology, then I'm sure she understands that."

"I suppose." He leans forward in his chair and growls when his gaze lands on Bethany.

"Leave her alone, Grey."

"Why the hell would you allow Bethany into our home?"

"Take a good look at her, handsome." He squints his eyes, then sits back with defeat in his shoulders. "She has dark circles under her eyes like she hasn't been sleeping."

He grunts but doesn't say anything.

"I'm not saying she's innocent, but I don't believe she deserves to be punished for the rest of her life either. She's done everything she can to help correct her mistakes—including agreeing to testify against Riley. I won't be part of tearing someone down the way I was."

"Fine, I get that. But is it necessary to celebrate with her too?"

"It's called forgiveness, Patch. Will she be invited to Christmas? No. But she put herself out there when she came and apologized in person, and now we can move through town without animosity."

"Hey." I look up to see Braxton grinning down at us. "Sun's down."

"Yup, and yet all these fuckers are still here." Grey scowls across the back yard.

"Grey, you know I love you." I grin when I hear Madi behind us. "But if you don't get your ass out of that chair so I can put up my feet, I'm going to cry for the entire town to hear."

He stands and helps her into the rocking chair, then smirks as she sighs.

"Think we can get Moose to build us a couple of these?" she asks Braxton.

"I'm sure he'd love to," he replies. They talk about the maternal glow of pregnancy, but I'm inclined to think Braxton has it too. "Come on, Grey. Let's refill their drinks."

My husband presses a kiss to the top of my head. "Need anything else?"

"No, I'm good." My smile grows as I watch him walk away, bickering with Braxton.

"It's nice to see you happy," Madi says. "But I agree with Grey. Bethany was a step too far for me."

"Be nice," I grin. "Funny how I'm the nice one in this scenario."

"You've always been nice. Oh..."

The backyard lights cut off, and I sit forward on my chair. "That's strange. I don't even know where the light switches are back here."

"Just sit tight," Madi says. "I'm sure Grey's on it." A moment later, the telltale ring of FaceTime comes from her phone. "Oh, it's Clover." She presses a button, and Clover's face comes into view. "Hey, Clove."

"Did I miss it?" she asks.

"Miss what?" I look out over the pool and see a light flicker to life in the yard. Then one by one, tiny orbs begin to glow all across the property.

"Here," Madi hands me a stick that has a wire attached to it. At the very end, a two-inch firefly blinks as if it's telling me a secret.

"What the hell is happening?" I ask as more lights flicker to life.

All around me and the property, these little fireflies glow, but mine appears to be the only one blinking.

My throat closes up, and the weariness of the last two months is replaced with pure adrenaline.

"No," I gasp as "Fireflies" by Owl City plays through hidden speakers.

Madi's eyes sparkle next to me as she holds up her own firefly. Even Clover is holding one up through Madi's phone screen.

"Guys, what's going on?"

Clover mimes locking her lips while Madi points to the yard that's now full of hundreds of little plastic light-up bugs.

Through teary eyes, one in particular catches my attention. It's the only one moving, weaving through all our guests and fireflies that appear to stand on their own or are hanging from trees.

And it's blinking the same pattern as my own.

Oh, Greyson. What did you do?

Blink, blink, double blink. It's the pattern of our love and my heart syncs to the cadence as Greyson slowly makes his way toward me.

"This is where we leave you," Madi whispers. Braxton appears and helps her to stand, and then I'm left all alone on the deck, peering out over the darkness pierced by fireflies.

And then Grey is standing at the edge of the patio, his firefly light speeding up the closer it gets to mine.

"In a field of static light, I was always meant to beat to the rhythm of your heart." He smiles, and my pulse takes flight.

"What are you doing?"

"Someone told me once that fireflies flash in a pattern to

attract their mate, but I've been following your light since the moment you crashed into my life, and now I want to bask in your glow for the rest of our days."

He drops to one knee, and Braxton slides out of the darkness to take his firefly from him.

"Grey, what are you doing?" I whisper. "We're already married. Get up."

He chuckles, and so do the people who are closest to us, but it's too dark to make out their faces.

"We are, but as is our custom, we did things all out of order. I never got down on one knee, and you never got this moment. I'm correcting my mistakes."

He reaches into his pocket and pulls out a ring box. My thumb covers the ring I'm currently wearing, and then I twist the diamond on my finger.

"I already have a ring, Grey."

He takes my hand in his. "You do. And when I gave it to you, I also told you that it was the one I could get on short notice."

Did he? I honestly don't remember much about that conversation.

"Even then, I knew you were it for me, Sav," he whispers so quietly that only I can hear him. "I didn't want to admit it, maybe, but I knew. That's why I had a trusted jeweler in London working on this." He opens the box, and candles begin blazing to life around us as Madi, Elle, and Braxton hurry to light them.

But then I see the ring. The one he's holding in his hands, and my world completely stops.

It isn't flashy, though it catches every glimmer of light. An emerald sits at the center, strong and unyielding, encircled by a halo of diamonds. He turns it slightly, and I catch sight of the band.

Leaning in, I study the intricate weaving of vines that create the band with interwoven tiny diamonds. It's like my life and his coming together in a beautifully crafted forever.

Then he turns it again, and I see the inscription: *Mea lux.* "Oh, Grey."

"After my sister died, I was cleaning out her room and found a diary of sorts. It's where she designed and dreamed. In it were jewelry designs for every important time in our lives—including this engagement ring. She created it without ever having met you, but it's as though she knew who you would be one day."

He glances up, his face overcome with emotion.

"She designed this ring for my future wife, and Ace pulled *mea lux* straight from her dreams for my future. She would have loved you, Savannah."

Tears clog my throat. I'm not sure how much I can take before I explode in a blubbering mess of emotion.

"And I love you more than I ever dreamed possible." His tone is like an ocean breeze—calm and steady. "You are my light, my love, my life. You're everything I never dared to hope for and everything I need to keep me grounded. You're the fire to my ice, the bark to my bite, the love of my life."

"I love you too," I choke out.

"Our start hasn't been conventional, but I'll spend every moment for the rest of our lives being the man you deserve and giving you a life better than any fairy tale. Savannah Monroe, will you do me the incredible honor of becoming my wife, again?"

If I could jump out of this chair, I'd already be straddling him. Instead, I nod, tears streaming down my face. "Yes. From now until forever, I am yours and you are mine."

His kiss is the seal of all our promises, and finally, I

understand the appeal of a Prince Charming and a happily ever after.

It just took this stubborn, beautifully broken man to lend me his pieces to create something whole.

Vaguely I hear our found family cheering in the background, but I'm fully consumed by Greyson Reyes—my one-time enemy turned eternal firefly.

Happily ever after to me.

EPILOGUE
GREYSON

One Year Later

"Fancy meeting you here."

Savvy whirls around to find me leaning against the building. "I thought you had meetings today?"

I stalk her slowly, loving how even now, her eyes darken with desire. "I did, and I do, but did you seriously think I wouldn't check on you, knowing what you were discussing with Dr. Collins today?"

Yesterday, she gave her impact statement to a courtroom packed full of people. Her brother sat behind Riley and didn't so much as glance in her direction once.

The last thing I wanted to do was come face-to-face with her family, but I did it for her, and it solidified what we already knew—we're better off without them.

Her features soften, and then she buries her face into the crook of my neck.

"How'd it go?" I ask gently, rubbing little circles on the small of her back.

I read her impact statements for both Riley and Kristen

last week, and they damn near destroyed me. She left nothing out in either letter. But Riley's was particularly brutal. She didn't hold back and detailed how every one of his decisions and cruelties had impacted her life.

I wasn't sure I could finish the letter, but I'm glad I did. It allowed me to be strong for her yesterday. The fact that she did it in person when she didn't have to is a testament to her strength and her resilience. And it showed me how far she's come.

Kristen and Riley were both found guilty. His convictions included attempted murder, stalking, and a host of other crimes; Kristen's was reckless endangerment for feeding him information that led to the attack on Savvy. While Kristen will see parole much sooner than I'd like, Riley will never be free again.

"It was hard, but Dr. Collins was patient while I got through it. Mostly we talked about Austin and how, even after hearing about everything I went through, he still didn't believe me. It'll take a while for that wound to heal."

"Yeah, baby, I know."

We've both been seeing Dr. Collins for about eight months, and when I'm not fighting my instinct to punch the guy, he's given me valuable insight into how to break old habits and toxic family cycles.

He's been an even bigger help for Savvy though. She sees him twice a week, and we do couples therapy once a month.

Since we've been working with him, she's slowly gotten healthier, and her relationship with food is improving every day. He's also been instrumental in giving me the tools I need to help, not hinder her recovery, which is all I ever really wanted anyway.

Savvy and I have become a team in every aspect of our lives, and because of that, we're thriving.

"Hey, I have news," I say.

She lifts her head to peer up at me. "Good news?"

"Yeah. It's good."

"Can it wait for like, ten minutes?" Her smile takes my breath away.

"It can...but why?"

Taking my hand, she drags me down the steps toward her car, the limp on her left side barely noticeable after months of rehab. "I want to show you something."

Her car beeps twice, and then she's jumping into the driver's seat while I fold myself uncomfortably into her passenger seat. No matter how much I push, she will not give up her ten-year-old Camry.

"Where are we going?" I ask when she heads out of town.

"Envy's Edge."

I peer at her thin yoga pants. "It's a little cold to be up there, isn't it?"

"No, Patch. It's not." Her words can still sound like an eye roll that makes me want to slap her ass until it's red.

Ten minutes later, we pull into the empty lot that over-looks southeastern Georgia. It truly is beautiful up here.

"What the hell is that?" I ask, finally noticing the small picnic set up to the side of her car.

"Now, don't get all bent out of shape. Braxton and Quinn rearranged your afternoon for me."

Rubbing my jaw, I narrow my eyes. "Did they now? So when you said you thought I had meetings..."

"I was stalling. I knew you'd show up at Dr. Collins' office today." She smirks, and I return it. She knows me better than I know myself. "Come on," she says, opening her door. "I want to hear your news first."

She beats me to the table, which frustrates me, and she knows it. I would have liked to help her sit, but when she wrings her hands together, I see her nerves, so I fall onto my side of the bench without complaining.

"Spill," she says, leaning over the table excitedly.

"Well, the Heartmark Podcast Awards were announced this morning."

Savvy frowns. I thought she'd be more excited about this.

"You, Madi, and Clover were all nominated in each of your categories, as were four other Sunshine Studio podcasts."

Finally, a smile breaks free. "They were? Oh my God. Clover and Madi will be so excited."

"And what about you, my dear wife? It's okay to celebrate your accomplishments too you know?"

She waves me away. "I know, but it's more fun to celebrate theirs."

"Dr. Collins would disagree," I grumble, but not wanting to put a damper on the afternoon, I put my feelings on the matter aside. "Your turn. What's your news?"

Her gaze dances around my face—nerves have her plucking at nonexistent lint on her sweatshirt.

"Baby, what's wrong?"

"Wrong?" she squeaks out the word. "Nothing's wrong. Here, Betty made you some meatloaf at the diner."

I frown as she pulls out a Styrofoam container from the basket that sits at her side. I take it, attempting to hide a grimace. I hate meatloaf.

My brows dip into my hairline when her tinkling laughter comes next.

"Oh, you big baby. It's a joke. It's a BLT on wheat, light on the mayo, just like you like."

"I'm confused," I admit. "Why are you teasing me about meatloaf?"

"Because you said once that meatloaf at the diner wouldn't cut it for our first date."

Unease settles into my shoulders. "I do remember saying that, but we're well past firsts, don't you think?"

"Most of them," she whispers. When she brings her thumb to her mouth to chew on her nail, I hit my limit for bullshit.

"Monroe," I bite out. "You haven't bitten your nails in six months. What has you all tied up into knots?"

She drops her hand from her mouth and scoffs. She still hates that I know all her tells.

"What is it, Savvy?"

"It's a lot, actually."

Just spit it out, sweetheart. I'm starting to sweat through my suit, and it's not a pretty look.

"I can handle it." I say to assure her, while silently hoping that I can.

"Well, Valen told me that the DeVanes and Ashfords are having some...money trouble in their casino's. Do you happen to know anything about that?"

Yes.

"I've stayed out of that just as you asked."

"Right. But your new BFF Roman, did he have anything to do with that?"

I shrug and work to control the twitch of my eyebrow that would alert her to my partial lie. I can't help it that Roman felt so guilty about Savvy's accident that he told me he would handle the other families.

I'm only pissed it's taken him an entire year to bring it to fruition.

"I'm not Roman's keeper, but he did mention that there might be some...unrest in Vegas. That's all I know." And it's the truth.

"Right, well, that brings me to my next bit of news. I picked a date."

I drop the water I had only just lifted from the table, and it spills all over my sandwich.

"You...did?" I ask cautiously. "A date for..."

She nods twice. "Our wedding." She's been putting it off until she felt she was in a good place with Dr. Collins, which I fully supported. I haven't even pushed her once since I asked her to marry me in front of half the town.

I guess it helps that legally we're already married.

Freaking Pops still hums the song "Fireflies" every time he sees me though.

"You did?" I confirm. I'm very careful not to push her. As much as I want her to have the wedding of her dreams, I wasn't lying when I said I am perfectly happy exactly as we are.

"October twelfth."

"That's eleven months away," I blurt, then I realize what date she chose. "Our anniversary."

She smiles, and her cheeks flush pink. "The anniversary of the first time we met."

"Our first fight." I laugh.

"And our first kiss." She blushes harder.

Damn, do I remember that kiss. It happened later that night at the inn. I was the fuse, and she was the match. We didn't stand a chance.

"It's a great date," I say honestly. "Are you sure?"

"Yes, but that also calls for a renegotiation."

I groan and push my soggy sandwich away. If she brings up a post-nuptial agreement one more time, I will chain her to our bed until she promises to drop it for good.

"Monroe, we've been over this. I'm not signing any kind of agreement over our marriage. It's done—we're married. What's mine is yours, and you are mine."

She rolls her eyes, and I huff out a breath. Over the last year, fighting with her has become much less fun, and I find myself caving just so I can see her smile.

If that's not love, I don't know what is.

"This is a renegotiation of our other terms."

"What other terms?"

She opens her to-go container and pulls out half of her turkey sandwich, then hands it to me before taking a bite of her own. I'd still prefer she eat her whole lunch, but she's in charge of this particular journey, so I sit in silent support and eat the damn turkey.

After she takes a bite, she places the rest back down and pulls out a folder, peers into it, then slowly slides it across to me.

I stuff the rest of the sandwich into my mouth, dust off my hands, and pull the folder forward.

Opening the cover, my lunch sits like molasses in my throat.

The Ray of Sunshine Surrogacy Center logo stares up at me, and I want to vomit. Or rage. I'm not entirely sure what emotion I'll go with yet.

"Explain," I grumble through a mouthful of food.

She chuckles, then reaches across the table and flips the page to a new one.

This one is about IVF, and no matter how hard I try to swallow, I can't get the food down.

I spit it on the ground instead.

"What is this?" I ask, and panic begins to curl in my gut.

I've spoken to Dr. Collins about this. Even if Savvy decides she wants children one day, she's not ready. Past trauma and her disordered eating take time to recover from, and I'm not willing to risk her health for anything. Not even a child.

"I've been talking with Dr. Collins—"

"So have I." The words are aggressive, but Savvy just offers a placating smile.

"I want you to hear me out, Grey."

I nod, but my vision is hazy. I will not risk her life. Never again.

"In therapy, I've learned that I let go of a lot of my hopes and dreams in an effort to shield myself from pain. One of those was the idea of me ever becoming a mother. The deeper I dig, the more I realize that it might very well be something I want someday."

I hear a *but*. There had better be a *but*. We're focusing on getting her healthy right now, not risking her life by putting a baby in her belly.

I reach across the table and hold her hand. It's silent encouragement for her to continue.

"But."

Thank fuck. There it is.

"I still have a lot of work to do before I can even think about bringing a child into the world."

"Savvy, we've talked about this. I only want what's best for you."

"I know." Her words are quiet now. "But what if a year from now, two years from now, I'm in a better place and decide I do want a child?"

"We can adopt or foster. There's lots of ways for us to

become a family that don't potentially harm you in the process."

"Or." She points to the IVF packet in front of us. "We could freeze embryos now...just in case. Maybe I'll get to a place where I feel strong enough to carry a child myself. Or maybe I'll get to a place where I'm ready for a baby, but a surrogate is the safer option."

I nod, silently reading the paper in front of me while she talks.

She continues, "Or maybe we'll decide that adoption is right for us, or that we really don't want children after all. My point is, I do want us to have options."

"Monroe, the only option I care about is the one that keeps you happy, healthy, and safe by my side."

"I know." She rises and joins me on my side of the table. "I'm not ready right now, but I don't want to regret anything in the future either. I'm just asking that we explore all our options while I heal myself."

"Don't you know by now, baby? I'll give you anything you want, however you want, as long as you're safe and I can call you mine."

She presses her face into my chest. "I am yours."

"And I'm yours."

"So," she says quietly. "You'll consider jizzing into a cup for me?"

My laughter shakes us both. "Anything for you, Savvy Sweetheart. Anything."

We sit in comfortable silence, picking at the fries in her to-go container and the extra pickles she got on the side.

"But," I say after a while, "if we do end up having a girl, I'm calling dibs. Her name will have to be Rose."

"How about Georgia Rose?" she counters. "You may be

named after colors, but Austin and I are named after cities. It's only right that she gets a piece of both of us."

"Your family doesn't count. They're fucking animals."

"Oh," she laughs. "And your family is so much better?"

"Fair. But at least we got Sage and Braxton out of it. Who do we get from your side?"

She's still laughing when I pull her into my lap. "I think it's a good sign that we can now joke about our shitty childhoods, don't you?"

I stare into her eyes, seeing a future so bright it outshines the trauma I spent years running from. "Yeah, I do. I think we're heading for a very healthy future."

"Oh," she says, sitting up straighter. "I had a dog named Giggy once. He was great. Granted, Giggy was short for gigolo, but that's not his fault."

"We're not naming our child after a male escort."

She sighs into my hold. "Our child."

I freeze. Did I accidentally just put pressure on her?

"Relax, Grey. Communication is key, remember?"

"I do. I can't help worrying sometimes though."

"That's why we'll talk everything to death."

I snort out an ungodly sound. "Just what I've always wanted."

"I know. But, Grey?"

"Yes, Monroe?"

"Saying 'our child' isn't as scary as I thought it would be. I... kind of like the sound of it."

"Me too, baby. If a child is in our cards, I'll welcome it with open arms."

"And...if it's not?"

I pull her more tightly into my hold. "Then it just means I have more room to hold you close. This, right here, with you, is the family I've always wanted, and I'm thankful for you every single day."

"Ditto, Patch." Her cool palms cup my cheeks. "I love you."

"I love you more, *mea lux*. I'll always love you more."

––––––––

This is much more uncomfortable than I thought it would be.

The horse trots around the park, and I feel every bump and pothole in my bladder.

It's taken five years, but baby Reyes will make her debut by morning.

"Come on, baby girl. I really don't want a C-section. Mommy's had enough surgeries to last a lifetime. Just this once, take it easy on me, will ya?"

Grey continues to rub small circles on my lower back where the pressure is unbearable.

Levi, who just turned six, and Atlas, who is four going on forty, sit across from us.

"Uncle Gway," Atlas says with more exasperation than even I've ever hurled Greyson's way.

The last thing Grey wanted to do was bring Levi or Atlas with us on this horse and carriage ride, but who can say no to these two? Levi is the spitting image of Braxton but with Madi's eyes. And Atlas? Jesus. That kid is Valen reincarnated as a bossy little soldier—but a cute one, with his mother's capacity for love.

"Yes, Atlas?" Grey's really reaching for patience here while also scanning the park for their parents.

"Are you hurtin' my baby?"

I snicker into my hands.

Ever since Atlas felt the baby kick in my belly, he's fought Greyson tooth and nail, declaring it *his* baby.

If you ask me, it's kind of poetic justice.

"Kid, you know I love you, but this is *my* baby. Savvy is *my* wife. Georgia Rose will be *my* daughter when she finally makes her appearance."

Atlas glares at Greyson. He's got the scary protector vibe from his father down pat. I wonder if they practice that look together in the mirror at home.

"But..." Levi says, and we all spin on him. The kid's about to heckle his uncle, and I mentally high-five him. Levi's been my little buddy since the moment he was born, and I'm proud to say he's inherited a little of my personality as well.

"You can't marry your daughter," Levi taunts. "Atlas could marry her."

"Over my dead body," Grey mutters.

"What's marry?" Atlas asks.

"You're sitting here, fighting me for my daughter, and you don't even know what marry means?"

"Grey," I admonish. At least the ridiculousness of this carriage ride takes away from the fact that my water won't freaking break. "He's four."

"Marrying means you love someone forever," Levi says, scrunching up his nose. "And you buy them a pretty ring, and you kiss. On the lips. Gross. Like how my dad kisses my mom. All. The. Time."

"Huh." Atlas sits back and swings his little legs beneath him. "Yup. Me and Georgia is gettin' mar-weed."

"We call her Rose, and no, you're not getting married." Grey barks. He's close to hitting his stress limit for the day.

Moose pulls the carriage up to the Chug, and Grey curses not so quietly. "Your rides end here, kids."

Valen and Braxton stand waiting on the sidewalk for their sons.

"Dad," Atlas yells, but Valen hears a war cry and sprints across the lot toward us as though there's an active threat against his son.

"What? What's wrong?" Valen asks, running his hands all over Atlas's body.

"I'm mar-weeing Georgia."

"Rose," Grey barks again.

"That's...nice, Atlas." Valen's face is full of mirth as he grins at Grey.

Grey and Valen have come a long way over the years, but Grey still holds a grudge for what Valen did to Clover.

Secretly, I think Grey loves Valen like a brother, but as all good big brothers do, he gives him shit. Nonstop. Every day.

"She's not even born yet. Can we stop trying to fudging marry off my daughter?"

"You know, Uncle Grey. Just because you say fudging doesn't make it any better," Levi says. "We all know you're really saying fucking."

My chin drops to my chest.

"And that's our cue to go," Braxton says, hauling his son out of the carriage. "Your mother is going to kill me if she hears that shit come out of your mouth. You can't curse, Levi."

"Pops says it's just a word and you shouldn't censor me." Levi pouts.

"Pops is a damn menace." Grey grunts.

"I have to pee."

"I'll help ya, Auntie Sway-ve." Atlas pulls out of his father's hold and offers me his little hand.

You have to give it to the kid—he's a little gentleman.

"First you want my daughter, and now my wife? Back off, man. Hasn't your father taught you anything about bro code?"

"I'm never being a bro, right, Levi?" Atlas looks up to his best friend with a grin. "Bros are for—"

"Hey," Valen cuts in. "What the hell is Pops teaching you boys now?"

"Crows," Levi finishes. "Bros are for crows 'cause we're gentleman."

"Pops is not babysitting Rose. Ever." Grey grumbles.

"Fine, honey. But I really do have to pee." He offers me his hand and helps me to stand, and I'm instantly soaked.

"Oh no. Auntie Sway-ve. You peed yer pants." Atlas points at my feet.

Valen and Braxton swing the boys out of the way, while I stand dumbfounded.

"What do you know? The carriage ride actually worked." I stare from the puddle to Grey.

"I'm going to be a dad," he shouts.

"I'm gonna be a hubband," Atlas says in return, his little fists held high in the air just like Greyson's.

"Geez, kid. Let a guy have a moment, would ya?" Grey shakes his head, then gently helps me out of the carriage.

He's much calmer than I had envisioned he'd be, and we make it to the hospital without incident.

It's when the doctor comes for the epidural that he freaks out.

"We should have gone with the surrogate. Why didn't we

choose one again?" If the doctor hadn't already told him to calm down, I know he'd be pacing beside me right now.

"Because we didn't want to miss any part of pregnancy, and I knew I was strong enough to handle this, Grey. Plus, you hated every surrogate you met."

"I didn't hate them," he grumbles. "I just don't think it's unreasonable to ask them to follow a specially curated diet."

"That's not why, and you know it," I admonish. "You wanted them to submit to daily drug testing."

"Mr. Reyes, I'm about to get started. Are you able to be supportive, or should we have you come back once the needle is in place?"

"I'm not leaving."

A very demanding nurse gets right in his face. "Let me explain how my delivery rooms work, Mr. Reyes. I don't give a damn how much money you have. My priority is your wife and your child. If at any point I think you're in my way, I will have you removed from this room. Is that understood?"

She manages to put the fear of God in him—or at least scare him into believing he might miss the birth of his daughter if he doesn't get his shit under control.

After my nurse's little speech, Grey sits at my side, holding my hand and not saying a word.

"Okay, Savvy. Push your hips out like you would for a cow pose in yoga."

I do, and I instantly feel the pinch and burning, but it's over relatively quickly.

"What now?" Grey asks once I'm settled back into the bed, no longer feeling pressure at my back.

"Now, she rests for as long as she can. You can watch the contractions on this screen, but hopefully, she'll get a little sleep before the work begins." The nurse studies him closely. "You could do with some sleep too, young man. I'll be back in a while to check her progress."

I nod sleepily. I've been so uncomfortable for the past week that I haven't slept much.

"Go ahead and sleep, baby. I'll be right here."

I smile at Grey and then close my eyes.

———

"Come on, Sav. We've got this. Just one more push, we can do it."

"We?" I seethe. "*We* can do it? You're not really doing anything, Greyson, are you?"

I'm not in pain, but I am terrified.

Terrified that I'm not feeling the contractions.

Terrified that I'm going to screw this all up.

Why is this so hard?

"One more push, Savvy. Bear down, and push," Dr. Reed says. I'd liked her right up until she told me it was totally normal to shit all over yourself during labor.

I can do this. I can. I can totally do this.

Greyson holds one of my legs and a nurse holds the other.

The doctors and nurses say stuff I don't understand, so I block them out, and then push.

I keep pushing and pushing, ready to meet my daughter.

"You did it," Dr. Reed announces, but I don't hear Rose cry.

Why isn't she crying?

"She's a happy baby," someone says. "Greyson, would you like to cut the cord?"

He smiles and steps away as my limbs begin to shake uncontrollably.

Why isn't she crying?

Then my body goes into full rolling waves of tremors.

What the hell is happening to me? I can't even ask because my teeth are chattering so much.

A moment later, Grey stands over me, holding a little bundle wrapped in a blue-and-white blanket. His face is pure, unadulterated love, and then it's filled with fear when he sets his gaze on me.

"What's wrong with her?" he asks, tucking baby Rose against his now-naked chest. "What the fuck is wrong with my wife?"

"Calm down, Mr. Reyes," Dr. Reed says. "She's going through withdrawals—delivering a baby is like putting your body through a marathon you didn't train for. This is completely normal. Place the baby on her chest. It will help her body regulate itself."

I'm nodding, desperate to see my daughter through the ocean full of tears filling my eyes.

"Right," Grey says, accepting help from the nurse to show me baby Rose for the first time.

She has her father's blue eyes and my dark hair. She blinks up at me, and I know in that moment that all my fears about motherhood were unfounded.

I will love this little girl with every ounce of my being for the rest of my life. I'll go without so she can have. I'll sacrifice so she won't have to. I'd lay down my life to pave the way for hers.

All the things a mother should always do, and it came so naturally to me, I never even had to think about it. I just know it deep in my bones—I was born to do this.

I clutch her to my chest while the nurse presses baby Rose's mouth to my nipple.

Grey stands at my side, watching me fumble through my first attempt at nursing.

I've never seen this expression on his face before, and I can't help but wonder if he's had a similar epiphany about parenthood.

The gentle smile on his face would suggest he has.

"You're amazing," he says gently, kissing my cheek, my eyelids, my nose, before pressing one to the top of Rose's head too.

"Mr. Reyes, I appreciate that you want to love on your girls, but your daughter is hungry. Please step back so she can latch on."

I'm expecting a fight, but what I get is humble acquiescence as he steps back and motions for us to continue.

"Thank you, Savannah. Thank you for this moment," my husband says through a cloud of emotion.

I lift my gaze from our daughter's mouth and make eye contact with Grey.

We communicate without words because in this moment, none are needed.

We understand each other on a molecular level, exactly as it was always meant to be.

"We did it," I cry.

"You did it, sweetheart. You were amazing."

"We made a family," I say, running my finger along Rose's cheek as she suckles.

"No, Sav. We were always a family—we simply expanded it."

"Yeah," I agree, unable to look away from Rose now. "We did."

As Rose attempts to nurse, my eyes droop and become heavy.

"That's normal," the nurse says. "Nursing can have a very

calming or tiring effect on moms. That's why we have her propped up. She's safe, but if you're too tired, we can take a break and do the other side later."

"No," I snap my eyes open. "I'm here. It's okay. I want to do this."

Grey smiles and sits by my side as I nurse our daughter. After a while, Rose falls asleep, and he lifts her from my arms.

That's how I find them an hour later when I open my eyes next.

Grey leans against the window with our little girl in his arms, whispering about love and life.

"Your mom is the one who really saved me though. She's the real superhero in our family. She's the strongest, most beautiful woman I've ever met, and she's going to teach you how to be strong and independent. I'll teach you how to play football and run a billion-dollar company. I have big plans for your future, little one."

"You don't get to plan her future, Grey." But I chuckle because he's sure going to try.

"Hey," he says softly. "How are you feeling?"

I can't take my eyes off him as he crosses the room to sit next to me. He's a natural-born father. He cradles Rose in the crook of his arm as though she's always been there. It's one of the sexiest things I've ever seen.

"I feel happy, Grey. And...peaceful."

His face breaks into a beautiful smile. "Me too, Monroe. With each gift you give me, I think my heart can't possibly take any more love. And then you prove me wrong. For that, I will forever be grateful."

"I love you, Greyson Reyes."

"And I love you more, Savannah Reyes. I will always love you more."

Do you want more grumpy billionaires in your life?
Check out *Love Notes & Lifelines*, a single dad, small-town
billionaire romance!

Or are you in the mood for a billionaire who thinks love is
the beginning of the end? Check out Lochlan Blaine in
Without a Hitch!

ACKNOWLEDGMENTS

To my friends and family: John, Ellie, Declan, Rory, and Finn—thank you for putting up with my emotional breakdowns, my weepy woes, my fear-filled tantrums—and those are just on deadline days. Thank you for being there for me, supporting me, and loving me through all life's ups and downs. I wouldn't be me without you.

To my TWSS family: Thank you for believing in me every step of the way...even when I come at you with my three-year plans. Having your support makes navigating this world so much easier.

To my agents, Flavia and Meire: Thank you for continuing to put me and my stories in front of the right people. I appreciate all you do.

To my team: Thank you for all that you do to keep the business of me running. Especially when I go AWOL for weeks at a time while drafting, editing, and all those pesky times in between. I appreciate each and every one of you.

To my friends: The Care Bear Squad, The Sassy Sprinters, and The Sanctuary—if the friend group chat doesn't have a name, I don't want any part of it. LOL. Thank you for keeping me sane, for encouraging, for pushing, for picking me up when I feel down. Having friends like all of you is what life is all about, and I LUV you all dearly.

To the readers: I wouldn't even be here if it weren't for all of you. Thank you for trusting me, for believing in me, encouraging me, and supporting me throughout this journey. I'm thankful for every email and DM you send my way. You make the hard days worthwhile, and I'm forever grateful for all your luv.

To HEA Author Services: Thank you for putting up with my midday texts, my late-night DMs, my panic-filled emails through every stage of the writing process. You help me grow as an author and as a person. I'm so thankful for your guidance and expertise.

Rae Fields: Thank you for once again coming in at the last minute to make sure my words make sense. I appreciate your friendship and help. xo

To Kari March Designs: Thank you for always seeing my blurry vision and turning it into something truly magical!

GET TO KNOW AVERY!

Hello, Luvs!

Want to hang out with me? I'm in The Luv Club every day
sharing my chaos, my mess, my life. Pop in to say hi, meet
the other luvables, and stay a while. It's the happiest,
kindest, messiest, most inclusive group on the internet and
I'd LUV to see you there!

https://geni.us/AverysLUVclub

ALSO BY AVERY MAXWELL

Standalone Romance:

Without A Hitch

Your Last First Kiss

Falling Into Forever

The Westbrooks Series:

Book 1 - Cross My Heart

Book 2 - The Beat of My Heart

Book 3 - Saving His Heart

Book 4 - Romancing His Heart

Book 5 - One Little Heartbreak - A Westbrook Novella

Book 6 - One Little Mistake

Book 7 - One Little Lie

Book 8 - One Little Kiss

Book 9 - One Little Secret

Single Dad Hotline Series:

Book 1 - Love Notes & Lifelines

Book 2 - Late Nights & Love Lines

Book 3 - Heart Strings & Hotlines

Happiness Ever After Series:

Book 1 - The Renegade Billionaire

Book 2 - The Elusive Billionaire